HONORING
THE ENEMY

THE HONOR SERIES BY ROBERT N. MACOMBER

HONORING
THE ENEMY

A Captain Peter Wake Novel

ROBERT N. MACOMBER

Naval Institute Press
Annapolis, Maryland

Naval Institute Press
291 Wood Road
Annapolis, MD 21402

Library of Congress Cataloging-in-Publication Data

Names: Macomber, Robert N., date, author.
Title: Honoring the enemy : a Captain Peter Wake novel / Robert N. Macomber.
Description: Annapolis, Maryland : Naval Institute Press, [2019] | Series: Honor series ; 14 | Series: Spanish-American war trilogy ; 2 | Includes bibliographical references.
Identifiers: LCCN 2018051297 (print) | LCCN 2018053914 (ebook) | ISBN 9781682474457 (ePDF) | ISBN 9781682474457 (epub) | ISBN 9781682474198 (hardcover : alk. paper) | ISBN 9781682474457 (ebook)
Subjects: LCSH: Spanish-American War, 1898—Fiction. | United States—History, Naval—19th century—Fiction. | BISAC: FICTION / War & Military. | FICTION / Biographical. | FICTION / Sea Stories. | GSAFD: War stories. | Historical fiction.
Classification: LCC PS3613.A28 (ebook) | LCC PS3613.A28 H676 2019 (print) | DDC 813/.6—dc23
LC record available at https://lccn.loc.gov/2018051297

27 26 25 24 23 22 21 20 19   9 8 7 6 5 4 3 2

This novel is respectfully dedicated to the memory of one of the bravest men I've ever known:

CAPT. CHARLES K. (CHUCK) CLINGENPEEL (CID/LCSO)

(1937–2013)

A soldier, lawman, adventurer, philosopher, mentor, and
dear friend who taught me so much, stood by me so often,
and made me a much better man.

The man who watches each day's sunrise with *anticipation*
of a great day ahead, and each day's sunset with *satisfaction*
of a great day done, can truly be said to live every day of his
life to the max.

—F/Sgt Chuck Clingenpeel, December 1976

An Introductory Word with My Readers

When writing this fourteenth novel in the Honor Series about Peter Wake, it occurred to me that both new and longtime readers might appreciate a timeline of our fictional hero's life until this point. It certainly has been far from dull. The source and informational notes arranged by chapter at the back of the novel have even more information on the places and people in the story. Readers who are interested in delving further into this fascinating subject can see my research bibliography, also in the back of the book.

Timeline of Peter Wake's Life from 1839 to Mid-1898

1839—Peter Wake is born into a seafaring family on the coast of Massachusetts on June 26.

1852—At age thirteen Wake goes to sea in his father's schooner to learn the coastal cargo trade.

1855—Wake is promoted to schooner mate at age sixteen.

1857—Wake is promoted to command of a schooner at age eighteen.

1861—The Civil War begins. At his father's plea, Wake remains a draft-exempt merchant marine captain on the New England coast. By 1862 his three older brothers—Luke, John, and Matthew—are already in the Navy and fighting the war.

1863—Wake loses his draft exemption and volunteers for the U.S. Navy. He is stationed at Key West and commissioned an acting master. Given command of a small sailing gunboat, *Rosalie*, he operates on the Southwest Florida coast and in the Bahamas against blockade-runners and is promoted to acting lieutenant. Irish-born boatswain's mate Sean Rork joins *Rosalie*'s crew, and the two men become lifelong best friends (as depicted in *At the Edge of Honor*—first novel of the Honor Series).

1864—Wake chases Union deserters from the Dry Tortugas to French-occupied Mexico. Later he marries Linda Donahue at Key West, with Rork as best man. Wake is engaged in amphibious operations against Confederates in Florida (as depicted in *Point of Honor*).

1865—Wake's daughter Useppa is born at Useppa Island. After the tumultuous end of the Civil War in Florida and Cuba, Wake is sent to hunt down ex-Confederates in Puerto Rico (as depicted in *Honorable Mention*).

1867—When volunteer officers are dismissed, Wake decides to stay in the Navy and is commissioned a regular lieutenant. He is one of the few officers in the Navy who haven't graduated from the Naval Academy. His son, Sean, is born at Pensacola Naval Station.

1869—While on a mission against a renegade American former naval officer off the coast of Panama, Wake relieves his captain of duty and is charged with mutiny. He is subsequently acquitted of the charge, but his reputation is permanently tarnished (as depicted in *A Dishonorable Few*).

1874—While Wake is involved in questionable activities in Spain and Italy, he is saved by Jesuits from further disrepute when a beautiful French woman enters his life. He later rescues the woman and other French civilians in Africa and is awarded the Legion of Honor by France and promoted to lieutenant commander (as depicted in *An Affair of Honor*).

1880—Wake embarks on his first espionage mission during the South American War of the Pacific and further cements his relationship with the Jesuits. He is awarded his second foreign medal, the Order of the Sun, by Peru. Before Wake can return home, his beloved wife, Linda, dies of cancer. He sinks into depression but then plunges into his work, helping to form the Office of Naval Intelligence (ONI) (as depicted in *A Different Kind of Honor*).

1883—On an espionage mission into French Indo-China, Wake befriends King Norodom of Cambodia, is awarded the Royal Order of Cambodia, and is promoted to commander. Wake and

Rork buy Patricio Island in Southwest Florida and build bunga-
lows there for use when they are on annual leave (as depicted in
The Honored Dead).

1886—Wake meets young Theodore Roosevelt and Cuban patriot
José Martí in New York City as he begins an espionage mission
against the Spanish in Havana, Tampa, and Key West. His deadly
twelve-year struggle against the Spanish secret police begins, as
well as friendships with Martí and Roosevelt (as depicted in *The
Darkest Shade of Honor*).

1888—A search for a lady friend's missing son in the Bahamas and
Haiti becomes a love affair and an espionage mission ending in
a perilous escape. Wake's relationship with the Russian secret
service begins. His marriage proposal rejected by his lover, Wake
falls back into depression and focuses on his work (as depicted
in *Honor Bound*). During a mission to rescue ONI's Cuban operatives from Spanish custody in Havana, Wake uses an introduction through Martí to forge a relationship with the Freemasons.
Barely escaping the Spanish secret police in Cuba, he manages
to save the lives of the men he was sent to find and liberate (as
depicted in *Honorable Lies*).

1889—Wake is sent to the South Pacific on an espionage mission
to prevent a war between Germany and America at Samoa. He is
awarded the Royal Order of Kalakaua by the Kingdom of Hawaii
and gains the gratitude of President Grover Cleveland but is
ashamed of the sordid methods he felt forced to use in Samoa (as
depicted in *Honors Rendered*).

1890—Wake learns that his 1888 love affair produced a daughter,
Patricia, who is growing up in Illinois with her maternal aunt
after her mother died in childbirth. Wake leaves ONI espionage
work and thankfully returns to sea in command of a small
cruiser. This same year, his son, Sean, graduates from the U.S.
Naval Academy as a commissioned officer.

1892—Wake has a love affair in Washington, D.C., with Maria Ana
Maura of Spain and is brought back into espionage work on a

counter-assassination mission in Mexico and Florida. He saves Martí's life and returns to sea in command of another warship (as depicted in *The Assassin's Honor*).

1893—In April, Wake is promoted to captain and Rork to the newly established rank of chief boatswain's mate. In May, Wake marries Maria, and his daughter Useppa marries her Cuban fiancé, Mario Cano, in a double wedding ceremony in Key West (as depicted in *The Assassin's Honor*).

1895—Wake's dear friend José Martí is killed in action while fighting the Spanish at Dos Rios in eastern Cuba on May 19.

1897—Wake ends seven years of sea duty with orders to be the special assistant to the young new assistant secretary of the Navy, his longtime friend Theodore Roosevelt. Together they ready the Navy for the looming war against Spain.

1898—Roosevelt sends Wake inside Cuba on an espionage mission against the Spanish during the tense confrontation before the Spanish-American War begins. He is in Havana Harbor when *Maine* explodes, and later that night kills his longtime nemesis, Colonel Isidro Marrón, the head of the Spanish secret police. After war is declared several months later, Wake leads a daring coastal raid against the enemy in Cuba. Afterward he is unofficially shunned for employing shockingly brutal tactics against the Spanish to accomplish the mission, save the lives of his men, and get them all home. Wounded during the mission, he convalesces in Tampa, nursed by his wife, Maria (as depicted in the first novel of the Honor Series trilogy about the Spanish-American War, *An Honorable War*).

As *Honoring the Enemy* begins we find Wake back in the thick of the Spanish-American War, somewhat recovered from his recent wounds. But instead of the ship command he deserves and expects, Wake is ordered to assist the U.S. Army's woefully unprepared and inept V Corps staff at Tampa in planning the invasion of Cuba.

A Note about the Memoirs

Peter Wake wrote his memoirs so his family and friends would know the truth of what had happened in his career. They are thus written with unusual candor and personal details. His descriptions and opinions of people may not be considered sensitive and tolerant in our modern age, but Wake was remarkably liberal for his time. His political assessments of personalities and events were frequently at odds with the norm back then but have proven to be uncannily prescient with our hundred-year hindsight.

The turn of the century was full of momentous events whose consequences dictated world history for the next ninety years. They changed all of us.

Robert N. Macomber
The Boat House
St. James, Pine Island
Florida

Preface

This is a memoir of men—and one very brave woman, my wife—
in the midst of war. My goal in recounting my experiences in Cuba
is to educate the next generation about what war is really like, for
they must not make the same miscalculations when facing future
confrontations. The most egregious error is supposing that we
Americans have exclusive possession of the moral high ground and
physical courage. In modern warfare, the cost of that sort of naïveté
is measured in the blood of thousands.

With startling rapidity, the onset of combat operations changes
long-assumed facts. Military plans never evolve as intended. Equipment never operates as expected. The enemy is never as incompetent,
or as invincible, as previously assessed to be. Fellow countrymen
and foreign allies turn out to be far less capable than they were
thought to be. Even Mother Nature enters the scenario. She is the
great equalizer, not caring a damn about nationality or military
status or politicians' bombast. Tropical terrain, weather, and disease
thwart momentum and crush morale.

Such was the situation in the jungles of eastern Cuba that summer of 1898. Within minutes of blundering ashore, the Americans
discovered all their prior assumptions were false. Like the sand
on Daiquiri's beach at flood tide, those comfortable notions disappeared—replaced by the rude reality of Cuba's incessant heat,
humidity, rain, disease, and insects. That was the first day. Soon
afterward the Americans learned in detail about the enemy's Mauser
rifles and Krupp artillery.

I was there from the very beginning. I endured the two most
significant battles of the war and witnessed the victories that made

the United States of America a world power. Back home, the nation rejoiced. But I knew how very close to a humiliating defeat we actually were.

The Spanish didn't have the luxury of arrogance in Cuba. They'd been fighting there for too long. All they had left was courage and skill. I saw it close up. And as the battles ground on, I found myself respecting and even honoring our enemy.

This volume of my memoirs tells why. Though written ten years after the events it describes, I still shudder at the memories of those days and nights in Cuba. It is my hope that future generations take these lessons to heart.

The next time we face a modern foe, we might not be so lucky.

Rear Adm. Peter Wake, USN
Special Naval Aide to the President
Washington, D.C.
13 September 1908

HONORING
THE ENEMY

1

The Hotel

U.S. Army V Corps Headquarters, Tampa Bay Hotel, Tampa, Florida
5:45 a.m., Monday, 6 June 1898

T HE TAMPA BAY HOTEL, Florida's premier tropical resort, is normally closed for the summer, when tourists tended to avoid the entire state. Built in 1892 and owned by railroad and real estate mogul Henry Plant, the hotel made a lot of money in the winter season. In 1898 it also made a lot of money in the summer, for war came to Tampa, and the shiny brass of the U.S. Army moved into the Tampa Bay Hotel.

The hotel's hot, musty rooms were now full of hobnobbing newspaper reporters, harried Army staff functionaries, serious-faced senior officers, and smiling politicians, along with a few insistent wives who regretted their decision to come to Florida in early summer. As I walked through the deserted public rooms at a quarter of six that June morning, not one of them was in sight. A general atmosphere of easygoing indolence pervaded everything. The place even *smelled* closed for business.

As I crossed the lobby I saw one man calmly noticing everything—Joseph Herrings. It didn't surprise me that he was there at that hour. He might turn up anywhere, at any time. A reporter for a German-language newspaper in New York, Herrings wrote about the Army's true military readiness and skills in articles that were disturbingly accurate. He cast a knowing smirk toward me before looking down and scratching something in his notepad.

My footsteps echoed loudly on the polished floor of the empty hallway leading to the Army staff offices. With every step my anger increased. The hotel was headquarters for an entire Army corps about to embark on a large-scale seaborne invasion of enemy territory—the first for the U.S. Army since the Mexican-American War half a century earlier. The lives of 17,000 American soldiers—and more important, *my* life—depended on what the various generals inside that hotel decided, if and when they ever got around to it.

I strode past the drowsy sentry, a less than impressive volunteer from Illinois, and entered the anteroom of the commanding general's office. I found it silent, too. Only one man was in sight, a smooth-faced lieutenant who seemed startled by my intrusion. He also appeared to have just arrived and was setting a glass of tea down on his desk. The ice shavings in it were an extravagance for which the resort was famous. *Savor it now, son*, I thought, *for there won't be any ice in Cuba.*

A pair of electric lamps illuminated the mixture of curiosity and pity on the lieutenant's face as he stood to greet me. Naval officers are rarely seen inside Army staff offices. But by the way he was studying me, especially the fresh scars on my face, I could tell I was no stranger to him. His manner indicated he'd seen me around the hotel while I'd been recovering from my wounds, though I'd tried to stay at the other end of the huge place. No doubt he'd heard the rumors about my ill-fated mission inside Cuba in late April. I could also tell that he probably had heard the rumor about where I was heading next; thus the pity.

The lieutenant quickly assumed a neutral expression. "Good morning, Captain Wake. I'm First Lieutenant Buford of the general's staff. We're honored you have officially joined us this morning, sir."

No more than two years out of West Point, I guessed. The shiny new aide-de-camp aiguillette braid on the left shoulder of Buford's immaculate uniform matched his gleaming silver rank insignia; wartime sped up the promotion system in both the Army and the Navy. I wondered if Buford ever visited his academy classmates sweltering in tents not a quarter mile away.

"Thank you, Lieutenant. I was told to be here at six for the chief of staff. I am a bit early, but it looks like the place hasn't yet opened up for the day. Is he around here somewhere?"

Buford caught my sarcasm. "Oh, we're open, sir. The rest of the staff will be arriving any minute. The chief of staff was looking forward to discussing the military situation in Cuba with you this morning, sir, but he's been called away on an important training issue in one of the regimental camps and doesn't know when he can get back. General Shafter will be here in a few minutes, though, and I know he also wanted to see you this morning."

He said it effortlessly, a very smooth lie. He followed with a reassuring smile to indicate all was well. I began to dislike First Lieutenant Buford. I knew his type. We had them in the Navy, too. They go far in their career without ever hearing a shot or making a deadly decision.

A training issue in one of the camps that requires a senior officer to solve? I knew better. The embarrassing fact was that there had been a drunken riot among some of the volunteer soldiers, barely quelled only a few hours before.

Buford gestured to a row of plush-looking red leather chairs near a potted areca palm. Having Army headquarters in a luxury hotel had its benefits.

"If you could wait here for the general, sir. It won't be long. Coffee, sir?"

"Thank you, Lieutenant," I replied as I settled into a chair and considered his adroit detour around the actual reason for the "important training issue."

Prostitutes had been found inside the tents of a newly recruited New York infantry regiment camped in the pine woods west of town. When the regiment's officers told the women to leave, the drunken soldiers suggested it was the officers who should leave. The confrontation went from insubordinate words to physical threats in seconds. It ended only with the desperate colonel's warning that he would bring in another regiment to kill the mutineers.

I'd heard all about it from a waiter serving me coffee thirty minutes earlier in the hotel's kitchen. He'd learned it from an exasperated messenger who was searching for an officer at headquarters to receive the regimental commander's request for help. The waiter thought it all quite funny. I thought it pathetic and wondered what the press would think of it when they arrived for their leisurely breakfast at the dining room in three hours or so. By noon the New York papers would have it via the wires. Then I thought of that smirk on Joseph Herrings' face and corrected my estimate. Maybe before noon.

The smiling lieutenant brought me a cup of very good Cuban coffee, some of the last brought in from the island before war was declared. He assured me we'd soon have much more of the stuff once we kicked those "cowardly little spics" off the island and took it over once and for all.

I merely nodded as I considered what an excellent target Buford's shiny shoulder braid would make for one of the "little spics" in the Spanish army.

2

The Army

U.S. Army V Corps Headquarters, Tampa Bay Hotel, Tampa, Florida
5:45 a.m., Monday, 6 June 1898

REGIMENTAL INSUBORDINATION was a rarity in the regular Army, but it was emblematic of the mob of raw recruits who had joined up for a patriotic lark after *Maine* exploded and sank in Havana Harbor. Unlike their professional counterparts, the volunteers flooding into Tampa from around the country showed little discipline or martial skill. Many had never fired their weapon. Some hadn't even been issued one.

The Army completely lacked the organizational ability to cope with the situation it suddenly faced: fighting a tropical jungle war in Asia and the Caribbean while defending the U.S. coasts from Spanish raiders. Army officers hadn't operated or supplied formations larger than a thousand men since the Civil War. In March, there had been only 28,000 men in the entire Army; 2 months later there were more than 100,000. Within another 3 months it would be more than 250,000. Across the country, Army camps run by overwhelmed officers sprang up haphazardly, placed more by politics than by military necessity or logic.

At Tampa alone, almost 30,000 soldiers had arrived in the past 3 weeks. Many still lacked shelter, provisions, supplies, clean water, and sanitary facilities. Most had never endured anything like the

95-degree heat, humidity, mosquitos, and rain of a Florida summer. Camp diseases such as dysentery were beginning to appear. The only item easily obtained was cheap liquor, some of which was little more than sweet-tasting poison.

Used to institutional ineptitude, regular Army soldiers quietly took care of themselves by scavenging for what they needed, much of it being the private or government property of the volunteers. As for the grog and the trollops, regulars were smart enough to keep those dubious pleasures out of their officers' sight.

Even worse for the Army, reporters were starting to sniff around and ask questions. The real danger wasn't members of the New York City press. Those worldly Hearst and Pulitzer men ignored the more sordid aspects of camp life. Some even quietly indulged in them. No, it was the reporters from America's small hometowns writing about how their beloved boys were being led and fed who had the generals worried. If word of what was really happening in Tampa got out, the endless supply of cannon fodder for the U.S. Army would evaporate like the hotel's famous ice shavings in the summer sun. This was the real reason the chief of staff wasn't in his office to discuss war operations. He was trying to keep the proverbial lid on a pot already boiling over.

The effort in Tampa was not an auspicious beginning for the great military crusade the national press and politicos had been promoting. I pitied the Army, for when they actually entered the jungles of Cuba and faced the well-armed, well-led, and well-supplied Spanish enemy their difficulties at Tampa would seem trivial. I wondered how they would cope.

So far, the war hadn't gone particularly well for me, either. I'd spent the previous month recuperating from a coastal raid concocted by politicians in Washington. I was heartily tired of fighting on land and more than ready for a naval command. I'd damn well earned one. But I knew it wasn't going to happen. I was a pariah in Washington because of what I'd had to do in Cuba to salvage that damned operation.

So instead of getting what I wanted and deserved, I was ordered to report to the Army, a not so subtle message of my superiors' disapproval. "Senior naval liaison to the V Army Corps staff" was my official assignment, presented to me as if it were a prestigious posting. That was just another lie, one among the many fabricated in Washington recently.

Thus I was sitting across from First Lieutenant Buford, who busied himself trying to look busy. He arranged piles of papers in neat rows on his desk while sipping his iced tea. I wanted to fling them all onto the floor in disgust. Such disagreeable thoughts were interrupted ten very long minutes later by a commotion in the hallway outside. The soldier stationed by the outer door, now fully awake, stamped the floorboards with his boots and slapped his rifle to present arms position. I heard somebody shout, "Morning, sir!"

The door opened, and in lumbered an obese, sad-eyed Army officer who was already sweating profusely at this early hour. It was none other than the senior commander of America's military effort to liberate Cuba.

The lieutenant shot up into perfect West Point attention. "Good morning, General!"

I stood up as Maj. Gen. William Rufus Shafter grunted something to Buford about the morning being anything but good.

The lieutenant politely gestured toward me. "Captain Wake of the Navy is here to report in, sir."

I announced myself to my new superior officer. "Captain Peter Wake, reporting as ordered, General."

Shafter looked at me for the first time. A slight smile of recognition crossed his face. He had probably seen me on the hotel's verandah. "Ah yes, the Navy. A fish out of water, eh?" he said, chuckling at his little joke. The lieutenant smiled appreciatively. I didn't. The general's chuckle faded away. "Yes, well, come on in, Wake, and we'll talk."

He turned to the lieutenant. "When the chief of staff returns, I want to see him immediately. In the meantime, Captain Wake and I need privacy."

"Yes, sir," said Buford. I followed the general into his office, a converted corner suite overlooking the hotel's colorful gardens. Behind us, an entourage of eager minions surged into the anteroom. The senior ones grabbed the fancy chairs, awaiting their turn with the great man.

Once the door was closed, Shafter plopped down with a sigh into a groaning swivel chair behind a large desk. Placing his valise on the desktop, he swung around to take me into his gaze and got right to the point. "Know why you're here, Wake?"

I found his abruptness surprisingly refreshing. Shafter was no fool. Fully aware of the Army's unpreparedness and his own ignorance of Cuba and the Spanish foe, he knew the daunting odds against succeeding in this assignment. The man had seen combat, from the colossal horrors of the Civil War, where he received the Medal of Honor, to the ruthless battles against cagey bands of hostile Indians on the western Plains, where he picked up his nickname, "Pecos Bill." But all that was long ago. He wasn't Pecos Bill anymore.

I'd heard that Shafter was chosen for this critically important command because he lacked political ambition and therefore posed no threat to anyone in power at Washington. This, in my opinion, was a point in his favor. I decided he could handle the truth.

"General, I *thought* I was getting a ship command, but instead I received official orders from the Navy Department to be the naval liaison for the Army expeditionary forces here in Tampa. I've recently learned, however, that I won't really be on your staff because you are sending me on a clandestine mission inside Oriente, Cuba, ahead of the invasion."

The general's eyes narrowed and hardened.

I went on, "Once there, I am to make contact with Major General Calixto García, commander of the eastern department of the Cuban Liberation Army, and be the liaison between his force and the American Army. I am to ensure that Cuban forces clear away Spanish forces from our invasion landing area near Santiago de Cuba. Once that is done, our regiments can come ashore unopposed and have the time and space to form up properly before facing the enemy. Otherwise, the landing will be a bloodbath."

Shafter's eyes were no longer merely hard. They were angry now, boring into me as I continued.

"I was selected for this assignment because nobody in the Army has my knowledge of Cuba and the Spanish enemy, my contacts among the Cubans, and my ability to move quietly in a foreign country. I was further told the invasion is in ten days, and your entire corps is embarking on makeshift troopships here at Tampa within two days. So obviously, neither I nor you have much time . . . *sir.*"

His ever-darkening expression made it clear that the general found my unenthusiastic candor disturbing. I didn't really care.

"You're right on all counts, Wake," he growled. "But how the hell do you know all this? It's confidential."

"From one of your staff officers, sir. He was drunk at dinner here in the hotel three nights ago."

I didn't elaborate that in his inebriated state the ignorant lout had told me he was jealous of my mission, which he declared would be "an exciting adventure." I also didn't add that he was one of the sycophants waiting in the anteroom.

"Really? And who was this officer with the big mouth?" Shafter demanded.

I shrugged. "Does it matter, sir? The entire staff knows the confidential invasion plans, and they all need to keep their mouths shut. Thousands of American lives will be in jeopardy when they arrive on that Cuban beach. Not to mention *mine* in setting all this up."

Before he could press further about his loose-tongued officer, I changed topics. "General, I've already arranged clandestine transport to Cuba and have to start my journey this evening to get there in time, so we'll need to conclude our plans for my mission right now."

He said nothing, appearing a bit taken aback by my attitude, so I continued my monologue. "I understand the exact beaches have not yet been chosen for the landing. Once your forces arrive at the Santiago area, I will send word out to your ship from General García's headquarters about recommended places to land. Also, I strongly suggest a preinvasion meeting ashore with you, Admiral Sampson, and General García when you arrive so the three commanders can work out last-minute details and eliminate any confusion over timing and responsibilities. Do you have any other information for my mission, sir?"

The proper way to put my last question would be to ask if he had any further *orders* for me, but I preferred to be unencumbered by such restrictions. Most generals and admirals have forgotten how to be innovative and nimble. Shafter had been a general a long time.

For a split second his face reflected extreme resentment and I anticipated a rebuke, but it soon faded into reluctant resignation. "No, I can't think of anything more, Captain Wake. I heard what you did in Cuba in April and was told you were the right man for this job. I can see they were correct."

I rose from the chair without seeking permission to do so, yet another breach of military courtesy. "Thank you, sir. I know your time is valuable, General, and you have a lot of officers waiting to see you, so I'll be on my way. Good luck, sir. I'll see you in Cuba."

He stood also, requiring an effort that was unsettling to watch. As I walked out of the office I wondered how this well-intentioned but profoundly unfit man could survive the Cuban jungle in the lethal fever season. How could any of the Americans?

3

Breakfast with a Hero

U.S. Army V Corps Headquarters, Tampa Bay Hotel, Tampa, Florida
6:52 a.m., Monday, 6 June 1898

I WAS HEADING PAST THE hotel's registration desk toward the elevator to my third-floor room when Col. Leonard Wood marched into the lobby. A renaissance man if ever there was one, the thirty-eight-year-old Wood was a handsome and cultured Bostonian, Harvard-educated physician, former football athlete, amateur naturalist, career soldier, Medal of Honor recipient, and Indian fighter. Now he was the commanding officer of the 1st Volunteer Cavalry Regiment, already nicknamed the Rough Riders by the press. His usually pensive face split into a wide smile the moment he saw me. Seconds later he was excitedly pumping my hand.

"Good to see you, Peter! Theodore told me you'd be here. I haven't seen you since our dinner at the Metropolitan Club. What was that, six months ago?" He raised a finger to trace the wound on my cheek. "Whoa, who sewed you up—a native witch doctor?"

I didn't get a chance to reply that it was a Navy boatswain with a sail needle, because another man burst through the doors: Wood's assistant regimental commander and my energetic young friend of a dozen years, Theodore Roosevelt. Until a month ago Theodore had been assistant secretary of the Navy and my direct civilian superior. Now he was a volunteer lieutenant colonel in the Army and one rank junior to me.

Upon seeing me, Roosevelt executed a flawless left-oblique march and stopped the regulation thirty-six inches from me, complete with clicked heels. He straightened to attention, his toothy grin tightening into mock solemnity. Looking me in the eye, he slowly rendered the hand salute.

I returned the salute, violating naval regulations, and told him to stand easy.

Then the sentimental dam within Roosevelt burst. He clasped my shoulders and announced in a voice they could hear back in the kitchen, "Oh, my *gracious*, Peter! I have waited such a long time to be able to do that! I am simply delighted to see you. Edith told me she'd had dinner with you and your lovely Maria here in the hotel last week. I've a thousand questions. How are the wounds?" He pointed at my cheek. "Say, that's a very impressive *Renommierschmiss!*"

I laughed. "It's hardly a dueling scar, Theodore. Just a couple of minor splinter wounds."

"No matter, it shows you've been in *action*. Let's get some breakfast!" Theodore spun toward Wood. "Do you agree, sir? We've a bit of time right now, and Peter can fill us in on what's what down there." With dismay he quietly added, "He's probably the only one around here who really knows a thing about Cuba."

Wood nodded. "Good idea, Theodore. Peter, the Army's buying, so please say yes."

"Very well, Leonard," I heard myself say, though I had little time and a lot to do.

A few minutes later we were seated, breakfast was ordered—my second of the day—and I was being interrogated about the enemy's leadership, strategy, defensive works, weaponry, transport, and communications. After I'd given my opinions on those subjects, which were generally positive, I was asked about the enemy's individual morale and fighting ability. Most Americans underestimated them. I didn't.

"The Spanish order of battle in Cuba totals about a quarter of a million troops. In my opinion, morale is generally low among the conscripts sent out from Spain to serve in Cuba, relatively high among the veteran regular soldiers on the island, and very high among the pro-Spanish island militia, the guerillas. The Spanish forces have fought a nasty war for the last three years. They won't run away from us, fellas."

I let that point sink in, then continued. "The regular soldiers are disciplined professionals experienced by fighting in Africa, the Philippines, and Cuba. They don't get rattled. If outnumbered they will withdraw in good order and make you pay for every foot of your advance. Forget what the American press says about them. Do *not* underestimate the Spanish army, gentlemen. Their regulars are deadly. All of their troops—regulars and militia—know the jungle and how to fight in it. Our troops don't."

"What's the best way to beat them?" asked Wood.

"Bait them to attack you over open ground, if you find any. Hit them with artillery and machine guns as they approach."

"Like you did at Isabela?" asked Roosevelt. He saw my surprise and added, "I heard about it from Woodgerd the day before I left to join the regiment."

A former Army officer turned mercenary, Michael Woodgerd was an old mutual friend who'd turned up at the battle in a new role: correspondent for William Hearst's newspapers. He'd been alongside me in the battle.

"Yes, but I was lucky. We weren't in the jungle. It was a coastal town with open ground. We were able to withdraw the men onto the ships at the dock before the Spaniards overwhelmed us. Then we escaped under the covering fire of the squadron.

"You won't have naval gunfire support once you move a couple of miles inland from the beach," I warned. "And moving artillery along jungle paths will be slow, if not impossible. Keep your machine guns well maintained and always ready. Forget your cavalry horses. They aren't used to the Cuban heat and forage, and there'll be no room for large cavalry formations to maneuver in the forests."

"No horses? Our boys won't like that at all," said Roosevelt. "Woodgerd told me the same thing, though. By the bye, he also informed me about the official government and press reaction to your victory at Isabela. To say I was angry is an understatement, but I was gone from power by then."

Because of the controversial tactics I was forced to employ to save my men against an enemy outnumbering us ten to one, the official reaction to the victory at Isabela a month earlier was to simply ignore the battle. Washington and New York considered my actions dishonorable atrocities unworthy of an American and worried what the public would think of my decisions. The entire affair was downplayed into a minor raid and skirmish with minimal comment, no mention of the tactics, and no accolades. The press also ignored what had happened, for it didn't fit in with their propaganda. Woodgerd, who had written a factual account supporting my decisions and tactics, quit the Hearst newspaper in a rage the day his editor refused to publish it.

"Don't worry about it, Theodore. The important thing is we accomplished the mission and got the Cuban exile battalion with its artillery into Cuba."

"And your new mission?" Roosevelt asked, with a noticeable tinge of hesitancy.

I took a moment to look each man in the eye before replying. I'd joined the Navy thirty-five years earlier to stay out of the Army. Now I was working for the Army because of these two men.

"You two damn well know what my mission is. You both recommended me for it. Without my consent or knowledge, I might add. I found out last Friday evening during dinner, from a drunken fool on the Army staff who let it slip. Shafter confirmed it a few minutes ago when I reported into V Corps Headquarters."

Wood looked worried. "Peter, we didn't mean—"

I held up a hand to stop him. "Don't say a word, either of you. I've had three days to calm the hell down. I've already arranged transport to Cuba for tonight. I just wish I had Rork with me."

Chief Boatswain's Mate Sean Rork was my best friend and thirty-five-year comrade in arms, the one man I trusted completely in perilous situations. We'd worked intelligence missions around the world and saved each other's life many times.

Roosevelt shook his head. "Blasted bad luck. Edith told me about Rork's fiancée marrying another man while you two were fighting the Spanish at Isabela. He's far better off without her, of course. I understand why he needed to go back to sea rather than face his old friends."

From a life filled with tragedy, Theodore knew grief well. He lightened his tone. "But I understand Rork's joined *Oregon*, right? A bully ship! And if I recall correctly, isn't your son Sean with her also?"

My son was a lieutenant and the assistant gunnery officer in the battleship *Oregon*. She was steaming with Admiral Sampson's blockade fleet off Santiago de Cuba.

"Yes, Theodore, they are both with *Oregon* waiting to battle the Spanish fleet, which is where I should be as well." I changed the subject. "Enough of me and the Navy. What about you two? What's happening with your regiment?"

Wood answered. "Our train got in Friday night after four days of travel. They originally told us it would be two days. When we finally arrived, we found total confusion. Nobody knew where we were to camp. Eventually we bivouacked a quarter mile west of the hotel."

He lowered his voice. "We're keeping the men busy with training and maintaining the camp conditions as sanitary as we can here. So far, only a few have succumbed to the various detrimental influences that seem to abound in Tampa. Haven't yet gotten word when we're loading on the ships or where in Cuba we're heading."

"In my opinion, this inaction degrades efficiency, sir," piped up Roosevelt. "Our boys are raring to go down there and show the world what an American fighting man can do!"

I didn't comment, for I knew they'd find out soon enough when they were shipping out, probably later that day. Instead, seeing an hour of my precious time had somehow quickly gone by, I stood to leave. "Gentlemen, I'm behind schedule and have to go. I'll see you next in Cuba. Theodore, your children need you, so don't do something stupid when you get into combat thinking you're being heroic. Understood?"

"Yes, sir!" he answered with a grin, but we both knew he would likely do just that.

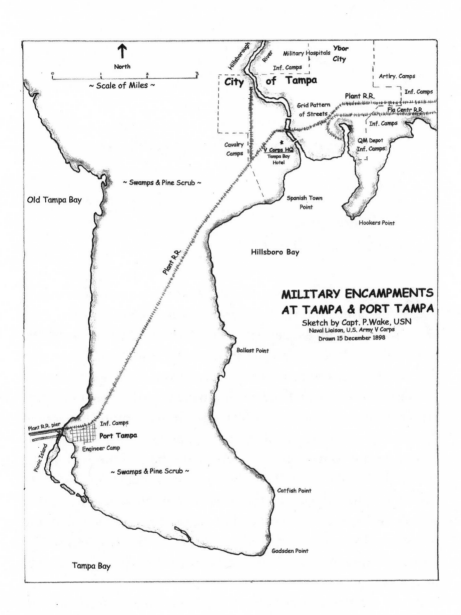

North
~ Scale of Miles ~

Hillsborough River

Military Hospitals
Ybor City
Inf. Camps

City of Tampa

Artlry. Camps

Plant R.R.
Inf. Camps

Grid Pattern of Streets

Fla Centr R.R.

Inf. Camps

Cavalry Camps

V Corps HQ
Tampa Bay Hotel

QM Depot
Inf. Camps

Old Tampa Bay

~ Swamps & Pine Scrub ~

Spanish Town Point

Hookers Point

Hillsboro Bay

MILITARY ENCAMPMENTS
AT TAMPA & PORT TAMPA

Sketch by Capt. P. Wake, USN
Naval Liaison, U.S. Army V Corps
Drawn 15 December 1898

Ballast Point

Plant R.R.

Plant R.R. pier
Inf. Camps
Port Tampa
Engineer Camp

Picnic Island

~ Swamps & Pine Scrub ~

Catfish Point

Gadsden Point

Tampa Bay

4
***

The Spreading of Joy

208 Lafayette Street, Tampa, Florida
9 a.m., Monday, 6 June 1898

AFTER CHANGING MY UNIFORM for a rumpled tan suit, I dashed out the back verandah of the hotel. Leaving the resort's idyllic gardens behind, I turned left on Lafayette Street and walked east on the iron bridge over the Hillsborough River to the center of town. Tampa was no longer the quiet, pleasant southern community it had been for many years, for the lure of government war money had transformed it from charming lethargy to cynical chaos. The results were vividly apparent to the senses.

Making my way along Lafayette past the locomotives at the South Florida Railroad Depot belching their dense, toxic clouds, I tried to ignore the competing stench from horse manure in the streets, leakage from overflowing regimental latrines, and the overworked sewer system designed for far fewer people. The city reeked of human and animal waste. The sights and sounds were no better.

At the intersection of Lafayette and Tampa Streets, traffic was in a state of bedlam. Four vehicles had just collided, one of which was completely capsized. Its horses had run off, and the cargo of bananas, strewn everywhere, was turning into a sea of brown mush and rotting quickly in the sun. A long line of Army commissary wagons waited on Tampa Street, the drivers half asleep, having given up hope of moving anytime soon. In contrast to the drivers, three dozen people of all colors and classes stood amid the wreckage, squabbling about who was at fault in Tampa's primary languages: English, Spanish, and Italian. Two frustrated policemen were issuing orders to which no one in the angry mob paid any attention.

On the crowded sidewalk it was no better. Wandering soldiers, some still drunk from the night before, swaggered or tottered along. Smug merchants and dapper government functionaries sidled through as disgusted young women tried to ignore the rude comments soldiers cast their way. It was only midmorning, but in the alleyways I saw thieves coldly searching the crowds for unwary souls. They could afford to wait. The day's incoming troop trains hadn't arrived yet.

After passing a bookbinder's shop, I came to my destination next door, a seedy-looking saloon. Half a dozen sullen soldiers were loitering outside waiting for it to open. They took no notice of me as I ducked into a narrow alley beside the saloon and climbed a rickety exterior stairway to the second floor. The door at the upper landing was unlocked, and I walked inside. It was pitch black compared with the sun's white glare outside.

"You are late. Rare for you," said a deep, disembodied voice somewhere to my left. I recognized the refined Creole drawl with its Gallic accent. "Unforeseen interruptions, Professor."

"Understandable. There have been a lot of those for everyone lately. I have the information you needed, but as usual it is not written down. Too many eyes and ears around here. Some of them belong to your enemy."

My eyes began to adjust to the gloom, registering a tiny candle providing a dim glow from a café table in the far corner. It was oppressively hot and rank in the room. Sweat poured off me. The room's only other occupant, a dark-skinned older man practically invisible except for his white hair, goatee, and gleaming eyes, lounged in a simple chair at the table. He wasn't actually a professor. The sophisticated manner was a practiced façade he enjoyed. I was one of the few who knew his real name—or at least I thought I did—though I always used the common moniker by which he was known in the Caribbean.

As he gestured to the other chair, smoke from a Cuban cigar wafted over me. His left hand was on a bottle. I could smell the sweet scent of rum on his breath.

"Thought you might want a taste of Dupré Barbancourt's very best, Peter. Might steady your nerves for what lies ahead—as it did for us in Haiti a decade ago."

When I didn't reply, he laughed disdainfully. "Too early in the day for you, Peter? Oh yes, you Americans have strict religious rules about such indulgences in the morning."

I ignored the bait. I also remained standing. This wasn't a social call. "No rum for me. I don't have much time and need a clear head, so just let me know the code names of my contact with the rendez-vous location, date, and time."

He seemed disappointed there would be no discussion of societal mores. The Professor could be quite mercurial when he'd been drinking. I'd seen him shoot a man for being impolite to a dog.

"As you wish. We shall concentrate on the business at hand. There is only one contact, Peter. No secondary contact or contingency plan is available. Times are perilous. Willing collaborators are few, and your enemies are many. The code name for your contact is Isidro."

"Isidro?"

He took a long pull from the bottle, then chuckled softly. "Ah, I knew you would appreciate the poetic justice of such a nom de guerre, not to mention the additional layer of anonymity it provides. Really, who among your considerable list of personal adversaries would think you'd use that particular name for the complete stranger who controls your destiny?"

His sarcasm did have a valid point. Isidro was the name of my nemesis, the Spanish secret policeman I'd killed in Cuba four months earlier, before war was declared. The bastard had been trying to kill me and my family for twelve years.

"Very funny. Where do I meet this Isidro? What does he look like?"

"Your rendezvous with Isidro is at Tánamo, on Cuba's northern coast. No specific time, but a very specific day. Just get yourself there. Isidro will know you have arrived and will contact you. You know the place?"

"Know of it. Never been there. What day?"

"On the twelfth of this month, no earlier and no later, for Isidro has other commitments. Which means you have only six days. Can you make it in time?"

"Seems I'll have to, won't I?"

He sensed my disapproval of the loose arrangements. His apology rang a little hollow. "*Je suis désolé*. It was the best I could do since you gave me such short notice."

I'd cabled him my request late on the previous Friday night, after the drunk let slip my mission. "You did well to get all this done in three days. No one else could've done it. *Merci*. So, what's your fee?"

He'd refused to discuss a fee earlier, though I'd asked in the cable. The Professor shrugged and took another pull of rum. "In this particular endeavor I had to be especially innovative. Called in some long-ago promised favors, of which certain people needed to be reminded. I also had to spread some joy to facilitate the rental of loyalty among the locals at your destination. One hundred British sterling pounds of joy, to be precise. That makes my total fee twelve hundred U.S. dollars. I presume I shall be reimbursed in the standard way?"

He knew $1,200 was more than triple the highest amount I'd paid in the past to get people into or out of Cuba. It was to be expected in the current situation, however, for war has a precipitous effect on prices.

I knew he wasn't lying to me. He wouldn't, for he literally owed his life to me. The Professor had a lot of mortal enemies of his own. He knew if he ever cheated me or I suddenly disappeared, his identity and last known location would be sent to those enemies. His life would be instantly forfeit, measured in hours.

"Yes," I replied. "Your fee will be deposited in the Nassau account at the beginning of next month, like the old days. Anything else?"

"Yes, a warning. The Oriente province is vastly different from Havana, Peter. Its people and culture are more like Haiti in many ways. This, naturally, means it is much like Africa."

"I'm well aware of the cultural similarities, Professor."

He chuckled again, this time with a touch of evil. "Yes, you have been in Oriente, but in the white cities, not in the remote, un-Christian, uncivilized areas. And this time you will not be so fortunate as to have me with you, Peter."

After a brief pause for dramatic effect, he continued. "Isidro is a curious character who possesses some highly unusual acquaintances who will be your guides across the mountains to the south coast. I am afraid they are of the type who will remind you of your painful experiences in Haiti."

Haiti—the one place in the world that would always haunt me. I couldn't forget my terrifying time there, though I'd tried for years. Poisoned surreptitiously by Vodoun sorcerers, I was thought dead by everyone, even though I was still conscious. My body was about to be buried when Rork saved me with an antidote made from bush medicines. I knew exactly the hazards to which the Professor alluded. A chill went through me.

He leaned forward in the chair. "You must remember this point very well, Peter: my money bought you an entrée with Isidro's entourage and further contacts, but you are the one who must cement that entrée into a *bond*. This is an absolute necessity, for those strange people will be your only protection in the wild mountains of Oriente on your journey to General García."

He knows about García?

He leaned back, taking another gulp, letting the rum swirl in his mouth as he watched my reaction closely. After a couple of seconds he leered through the gloom at me. "Oh, don't look so surprised, my friend. Of course, you are headed for García. Why else would any American go to Oriente these days? Just remember what I said. Do not antagonize your guides."

Using every ounce of willpower, I merely uttered, "I'll try to remember that."

His reply was equally nonchalant, rendered partly in in his native Haitian Creole. "Then it is time to say *bòn chans, zanmi mwen . . .*"

That last phrase, "good luck, my friend," he uttered with obvious insincerity. I responded with a standard line in the same lingo, another recollection from that sinister time of my life. "*Volonte BonDye.*" God willing.

With that said, I walked out the door into the brilliant sunlight. Heading back through the pandemonium of the streets to the grand hotel, I walked more quickly than before. Maria was waiting for me in the cool, clean, gentle quiet of our room. I needed to hold her. I needed to feel her love. To feel normal.

I also had to purge those memories of Haiti from my mind.

5

Au Revoir, Not *Adieu*

Tampa Bay Hotel, Tampa, Florida
10 a.m., Monday, 6 June 1898

OUR CORNER ROOM ON the third floor was one of the hotel's finest, certainly the equal of General Shafter's at the other end of the quarter-mile-long building. It was spacious and lavishly appointed with the latest in amenities, and Maria and I had resided there quite comfortably for the previous month while I recovered from the flesh wounds on my face, chest, and torso.

This entirely agreeable convalescence was courtesy of my wife's wealth, for I could not have paid for it on my naval salary. This is not to say that our usual living arrangements were as opulent. Quite the contrary, for we both preferred a simple home life. Up in Alexandria, Virginia, we lived in a small cottage. Our retreat down at Patricio Island in Florida was an even smaller bungalow.

When I finally reached the posh room, my suit was drenched with perspiration and I was ready for a cool drink. But our room wasn't the refuge I'd hoped for. Far more important worries awaited me there.

Maria had tried to be supportive since I'd told her the previous Friday night about the general aspects of my new assignment. "Admitted to her" would be a more accurate description, for she had intuitively known I was returning to the war in Cuba—a war

24

against her native Spain. She'd confronted me about it before I could figure out a way to bring it up.

When I entered the room, she was sitting in a chair by the window, crying. In the garden below, soldiers were going through the ritual of changing the guard. Standing behind her, I held her shoulders and kissed her neck. She was trembling as the sergeant of the guard bellowed his commands, putting on a show for the staff officers and reporters assembled on the verandah.

Maria's tears grew into wracking sobs when she looked up at me. I could see she needed to unload the burden weighing on her heart. It started slowly in a whisper, rapidly increasing to a torrent of despondency. She reached up and clutched my hands.

"Peter, I am trying to be brave for you, but it is so impossibly difficult to smile when I must cry—when any sane person would cry. Everyone and everything around us has become insane. The world is insane. All because of this war madness over something called national honor. I have lost so much. My darling son Francisco, a priest who never hurt anyone, is dead, murdered by a monster who called himself a proud Spaniard. My other son, my little Juanito, is a prisoner of war languishing in a filthy camp a thousand miles north of here."

She paused, but I said nothing. She had to let it all out.

"And you, my *husband*, the center of my being, who came so close to dying from Spanish guns, are now scarred by them for life. Our very best friend, Rork, is somewhere out there on the ocean with our young Sean, waiting to fight the Spanish navy. And last night our well-meaning but stupidly naïve friend Theodore actually told Edith he needed to face the enemy to prove himself a good American man. I just spoke with her. She is sick with fear he will die or be maimed. All of this misery, and why? Because some Spanish idiot sank a warship? Or even worse, maybe it was an accident caused by some American idiot?"

Maria knew I doubted the official U.S. explanation that a Spanish mine had destroyed *Maine* at Havana back in February. I thought it might have been a spontaneous combustion in the coal bunker, which had been filled with notoriously unstable bituminous coal.

The bunker was adjacent to the ship's forward magazine, which then exploded. Many naval officers had thought and said the same thing at first; now they all echoed the official conclusion.

In her anger, Maria's fingers dug into my hands. "Every day I see more and more sick boys in the Army hospital, Peter. Now we have wounded sailors coming in from the small battles around the Cuban coast. Soon the big battles will be fought, and then it will be *thousands* of boys coming into the hospital. No one is prepared. We are so short of nurses, even someone useless like me is needed to tend to the patients."

Maria was not a trained nurse. In an effort to do something positive after Francisco was killed she had volunteered to help organize Red Cross hospitals in Washington and Tampa while I was away at war. Since there weren't enough trained nurses, she'd pitched in to help, learning by doing. By all accounts she was good at it, but the work had taken a fearful toll on her heart.

"I can't do it anymore, Peter. I keep seeing your face, or Sean's, or Rork's, or Theodore's, on each one who arrives. I am so frightened . . ."

Her anguish overcame her. She was unable to speak or even look at me. I wasn't sure what to say or do. I knelt beside her chair. Turning her to face me, I pulled her close, gently suggesting, "Perhaps some time away would be good. You could go home to Alexandria."

She shook her head wearily. "No. It is too near to Washington, where the most truly insane are urging all this on. On the street, people stare at me with contempt, for my Spanish blood stands out. At least down here in Florida there are so many with Spanish blood that I am not a curiosity. Here, I am busy helping the sick and wounded who bear the consequences of this insanity and ignorance."

Her anger had stopped the tears. Suddenly, she seemed emptied of ire as well, asking in a small voice, "How much time do we have left before you go?"

"A little less than two hours, dear."

Her hand lightly touched my face. "Promise me you will come back, Peter. You promised before and came back. So, I need to hear you promise me again, right now."

I kissed her, lingering on her lips, savoring her taste, her scent, everything about her. I followed with a vow from my heart. "Maria, I promise to come back to you. I promise we will get through this and be stronger for it. I love you. No outside insanity can ever part us. We have a lifetime ahead of us. And someday soon we'll be able to tell our new grandchild our wonderful love story."

I was rewarded by a smile. "Oh, it would be wonderful if you are back in time for Useppa's baby in November. I am looking forward to having a new little life to love and guide. We will be good grand-parents, won't we? Oh, how I cling to that future joy, Peter. It is the only pleasant part of my life these days."

I saw by the clock on the dresser that it was half past ten. "I know it's early, but why don't we have something to eat, and perhaps a glass of wine. Then we can rest a bit in our big bed over there. What do you think?"

She favored me with one of her delicious laughs, part innocent and part naughty.

"Sailors! Do all of you think like this?"

"I have no idea whatever you mean, my darling," I replied. "Are you suggesting we do something other than *rest* in that big bed?"

"Yes, I am, and I suggest we do it now," she giggled. "I shocked the hotel by requesting our luncheon food and wine be here at eleven-fifteen. Until then you, my dearest husband, will get a reminder of why you should come back to me."

"I love your reminders."

"Thank you. Here is another. When you walk out of this door later, we will say *au revoir*, not *adieu*, and the next time we see each other we will immediately run right back into this bed, as if we never left. Those are *my* orders, Captain Peter Wake, of the famous United States Navy."

"Aye, aye, ma'am!"

For the next ninety minutes the insanity of war, Maria's fears about me in Cuba, and my nightmarish memories of Haiti disap-peared from the luxurious corner room on the third floor of the elegant Tampa Bay Hotel. There was only our gentle love.

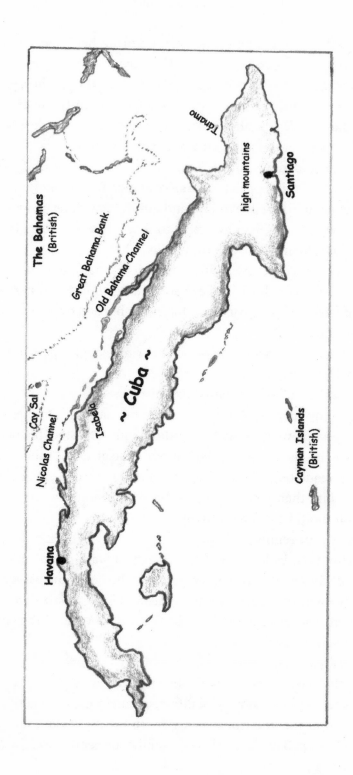

6

Back in Cuba

Tánamo Bay, Cuba
Sunday, 12 June 1898

SIX LONG, HOT, TENSE DAYS later I arrived just after dawn. It wasn't a triumphant return for me. The freighter captain had no wish to tarry an extra moment while transporting a spy in a war zone, so I was quickly dumped from the dinghy like trash on the rough shell-and-coral beach at Tánamo Bay. Five minutes after the dinghy returned, the ship was gone.

It was oppressively hot and humid on the beach, with not a ripple of wind on the water. The mangrove jungle behind the beach stank of rotting vegetation and some dead animal. My clothing—the faded tan cotton suit of a humble Cuban merchant—was already soaked with sweat.

Fifty feet away, the head of a seven-foot-long crocodile protruded from the mangroves, its narrow, toothy jaws slightly open, as if having a private laugh at my expense. It slowly turned to watch me, an intruder in its domain. Cuban crocodiles can be very aggressive, as I remembered well from back in February, so I slowly backed away from the reptile's part of the shoreline.

I found a muddy path leading from Punta Gitana inland through the dense tangle of mangroves. As I headed southeast on the pathway, a cloud of mosquitos and no-see-ums emerged to plague every exposed part of my body. My destination was the village of Tánamo, which my rudimentary map indicated was about three miles away. Once there, it was my intention to keep a lookout for any enemy Spanish or friendly Cuban forces and scout out a secure place to hide for the day while I waited for Isidro to find me.

Trudging along, I put away memories of the past six weeks of marital affections, soft beds, good food, decent libations, and intriguing conversations. They needed to be forgotten, not lamented or dwelled upon. I was in the jungle in enemy territory, and I needed to focus on my mission. From harsh experience, I knew that tomorrow, and each damned day afterward, conditions would get only worse.

At this particularly demoralized moment a squall line arrived. I'd been watching it come down a hill in the interior. This was not simply a heavy shower, as happens in northern climes. In the tropics, rain is a deluge. The cascade had enough weight in it to make me bend over with the strain of fighting my way through it as I slogged through the mud it churned up.

Visibility was cut to fifty feet ahead on the path. My ears, mouth, eyes, pockets, and shoes were filled with water. The sound, sight, feel, and smell of pounding rain drowned out all other sensations. Even the bugs fled. Behind the first squall was another, then another and another. No respite, no sun, no end in sight.

Nothing on my person or carefully stowed in my seabag escaped the penetrating rain. I could predict the results. None of my possessions would be dry again for the duration of my time on the island. Mold and fungus would be apparent on everything by tomorrow. My weapons would rust in two days if not cleaned and oiled carefully. Within three days the fabric of my clothing would begin to deteriorate. In a week or two I'd be in filthy rags, able to carry less and less on my shoulders as the skin sores spread.

I was back in Cuba.

7

Isidro

Tánamo, Cuba

Sunday, 12 June 1898

A S ALL ARMCHAIR STRATEGIES inevitably do when they meet reality in Cuba, mine soon fell apart. It happened only a mile from the beach where I landed.

Sloshing through ankle-deep mud, the incessant rain having succeeded in beating down my stamina, I moved in a trancelike state, my eyes staring down at the mud just in front of me. My senses thus diminished, I literally ran into the man blocking the path.

Charcoal black and slit-eyed, his skinny body barely attired in tattered underwear, he stood with arms akimbo holding a long machete. His countenance was decidedly unfriendly.

I offered my apologies in rough Spanish, but he said nothing. He only stood there, mutely glowering at me. The reply came from someone right behind me.

"Norteamericano?"

Turning around, I found the speaker to be like the other man in physique and attire. But this fellow clearly had some status, for he brandished a large revolver, which was leveled at my face. It was a Model 1884 Obrea Hermanos .44 caliber, the standard pistol for Spanish army officers. The custom-made pearl grips and gold retainer cord marked it as the former sidearm of a wealthy senior officer. Unlike everything else about these two scoundrels, the revolver was clean and in good shape. I judged it to be a recent addition to his other weapon—a large cane knife wedged in his rope belt.

My response to his question would be full of consequence, depending on the man's alliance of the moment. Obviously he was of African Cuban origin, and I guessed him not to be in the regular Spanish army. But was he a guerilla in the pro-Spanish militia, and thus in possession of a valuable pistol presented to him by a grateful commander? Or was he one of the famous Mambi peasant warriors in the Cuban Revolutionary Army with a revolver "liberated" from a dead enemy?

If he belonged in the former category, I would shortly be joining the many dead of the island, after an excruciating interview to extract whatever information my brain contained. But he didn't look the part. The guerillas generally wore faded blue cotton uniforms, and most of their officers and sergeants were of a higher social standing than the peasant before me. I decided he wasn't in the Spanish side of the equation. He looked and acted like a Mambi. If I could convince him I was an ally, I would be rescued. Maybe he even knew Isidro.

I presented my most genuine smile. "*Sí, señor. Soy norteamericano.*" No reaction. He simply stared back at me.

It was then I realized my assessment was completely wrong. These fellows weren't affiliated with either political camp. With incredibly bad timing, I'd managed to stumble upon a gang of bandits whose only allegiance was to themselves.

His bland expression morphed into a sadistic sneer as he cocked the big revolver's hammer. In crude rural Cuban Spanish he demanded all I had.

I heard others coming out of the mangroves behind me. Their words, in the same grumbled patois, were indiscernible in the noise of the downpour, but their tone was unmistakable—an eager debate on what type of loot was inside the seabag slung on my left shoulder. Knowing my future was limited whether I volunteered my property or not, I decided to demonstrate to the boys a *ruse de guerre*.

Portraying abject fear was not hard to do under the circumstances. With terror-struck eyes and sobbing pleas for my life, I held up both hands in the universal gesture of surrender. Someone behind me muttered something uncomplimentary. Everyone but me laughed. Even Revolver Man's sneer softened a bit, since it was readily apparent I was only a sniveling old gringo lost in the wilds. No menace to anybody. I could tell he was looking forward to the fun of stretching out my demise.

Their smug complacency provided the right moment for me to employ a maneuver taught to me by an ex-penitentiary inmate whose forgery skills I sometimes utilized as well. Speed was crucial.

With my left hand, the closest to the revolver, I seized the barrel and pushed it up in an arc away from me. At the same time, my right hand also grabbed it, completing the arc so that it was now pointed at the brute's face. My movement was so unexpected that he had no chance to make the conscious effort to stop his involuntary reflex to pull the trigger as his hand was jerked up. That failure led to his instantaneous death from the face wound he'd wanted to give me.

Spinning around, I confronted his companions with their former leader's weapon. Evidently, they'd never seen anyone actually fight back in a robbery and didn't know quite what to do at first. Fortunately, I did. Three of them holding firearms—two revolvers and an ancient shotgun—received a bullet each. My initial acquaintance among them got a bullet too. The others decided discretion was the better part of valor and hastily retreated back into the jungle before the gun smoke cleared.

Before they could regroup I headed up the path at the double-quick. I needed to reach an area where high ground would afford me some concealment and rest, and hopefully some respite from bandits and the damned insects. Half-walking, half-running up that meandering path, I spent the next hour cursing Cuba, the Cubans, the Spanish, politicians of every breed in Washington, the U.S. Army, and most especially the man who'd sent me on this insane endeavor, Maj. Gen. William Rufus Shafter.

No one followed. At long last the thick mangrove forest gave way to fields of young sugarcane. Altering course to cross the field on the right, I headed toward a copse of banana and mango trees. With the last of my strength, I climbed the tallest mango. Stretching my body precariously across three sturdy branches, I pulled several rain-soaked branches over me for camouflage. Every muscle protested until I could finally stretch out and relax, intending a catnap of an hour. The moment my head rested on the largest limb, however, I fell into the slumber of the dead, not caring what might happen next.

I awoke to find someone throwing mangoes at me. It was still raining. Four young men who looked to be in their early twenties stood in a half circle looking up at me, conversing among themselves. Their skin color varied from ivory to ebony, they looked well fed, and their language had the slower pace of eastern Cuba, but with proper grammar. They weren't peasants or bandits, for they were outfitted in the clothing of the tradesman class in a town.

The fellow who'd thrown the mangoes had a nascent beard trying to cover his round face. None of them had weapons showing or even appeared threatening, but I've been fooled before. Besides, they were the right type to be in the pro-Spanish militia.

I waved at them, smiling innocently, as my right hand inched toward my trusted Merwin-Hulbert revolver.

The bearded fellow became my chief inquisitor, asking the obvious question of why exactly I was up in the tree. Though asked pleasantly, his question had no plausible answer on my part. How exactly do you explain being a foreigner hiding up in a tree in a country at war unless you are a spy?

To gain time to come up with an explanation, I decided to play dumb, an admittedly natural talent of mine. Making a pleasant "Uh?" sound, I put my head down on my hands on a tree limb to pantomime sleeping. Then I waved for them to go away. My dramatic efforts got a chuckle from others in the audience, which I thought a good beginning.

Just as my brain began fabricating a lame lie about being a British tourist, my interrogator had another question. This one stopped me cold.

"Why didn't you bury them?"

Then one of the other young men surprised me with a perturbed comment in good English. "We had to stop and take time to bury your mess so the Spanish would not find the bodies and know you are here. It was a waste of our time."

My alibi thus evaporated, I warily asked, "Are you Isidro?"

"Who is that?" the young man replied.

Not the right answer. I put my finger on the trigger.

At that moment the youngest-looking of the bunch, who had been silently watching all this while leaning against a banana tree, stepped forward. He took off a wide-brimmed straw hat, unleashing a cascade of long, shiny, dark hair, then looked up at me. I was stunned yet again. He was actually a *she*, a beautiful young lady of perhaps twenty years. She was clad in the same rumpled cotton trousers, shirt, and coat as the others. Her garments were loose fitting, but now that I saw her face, I recognized the shape of her gender.

"I am Isidro," she said brusquely in flawless English. "Do not tell me your real name. I will not tell you mine."

"How did you know I was here?" I asked, still trying to make sense of this development.

"We have watched you the entire time since we first saw your ship enter the bay."

"Then why didn't you meet me on the beach?"

"We expected you to come by small boat so you could get past the Spanish lookout post at the mouth of the bay in the darkness. But you came in by large ship in the daylight, so we had to eliminate the Spanish lookout post first so they could not alert their commander in the town. That is why we were late in getting to this side of the bay. Then we found the bodies and had to hide them, which took more time. We followed your footprints to this tree. You made it easy to find you."

Damn. I hadn't known anything about a lookout post. The Professor's words came back to me: *Just get there and Isidro will know it. He will contact you when you arrive.*

"So *you* will take me across the mountains?" I asked her.

She bristled visibly at the incredulity in my voice, but then got down to business. "We will talk about that later. There is no time now. When the lookout post never checked in on their telephone line an hour ago, the Spanish garrison sent a patrol to their location. Now there are patrols everywhere. One of them is a kilometer away and heading here. Climb down from the tree. We are leaving now."

The woman started walking off, trailed by her companions. I misjudged the height and dropped down, landing with a grunt and falling over to the ground. They didn't even look back. Miraculously, nothing was broken or sprained other than my pride. I didn't dawdle, however, and ran to catch up with my strange new protectors.

8

The Society of the Night

Tánamo, Cuba
Sunday, 12 June 1898

I HAD YET TO SEE A WEAPON among them, but I had no doubt they carried concealed blades and probably pistols. My new acquaintances didn't give me their names or speak among themselves. They made their way quietly and deliberately along the trail as it ascended into some hills. Each constantly surveyed a different sector of the surrounding terrain. Such extraordinary operational discipline made it obvious these were veterans.

It was an odd feeling to be old enough to be "Isidro's" grandfather, not to mention a senior naval officer, and yet take orders from this unusual young lady. Her male subordinates complied with her few directions without hesitation or complaint. Whatever her real identity might be, she was a remarkable leader in a very dangerous environment.

Our route stayed away from the main roads, never going in or near a village. She knew the landscape as well as how to organize a transit through enemy territory. One of her men was fifty yards out in front, one an equal distance to the rear. When we crossed open fields she sent the other two out to the flanks, quietly but repeatedly admonishing them to be alert.

I thought about trying to gain more understanding of her circumstances through conversation, but her demeanor didn't invite unnecessary chatter. It's a trait I usually appreciate, but my increasing curiosity, in addition to the fact my life was in her hands, made me want to know more about this woman who was much younger than my daughter.

By midafternoon we were several hundred feet up in the high foothills of the Sierra de Cristal mountain range. The coastline spread behind us to the north, with the many coves of Tánamo Bay branching out to small villages, most of which weren't on my map. Ahead of us to the south, everything looked to be uphill—not an inviting sight for me.

Happily, the rain had ended, or the trek would have been even more arduous. As it was, we stopped every hour for exactly ten minutes, each of us getting a large bite of cold stew (sugarcane, chicken, beans, and rice), a swig from a gourd of rum-laced water, and the chance to lie down. The woman was the last to sit down and the first to get up, displaying a fortitude bordering on either obsession to dominate us or fear of the enemy—I never determined which.

The sun was behind a nearby mountain when she called a halt at 5:21 p.m. We were on a narrow animal trail near a tall jacaranda tree, its delicate lavender blooms strewn around us. Our leader went off alone, climbing rock to rock up the steep slope beside the trail. A hundred feet above us she called down for us to follow. The others made it look effortless. I was gasping for air the whole way. When we got up to her position, she informed us we would remain there until my contact arrived.

My contact? This was news to me. Though she'd never answered my original question on the subject, I'd had the impression since then that *she* was my contact and guide for the journey across the mountains to General García's army. Annoyed, I asked what else was in store for me.

Ignoring my attitude, her reply contained only the minimum information. "When the sun's rays leave the top of Loma Quemada, our task is done and we will leave you. Your walk into the high mountains will be with someone else." She nodded toward a conical peak, taller than our own, several miles to our east, the upper tip of which was still bathed in light from the sinking sun. I calculated it would be only a few minutes before the entire hill was in shadow.

We waited in silence for whoever was coming. Sure enough, when the last shaft of sunlight disappeared, a birdcall screeched out from someplace below us. The woman—I cannot bring myself to use a male alias for someone so lovely—echoed the call. After a few minutes I heard rocks falling and people scrambling below us. The sounds grew closer until the head of a disheveled black peasant carrying a shotgun appeared before us. The leathery face told me he was at least seventy, maybe more, but his physique was thin and strong.

There was no sign of recognition or dialogue between the man and my female guardian. He simply looked around and then sat down, cradling the weapon, his ancient eyes studying me. Two more men arrived. One was very dark skinned, big boned, and young, a ferocious-looking brute whose gaping mouth showed few teeth. The other was teak colored, dressed a bit better than his cohorts, and obviously better fed. He acknowledged me with a cordial nod. Once he sat nearby, the woman got up and, without a word of farewell, led her comrades down the slope to the trail.

I watched them descend, intrigued by the mystery woman. I deduced that she was a person of privilege and education, and her manner indicated she was used to demanding respect and commanding servants. She was no stranger to the countryside, perhaps the daughter of a rich plantation family. Surely she was no criminal, so how did she know the Professor? Was she a rebel doing her bit for the cause of independence? Perhaps. But why? Not many plantation owners were supporting the revolution, which was likely to damage their prospects if successful. Was it for revenge, money, lofty ideals, love? I never discovered the slightest clue. In all my clandestine undertakings around the world, she was the most remarkable contact I've ever had, man or woman. The enigma of her background and motivation remains unsolved to this day, for I never saw or heard of her again.

"I am Jorge Acera. I take you across mountains," my new keeper declared once the previous crew had disappeared from sight. He didn't bother to introduce the other two. Acera was a large, muscular mulatto man in his early forties sporting an imposing mustache; his English wasn't fluent or school-taught but was easy to understand nevertheless. I surmised he'd learned it in commerce with Americans, perhaps in Havana or Santiago.

"Good to meet you," I said. In a flash of inspiration, I picked my own pseudonym. "My name is Hermann Jacobsen."

He gave a speculative look to show me he knew it was an alias, then said, "We must go now, *Hermann*, to meet people to protect us on journey."

"More people? I thought you were my protection."

"I am your guide. They will stop problems."

Stop problems? He didn't elaborate. "How far will that be?" I asked.

"Long walk," he said impassively, clearly tired of my questions.

Jorge's description understated both the distance and the difficulty. I guessed it at ten miles consisting of a tough ascent through thick scrub to a jagged ridgeline running east and west. I was offered assistance on carrying the seabag but followed my rule of keeping its contents close to me, even though the weight was staggering. For the hundredth time since I'd landed in Cuba I wished Sean Rork was with me. He is immensely strong with the enviable ability to bear any fatigue with humor. My own sense of humor deserted me about a mile into the "long walk."

During this hike, no one spoke. I was glad of it. The conditions demanded far too much respiratory effort to talk and mental power to even think. Much better to disengage my mind, plod one foot in front of the other, and thus lose track of time and distance. Eventually I would either get there, somebody would tell me to stop, or I would die. After a while, it mattered not which.

The only positive developments were the altitude's cooler temperature, drier air, and lack of biting insects. My rough estimation was around 1,200 feet. At the top of the first ridge, I saw much higher ridges in front of us. Not another soul was in sight the entire time, though in the dimming light several thin smoke plumes could be seen rising from the jungle valleys.

At a little after 9 p.m. Acera held up his hand. We stopped in the pitch-black jungle; or rather we collapsed in individual heaps on the trail. With perverse satisfaction, I saw the others were also exhausted, though their burlap sacks of provisions were far lighter than my burden. We set up no lookouts, perimeter guards, fire, or tent. I thought this imprudent but hadn't enough energy to complain to our taciturn leader.

Starshine provided just enough light to make out forms close by, as long as I didn't stare at a single spot for too long. A sliver of moon came up after we stopped, greatly enhancing visibility and depth perception. It was then I noticed a circle of yellowish mud smeared on a tree next to the trail. Our stopping point was not randomly chosen.

After resting for some time, the three Cubans abruptly sat up. Acera quietly mouthed to me, "They are around us now, Hermann. Stay calm."

Sensing nothing, I sat up too, and whispered back, "Who are you talking about, Jorge?"

"The Abakuá," he said reverently.

I vaguely knew of them. "The Ñáñingo Society of the Night? I thought they were mainly around Havana, Regla, and Matanzas over in the western end of the island."

He hesitated, evidently surprised by my knowledge, then said, "Yes, in slave days. Most are still there. Some escaped western plantations and came to high mountains here. They live free in mountains, far from Spanish. Not trust white men." Acera was watching me intently, gauging my reaction. "The Abakuá live in the old African ways. They mixed with Haitian slave people here. All of same tribe in Africa long time ago."

"Descendants of the Igbo and the Efik people of Nigeria," I whispered. Instantly, the terror of that night with the Bizangos in Haiti returned to me. I tried not to show my dread in front of Acera. The Professor's warning pounded in my brain: *They will remind you of your painful experience in Haiti and bring back your fears. If you allow them, those fears will consume you. Do not let that happen.*

"Yes," Acera replied. "Not many white people know of the Night Society. Show respect to these men. They own our lives."

"I understand," I said as a chill wind ruffled the trees above us. The roaring sound of a squall quickly got louder until the storm was upon us. Icy rain poured down on us and swept down the mountainside.

I sat there shivering in the dark.

9

Africa

Sierra de Cristal Mountains, Cuba
Late Sunday Evening, 12 June 1898

W E WAITED FOR THIRTY silent minutes. The sky cleared enough for me to see my companions in the silvery moonlit gloom. They didn't seem frightened but rather intensely alert, waiting for the inevitable.

Then the faces of twenty men materialized in the bushes nearby. They stepped forward without a sound and encircled us closely, eyeing us with undisguised scrutiny. The Abakuá were dressed in faded gray or white clothing. Most carried a large knife or machete. Several wore blue rayadillo cotton Spanish army tunics that still showed the bloodstains of the former owners. Many of them carried feathered or furry talismans. One of them was dressed in red and was more assertive than the rest. The others kept one eye on him.

I sat without moving, my right hand on the revolver in my pocket and my left hand on the shotgun inside my seabag. Acera and his two companions did not appear defensive, however. Each stood and bowed his head in respect to our new friends. Or was it submission? Releasing my grip on the shotgun but keeping my hand on the pistol, I followed suit.

The Abakuá man in red ignored the others and jutted his chin at me. I realized he was studying the scars on my face. Then, in a deep, rumbling, accusatory tone, he said, "*Entemio macarará, aguerise?*"

It wasn't Spanish, Haitian Kreyol, or anything else I recognized, and the tone wasn't friendly. Acera quietly explained. "He talks in Abakuá words, saying: 'White foreigner, what your name?' You must answer him."

I looked at the Abakuá headman and said, "Hermann."

The Abakuá thought about that before nodding to his assistant, who walked over and looked into my seabag, touching the pistol and shotgun within but not removing them. He uttered to his boss, "*Etombre, cananasú.*"

"*Efembe,*" was the answer I heard, followed by a fast gibberish to Acera, whose multilingual skills were far superior to mine.

"They like pistol and shotgun, and you," announced Acera.

The boss next spoke to Acera in a strange version of Spanish I also couldn't understand. Acera translated for me. "He knows you here to fight Spanish. He likes that. His Spanish name is Felipe Velez. He take us across mountains to Jamaica."

Jamaica? That makes no sense. Was there some sort of miscommunication of my needs between the Professor, Isidro, and Velez?

I was about to speak up, but I held my tongue when I saw Acera didn't seem fazed by the news. He bowed again, saying to Velez in Spanish I could understand, "Thank you, sir. We respect your Abakuá fraternity of brothers and appreciate your help in taking us to Jamaica. The second donation to your community is ready. It will be delivered upon my return."

Velez nodded at Acera, then locked eyes with me and pointed to the ground. He spoke slowly in Spanish for my benefit. "You sleep now. We leave before the sun rises."

That having been said, we made camp for the night. Acera's men laid down under a bush while their boss had another discussion with Velez. I found a place under a palmetto frond that kept some of the intermittent rain from my face. Half the Abakuá men disappeared, presumably on guard or scouting duty. The others set up a crude shelter framework of vines about fifty feet from us and quickly wove banana leaves over it, then sat under the shelter in a tight circle. No fire could be made, but the wet weather didn't stop them from a jolly discussion of something in their lingo.

"Jamaica is village north of Guantánamo on coast, Hermann," explained Acera when he returned and stretched out beside me under his own palm frond.

Then he added an admonition. "Do not go where Abakuá sit. Private—not for you. They celebrate good fortune of my money. They ask spirits for protection on the journey. Do not worry, Hermann. They do not think you are enemy. Abakuá leopard warriors of the night give word of honor to protect us."

I was still fighting off memories of Haiti, so I fervently hoped Acera was right. In a few moments the Abakuá men began chanting, accompanied by half a dozen small, homemade instruments. Several of the men left the shelter and began dancing, their shadowy figures scarcely perceptible in the dark.

The resulting rhythm and melody were undiluted echoes from Africa reaching deep into the human soul. Even without knowing the Abakuá language I understood the meaning—not aggression but rather contentment.

Acera explained about the music. "Very old, from Congo and Niger people. Here in Cuba called *Changüí*. The box is *marimbula*, gourd is *güiro*, the little drums *bongós de monte*, and small guitar is *tres*. The song is Bantu words of Igbo people. Only Abakuá know."

"When will they sleep?" I asked, wondering what those fellows were drinking.

"They dance with ancestors in Africa now," explained my teacher. "No need sleep. They have strength of Mokongo, warrior spirit of Abakuá people."

With that, my lesson ended and he turned over. Inside of five minutes Acera and his men were snoring. Such trusting repose did not come to me, though I certainly needed it. Instead, I passed the night listening to the sounds of Africa, remembering the horror of Haiti, and thinking about how far I had come since my morning arrival in Cuba.

In my quest for sleep I tried to force my mind onto pleasant subjects, visualizing Maria and me enjoying breakfast at our hilltop home on Patricio Island. But it was all to no avail. My mind kept reverting to the myriad details of the impending operation. Aside from my unsettling location and companions, I anticipated many difficulties to contend with once I reached García's army. If I did.

The entire situation was depressing. I'd been traveling for six days after leaving Tampa but wasn't even close to my ultimate destination. Once I arrived, I had a daunting list of tasks but little time to accomplish them. The invasion force was to have sailed from Tampa on the eighth and was expected to land on a beach somewhere near Santiago on the sixteenth.

I had only three days left to cross the mountains, find General García, coordinate a meeting between him and Shafter, and get the Cubans to displace the Spanish from wherever the Americans were coming ashore. But instead of beginning to accomplish my tasks, I was stuck in the middle of Oriente's mountains, completely at the mercy of savages.

As I lay there on the mountain, chilled in my wet clothes and surrounded by frightening alien sights and sounds, the entire mission seemed damned impossible.

10

Civilization

Jamaica, Cuba
Wednesday, 15 June 1898

FOR THE NEXT THREE DAYS the Abakuá held themselves
aloof from the rest of us. We, especially I, were considered
mere cargo to be safely delivered to a place. Beyond that goal,
they cared not a bit about us.

The Abakuá insisted on maintaining a brisk pace all day and
well into each night, with periodic stops to lie on the ground and
rest our muscles. The slopes were brutally steep, the jungle thorns
impossible to avoid. All took a toll on me. The pace of the column
necessarily slowed as my constitution faded. I was discouraged
and embarrassed, but the going was extremely difficult and I just
couldn't keep up. No one said a negative word to me, but their
condescending manner spoke volumes. Eventually, my strength
declined to the point where I even gave up carrying the seabag. I
did manage, however, to insist that Acera's man lugging it stay right
in front of me.

Our provisions during this ordeal were primitive, to say the
least—a bite and a gulp at each stop. The food was an unrecognizable mush of fruit, vegetable, and some sort of roots, carried in sacks

and scooped out into our hands. The drink was rainwater carried in a gourd and dosed with rotgut aguardiente, cane liquor.

By the third day of this misery my clothing was sopping wet, sprouting mold, shredded by the thorns, and impregnated with slime. Boils and sores were popping up everywhere on my skin, including the most sensitive areas. Chigger bites festered. None of these minor wounds showed signs of healing. Without an antiseptic they would change from minor annoyances to potentially deadly sources of infection. Internally, even worse signs began, for my stomach and bowels were showing the unmistakable symptoms of dysentery. But the most distressing factor was my fading mental acuity. Making the simplest decision became a supreme, demoralizing effort.

Late on the night of the fifteenth, when Acera estimated we were eight miles from the village of Jamaica, Velez called a halt. We had crossed through the highest passes of the mountain range the night before. We were still up in the foothills on the southern side but were steadily descending. At that point we reached the very edge of Abakuá territory, beyond which they would not go.

Velez informed us his word had been upheld. They were going home now. Before heading off, Velez leveled a warning gaze at me. He cautioned us in Spanish against divulging details of any of themselves, their secret routes through the mountains, or their stopping places. My earnest pledge to obey Velez's command seemed to mollify the Abakuá men. Within seconds they melted into the tangled forest as wordlessly as they had first appeared and were gone. Even in this memoir, written so many years later, I have kept my word, providing only a general narration without details of the men or route. In truth, I could not do much more because of the state of my mind at the time.

Peering ahead through yet another torrential rain shower, Acera informed me there was a road leading to Jamaica, but it would be deep in mud. He knew a much faster way to get where we needed to go. Our destination was a farm outside the village belonging to a friend. Our route of descent to Jamaica would be by water, he explained, and set off without offering further details.

The other two fellows and I followed Acera through the black night to a rampaging creek. I heard it before I saw it. Acera grabbed a small log from the debris on the bank, thrust it into my hands, and gave me a somewhat reassuring pat on the back. Then he grabbed another log and held it to his chest. He announced in Spanish he would go first, then me, then the others. I was not to worry, he promised, for it would be a very short ride and he would be there at the end to pull me out. I was to hold tightly onto my log and keep it pointed in front of me because there would be many rocks.

Acera stepped off into the watery turmoil and was instantly whisked away into the darkness. The older of his men, who evidently didn't get the order of precedence, stepped in front of me clutching his log and jumped into the turbulence.

That was fine with me, for I was still adjusting my grip on the damned log, which seemed a bit too small to carry both me and the seabag tied to my left wrist. With no warning, Acera's other man, the young toothless gent, shoved me into the rapids and splashed in after me. I barely held my grip on the log as I tried to keep my head above water while smashing into rocks, tree limbs, and the seabag. I lost all my senses in the watery blackness except for repeated jabs of pain while desperately trying to get a gasp of air into my lungs. This torture seemed to go on for miles.

How I emerged from this unique version of hell I do not precisely know. I regained my wits on the bank with one of Acera's fellows, the same bastard who'd pushed me in, kneeling over me and tapping my face. Helping me sit up, he pointed toward a faint radiance not far away. My eyes finally recognized it as the glow of a lantern. It was coming through a window of a home, the first real dwelling I'd seen since my ordeal through the mountains began.

The intoxicating scent of cooking food, real civilized food, wafted over us and energized me enough to stand up. I took stock of my surroundings while Acera explained we were at our destination: a fruit farm two kilometers north of Jamaica. The town of Guantánamo was another fifteen kilometers to the south, and the bay of the same name was twenty-two farther. He also announced it was safe to approach the cabin because two goats were tethered to a fence in front, the signal no enemies were around. The four of us trooped toward the house, my every step hurting, but not enough to stop me from getting to that food.

Five minutes later, as I limped onto the front porch of the tiny wood-frame home, Acera introduced me—as an American warrior sent to help liberate Cuba—to the ancient mulatto couple who owned the place, Arnoldo and Olga. After that description, which I knew my ragged appearance didn't support, I was immediately the man of the hour and treated accordingly.

Arnoldo and Olga were the salt of the earth. He had a farmer's lean build and weathered face. He moved with the quiet dignity of an old soldier, which Acera said he was, having fought for Cuban freedom as a sergeant with Céspedes' original band of men back in '68. Arnoldo walked with a slight drag of his left foot, a wound from those days, and also bore a scar on his arm from a wound picked up in 1880 while he was a lieutenant during the second war for freedom. The wounds were badges of honor among his fellow Cubans.

Rotund little Olga was sweetness personified, everyone's vision of an angelic grandmother. In the age-old Cuban manner of hospitality, which is unequaled in the world, she took every care for me, fussing continually over my comfort.

Embarrassed by our decrepit condition, the four of us shed most of our mud-stained rags, keeping on only what was needed for modesty. Far too tired and sore to converse, we dropped our sick, starving bodies onto the boxes and chairs arranged for us on the tiny porch. At last, Olga came out and announced in graceful Spanish that dinner was ready, with an added apology that their home's table seated only two.

Acera's men went in first and wolfed down their food. Acera and I were next, our hosts insisting they would eat last. The simple feast of rice, cassava, and beans, accompanied by coffee with a stick of sugarcane, tasted better than any spread I've had in the fanciest dining rooms of Washington.

Touching the fresh abrasions on my face and arms and the older wounds on my cheek, which had reopened, Olga clucked her concern, declaring I would have a bath after dinner. I was astonished to find the bathtub in their back room was a real ceramic one, not the horse trough I expected. After much dashing about on Olga's part, it was filled with steaming water from the stove, made fragrant by floating jasmine and gardenia flowers and enhanced by a bar of actual Spanish milled soap on a side table.

Once shed of my remaining rags and immersed in the fragrant, soapy water, I let out a sigh that could've been heard in far-off Havana as my skin and muscles untensed. Initially, my wounds hurt even more, but then the soapy water worked its magic. The pain and inflammation lessened, then disappeared.

Arnoldo removed my filthy rags and spread out the contents of my seabag near the tub to dry, instinctively knowing I wanted to remain in sight of my weaponry. He returned with a set of his own clothes for me to wear while the indefatigable Olga laundered my spare set from the bag. During the journey, my frame had lost all of its excess weight, so I surmised that though they might be tight, skinny Arnoldo's clothes would probably fit.

Lastly, my new friend brought me Olga's finest possession, an intricately stemmed glass of green crystal filled with Matusalem sipping rum, a bottle of which had been hastily obtained from a more affluent neighbor half a kilometer away. This pure nectar was the perfect culmination of my recuperation regime. My body began to feel human again. My mind started functioning normally. Self-confidence began to regenerate. *Yes,* I told myself, *I* will *hold Maria again.* I felt a smile form on my face.

As I was basking in my resurrection, a commotion erupted out in the main room. I heard a stranger's voice, deep and insistent. I reached for my revolver on the chair beside me and had it in hand when the door opened.

Acera leaned in and declared, "Cuban Liberation Army officer here now, Hermann. My work done. I go home now." He then cheerfully included, "My name no Jorge Acera, like you no Hermann Jacobsen. *Vaya con Dios, mi amigo.*"

He came over and shook my hand, then went out the door and back to his life. As was true of so many I encountered on this odyssey, we never met again. I have often wondered about him.

Seconds later, my newest Cuban liaison entered my bathing room. This one was completely different from Acera in every way. A serious-faced fellow, he marched in wearing the neat butternut-colored uniform of a staff officer in the Cuban Liberation Army. The small aiguillette draped from the left shoulder indicated that he was aide-de-camp to a very senior general.

Middle-aged, trim, short, with a pencil-thin mustache and European-style goatee, he was the opposite of the hulking, slow-moving Acera. His shiny onyx eyes were piercing, his chin and nose refined, and his manner confident. Even before he spoke, I knew he was a man used to making decisions and expecting them to be carried out. Looking down at me in the tub, he surprised me with effortless English spoken in a clipped New England accent.

"Good evening, Captain Wake. Welcome to Free Cuba. I am Major Alonso Fortuna, aide-de-camp to General Calixto García, commander of the Cuban Liberation Army of the East. I have been given the honor to be your liaison officer. General García sends his compliments, sir."

A bit overwhelmed by his unexpected and impressive entrance, and my own less than formal situation, I blurted out, "Well, thank you, Major. Ah, it's an honor for me too, though I fear you have me at a disadvantage regarding attire."

He looked away, embarrassed. Clearly, my inane comment wasn't the right way to start a military campaign, so I quickly followed up with something more appropriate. "Forgive my befuddled mind— it's been a long journey. Please sit down in this chair, Major. I'm sure you had a difficult trip here, too. I must say that it's a distinct privilege to be the U.S. liaison with the legendary General García. But before we go into that, I must first ask: Harvard, Yale, or Dartmouth?"

He grinned. "Does it show? Harvard University, sir. Class of '93. Civil engineering."

Hmm. Men trained in construction also understand the principles of demolition—a skill that might come in handy. Aloud I said, "May I offer you a glass of this excellent Matusalem?"

"You may, sir. Thank you very much. It is one of Cuba's very best rums."

Another, less ornate, glass was procured and filled. Fortuna sat in the chair near the tub. After the obligatory toast of "*A una Cuba libre*," I inquired, "When do I meet with the general?"

"We will leave in the morning, sir, after your aide-de-camp arrives from the U.S. Marines at Guantánamo Bay. I do not know his name. I have been told he should get here about dawn."

I digested that tidbit. *A Marine aide-de-camp? Why? That wasn't in the plan. And the Marines are at Guantánamo Bay? That wasn't in the plan either.*

"Major, you mean the Marines have landed at Guantánamo? The invasion has already started?"

"No, sir. Not a full invasion. Only six hundred Marines and sailors from three of your warships. Once ashore, they united with some of our forces, and together they have been fighting the Spanish to secure Guantánamo Bay to be used by your fleet as an anchorage and coal depot. Last night the enemy was finally defeated and has retreated inland."

"Where is our fleet now?"

"The main U.S. battle fleet is still off Santiago blockading the Spanish ships inside. We have not yet seen any U.S. transport ships carrying invasion troops."

This wasn't the plan I'd heard at V Corps. The effect of the rum and my exhaustion faded. I needed immediate information on the situation around Santiago, and I had to assimilate it calmly, understanding the possibilities for action. There was no time to wait.

"Let me get dressed, Major. Then you will give me a detailed situation report about everything going on ashore and afloat in this region."

Once we had settled ourselves on the porch, Fortuna began his briefing with a description of the Spanish army's order of battle in the Santiago area—around 17,000 men. Another 40,000 soldiers were scattered within 200 miles, throughout the eastern half of the island. Then he described Santiago's defensive positions, which included concentric rings of recent earthworks, modern fortifications, and older forts, augmented by both modern and ancient artillery. Next came information on the enemy's ammunition supplies, provisions, communications, and transport.

Last came the most important part, the personalities of the Spaniards' commanders. The men in charge were smart, battle-hardened professionals who had arranged formidable defenses. They would use every asset and man to defend Santiago, making the Americans and Cubans pay in blood for each yard gained toward the city. It would take a large army to capture the ancient city and then destroy the Spanish fleet—the main reason for this campaign—at anchor in the bay.

Next, Fortuna summarized the order of battle for the Cuban forces. It was a depressing contrast. They numbered fewer than half the Spanish forces, were lightly armed, and lacked modern auxiliary support. The Cuban Liberation Army relied on the local people and the land for supplies and provisions, plus what they could capture from the Spanish for weaponry, ammunition, and equipment. They controlled the countryside but weren't strong enough to attack the fortified city.

Fortuna's summary was bleak but not unexpected. So far, it was a stalemate. The only new development was the U.S. Marine incursion at Guantánamo Bay. The combined forces had come close to defeat several times over the previous five days, but the situation now appeared much better, due primarily to the incredible determination of the Marines, sailors, and Cuban soldiers. I knew

Guantánamo Bay had good potential as a sheltered support base for naval operations, but still, the victory there was a minor show compared with overcoming the strong Spanish defenses at Santiago.

Four hours later we were done. Fortuna slept on the floor in the front room. I was given the only bed in the dwelling, located by the sole window in the back room. I accepted without protest and fell into it gratefully. I was also grateful for the mosquito net draped over the bed. The dinner, bath, rum, clean clothes, and bed were heaven sent. My last conscious thought was self-congratulatory—I'd made it back to civilization.

Albeit in the war zone . . .

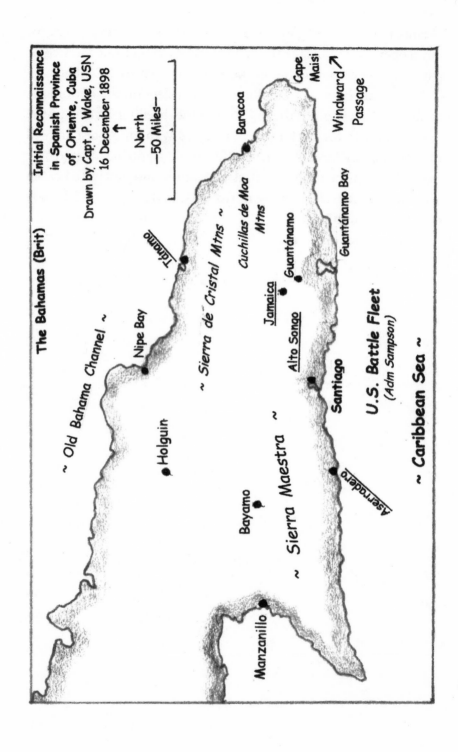

Initial Reconnaissance
in Spanish Province
of Oriente, Cuba
Drawn by Capt. P. Wake, USN
16 December 1898

North
—50 Miles—

The Bahamas (Brit)

~ Old Bahama Channel ~

Nipe Bay

Holguin

Bayamo

~ Sierra Maestra ~

Manzanillo

Tánamo

~ Sierra de Cristal Mtns ~

Cuchillas de Moa
Mtns

Baracoa

Cape
Maisí

Windward
Passage

Guantánamo Bay

Guantánamo

Jamaica

Alto Songo

Santiago

U.S. Battle Fleet
(Adm Sampson)

~ Caribbean Sea ~

Aserradero

11

Reinforcements

Jamaica, Cuba
Thursday, 16 June 1898

I WAS DREAMING OF MARIA. But why was she speaking in an Irish brogue? No, not Maria. Someone else. I couldn't make out what he was saying at first, then I heard it again. This time I could make out the words clearly, along with the mocking attitude.

"Damn if he don't smell like he drowned in a distillery, God bless his heretical soul. Not good at all for one o' the senior officers'uv Uncle Sam's navy. Lollygaggin' about like a drunken lout. Why, it ain't proper nor fair, especially when me own throat's as parched as a Baptist's."

Intense pain filled my head. Then I recalled the reason—I'd had a lot of rum the previous evening, somewhere around four full glasses of it. Or was it more? Warily opening my left eye, I registered that the room on that side of the bed was lit by a lantern. It was held by the master of the house, who looked perplexed. Beside him was Major Fortuna, concern clouding his face.

From elsewhere in the room the same scolding voice intruded again as a wave of warm, stale breath washed over me. "'Tis an idle bugger you've become. Whatever would hizzoner Admiral Sampson say if he saw you now?"

The major glanced nervously at the right side of the bed, where the voice was coming from. I opened my right eye and found a big, beaming face inches from mine. I knew the leathery mug well, for it belonged to none other than my best friend, Sean Aloysius Rork, Chief Petty Officer, U.S. Navy. He chuckled at my discomfort. I winced in cranial agony.

"Damn glad you're here, Rork," I moaned. "I presume you're my new aide-de-camp. Now go away. It's not sunrise yet." I rolled over and buried my face in the pillow.

He didn't go away. "Well now, ain't that a fine welcome aboard from me old shipmate an' best pal in the whole world? The very same man whose miserable life was saved by none other than the likes o' me, right there in the scorched desert sands o' Africa. To think he treats me in such a manner. Makes me feel a bit . . . unwanted."

Then the insensitive scoundrel started shaking my ankle. "Aye, boyo, 'tis time to shake a leg an' get that rum-soaked carcass o' yours under way in proper naval fashion. There's a war to fight, laddie. An' we're just the men to do it."

I wasn't impressed. "It's dark outside. The war will wait until daylight."

He shook my shoulder next, the one he knew still throbbed from a wound in Indochina years before. "Up an' at 'em tiger, lazy days're over!"

I was getting really irritated by all this and about to let him know it in no uncertain terms until I heard Arnoldo and Fortuna conversing worriedly in Spanish. For some reason that touched a nerve, having an audience to my weakness and Rork's sarcasm was too much to ignore.

I slowly sat up. Piercing the others in the room one by one with a nasty glare, I stated, "All right you heartless sonsabitches, you got me up. What the hell time is it, anyway, Rork?"

"Already gettin' late in the day, sir. Three bells in the mornin' watch. An' the lovely lady o' the house is makin' us a breakfast fit for an archbishop. Aye, that'll get rid o' the Devil's work in your head."

Five-thirty in the morning? I'd had only two hours' sleep. I studied Fortuna more closely. The major didn't even have the decency to look hung over. Of course, he was at least fifteen years younger than me, but still, he shouldn't look so damned chipper.

The Cuban officer straightened. "Sorry for waking you this early, sir, but your men got here earlier than expected."

Men? There were more than Rork? My bewilderment cleared when I became aware of a young man standing in the shadows by the door in the dusty brown and blue fatigue uniform of a U.S. Marine. He stepped forward to the foot of the bed and came to attention. In his right hand was a Navy Lee rifle, which he stamped down to the dirt floor to the position of order arms. His wide-brimmed slouch hat was tucked under his left arm.

"Second Lieutenant Edwin Law, United States Marines, reporting in as your aide-de-camp, sir. Commander McCalla sent me and Chief Rork from Guantánamo Bay to assist you."

This was new. Rork and I were used to working alone. Well, Lieutenant Law looked intelligent and fit. Maybe having him along might work out. "Welcome aboard, Mr. Law. Do you speak Spanish?"

"No, sir. But I am picking up some of the basic lingo from Chief Rork."

I glanced at Rork, whose face was impassive. "I imagine anything Rork has taught you is not meant for polite company, so be careful using it. Listen, I need you to keep watch around us as we progress on this mission. If you see something that appears threatening, let Chief Rork or me know immediately. Be prepared for action at all times."

"Aye, aye, sir," he replied in a matter-of-fact way.

I turned to Rork. "So, Bowman's down there at Guantánamo Bay?"

"Aye, sir, the legendary Commander Bowman McCalla himself, in the flesh. He's in charge o' the shore party o' sailors an' Marines, just like those ol' days at Panama. This time, he's been kickin' the Spaniardos out o' the area at the mouth o' the bay. The good lieutenant here was in the thick'uv it all. 'Twas a dicey deal, but that fine anchorage is ours now, sir. Our ships don't have to go to Haiti for calm water to re-coal or resupply anymore."

It suddenly struck me Rork shouldn't be there. "Wait a minute, Rork. I thought you were serving in *Oregon*, with my son. Why were you ashore at Guantánamo?"

"Aye, I was in *Oregon*, sir, an' glad to say me godson, young Lieutenant Sean Wake, is doin' us both proud in that grand ship. They made a hell'uva dash around the Horn to get here. O' course, that was afore I joined her at Key West."

"That doesn't answer my question, Rork. *Oregon*'s blockading the harbor over at Santiago where the Spanish fleet is, so how the hell did *you* end up ashore here?"

"Well, sir, that's a bit'uva tale. But the short story is this: I was mindin' me own business with the lads in *Oregon*'s goat locker when a chief yeoman said somethin' about the admiral's orders to Commander Bowman to go raid Guantánamo Bay an' secure it as a Navy anchorage. What's this, I think? Sounds like some fun. Battleships can be a bit dull, don't you know. No real action most o' the time. So I got meself volunteered by *Oregon*'s captain to go over to *Marblehead*, Commander McCalla's ship. Pretty soon we were ashore at Guantánamo Bay an' hip deep in Spaniardos. Nary a dull moment!"

He paused and I glowered, for I knew there was more to it. "And?"

"And then last night durin' a poker game, me ears happened to hear a Marine sergeant say that the good lieutenant here was bein' sent inland to meet a Yank Navy captain who'd snuck ashore to be the liaison with the Cuban army. Well, only one man in all'uv Uncle Sam's Navy fits such a description—an' that's *you*. Had a gam with Commander McCalla, an' he thought it a capital idea for me to come along an' lend a hand. He said to remind you about the drink you've owed him for two years."

The comment was pure Bowman McCalla. "And I seem to recall he owes me about five."

"Aye, an' I'm thinkin' the both o' you owe me a whole cask o' the good stuff. Heard it was a hell'uva a walk you had to get here. It's good to be back together, sir."

Rork innocently lifted an eyebrow as he rubbed his left wrist. "An' even though we're lucky to have Mr. Law along on this risky caper, we just might be needin' some o' me own special assets as well."

Confusion flashed across Law's face. I could see the lieutenant wondering what he'd gotten into, and who the hell he'd gotten into it with.

Rork was referring to his "appliance." Though it appears real, his left hand is actually made of India rubber that is configured in a permanent grip. It allows him to use the hand to hold an oar, a belaying pin, or a bottle. Every year the hand is finely repainted, complete with faked hairs and freckles, by a lady friend of Rork's who works on the street outside the Washington Navy Yard. You have to be very close to the hand to realize it is a replica. If you are a foe, by that time you are far too close and it is far too late, for there is a silent and very deadly weapon inside the hand.

Underneath the rubber exterior is a five-inch-long marlinespike protruding from a wooden base. It is mounted at the end of a soft leather sleeve strapped down over the stump of Rork's amputated left forearm. That wound was incurred in 1883 from a sniper at the Battle of Huế in the empire of Vietnam. Rork's life was saved, and his appliance constructed, by surgeons and metalsmiths on board a nearby French warship. Rork misses his left hand, but he also relishes his appliance, which can be removed in seconds to expose the spike.

I heard Olga sputtering protests out in the front parlor, then a Cuban soldier arrived in my room, escorted by one of Major Fortuna's detail. After a rapid-fire dialogue between them, Fortuna received a page of notepaper. It had hieroglyphics across it that I recognized as a Masonic cipher. Many of the Cuban rebel leaders were Freemasons. Presumably, so was Fortuna.

The major turned to me. "This man is a courier from General García, sir. The general is moving his personal body of four thousand troops from Holguín toward Santiago, where they will unite with the five thousand in that area. The message states the general is nearing Alto Songo, north of Santiago. He will expect us there late tomorrow night for a meeting."

"How far away from here is Alto Songo?"

"Because we must go around the town of Guantánamo, which is still controlled by the Spanish, the journey will be about seventy kilometers, some of it on good roads and some on rough ground. There are trails through the rough areas. By using fresh horses at intervals we can ride the entire way and make it in time."

Horses? I didn't like the sound of that. Rork looked as apprehensive as I felt. Like many sailors, we are not versed in equestrian skills and have little trust in the beasts. On several past missions, horses and mules proved a constant bane to us while our comrades riding alongside had no trouble. For some reason, the damned creatures never follow my orders.

Fortuna extracted a topographical map from inside his tunic and unfolded it for us, tracing the route we would take. The map was crowded with elevation lines depicting mountains. The only alternative to horseback was walking up and down hills all the way to Alto Songo. The very thought of it made my knees hurt.

My old friend was grimacing at the map, so I tried to cheer him up. "Well, Rork, looks like you joined this shindig just in time to enlist in the cavalry. Aren't you glad you volunteered?"

"Oh joy, sir . . ."

12

The Great Man Himself

General García's Headquarters, Northwest of Alto Songo, Cuba
Friday Evening, 17 June 1898

W E GOT TO THE GENERAL's temporary headquarters late at night, after the predictably painful cross-country ride on diminutive Cuban ponies. We exchanged them for different ones every twelve kilometers or so, but the entire bunch proved that our equestrian luck hadn't changed. Each set of steeds was as unhappy with Rork and me as we were with them, and they let us know it for the entire route. Wandering off to sniff a bush, refusing to budge, or whirling about in a fit, they were the most cantankerous beasts I've ever sat on anywhere in the world. The war elephants I rode in Cambodia were easy compared with these delinquents.

Our Cuban comrades, naturally, got along easily with their mounts and barely contained their mirth at our incompetence. They repeatedly reminded us of our good fortune at having this luxurious mode of transport, for horses were getting scarce in the rebel army. Feelings of gratitude escaped me when painful saddle sores overcame all my other senses. Before the first hour had elapsed, I was seriously considering shooting the damned pony, burning the leather thing atop it, and walking.

By the time of our arrival I was in a deeply foul mood, bowlegged, and chafed beyond belief. Rork was in the same shape, but young Edwin Law looked none the worse for wear. He prudently kept quiet on the subject.

The man I had come all this way to see was spending the night in an old farmhouse similar to Arnoldo and Olga's, but García's hideout was pockmarked with bullet holes. The nearby barn was a pile of charred ruins. It was sadly typical of the entire area, devastated by both sides in the previous three years of warfare. The smell of burned sugarcane hung funereally in the air. There was no fruit on the trees, no livestock in the fields.

Major General Calixto García emerged from the house as we rode up. Having changed an hour before, Rork and I were in uniform, the first time for me since Key West. General García was not in military garb, attired instead in a white linen suit with long riding boots, and bareheaded. He was an impressive sight nonetheless.

I knew him to be two months younger than my age of fifty-eight. But thirty years of war had aged his face and hair enough to make him appear ten years older. Still, he was no doddering old man. Clearly, García was every inch the officer in command. From his tall, well-built frame to his august manner, Calixto García created a memorable first impression. His tanned face was topped by snowy hair. An enormous white mustache effectively concealed any smile or frown. A bullet scar formed a small depression in the center of his forehead. But of all his stark features, even the scar, his intimidating eyes were the most arresting. That was where his emotion could be readily gauged. As I came to see over the ensuing days, those eyes could be evaluating, skeptical, and sometimes pitiless.

As Fortuna dismounted to introduce me, torchlight illuminated the famous general. I noticed his dark eyes carefully appraising my inept riding style, clumsy dismount, and labored approach through his guards and staff. Among these veteran soldiers I felt every inch the foolish yanqui sailor.

Calixto García didn't have time for fools, yanqui or otherwise. Second in command of the entire Cuban Liberation Army, he specifically commanded the Eastern Department, which occupied the entire eastern half of Cuba. This department was composed of the First Corps (two divisions of six brigades comprising thirteen regiments) and the Second Corps (four divisions of eight brigades comprising eighteen regiments) in Santiago Province. He also had under his personal command the Third Corps (two divisions of four brigades comprising eleven regiments) in Puerto Principe Province. His command covered three hundred miles of the length of Cuba, a massive responsibility that he had shouldered for years.

To accomplish this García had about 20,000 men deployed throughout the eastern part of the region, supported by a population filled with supporters of the rebel cause. He had lost thousands of men to combat and disease since the 1895 start of the latest "hot war"—the third such period of open warfare during the thirty-year struggle for independence. But amazingly, even though outmanned and outgunned by the Spanish, the Cubans never gave up, even when offered amnesty.

When I met him, García controlled several small cities in addition to the countryside as a whole. At Santiago, he had the Spanish forces mostly bottled up behind their fortifications, able to make only an occasional patrol outside their lines. The Cubans were winning the war the slow way, through incessant attrition. It was a case of which side could outlast the other.

"It is a pleasure to meet you, Captain Wake," García said in Spanish, translated by Fortuna.

The major translated my reply into Spanish as I spoke. "It is a long-awaited honor for me to meet you, sir. I am here to serve you as the United States' liaison. Please allow me to introduce my aides. Lieutenant Edwin Law of the United States Marine Corps, and Chief Bosun Sean Rork of the United States Navy. And thank you for sending me Major Fortuna, a first-rate officer."

García glanced at the major and nodded. "Yes, he is. Your country has many also. More than a month ago I had the pleasure to meet one of them, a lieutenant in your Army who brought me a message from your president in Washington. The lieutenant's name was Andrew Rowan. Do you know him?"

"No, sir, I do not know Lieutenant Rowan, but I was apprised of his mission to let you know we would support your army as soon as we had mobilized our own invasion force. I have confidential information of my own, sir. May we speak in private?"

We went inside to a tiny, windowless room in back, passing by a young colonel whom I later discovered was García's son Calixto Junior, already a blooded veteran of combat. Fortuna came in and translated while Law and Rork stood at parade rest inside the doorway, watching outside for any signs of trouble. The general, Fortuna, and I sat at a small table. An oil lamp supplied a modicum of radiance to the stifling room, along with some putrid smoke.

Never taking his eyes off mine, García nodded for me to begin.

"Sir, I have been assigned to facilitate the interaction between our two forces. I was sent on this mission by Major General William Shafter, who commands the 17,000-man Army corps assembled at Tampa for the invasion of Cuba."

García showed no reaction, so I went on. "General Shafter presents his respects for the courage and skill of your men. He is looking forward to meeting you in person and serving alongside you in this great cause. The invasion is planned for this area of Cuba."

None of the sentiments I attributed to Shafter was true. Shafter had told others he considered the Cuban rank-and-file soldiers a bandit rabble, like the Indians he fought for years out west. But in the Hispanic culture, mutual respect is the foundation of relationships. I had to establish it at the outset, even if it involved some invention on my part.

García cut through it. "Only 17,000 men to invade Cuba?" He raised his eyebrows in disbelief. "When are these men arriving?"

"They are only the first formations that will be arriving, sir. One hundred thousand additional troops are being assembled around our country right now. They will reinforce General Shafter's men. Another 50,000 men will be sent to occupy the Philippines."

"Captain Wake, the Spanish have 240,000 men under arms across Cuba. The usual ratio of attacking force against fortified defenders is five to one. You have a country of millions, and yet it sends only 17,000 to attack the Spanish at Santiago?"

He was right. Seventeen thousand was far too few according to accepted military doctrine. I dared not tell him the entire U.S. Army had consisted of only 28,000 men until March, and I certainly remained mum about the quality of the new volunteer units. Instead I mentioned the one force we had that *was* ready. "Yes, sir. But in addition to our soldiers there is our famous fleet, sir. The U.S. Navy's guns will provide very effective support to the Army operations along the shoreline. Combined, the forces of freedom will win."

García's doubts continued. "We heard the *norteamericanos* would invade at Havana a month ago, before the fever season. The fevers will start here in the middle of July. For foreign troops it will be a deadly disadvantage. Why invade here, and why now?"

I couldn't tell him the real reason for the change of strategy, or my role in it. In February, while I was in Havana on a clandestine intelligence mission, my operatives had given me the Spanish defense plans for the city. They showed the defenses were far too strong for an untried American Army of volunteers to subdue. By the third week of May, a month after war had been declared, my report and the opinion of other senior officers had finally convinced those in charge in Washington of the sheer folly of their notion of attacking Havana. This and, most important, the arrival of the powerful Spanish fleet at Santiago had shifted the invasion scheme eastward to Oriente Province.

All of this was highly guarded information and not to be shared, even with an allied army commander. The Spanish still didn't know we had their defense plans for Havana—very few American Army or Navy officers did either—hence the need for utmost secrecy cloaked in plausible falsehoods.

"Yes, sir, originally, the invasion was to be near Havana, but it is now thought better to come in near Santiago, with the objective of destroying the coastal forts to enable us to eliminate the mine-field at the entrance to the harbor. Then we can destroy the Spanish fleet inside. After that, the city will fall. From Santiago we will march west together to liberate the length of the island and capture Havana. The invasion force will arrive offshore any day now—many transport ships."

"Where will they come ashore?"

"A location has not been chosen yet, sir. Before the U.S. forces come ashore, General Shafter desires a meeting with you and Admiral Sampson, who commands the naval force blockading the Spanish squadron inside the harbor at Santiago. General Shafter wants your opinion of where to land and also needs the help of your men to clear that landing place of any Spanish troops, so his men and supplies can get ashore."

"The Spanish defenses around Santiago are very strong. It will have to be away from the city. What kind of area do you want for this landing place for your soldiers?"

"It will have to be a gentle beach, sir, with little or no surf. And it needs to be near a road leading to Santiago through relatively flat terrain."

He took a moment to think. Then, looking at me but speaking to Fortuna in Spanish, he said, "It has to be east of the city, then, where the beaches are less rocky, the land is flatter, and my regiments have more control. The Juraguá Iron Company has a small rail line along the coast there leading from its open pit mines to its pier inside Santiago Harbor. The railroad is not in good condition because of the war, but it could be useful. To the west of Santiago the land is very mountainous and difficult for a large army to traverse, with few beaches and no pier, except for Cabañas Bay, which is heavily guarded by Spanish troops and guns."

After Fortuna had translated that for me, the general raised a finger to make his next point. "However, I would suggest the proposed meeting with your general and admiral be made far west of the city, at Asarradero. We have control of that area. It is closer to my main headquarters in the Sierra Maestra. Meeting there will also serve to divert Spanish attention away from the true landing place east of the city. We must keep the enemy deceived as long as possible to preserve surprise for the invasion."

The three Cuban officers went into a discussion of suitable landing places. Cubans speak Spanish rapidly. With several talking at once, it was too much for me to follow. All I was able to catch was a debate over the merits of places called Siboney, Juraguá, and Daiquiri, none of which I knew a thing about.

The general ended the discussion abruptly and returned his attention to me.

"Captain Wake, the possible landing places will be examined tomorrow by officers of my staff. They will have a recommendation for you tomorrow night."

"Thank you, sir. If I can assist in any way, please let me know."

He waved his hand dismissively. "No, no, you have done enough for now. You need rest, for when your general and his soldiers arrive, you will be very busy."

García said his next words slowly, his tone more emotional, more deliberate. I didn't need Fortuna's translation to understand him. "Captain Wake, what I see in your eyes supports what I have heard about you. I know of your personal friendship with our martyred apostle of freedom, José Martí, may he rest in peace; of your designation as a 'friend of Freemasons,' of which I am one; of your long battle against Colonel Marrón's secret police in Havana; of your championing of our cause for years in Washington, to the detriment of your career; of your charming Spanish-born wife; and of your hard-fought victory over the Spanish at Isabela two months ago. I thank you, on behalf of all Cubans."

If he knew that much about me, he also knew I spoke a bit of Spanish, something I had taken care not to divulge so far while inside Cuba. I found it intriguing that he never mentioned it in his recital of my past and decided to maintain my pretense.

The general continued, "And now, Captain Wake, you, Major Fortuna, Mr. Law, and Mr. Rork will be my guests for dinner. Allow me to show you the hospitality of my country."

García's eyes softened for the first time. With a mischievous twinkle in them he asked me, "As you and Mr. Rork are sailors, may I presume you do not mind beginning with a taste of our Cuban rum?"

I was still recovering from the drinking bout two nights earlier, but Rork raised a hopeful eyebrow. He'd been at sea for a very dry month. "Thank you, General," I said. "We would be delighted to have a taste of Cuba's rum, sir."

The rum arrived, and I stood to offer the first toast. "To the Republic of Cuba. Soon she will finally, and forever, be free of oppression!"

The general raised his glass in approval, tossed down his rum, and said in halting English, "I know your blood is not Cuban, but I think your heart is. You are one of us, Peter Wake, and we are glad to have you here."

I'd passed the test of trust, upon which everything in the future rested.

13

Decisions of War and Love

Asarradero, Cuba
Saturday, 18 June 1898

SEVERAL HOURS LATER, the general and his staff headed off to inspect the Cuban units in the mountains north and west of Santiago. He was true to his word, though, and set the reconnaissance of the beaches into motion. Using couriers and signal lamps he sent word to a Cuban officer stationed on the eastern side of Santiago who had been a topographic engineer in civilian life and was trained to examine land for potential uses. By dawn the next day the engineer was surveying potential sites. I found it an amazing demonstration of communications.

We caught up with García and his staff at 10 p.m. west of the city near the coastal village of Asarredero. The journey was an exhausting twelve-hour-long circumnavigation of the Spanish defenses at Santiago, mostly on those damned ponies.

As we finally trudged into García's headquarters I surveyed what I could see of the locale. The camp was on the side of a mountain overlooking Asarradero a thousand feet below next to a tiny beach. To the south there was nothing but the black expanse of the wide Caribbean. Eighteen miles to the east, out of sight behind our mountain, the U.S. fleet waited in front of Santiago Bay.

After we set up our tent, Fortuna was summoned to the general. He returned an hour later with the report that Daiquiri, about twenty miles east of Santiago, was recommended as the best landing place. It had a small pier and beaches with an easy slope, and there were only about three hundred Spanish infantry in the general area. A narrow road wound inland to the coastal road that led to Siboney, where a main road led inland toward Santiago. Farther west along the shoreline from Siboney the coastal road paralleled the small railroad track García had mentioned, and both turned northwest toward Santiago close to the harbor entrance forts. Siboney was deemed the second landing location. It had the same basic characteristics and included a more substantial pier.

Fortuna showed me a Spanish government map of the coastal area along with the engineer's detailed sketch maps of each location. Neither showed the depth of water or type of bottom, but I was assured there was enough water for small boats and barges to land at both places. In the absence of contrary evidence, I decided the Cubans' assessment was right and informed Fortuna of my agreement with the selection, and he in turn departed to tell the general.

Elements of the Cuban Liberation Army would move toward those locations and await word from Shafter to secure them. The American landing would begin at Daiquiri. Siboney would be taken after that by the forces moving overland from Daiquiri and others coming directly ashore. From there the Americans would march along the coastal rail and vehicle roads toward the coastal fortifications at Santiago, capturing them under the cover of direct naval gunfire support. Control of the forts would enable the U.S. fleet to neutralize the mines and enter the bay, where they would eliminate the Spanish warships hiding inside.

While Fortuna was off with the staff, I took the opportunity to make a more in-depth assessment of the Cuban soldiery camped around us, which I put into a memorandum for Shafter's eyes. He needed to understand his new allies.

The famous Mambi soldiers had been with García from the beginning and were a grim-looking lot. Most were peasants of various dark skin shades and ethnicities. Many walked with a slight stoop, as if their bodies were molded by a life of heavy labor. They kept their eyes cast impassively downward when carrying a burden yet were keenly watchful of all around them when on patrol or attack. Their short, thin frames were deceptively strong, able to carry impossible loads for long distances. For packs they carried bags made of palm burlap, into which went their ammunition, food, and few personal possessions. Most looked and smelled like they hadn't had a bath for a year.

Every man carried the ubiquitous cane knife, or machete, and was an expert with it. Most but not all had old family shotguns or rifles captured from the Spanish. Their marksmanship was not all that precise, but they seldom fired unless in close range anyway. These men preferred the blade on their rope belt. Interestingly, I never saw them engaged in an internecine fight in camp. When they got orders to attack the Spanish in battle, though, they were absolutely fearless, almost crazed.

At the mess tent, actually a hastily set up lean-to, I got half a boiled potato and a slice of mango, both of which were well past ripe. This was a veritable feast, made available to me only because of my rank and nationality. Normally I would shun such favoritism, but right then my morals took second place to my hunger. I consumed it in an instant and was damned grateful for the chance.

Here and there around me, groups of weary Mambi warriors sat by small fires. They kept their voices low. Their talk was short-winded, peppered with foul words. There was no music, no laughter, no reminiscences from the march.

No one had the energy left for light-hearted banter. Dragging mules, equipment, field artillery, supplies, and your own gear up and down mountains in the tropical summer heat and humidity saps the spirit of the strongest man. These men had just done it from Holguín, across 2,000- and 3,000-foot mountains to Alto Songo, then onward to Asarradero—110 miles in all.

I'd seen tough soldiers at war in Africa, Asia, and South America, but none were tougher than the Mambis of Cuba. After weeks of such toil, humans become machines. Their emotions fade into a colorless resignation to their place in life. Time becomes irrelevant, for the next hour and day and week will bring nothing but the same. The astonishing thing for me was that the Cubans weathered it all without signs of mutiny—even after the Spanish offered them amnesty if they surrendered. Was it any wonder their enemy spoke of them with respect?

As I passed each small fire, something extraordinary happened. The huddled men straightened up with pride and greeted me as if I was a valued comrade. I was merely a symbol of the rich yan-qui colossus just to the north, of course, but that was something new and encouraging for them. I was the first of the long-hoped-for *norteamericano* reinforcements. Many of the Cubans thanked me for being there alongside them. Word had spread. I was proof the rumors were true. They weren't alone anymore. The end was in sight, and the dream of freedom would soon become a reality.

These simple displays of gratitude made a great impact on my heart. I hoped our soldiers would stand up to these expectations, but my experience in Tampa had jaded my opinion of the U.S. Army's efficacy. Not because of a lack of fighting spirit in the men, but because the senior officers were so ill prepared and lacking in skill.

When I got back to our part of the camp, Law was asleep. Rork sat alone next to the red glowing coals from our dinner fire. I hadn't seen him since we first arrived at the Cuban headquarters camp because he'd been out searching for kindling for the fire. He looked more than tired, as if in the grip of melancholia.

"Aye, you're back. They figure out a landin' place yet?" he asked absentmindedly.

"Yes. It'll be Daiquiri. Gentle beach, small boat pier, road inland that meets the coastal road, relatively remote, with few of the enemy about. Siboney is the second landing place. How are you feeling, Sean? You look really worn out tonight."

"Ooh, indeed, sir. These ol' bones're achin' up a storm. The friggin' pony rides don't help any. Me backside feels like it's been keelhauled.

An' me head's still gettin' past that soiree last night with the general. The ol' sod can really put 'em away. Hell'uva drunk, it was."

There was something else bothering him, though. I could tell by the way he'd avoided looking me in the eye since we were reunited back at the farmhouse at Jamaica. His usual humor, always present even in the direst of situations, was lacking too. Rork could be reticent in revealing his wounds, both physical and sentimental. I guessed the reason but waited for him to tell me. Meanwhile, I looked up at the constellations, clearly visible now that the rain clouds had cleared away.

When Rork did open up, it came as a murmur. "Ah, well, there's somethin' needin' to be said by me, sir. Been weighin' heavy on me mind."

Only two coals were still red hot. As Rork poked at them with a stick, I said, "Out with it, my old friend. Sean to Peter, with no rank. We're too old to beat around the bush."

"Aye, Peter, that we are. Well, been meanin' to apologize for me behavior back at Tampa in May. But we've not been alone for me to speak me mind. Truly sorry for leavin' you in the lurch after readin' that letter from me Minnie. Truly thought she was the one, an' had me heart set on finally bein' happy like you an' dear Maria. Had the weddin' set an' all, or so I thought.

"That damned letter got me feelin' so bloody empty an' full o' tears, I just couldn't face anyone, not even you, me own best friend. Left that wee note for you an' took French leave right then an' there for the fleet at Key West. Had to get out to sea an' away from the whole bleedin' mess."

"Sean, I got your note and also heard about the letter from your fiancée. I understood immediately, and I probably would've done the same. Hell, I was impressed at how you ended up in *Oregon* just when she became the most famous ship in the Navy."

He exhaled deeply, as if ridding himself of guilt. "Thanks for understandin', Peter. Aye, Captain Clark got me in *Oregon* an' set me straightaway to work. There was a fair amount to be done after that

14,000-mile voyage, let me tell you. An' seein' young Sean doin' so well as an officer took me mind off me own heartache."

"Your heart'll mend, Sean. The right lady will come along one of these days when you least expect it."

"Aye, they say hope springs eternal, so maybe there's a woman out there for me. She'll have to be half blind, o' course, to face the likes o' me every mornin', but all she'll really need is a good heart an' soul."

He yawned. "Well, I've had me say, an' now me ancient bones're tellin' me 'tis time for us ol' men to be turnin' in, Peter. God only knows what the hell we'll face in the morn."

That night sleep once again eluded me, for my mind was preoccupied with all that was happening. The Cuban Liberation Army had been in communication with Admiral Sampson in the battleship *New York* since the fourteenth, providing intelligence on the enemy's ships, forts, and regiments at Santiago. In addition, the Cuban army's requests for arms, ammunition, medical supplies, and uniforms were approved and fulfilled immediately, delivered by USS *Suwanee*, a 165-foot lighthouse tender brought into the Navy for the war.

This support had cemented my status with García's staff and soldiery. Upon my arrival at Asarradero I began sending my own messages to Sampson, including intelligence assessments and a suggestion for a preinvasion meeting ashore between General García, Shafter, and Sampson. Indeed, Sampson immediately proposed meeting General García that very day, Sunday the nineteenth. When García agreed, the admiral steamed *New York* to the coast in front of Asarradero late that afternoon. García, Fortuna, and I were brought out to her in the ship's steam launch. Law and Rork stayed on the beach with orders to keep watch on everything happening around them.

The general, rigged in his best uniform for the first time since we'd met, was given the full display of ceremonial naval pageantry and treated with the utmost respect by all on board. He and Sampson got along well from the start. Afterward, Sampson confided in me that he was truly moved by García's professionalism. There was nothing of the sycophant about him. He was a soldier's soldier, just as Sampson, one of the smartest officers in the Navy, was a sailor's sailor.

Sampson also favored me with congratulations for my work inside Cuba, adding that he wished I would be commanding one of his cruisers when he had to fight the Spanish fleet but knew my present mission could help make the overall American operations in Cuba far more successful. After an hour and a half on board, the Cuban general and I left the clean, ordered, and well-fed world of an American warship and returned to the filthy squalor of an army camp in the jungle.

Leaving that ship took all my willpower.

14

Find a Bigger Mule

Asarradero, Cuba
Monday, 20 June 1898

IT WAS BARELY LIGHT the following morning when the cry
of a messenger woke my entourage and me. The message had
come down from the Cuban army lookout post atop 3,600-foot-
tall Loma del Gato, just to our east, via relay runners. Emerging
from our tents, we heard cheers breaking out through the camps
before we heard the news. A great armada of thirty-seven American
troop transports had arrived in the night and was covering the sea
beyond Admiral Sampson's blockading battle fleet.

An hour later I saw a Navy steam launch down at the beach. In
another hour a breathless naval lieutenant arrived at the top of the
slope looking for me. He handed me a dark blue envelope sealed
with gold wax. My companions gathered around at a respectful distance as I read the message inside from Admiral Sampson.

> 7 a.m., 20 June 1898
> Captain W,
> The army has arrived. I will be meeting with Gen S on his
> ship at 10 a.m. There, I will suggest a conference later today
> with him, Gen G, and myself at your location. Confirmation

and details on time will be sent to you after my 10 a.m. mtg with S. Please advise your principal and make necessary arrangements. Send confirmation of receipt of this message, with concurrence by your principal.

    W.T.S.

This was exactly what I had proposed from the beginning. The American general and admiral needed to come ashore, away from their comforts, so they could see and feel the challenges of the terrain and climate. They also needed to understand the strengths and deficits of their Cuban allies.

It was by then almost 9 a.m. Fortuna and I went straight to General García to tell him the news. To our great surprise, we discovered he was not there. Not knowing when Shafter would actually arrive, he'd gone to inspect a brigade that had recently been in battle and was several miles away in the higher mountains.

I uttered a very blue oath at my bad luck as Fortuna set out to find Major General Jesús Rabí, the second in command. Rabí beamed in delight when he heard Sampson's message. He immediately issued orders for the reception of the American commanders and sent out several officers to locate García and get him back as soon as possible.

With my aides, I descended to the beach and gave my simple written reply of acknowledgment to the lieutenant. There was no wind and not a cloud in the sky that day, the sun making the place a humid oven. In spite of the heat, the Cubans on the beach were far more optimistic than I'd ever seen them, for somehow word had spread about the meeting. My companions and I waited in the shade of a coconut palm for Sampson's next communication while we studied the transports milling about offshore. In these temperatures, we knew it would be hellish belowdecks in the transports for Theodore Roosevelt's men, and even worse for the horses.

Sampson's next message arrived at noon and simply said, "2 p.m." Fortuna passed the word to his superiors. Soon the beach was filled with Cuban officers and men practicing formations of long-forgotten, if ever learned, ceremonial drills. It was decidedly *not* their forte.

Just before the appointed hour, General Shafter's ship, the Ward liner *Seguranca*, steamed up and stopped a couple of miles away. She was escorted by *Gloucester*, a sleek little gunboat. Up until three months prior, *Gloucester* had been the yacht *Corsair II*, prized possession of financier John Pierpont Morgan until he sold her to the Navy for war duty. Since then she'd done fine work raiding Spanish ships and positions along the Cuban coast. My friend Richard Wainwright, whom I'd last seen on *Maine* the February night she exploded in Havana, was now in command of her.

At 2:07 p.m. an armada of small boats approached the beach from the liner. First to arrive was a launch full of stern-faced Marines, who scrambled out and trotted up to dry sand. They formed up in a double line at port arms, their bayoneted rifles loaded and ready for action. I noticed Lieutenant Law watching their technique with a critical but approving eye.

Next came a boatload of chattering correspondents, who targeted the most impressively uniformed Cuban in sight, apparently in the belief he was General García. He wasn't. He was the sergeant of the color guard and was visibly confused by the sudden attention. Fortuna quickly straightened out the misidentification and told the newsmen to stand in a group off to the side. None of them did.

Two boats of armed sailors and Marines arrived and drifted just off the beach, ready to come ashore if needed. The fourth boat contained the usual hangers-on in the general's staff, along with two foreign military attaché observers and the reporter I'd last seen at the Army headquarters in Tampa, Joseph Herrings. The boat grounded a few feet from the dry sand, and Cuban soldiers rushed out to carry the passengers to shore. The visitors stared at the strange scenery and inhabitants, their faces not reflecting admiration of what they saw. I remembered several of the staff officers from the Tampa Bay Hotel, including the idiot colonel who'd spilled the beans on my secret assignment. He was the picture of misery as he and the others were carried through the shallows on the backs of the grinning black Cuban soldiers.

Herrings waded ashore by himself, looked around at the spectacle, and began noting it all in his little book. He didn't look impressed.

After this vanguard was ashore, the launch with the admiral and general came in. When the boat crunched on the sand bottom, most of the crew went over the sides and waded up to the beach, where they stood in a line opposite the Marines. Sampson, who has always been trim and light of build, walked forward, stepped up onto the launch's bow, and jumped off into the ankle-deep water. He was followed by his chief of staff, Chadwick, an old naval intelligence colleague of mine, and a staff lieutenant. That left the general and the coxswain still in the boat.

General Shafter stood up, giving a casual wave to the onlookers. A hush fell over the crowd as they took in his immense size. I doubted if any Cuban had ever seen a man that large. There were no fat men in the Cuban Liberation Army; everyone, from García down to the lowest private, was perpetually on the verge of starvation.

Fortuna gasped in horror. Turning to me, he quietly said, "Sir, as you know, it is over a mile to our headquarters camp, and a thousand feet up. Please excuse me, but I have to find a bigger mule." Then he was gone. Beside me, Law struggled not to react. Rork muttered under his breath something very obscene about the U.S. Army.

Shafter looked from the gunwale to the shallows, obviously perplexed as to how he was going to get ashore. Simply stepping up onto the gunwale and jumping down into the water was out of the question for him, as was the option of scampering up to the bow and leaping off as Sampson had. He conversed quietly with the equally perplexed coxswain, who I saw respectfully shake his head. Shafter turned his eyes toward Sampson on the beach. For a fleeting moment the admiral's face betrayed no acknowledgment of Shafter's plight, and I got the sense he didn't like the general. Then Sampson looked expectantly at me.

Using my Spanish for the first time on this mission, I asked a nearby Cuban colonel to get some of his men to carry the boat into shallower water. In a flash, orders were bellowed and a mob of half-clothed Cuban soldiers and U.S. sailors in white uniforms splashed out to the boat. I nodded to Rork, who went in the water too, calling for the sailors in the boats floating off the beach to come in and help.

Taking charge of the operation by using the crude Spanish curses he knows, as well as a few in English, Rork quietly suggested to Shafter, "Mornin' sir. Perhaps it'd be best for you to be seated 'til we get the boat up to the beach."

The coxswain, receiving a curt nod from Rork, jumped into the water to join the crowd of men along the sides of the boat. Rork then got all the Cuban soldiers and American sailors lifting and pushing together on the count of three. With loud grunts and curses the heavy launch lifted and lurched forward until the forward half was dropped on dry sand and the deed was done.

Then the commanding general of all American Army forces in Cuba, which at that point numbered about five staff officers, stepped ashore on the island he was supposed to liberate from Spanish oppression. A wave of lackluster applause came from the still gaping Cuban throng. Someone shouted, "*Viva los norteamericanos.*" But it came out sounding rather perfunctory. No one echoed it.

After wringing out his handkerchief, Shafter mopped his brow. In an uncertain gait he made his way through the soft sand past the saluting American Marines and sailors to Admiral Sampson. Once together they headed for the official Cuban reception party, led by Major General Rabí and Brigadier General Castillo. On the eastern side of this group stood the Cuban honor guard and the American press, one of whom was trying to set up a camera tripod to record the moment for posterity. On the western side were Shafter's staff, Lieutenant Law, a soggy Chief Rork, and me.

Shafter and Sampson stopped a few feet short of the Cuban generals. Someone shouted out an order in Spanish, and all the Cubans on the beach came to attention, as did the gathered Americans, rather belatedly. The U.S. Marines, of course, accomplished the drill magnificently, snapping their rifles into present arms in unison, the sling buckles and hand slaps providing a nice percussion to each movement of the evolution. The performance openly impressed the Cuban soldiers.

About this time, a harried-looking Fortuna reappeared, slipping through the crowd to stand beside and translate for Rabí. Castillo, who had lived in the United States and was fluent in English, stood on the other side of Rabí. The Cuban generals, both of whom were combat veterans and war heroes, stepped closer to Rear Admiral Sampson and Major General Shafter and rendered a perfect hand salute. The American admiral reciprocated. Shafter switched the handkerchief to his other hand, straightened a bit, and offered a quick return salute.

More orders were shouted, a drum rolled, and the Cuban honor guard presented arms—not as well as our men but better than I thought they could. The flags of Cuba and the United States were brought forward, and several bugles sounded a salute of sorts to the colors. Afterward, Rabí and Shafter gave mercifully short speeches containing nothing of substance.

I was hoping for a moment to advise Shafter on the situation, but the only interaction between us was a polite exchange of greetings—once I reminded him of who I was. He appeared not to remember my mission either, so I reminded him of that as well.

I thought that would spark some interest on his part, but he merely said, "Yes, well, Wake, please let my staff know what you've learned about the situation around here. They'll factor it into the plans."

"Aye, aye, sir," I said as he turned away toward a beckoning staff officer.

The gathering turned into a procession, with senior officers of both armies mounting mules for the ascent up the mountain. The mule Fortuna had arranged for Shafter was the largest I'd seen in the camp but still nothing near the size of the usual American mule. The general looked at the creature doubtfully. A stump was brought over for him to step on while mounting the crude saddle. The agony in the mule's eyes incited pity even from me, a sworn enemy of the genus. For my money, that damned beast deserved a medal, sainthood, and full pension for the rest of his life for carrying that horrific load more than a mile and a thousand feet up in elevation.

Our caravan moved at a slow pace along the trail. All the American officers on muleback were led by grooms; the Cuban officers handled their own mounts. Right behind us, the Marines ascended the mountain on foot. The entire route was lined with Cuban soldiers, who brought rifles, shotguns, or whatever weapon was in hand to the present arms position as General Shafter passed them. There was pride and determination in their eyes, but I could tell the sweltering American officers never noticed it. All they saw were black-skinned natives in rags.

15

Council of War

Asarradero, Cuba
Monday, 20 June 1898

W HEN WE FINALLY reached the top, everyone dismounted. Many of the American officers rubbed their
backsides and complained about the small size of
the Cuban mules and the discomfort of the rudimentary saddles.
Shafter led the grumbling. As the general unburdened the mule, he
looked disdainfully at the lean-to huts of the Cuban generals.

I was standing close by him when he quietly muttered to one
of his staff, "Humph, this place resembles Indian cantonments I've
seen, but with even more disorder. I suppose they can put it up in an
hour and vacate it in a minute."

The foreign military observers went even further in denigrating
the camp. They dismissed in racial terms the probable fighting qualities of Cuban soldiers based on what they'd seen of the men and
their camp. They were ignorant of what the Cubans had actually
accomplished, which was nothing short of astounding.

True, the Cubans weren't European parade-ground puppets—
they were combat-hardened jungle fighters who survived on wild
fruit, greens, and a little rice. It was all I could do to remain polite

in the face of such sneering arrogance by my fellow Americans and the foreign officers. As I was trying to think of something positive to say, I heard cheers emanating from another trail on the northeast side of the mountain. Major General García was returning at last from his inspection tour of the frontline brigade.

Unlike the visiting dignitaries, he was not in full uniform. Instead he was in his usual long-sleeved working rig—a faded blue uniform fastened up to the neck, with two buttons undone in the middle exposing his under vest. He wore neither rank insignia nor side-arm. Beside the resplendent American admiral and general and their staffs, García looked like an elderly servant, even though he was no older.

Fortuna translated as the Cuban general embraced his friend of one day, Admiral Sampson, then gravely saluted General Shafter. "Welcome to Free Cuba and my humble campaign headquarters, gentlemen. Forgive my late entrance, but when I learned of General Shafter's sudden arrival I was many kilometers away inspecting a brigade that has seen heavy fighting this last week. They won the fight but took many casualties."

Shafter offered polite congratulations on the victory and in the next wheezing breath suggested they get on with the council of war. Accordingly, García, Sampson, and Shafter adjourned to the thatched hut belonging to Major General Rabí, a veritable palace compared with the other huts nearby. They sat on empty ammunition crates arranged in a circle around a rough table. Fortuna brought in a topographical map of the area along with the survey sketches of Daiquirí and Siboney. García motioned for me to enter also, but the other staff stayed outside looking in at us.

García began, with Fortuna translating. "General Shafter, I want to start by saying the Cuban Liberation Army will do all in our power to assist your army. All Cubans are very grateful to the United States. I hereby place myself and my forces at your disposal. We will ensure a safe landing for your men and equipment. Together we will then execute an advance on Santiago. Let me add my appreciation for the excellent work of your liaison, Captain Wake. His insight has been invaluable."

"Yes, well, thank you for your generous offer of support, General García. I am quite favorably impressed by your élan. And, ah, yes, Wake is a good man," Shafter rattled off vacantly. "As for you being subordinate to me, I do not have authority to order it. But if that is your wish, so be it. I am sure there are many functions your people can fulfill."

Fortuna was translating, but García clearly caught Shafter's negative tone even before the words were put into Spanish. He nodded politely anyway.

Because of their ability in English, Castillo and Fortuna then explained to Sampson and Shafter the latest details of the Spanish order of battle. Each subject was covered concisely. Shafter listened intently, asking some pertinent questions on enemy logistics. I was pleased to see that, for it's the sign of a good commander.

When the briefing ended, Shafter thanked Castillo and Fortuna, then turned to General García. "Now, I need to address the initial war operations. General García, where do you suggest we land our troops?"

"Daiquiri first, then Siboney."

García nodded to Castillo, who explained the reasons for recommending Daiquiri and Siboney. Fortuna took over with a detailed description of the coastal terrain and roads, particularly the railroad line and adjacent road that ran west along the shoreline toward the Spanish fortresses at the mouth of the bay. He continued with details on the inland approaches to Santiago from that section of the coast, referring to sketch maps of each location. During the entire time, Sampson observed everything closely but contributed neither question nor suggestion. His lack of engagement puzzled me, but then again, this was primarily an Army show.

Shafter asked his Cuban counterpart, "General, when do you propose we do this?"

"Very soon, General Shafter," García replied. He gestured toward me as Fortuna put it in English. "Perhaps Captain Wake has an opinion, for he is the one man who best knows the military and naval capabilities of everyone involved—the Americans, Cubans, and Spanish."

It was my first inclusion in the discussion. All eyes turned to me—the Cubans expectantly and the Americans somewhat warily. The latter's expressions indicated they thought of me merely as a sailor interfering with Army operations who had perhaps "gone native" and was overly enamored of the Cubans and their cause. I did have the reputation in Washington as a supporter of Cuban independence, so their apparent attitude didn't surprise me. In any event, in that hut on the mountain in Cuba, I was well past caring what an American general and his staff thought of me.

"We need to start landing troops within two days at the most, sir," I said. "There are only a few feasible landing places, and the Spanish have detachments watching each of them. The Cubans can secure Daiquiri and block the Spanish from reinforcing their outpost there, but they only have enough ammunition, supplies, and food for a couple of days of fierce fighting on a large scale. If the enemy realizes our planned landing location and puts it under a major attack of three or four thousand men, the Cubans will need American relief within three days. Naval diversions along the coast will help confuse the enemy, but not for long."

Shafter's eyes hardened as he asked the next question in a low voice. "Captain Wake, as General García has said, you know the Cuban and Spanish culture, as well as the local situation and forces. You know them better than any of my officers, which is why you were sent inside Cuba ahead of us.

"I expect your candid answer to my next question before I commit the lives of 17,000 American men to this enterprise. If I accelerate the campaign and begin landing two days from now on the twenty-second, do the Cubans actually have the strength and skills to hold Daiquiri and Siboney long enough for us to land all our troops and equipment? If the Cubans fail and the Spanish get through, my men will be caught in a bloodbath on the scale of Fredericksburg."

Fortuna's translation into Spanish for García was far less pointed, but everyone there sensed that Shafter's thinly veiled real question was whether the Cubans would fight a toe-to-toe battle with the Spanish. It was a valid point that needed answering.

"General Shafter, during the last three years the Cuban Liberation Army has repeatedly overcome daunting odds against a modern European army. They've done it all on their own with little outside help due to the U.S. arms embargo, which ended only recently when we got in this war. The Cuban people have been struggling for this moment for thirty years. These men around you may not look like much, but they are no strangers to combat and death. They know their own people are watching what will happen here. This place and time will determine their future freedom. It is now or never."

I paused to let the meaning of my preamble resonate, then emphasized, "I have absolutely no doubt that General García's soldiers will clear and hold Daiquiri, and Siboney also, for three days or until every single one of them is dead. For our part, we Americans need to strike hard and strike fast, before the Spanish can react in force from Santiago."

For the next few seconds, the only sound in the hut was Shafter's breathing. Fortuna translated my words verbatim for García, who grimly nodded his concurrence to the mammoth blond American general, the outsider to whom he had pledged everything.

Shafter pounded a fist on his knee. "Very well, then. I concur. Our invasion force will land the day after tomorrow at Daiquiri. Once ashore, they will move west and meet our reinforcements as they land at Siboney, then consolidate and move west toward Santiago. And now, we need to get the details of the naval diversions and actual landing decided, for this will be a complex movement involving Cuban troops, American warships, and my army."

Other staff officers were brought in. Available manpower, transport, provisions, ammunition, diversions, and communications were analyzed. When it came out that the Cuban forces were starving, which was why García offered no refreshments other than coffee to the distinguished American visitors, Shafter summoned a colonel and ordered him to get two thousand U.S. Army rations ashore by sunset. García couldn't hide his surprise at the American general's ability to do such a thing and expressed his sincere appreciation. Outside the hut I heard the joyous word spreading—food was coming.

I must admit that General Shafter impressed me with his administrative ability during the processing of planning out the details. Once the options were laid out, he made rapid decisions. He then formed a methodical progression of operational orders for all the components of the campaign, even while under obvious physical distress.

This discomfort became more manifest as the meeting went on. Sweat ran profusely down his reddened face and plastered his hair to his scalp. Periodically he stood up to stamp a foot, massage a thigh, or stretch his back and neck. The Cubans discreetly pretended not to notice. I feared the man was in real trouble, but he stoically carried on with the crucial decision making.

The process continued with only one interruption. A newspaperman was caught standing near the back of the hut, eavesdropping on the discussions. He was removed at once, his protests ignored by an American staff officer who threatened to arrest him. Thereafter, a Marine was stationed there to guard against further intrusions.

An hour later, at 4 p.m., the planning for the operation was over. Lt. John Miley of the Army staff, a squared-away sort, was brought in during this final phase to take notes. His mandate was to reduce the voluminous notes into a concise document and distribute it at dawn to the U.S. Army commands, Admiral Sampson, and the Cuban high command.

At the end, Shafter recited the operations plan to the conferees without referring to notes, including dates, times, places, and units. When finished, he gave a polite thank-you to the Cuban generals and raised his ponderous bulk up off the crate, plainly anxious to leave.

There were no mutual congratulations among the participants, only handshakes and resolute countenances. Each officer, Cuban and American, knew his fate rested on everything in the plan working perfectly, a near impossibility in war. Everyone rose to head outside to the clearing where the mule train waited for the long descent.

It was still beastly hot. Several of the American staff spoke longingly about having something cool to drink back on the ship. Shafter had a slight limp as he approached his mule, which I saw was a different animal from the one that had carried him up the mountain.

García walked over to Shafter and embraced him in the Cuban fashion. Everyone else grew quiet as the two generals held a silent handshake for a long time. García's unwavering eyes conveyed the burden Shafter shouldered in addition to his military responsibilities—Cuba's freedom now depended on an American victory. Shafter put his other hand atop García's in a firm clasp, a solemn acknowledgment.

Then Shafter turned away, ending the momentous scene. With Lieutenant Miley's assistance, the general got atop the mule. On the ground beside him, an old Cuban man held the reins. The column headed off. When the last of them plodded down the winding trail, I stood at the crest of the little plateau and watched their descent. The Cuban troops on the trail had waited in the sun this entire time. They saluted again as the procession of American officers passed by them.

García walked over to me, took my hand in his, and quietly said something that means everything to a Cuban. The memory is one of my proudest possessions.

"*Muchas gracias, Peter, mi querido hermano.*" Thank you, Peter, my dear brother.

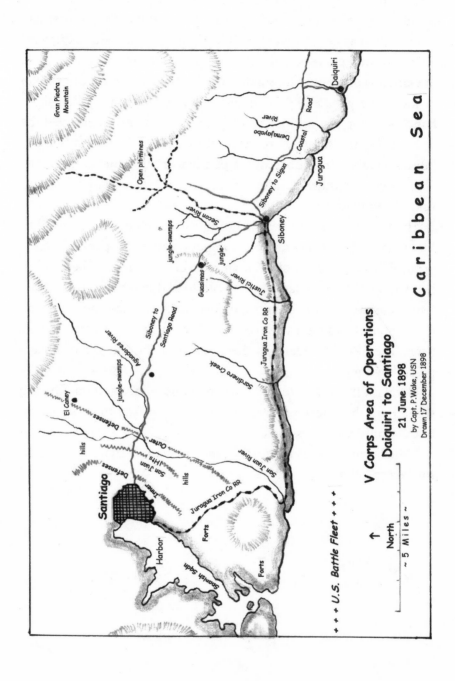

V Corps Area of Operations
Daiquiri to Santiago
21 June 1898
by Capt. P. Wake, USN
Drawn 17 December 1898

North
~ 5 Miles ~

+ + + U.S. Battle Fleet + + +

Caribbean Sea

Gran Piedra Mountain

Daiquiri

Demajayabo River

Coastal Road

Juragua

Siboney to Sigua

Siboney

Open pit-mines

Secon River

jungle-swamps

Guasimos

jungle

Justici River

Juragua Iron Co RR

Siboney to Santiago Road

Aguadores River

Sardinero Creek

jungle-swamps

El Caney

Defenses

hills

San Juan Hts

Outer

hills

San Juan River

Santiago

Inner Defenses

Juragua Iron Co RR

Harbor

Forts

Forts

Sbanish Sqdn

16

The Liberators

Daiquiri, Cuba
Wednesday, 22 June 1898

ENERAL SHAFTER'S INVASION plan was complicated,
requiring close coordination of various efforts in spite
of difficult terrain, cultural differences, lack of logistical
assets, communication barriers, and commanders completely inexperienced in large-scale landing operations. With all that going
against it at the beginning, I was amazed that the plan's execution
began exactly as had been outlined in the mountainside hut two
days earlier. The initial stage commenced very early on Tuesday, the
twenty-first, when several movements by more than six thousand
men in the Cuban army were set into motion.

Major General Rabi led three regiments in a feint toward Cabañas
Bay, just west of Santiago. Brigadier General Castillo and a thousand Cubans in two regiments were taken by troop transport in
the opposite direction to Demajayabo, a tiny village near Daiquiri,
where they were landed and sent on a flanking move to the east to
remove the Spanish from the landing site at Daiquiri. Concurrently,
General García marched four thousand of his Cuban troops toward
Asarradero from their inland camp at Palma. Once there they were
to be embarked on ships on the twenty-fourth, heading directly to

Daiquiri as reinforcements for the Americans, who would have already landed on the twenty-second.

My assignment by General Shafter—given as a thirty-second verbal order while he walked to his mule—was to go overland to the invasion site, reconnoitering the eastern defenses of Santiago en route. García, my nominal superior, acquiesced in letting me go. I thus had no time to waste, so my companions and I left Asarradero immediately after Shafter's descent from García's headquarters.

It was another miserable trek, with this one having the added burden of being very close to the Spanish lines and under constant threat of attack. What we learned when studying the enemy defenses was not reassuring. The entire perimeter around Santiago was professionally arrayed with barbed-wire entanglements, trenches, fortified Krupp artillery batteries, blockhouses, and Maxim machine guns—and full of Spanish soldiers. The defensive works were deep and mutually supporting. We could find no weak points on the northern and eastern sides.

The U.S. Navy had its role in all this, too. On the twenty-first, the day after the generals' conference, the sole oceanic telegraph cable from Oriente to Haiti—which the Navy had severed a month earlier to deprive the Spanish of its use—was repaired at Playa del Este, east of Daiquiri, and brought into service for the American forces. From Haiti the cable went to Nassau, in the British Bahamas, and from there to Florida. Shafter soon had instantaneous communication with government leaders in Washington.

At dawn on the morning of the invasion the Navy began diversionary bombardments all along the coast. The battleship *Texas* attacked Spanish units at Cabañas Bay and dueled with the Socapa batteries on the west side of the entrance to Santiago Harbor. *Eagle* and *Gloucester* attacked the small fort and the railroad bridge at Aguadores. *Annapolis, Hornet, Helena,* and *Bancroft* attacked Spanish infantry in the Siboney area. The main battle fleet steamed in close to the entrance to Santiago Harbor, lobbing shells at the eastern fortresses and up into the bay to dissuade Spanish warships from coming out to disrupt the American landing operations.

While these naval sideshows were being enacted, the primary U.S. effort was being directed at the sleepy little village of Daiquiri to the east, where I had arrived two hours earlier. General Castillo, who had raced ahead to lead the local Cuban forces, welcomed me heartily at his position on a hill overlooking the village and shoreline. He pointed out to sea. "General Shafter is keeping his promise. Right on time."

The Caribbean was covered with ships. A dozen transports loitering about four miles off Daiquiri's beach were lowering boats. Another dozen steamed in from the west. Closer inshore were the navy's warships. *Detroit, Castine, Wasp, New Orleans, Scorpion, Suwanee,* and *Wampatuck* were unleashing a furious bombardment on the village and the beach, cratering the entire area, setting the flimsy thatched dwellings alight, and making the ground constantly tremble. Shrapnel scythed down trees and bushes in the nearby forest.

It was a remarkable display of brute American strength, and it gave heart to the Cubans, who had never seen anything like it. With a frightening roar and swirling machetes, Castillo's Mambis went charging forward toward the closest Spaniards, about two hundred soldiers who had gathered near the narrow road leading inland to escape the bombardment. The Spanish infantry were overwhelmed in seconds. Caught between the high explosives of the Americans and the vengeance of the Cubans, they rapidly realized the hopelessness of their situation. The entire unit fled up the road at a run.

This was right about when the grand plan began to unravel.

The Spaniards' retreat left Castillo's men in control of the area. I heard the welcome sound of cheers from the various Cuban units celebrating the first combined allied success. The American warships didn't know of this good news, however, and began to bombard the Cubans, the only targets left. The cheering stopped. The Mambis scrambled en masse to the safety of the jungle behind the village.

Castillo's staff carried a large Cuban flag, but the men on the ships couldn't see it. Rork seized the red, white, and blue banner and ran to a clearing near our position, waving it madly back and forth toward the ships. A shell exploded near him. He bellowed a storm of vile curses that only an American Navy boatswain can conjure up. The nearest ships were a quarter mile or more away from us, but I wouldn't be surprised if they could hear every word. After another two harrowing minutes—a long time when you are being shot at—the guns stopped. The ensuing silence was eerie, the only sound being the crackling of the burning village.

At a little after 9 a.m., the first boatloads of American soldiers arrived at the narrow iron pier. Law, Rork, Fortuna, and I walked down through the village to greet them. They were regular infantry from General Lawton's division and expecting the worst, cautiously scanning the area as they leaped one by one off the boat whenever a swell lifted it close enough to the pier. Fanning out across the pier they began heading toward us, the incredulous sergeant in charge blurting out, "Who the hell are you fellas? Y'all wannee makee surrendero?"

Rork was about to admonish this gross breech of discipline, but then the sergeant saw our insignia and quickly added, "Oh, hell, you're Americans. Very sorry, sir! I thought you was the enemy trying to surrender."

The sergeant's confusion was completely understandable. Our uniforms were less than pristine, having been worn continuously for the last several days. Rork grumbled something under his breath about sergeants.

The sergeant asked Rork, "What're you sailors doing here on land?"

I could tell Rork was about to give a colorful but insulting answer, so, seizing the once-in-a-lifetime moment, I announced nonchalantly to the new arrivals, "Good morning, men. On behalf of the United States Navy and the Marine Corps, we welcome the U.S. Army to Cuba. We're very glad you've finally come to join us in the war."

The sailors manning the boat laughed. The soldiers looked at the sergeant for their response. The sergeant was still confused, my dry wit going right over his head. He'd expected a fight, not humor, and peered about looking for the Spanish.

Then he answered the only way he knew. "Yes, sir."

"Sergeant," I said, "as far as the enemy goes, they've been removed for you by the Cuban Liberation Army, so please clear this pier and make room for the soldiers following behind you. Chief Rork here will show you where to go. Just follow him."

The sergeant acknowledged my order and told his men, "Well boys, I guess we'll just follow the Navy. They know where we're supposed to go."

Rork gave me a perturbed glance. "Where do you want 'em, sir?"

"Put them across the road to the village, Rork. Then return here."

After Rork led them off, I surveyed the scene. Things were happening rapidly. At least ten Navy steam launches towing five or six launches each were heading for the pier. Another eight launches were already arriving, each vying to land troops as quickly as possible. Two other launches had turned away from the confusion near the pier and were trying to run up on the beach. Even though the sea was calm, there was a gentle undulation that gained in height as the water got shallower and culminated in four-foot-high breakers on the underwater coral ledge a hundred feet off the beach. I saw Rork waving them away, pointing to the overcrowded pier. *Oh hell*, I thought, *it's low tide*. The tidal range on this part of the coast wasn't much, but it was enough to hinder or help.

Law read my mind. "This wasn't planned very well. I'd better go take care of the confusion on the pier, sir."

"Good," I told him. "Once the tide comes up a bit, the boats can go over that coral."

Rork returned to where I stood and gave a more colorful assessment of the American invasion. "The damned Army's cocked this one up by the bloody numbers, sir. Look there, these poor bastards're wearing heavy wool uniforms. An' that sergeant just told me his lads've drunk all their water on the way here from their ships. Some're already startin' to drop from the bleedin' heat. An' even their officers've not a blessed clue as to where to go or what to do. Nobody's told 'em."

"Yeah, I know. The Army hasn't done a landing like this since before the Civil War, Rork. They're learning as they go."

He huffed in disgust. "Look at that. Can you believe the Army brought only one cargo barge to bring horses an' supplies to the pier—one bloody barge for an army o' 15,000 men? Aye, an' look out there just now, sir. Those soldiers're pushin' their horses off the ships! They're hopin' they'll swim in to the beach, but they aren't. This thing is a proper total bollocks, it is."

I followed his pointing arm. The transport *Yucatan*, a hastily chartered merchant ship now crammed with soldiers, had anchored only a quarter mile away, by far the closest in of the transports. Several panicked horses were swimming in circles alongside the ship, their hoofs flailing the water frantically. As others were dumped overboard, soldiers lining the rails shouted commands at them, to no avail. One circle of panicked horses headed out to sea.

Fortuna stood next to me, his face furrowed in concern. I had to agree with his unsaid estimation—so far the liberators were not very impressive. I wondered what Castillo, up in the hills, thought about what he was seeing.

"Bloody friggin' hell," muttered Rork to no one in particular. "It's gonna be a long friggin' day."

17

In the Arena and
Daring Great Things

Daiquiri, Cuba
Wednesday, 22 June 1898

AN HOUR LATER I was standing on the pier when a flash
of light caught my eye—the glint of sunlight off spectacles in one of the approaching launches. A moment after
that I heard an unmistakable voice. It was none other than Lt. Col.
Theodore Roosevelt rattling off his opinions to Col. Leonard Wood
sitting beside him near the stern.

"I simply *cannot* believe the confounded lack of proper preparation on the part of the corps staff. Don't they read history—or even
the newspapers—to learn how the British do things? Egad, Colonel,
even the black Zulu armies of *Africa* are more organized than this!
I just thank the good Lord above that our Navy is here to get us
ashore with their boats. Speaking of that, who are those fellows yonder on the pier? Why, they look like Navy men!"

In the next second he was pounding the boat's gunwale. "Look
there, Colonel Wood! Do my eyes deceive me or is that Peter *Wake*?
Yes, it bully well *is* Wake, and by Gumphrey, he's got Chief Rork with
him, too!"

I had Rork clear a space at the pier for the approaching boat, in which Theodore now stood in his self-designed uniform, a British-looking khaki affair with lots of pockets. He flashed his famous grin at me while waving an outlandish flat-sided slouch hat.

He jumped onto the pier first, Colonel Wood following with far more dignity. Roosevelt suddenly stopped, his mien changing from elation to stoic determination. Coming to attention, he saluted me.

"Lieutenant Colonel Roosevelt, of the First Volunteer Cavalry Regiment, sir. Good to see our Navy here!"

Seeing this martial exhibition of respect, everyone around us went to attention. Except Wood, who was scanning the hills for the enemy. Even the soldiers perched precariously in the boat tried to stand still. I hastily returned the salute before any of them fell overboard.

"Thank you, Theodore," I said, at which he beamed and pumped my hand vigorously.

I disengaged and announced, "Welcome to Cuba, gentlemen. The Cubans pushed the Spanish out of the village several hours ago, and we have a defensive perimeter set up inland. You can assemble your men over there, under the shade of those trees, before heading inland."

I motioned toward a shrapnel-mangled laurel tree on the other side of the village. Wood's eyes continued to dart everywhere, taking in the pandemonium on the pier and beach.

Turning to Roosevelt, I said, "You're six days late, Theodore. You and the Army were supposed to be here on the sixteenth."

"It's a long, incredibly frustrating story, Peter," he replied with an angry harrumph. "Total chaos from the moment we said good-bye in Tampa. I'll tell you later. But first I must attend to the task of assembling our troopers and finding my horses."

Wood interrupted. "While you're getting that done, Theodore, I'll go find General Young's brigade headquarters. Peter, do you know where they set that up?"

"He's not ashore yet, Leonard," I said. "Looks like you are the senior Army officer here right now. Yours is also the first cavalry regiment.

The soldiers who landed this morning told me they're in Lawton's infantry division."

His eyes hardening even more as they surveyed the ineptitude around us, Wood calmly said, "Thank you, Peter. Then I suppose I'll find a spot to set up *our* headquarters. I'm sure the general will be arriving shortly. Perhaps we can meet later on, when things are sorted out. I'd like to hear your view of the situation."

Wood, Roosevelt, and their cavalrymen formed up in a column and marched inland from the pier. Only a few of their horses made it ashore, and those were for the senior officers only. They would be cavalrymen in name only.

The morning wore on as hundreds, then thousands of soldiers gathered in the ruined village. So many were coming ashore that some boats gave up on waiting for space at the pier and again tried to run the surf to the beach. Most made it, but one loaded down with black soldiers and a mound of supplies capsized. Two of the soldiers didn't come up from the bottom. Capt. Bucky O'Neill, commander of a cavalry troop in Roosevelt's regiment, dove in to save them, to no avail.

By noon I had gladly relinquished my duties to an Army provost colonel, one of the many colonels I saw wandering around. Rork, Law, and I headed up into the hills away from the confusion. In the later afternoon, my tired little band—minus Fortuna, whom I had sent to check back in with General Castillo—found the camp of the 1st Volunteer Cavalry. We were greeted by Theodore, who was full of vim.

They'd found a little open area of scrub between the thick jungle and a stagnant pool of putrid water. Theodore reported the pond contained an excellent specimen of *Crocodylus rhombifer*, the small but very dangerous Cuban caiman, adding with disdain that he disliked all reptiles, especially the kind with teeth. Then he beckoned us to gather around the campfire and share their meal.

Wood was at a regimental commanders' conference with General Young. Law and Rork politely declined Roosevelt's offer, heading for another campfire. That allowed Theodore and me to eat in privacy.

"I apologize for the rather sorry state of our cuisine, Peter," Roosevelt said with a chuckle. "We are reduced to some barely reconstituted beans with rice that appears to be of antique vintage. We also have a can of something purported to be a type of meat. The cook says it is tinned beef, but the consensus among the patrons of this august regimental establishment is that it's a considerably smaller animal, one that *barks*."

I examined the contents of the pot. He was right. The congealed mess was unappetizing, but I didn't care. I wearily dropped to the ground and took the proffered tin plate from him. "It's better than what the Cuban soldiers and my crew have been eating, Theodore. We were lucky to get some wild greens and a rotten sweet potato."

Theodore was lost in reflection. "Ah, Peter, your diet brings to mind King Solomon's Fifteenth Proverb, verse seventeen: 'Better is a dinner of herbs where love is about, than a fattened ox where hatred reigns therewith.' And in all the years since that proverb was written, man has shown that the love of comradeship in the field of battle has no equal."

I didn't have the energy to reply, but it didn't matter. He wasn't done. Next he gave his opinion of the press coverage of the war. "The press has been focused on superficial matters. An army marches on its stomach! The lamentably *meager* provisions of your beloved Cuban Liberation Army have not generally been mentioned in the New York newspaper dispatches. Perhaps they should be. I will remind some of the correspondents accompanying us. I have a rapport with them, you know. Kindred scribes."

"All help is appreciated, Theodore. The Cubans need it."

"I fully concur, for I met some of your Cuban fellows today. What a sight they were. *Brigand* looking rather than soldierly. Really, a more ragged gang of tatterdemalions my eyes have never looked upon. More important, I found them armed with every type of dilapidated gun and blade, some as ancient as this so-called food. I suppose they might be good as scouts for our army, though. They do know the lay of the land."

He meant no ill will, but I was tired of the condescending attitudes from almost every Army officer coming ashore that day. "They may not look like much, Theodore, but they're pretty damn good at *killing* the enemy. They've been doing it in three wars over the past three decades. I just hope our troops turn out to be as good at it as the Cubans. Talk is cheap."

He physically recoiled from my comment, realizing he'd given offense.

"My dear Peter, everyone knows of your sincere *affection* for the Cuban cause of freedom. My comments meant no disrespect to you or them. The fact remains, however, these seminaked peasants do not presently have the same arms, equipment, or training as do the Spanish, or any other modern army. The Cubans fight in a primitive bandit form. Thus they have remained at an impasse with the Spanish. Without our military might they shall have neither victory nor freedom."

He was right, of course, damn him. The Cubans *were* in a stalemate. The Americans would have to shoulder the heaviest load of fighting to gain a decisive victory. "Time will tell on that score, Theodore."

He yawned. "Yes, it always does. I only hope my courage does not fail when facing the proverbial elephant."

"You'll do fine. Just don't do anything stupid and get killed. I'll catch hell from both Edith and Maria."

"I shall do my best! Though I am mighty fatigued right now, Peter, I need to stay conscious long enough to hear your latest observations about the enemy. How do we fight them? What is their weakness when in action?"

"It's much like what I told you in Tampa. Their soldiers wait to be told what to do. Strike fast, and their reaction time will be slow. Their average marksmanship is relatively poor, with rounds going high and a little to the right, so stay low to the ground. They usually fire in volleys. They also don't like to fight close in. Try to quickly flank them and come in on them from the side or rear. Frontal assaults won't work; the Spanish are too heavily armed. Some of their local loyalist militia units—they're called guerillas—have sharpshooters. One of their favorite tactics is to hide in up trees until you go by, then shoot you from behind. So always have a man looking up in the trees as you advance. Hit them in the trees with volley fire the moment you see them."

"Thank you for the practical suggestions, Peter. I will pass them along to Leonard. We'll be ready when we meet the enemy." He yawned again, stretching his arms. Taking off his spectacles and carefully stowing them in a top pocket, he said, "You know, I brought along no less than five pairs of these indispensable little items. I wonder how many I'll lose on this campaign? Probably all of them!"

Amused by his self-deprecation, Theodore laid his blanket roll beside the fire. I remained seated, Indian-style, poking the coals.

"I fear I must allow slumber to override hospitality, old friend," he said as he slapped a mosquito on his neck. "It's not the company, I assure you, but today's exertion in the face of daunting incompetence has tired me. But despair has no hold on me, for at long last we are here, in *Cuba*! We are warriors actually *in* the arena and actively daring great things. Like Lafayette and von Steuben, we are in the midst of the great liberation of a people! Come what may, you and I will always have that, for the rest of our lives."

In response to the typically romantic Roosevelt hyperbole, I simply said, "Goodnight, Theodore. Sleep well. You'll get your wish about seeing the damned elephant in the arena soon enough."

His reply was a blissful snore.

18

The Grand Strategy

Siboney, Cuba
Thursday, 23 June 1898

ARLY THE NEXT DAY, the twenty-third of June, the Army started landing troops at Siboney. This was done in a state of bedlam similar to that at Daiquiri, but fortunately the safety of this second landing was once again guaranteed by the Cuban Army's forcible ejection of the Spanish from the area. That, combined with a naval bombardment of the Spanish fort and an American advance guard coming overland from Daiquiri on the Spanish rear, soon secured the area. Equally fortunate, the Cuban troops were not subjected to accidental U.S. naval gunfire.

An American general headquarters of sorts was quickly established at Siboney—without General Shafter, who chose to remain comfortably on board his ship for the next several days between periodic visits ashore. By that first afternoon at Siboney, troops and heavy supplies were coming ashore slowly but steadily onto the pier or directly over the beach. Fortunately, the weather, something I'd worried about, stayed benign, for this would be the main landing place for the American troops and supplies.

The march toward Santiago began that same afternoon, though it did not follow the original plan, or even any coordinated movement.

The advance resulted from an impromptu race to see which American outfit could shoot a Spaniard first. The winner turned out to be the dismounted cavalry division, which had forged ahead of Lawton's infantry division on the six-mile march from Daiquiri to Siboney.

The plan had called for everyone, including the cavalry brigades, to rest and regroup upon reaching Siboney. Instead, the cavalry continued onward, taking a hard right turn at Siboney onto the inland road to Santiago. That right turn proved fateful. The first real contact with the enemy took place three miles up the road near a nondescript place called Las Guasimas in the hilly green jungle behind the coast.

The unit to achieve this distinction was the division's 2nd Brigade, commanded by Brigadier General Young. It consisted of the 1st Cavalry Regiment (white regulars); the 10th Cavalry Regiment (Negro regulars); and the 1st Volunteer Cavalry Regiment, the "Rough Riders," led by Wood and Roosevelt. The opening encounter was an exchange of potshots between the adversaries' scouts.

None of this, of course, was part of the methodical shoreline advance Major General Shafter had articulated so impressively two days prior at General García's mountain camp. Shafter wanted his entire army to land, consolidate at Siboney, establish supply bases and transportation, and afterward move forward in a well-controlled mass toward the enemy. That grand strategy echoed Gen. George B. McClellan's ponderous plan for the Army of the Potomac thirty-six years earlier in northern Virginia.

The commanding generals in both those scenarios, however, had not taken into account the aggressive personalities of some of those involved. For George McClellan in 1862, that person was his brilliant enemy, Confederate general Robert E. Lee. For William Rufus Shafter in 1898, it was former Confederate major general Joseph "Fightin' Joe" Wheeler, the commander of the cavalry division and second in command of the entire V Corps. There was nothing Shafter could do about his number two, appointed by the president for the political purpose of bringing Southerners into the war effort.

This crucial factor made Wheeler untouchable and, for Shafter, barely controllable.

Even at sixty-one, the trim and bandy-legged Wheeler had the irrepressible soul of a true warrior. He acted and thought like a soldier. This was to be expected, for he'd been one since he was a seventeen-year-old reporting in at West Point in 1854. Two years after he graduated and was commissioned, the Civil War arrived. Wheeler took the side of his native South, and his service in the Confederate army was legendary. Wounded three times, with sixteen horses shot from under him, young Joe was regarded as personally fearless and tactically brilliant. Many thought him one of the top two Confederate cavalrymen.

Wheeler was the opposite of Shafter in more than appearance and regional accent. There wasn't a cautious or calculated bone in his body. He was a cauldron of fire trapped inside a diminutive form. His flinty eyes, balding head of wispy white hair, and shaggy gray beard gave him a wildly dangerous appearance. A shrewd judge of men and situations, Wheeler's coiled inner spring demanded similar energy from everyone around him. Theodore Roosevelt saw a kindred soul in Wheeler and loved him.

I wasn't with any of these various worthies, for I was busy with my job as American liaison with the Cuban Liberation Army, which so far had been doing all the heavy but unsung work. Because of my assignment I was several miles out ahead of the American forces, and thus as unaware as Shafter of the Americans' race to shoot Spaniards. Law, Rork, Fortuna, and I had tramped through the humid jungle along with some Cuban soldiers heading for Colonel Carlos González Clavel's battalion, veterans of three years of hard fighting, which was keeping an eye on the closest enemy formations astride the road from Siboney to Santiago.

I respected Clavel, a no-nonsense commander in Brigadier General Castillo's division, whom I'd last seen the morning of the American landing at Daiquirí. It had been Clavel's men who had cleared Daiquirí and later Siboney. They also had formed the vanguard in front of the allied forces' advance westbound from Daiquiri to Siboney and beyond.

"The Spanish are withdrawing their troops from the coastal area, Captain Wake," the colonel advised me when I reached him at 2 a.m. on the twenty-fourth. "Come, sit over here while I describe the situation for you."

We sat under a mango tree long since picked clean of its fruit. By the dim light of an oil lamp he unfolded a sketch map, then began briefing me. "The Spanish commander is General Antero Rubín, and he is no novice at combat. Rubín has a rear guard of almost nine hundred Puerto Rican loyalist soldiers along with some Spanish conscripts. They are all in good entrenchments along the high ground near Las Guasimas. We are now on the eastern side of the Spanish position"—he pointed to the map—"here. As you can see, we have spread out to the east from the road, which is on our left. American reconnaissance has just been seen coming up the road. They can join the left end of my battalion."

I presumed the reconnaissance to be inland flank pickets of the coastal advance. "Can you get around that eastern flank and attack the Spanish rear, Colonel?" I asked.

He shook his head. "No, Captain. It would mean climbing a cliff in open sight, which would give away our intentions. The alternative is to march through the jungle to go around the mountain, but that would take too long. To make a frontal uphill attack on such entrenchments would be complete folly. That is exactly what the Spanish always want us to do, but I learned that lesson long ago. They outgun us, so we must outsmart them."

"That leaves the Spanish blocking the road."

"The Spanish will be removed, but not by force," came the colonel's surprising reply. "I think they will be withdrawing from the entrenchments soon. My scouts tell me the main body of the enemy is already gone, including two of their four Krupp field guns. Two more are still here, on that hill." He pointed to a hill west of the Spanish position. "The Puerto Rican rear guard is packing up their equipment as we speak."

"Why would they retreat?"

The usually serious man allowed a half-smile as he explained. "Simple. None of the Puerto Rican volunteers or the Spanish conscripts wants to be left behind in the jungle to face the Cuban Mambi and the Americans alone. They are also afraid of your naval guns."

I didn't tell him that this far inland—more than three miles—we were at the farthest edge of our guns' effective range, or that no signal relay system to the coast and the Navy's ships had been set up. The planned coastal route of advance would have allowed observers on the ships to see the battle conditions as they occurred, and therefore no relay system was needed. But direct observation would be impossible here.

Instead of telling him what the Americans *couldn't* do, I asked, "When do you think the rear guard will leave?"

"Probably later today. They will march west along the main road and reform in even stronger positions closer to their main defenses along a plateau called San Juan, on the eastern approach to Santiago city."

"So we just let them go?"

"Yes. I think it is far wiser to let them vacate their positions at Las Guasimas. But do not worry; once they are in open column on the road they will be vulnerable. Then we will attack. With the new reinforcements of Cuban soldiers who accompanied you here, I now have eight hundred men. They will be enough to conduct a successful ambuscade on the Spanish when they are exposed on the road."

"That makes a lot of sense," I replied with admiration for the Cuban officer's smart tactics. "You'll have a great victory over the Spanish and protect the right flank of the allied army's advance along the coast."

Since I knew Shafter wanted to consolidate his corps in the Siboney area before moving on Santiago, I was certain Colonel Clavel had time to wait for the Spanish to withdraw from the positions and then attack them. But of course I didn't know that the plan would fall apart because Fightin' Joe Wheeler and his "foot cavalry" had arrived on the scene.

19

The Jungle

Las Guasimas, Cuba
Friday, 24 June 1898

AN HOUR BEFORE DAWN, I resolved to personally report this new information about the Spanish positions back to American headquarters. Initially I was going to send Lieutenant Law with the message, but then I decided to return to the beachhead myself. I wanted to gauge the status of our troop and supply consolidation at Siboney. After ascertaining this information I would return inland the following morning, better able to advise the Cuban commanders on how to help the overall campaign.

The first light of day was beginning to filter through the trees as my men and I headed around to the west side of the Cuban positions. We followed an ancient, barefoot Mambi guide named Noveno along an animal path that trended to the southwest. He and Fortuna had worked together before and seemed to have an unspoken bond, much as Rork and I had.

Clad in odorous tatters that barely covered his bony frame, Noveno had dark brown skin that was wrinkled in deep furrows; his head lacked so much as a strand of hair. Born a slave seventy or more years earlier, Noveno knew the area intimately. He moved slowly but smoothly along the jungle path without making a sound. As his watery, yellowed eyes squinted through the jungle's miasmic gloom, his head constantly swiveled to see, hear, and smell things far beyond our meager abilities to detect.

To evade Spanish patrols, we furtively crossed the badly rutted main road. Grandiosely called the Camino Real—the Royal Road—its deplorable condition was symbolic of the demise of Spanish public works in Cuba. Our path led down into a thickly tangled valley toward the side of a low ridge.

As we moved along the narrow track, Noveno's impassive face showed a slight smile as he pointed out a Mambi trap just ahead. Fortuna explained it to us as we slowly edged our way around it. The trap was an *anon* tree right on the path. It had a dozen ripe green fruits hanging within easy reach, unusual in an area where most of the fruit trees had been stripped by soldiers desperate for food. Intertwined with this irresistible lure was a *guao* vine, Cuba's version of poison ivy, and a *pica-pica* vine, whose tiny hairs also produced a rapid and terrible itching rash.

The immediate flailing and commotion that would result if anyone reached for the *anon* fruit and touched the vicious vines would then unleash the pièce de résistance—an artfully concealed hive of *avispas tarantulas*. Several of the two-inch-long black-and-red wasps, which prey on tarantulas and have stings among the most painful known to man, were crawling over the hive. The sight was unnerving. I had to force myself to ignore the instinct to flee. After this lesson in Mambi warfare I kept an especially watchful eye on where I trod.

At last we began to ascend the ridge. The vegetation thinned out a little, and I saw an intersection with a wider trail a few yards ahead. My mental map told me turning left onto it would take us three miles southeast to the American lines at Siboney. Turning right would take us to the enemy lines no more than a quarter mile up the trail.

Just as we were about to turn left, a raucous squawking sounded in the trees above us. *Rota-tata-tata-too!* Noveno stopped in mid-stride, his left foot in the air and right hand pointing up. The rest of us instantly halted where we were. The squawking stopped. Noveno mouthed the word "*arriero.*"

Fortuna gestured toward a long-tailed brown bird in a tree to our right, softly explaining to me, "The Mambis' lookout bird. He alerts them when someone is moving quickly in their area."

Suddenly, the usually incessant jungle sounds—birds squawking, frogs croaking, insects whining, land crabs skittering, and other creatures moving in the undergrowth—ominously ceased.

I heard sounds of movement ahead. Noveno's head slowly pivoted around, his eyes focusing forward. Lowering his body to the ground, he cocked his head to hear better, then sniffed the air. All of us knelt down on the animal path watching Noveno, who had his head turned to the right.

The sound came again, closer now. It was on our right side this time, identifiable as the clank of metal and a gurgle of liquid. Even I could identify the source—a soldier's rifle stock hitting a half-full canteen as he walked along. It was followed by an angry admonition in oddly accented Spanish. The sergeant was angry.

"*Puertorriqueño*," Fortuna whispered in my right ear. "*El enemigo*."

Noveno raised four fingers on his left hand, then moved it from left to right. A stone's throw away, an enemy patrol of four Puerto Rican soldiers—part of General Rubín's force—came into sight, visible from the waist up. I deduced they were returning to Las Guasimas after a patrol toward the American lines at Siboney.

Suddenly, farther to the left, I was surprised to hear the drawl of a West Texas cowboy only fifty feet away. "Jimmy, see that one there? Ah'm puttin' a round up that bastard's ass afore he gits away." The Texan's Krag-Jorgensen rifle cracked twice.

My companions looked at me questioningly. There weren't supposed to be any American troops in the immediate area yet. *Is it the reconnaissance patrol? They're supposed to be back on the main road behind us, to the east.* I heard more American voices from the left.

A concerted volley of Spanish Mauser rounds exploded to our right. In the dense jungle it was impossible to pinpoint shooters, especially with the smokeless powder the Spanish army used. Several Krags replied from the left with their own barrage of bullets.

Just then, Hotchkiss light field artillery opened fire from behind and to our left, back near the main road. None of this was making sense. *Why are our guns this far out in front of our lines? You don't bring artillery along on a reconnaissance.* The rounds exploded somewhere to the north in muffled thuds, the concussion absorbed by the jungle. They were quickly answered by Spanish Krupp 75-millimeter field artillery from the northwest, behind the Spanish-held hill.

One of the Krupp rounds burst in the air close behind us, and I could hear shrapnel cutting through the trees as a cloud of green leaves showered down on us. One piece slashed a tree trunk near me.

A furious artillery duel erupted, the steady booms and thuds accompanied by Spanish rifle volleys. The artillery was joined by a free-for-all of independent rifle fire from both directions—a hail of Krag, Mauser, Hotchkiss, and Krupp projectiles. Shrapnel zinged through the air like angry bees. Everyone, except us, was firing.

Noveno turned around and looked at Fortuna questioningly. Fortuna shrugged and in turn looked at me. "Is General Shafter attacking *here*, sir? I thought he was advancing along the coast."

"I don't know *who* this is, Major. But we need to get out of here."

"Back to the northeast and the Cuban battalion, sir, or back to the south and Siboney?"

Another volley came from the Puerto Ricans on our right, and a round thudded into the tree between Rork and me. The big Irishman swore in Gaelic. The nearest Americans were somewhere on the main trail ahead of us, so I decided that direction was the best option.

"We'll go up to that main trail ahead, turn left, and get the hell back to the American lines!" I shouted above the rising din. "I'll lead so the Americans see my uniform. Follow me and *stay low!*"

They didn't need any further encouragement. We ran as fast as it's possible to run down a twisting goat path in a tropical jungle full of thorny bushes and Mambi ambushes. Turning left at the main trail, we ran even faster, all while crouching below the rain of white-hot Spanish shrapnel bursting above us. We'd gotten a few yards down the narrow trail—only the width of two men—when we saw the first dark-shirted troopers coming our way.

"Don't shoot! We're Americans! Americans!" I shouted, echoed by Rork and Law. We slowed to a walk—hard to do as Spanish bullets continued to zing toward us from behind—so the troopers could see us clearly. I called out to them, "We've got Cuban troops with us. The Spanish are farther behind. What regiment are you?"

"First U.S. Volunteer Cavalry!" someone shouted back. The troopers knelt down on one knee, leveling their rifles toward us. We kept walking toward them.

I saw a big sergeant among the troopers and recognized him as Hamilton Fish. In contrast with the majority of the regiment, Fish was a wealthy New Yorker, grandson of President Grant's secretary of state, and one of Theodore's college athlete friends. Fish had been allowed into the regiment because of his physique and intelligence. Standing beside him was Capt. Allyn Capron, a highly respected regular officer of ten years' service. I'd met both men at Theodore's camp near Daiquiri.

"Captain Wake? Is that you, sir?" called Capron.

"Yes, Allyn, it is," I replied as calmly as my pounding heart would allow. I passed the line of troopers and shook Capron's hand. After our sprint I was a little short of breath, but managed to ask, "What's your regiment doing this far inland?"

"Looking for the Spanish, sir. The whole brigade's on the move. The other one is behind us somewhere."

Well, so much for the grand plan. "Where's Colonel Wood?"

"Right here, Peter," Wood answered as he rounded the bend of the trail with about twenty more troopers. His men fanned out on both sides of the trail, eyes anxiously searching for targets. Behind them was a long column of more men in dark blue, rifles at the ready.

Wood wasted no time on pleasantries, for those days were past. "What do you know of the enemy?"

"They're fifty yards up this trail. You're facing a picket line of about two platoons of Puerto Rican infantry spread across the trail and into the jungle to the east. About a quarter mile farther behind them are the main Spanish defenses—nine hundred men of several regiments entrenched in a semicircle around a steep hill. They are also dug in on another steep hill to the north. The main road heads northwest between the two hills. I think we're near the left flank of their defenses on the nearest hill, but I'm not sure."

"The artillery?"

"There are at least two Krupp 75s just behind that main line. They're firing at our Hotchkiss guns over on the main road, where I take it we have other regiments."

"Yes, there are two regular cavalry regiments over there on the main road. We're covering the left side of the brigade. Where are the Cuban troops?"

A volley of rifle fire from the Puerto Rican troops behind us flew over our heads. Ducking down, I answered Wood. "There's around eight hundred Cubans under Colonel González Clavel far over on the right, about a mile and a half to two miles to the northeast. They're near the *right* end of the Spanish defense line, which is a steep cliff on the far hill. The Spanish were beginning to withdraw their main force from the trench line, but there's still a strong rear guard in position. The Cubans aren't strong enough for a frontal assault on the Spanish defenses, so Colonel Clavel told me he planned to wait until the Spanish vacated the entrenchments and then attack them when they were exposed on the road to Santiago."

Wood addressed Capron. "Allyn, now that you've heard Captain Wake's intelligence, continue your movement up this trail. I need detailed information about the enemy's disposition and the terrain, both ahead and along the hill to the left. Our regiment will advance up this trail, with elements flanking either side."

Capron, Fish, and the others hurried up the trail. More men arrived from the south and took up temporary defensive positions, ready to move on command. I looked down the trail to the south. It was jammed with American soldiers heading our way.

After Wood finished giving orders to a staff officer, I said, "Leonard, nobody up here was expecting the Americans for another couple of days, and then only to secure this area as a flank while the main force moved west along the coast. Obviously, the situation has changed. What's going on? General Shafter's moving faster than I thought, plus this advance is much farther inland than we thought it would be. Navy guns can't reach this far. Is his headquarters around here someplace?"

"No, he's still back on the ship. The follow-on regiments and supplies are unloading back at Siboney. Some are heading this way, not on the coast rail line. General Wheeler's the senior general ashore. He decided to keep the enemy off balance and moved the cavalry division forward toward Las Guasimas. The infantry divisions are still in Siboney. This is not supposed to be the main corps advance; it's a reconnaissance in force to probe the Spanish defenses."

I could tell Wood was giving me the official version. He was a regular Army officer, so I knew he wouldn't tell me his personal opinion, but I could well guess it.

"Leonard, I've got to tell the Cuban commanders what's happening."

"We in General Young's 2nd Cavalry Brigade are the front of the cavalry division. My volunteer regiment forms the left side of the brigade's advance. General Young and General Wheeler are with the regular 1st Cavalry and the regular 10th Cavalry on the main road with a battery of Hotchkiss 3-pounder field guns. They are the main effort of the operation. The division's 1st Brigade under General Sumner is about two miles behind, coming up from Siboney right now. The infantry divisions are still back at Siboney."

The sound of rifle fire punctuated by cannon booms was incessant now, mostly over on the right but increasing again in our area. Few around me were paying much attention to it; some even laughed with nervous contempt. Suddenly a tree branch beside me was shredded by Mauser rounds. Everyone ducked.

"That's the third time," muttered Rork. "Little buggers aren't that bad at it."

Wood continued his assessment. "Look, my regiment can't wait for the Spanish to leave their trenches. It's too late for that. The brigade has already started its attack along the main road, so we've got to forge ahead up the trail and pressure this flank of the enemy. Major Brodie and I are taking the left side of our regiment's advance along this ridge, and Lieutenant Colonel Roosevelt will handle the right side in the valley."

"I would be delighted if Captain Wake and his men could go with me, sir," interjected a disheveled Roosevelt, who had appeared out of the mass of soldiers on the trail. He wiped his fogged spectacles with a monogrammed handkerchief and briskly grasped my hand, quickly nodding to Rork.

"Fine with me," said Wood as he left us and headed up the trail at the head of his own contingent. "Just get your troops moving, Theodore," he called back. "And make solid contact with the left side of the regular regiments over there in the jungle valley."

None of what I had just heard sounded good to me. Shafter wasn't ashore yet, the original plan wasn't being followed in the least, and with Wheeler out on the front line, no one with any real authority was making command decisions back in Siboney as to where and how the Army forces would advance. I decided there was no reason to return to Siboney. Staying with Wood's regiment seemed safer than wandering around the jungle by ourselves trying to find the Cuban battalion and perhaps getting shot by mistake.

The left side of the trail was more open scrub, inclining up a ridge that ran parallel with the trail. The right side descended into the jungle we'd just emerged from and was crawling with enemy patrols. I glanced at Rork, for I value his intuition at times like this. He shook his head in disgust and started off behind Roosevelt, who was already heading up the trail and peering off to the right. I guessed he was looking for an opening in the green maze through which to take his troops into the valley.

"I suggest we follow the goat path. It's just ahead to the right. It's a hell'uva lot faster than cutting a new route," I said to Roosevelt. "The vines and bushes are too thick."

"A goat path, eh? Excellent idea—as I would expect from a man of your experience! No sense in useless expenditure of effort," he replied with a grin. "Save that for dealing with the enemy. Say, would it be too much to ask if you would kindly lead the way to your providential goat path, sir?"

"Very well, follow me," I said, without much enthusiasm.

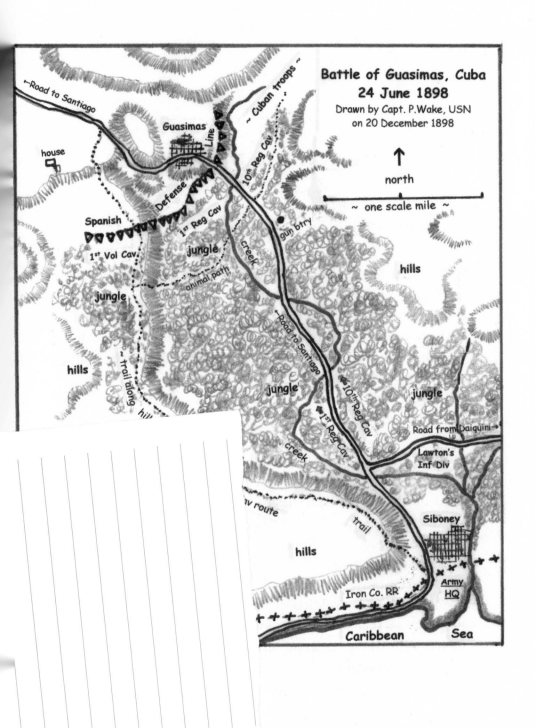

Battle of Guasimas, Cuba
24 June 1898
Drawn by Capt. P. Wake, USN
on 20 December 1898

north

~ one scale mile ~

Road to Santiago

house

Guasimas

~ Cuban troops ~

10th Reg Cav

Defense Line

Spanish

1st Reg Cav

1st Vol Cav.

gun btry

jungle

animal path

creek

jungle

hills

hills

~ trail along hills

Road to Santiago

jungle

jungle

1st Reg Cav

10th Reg Cav

Road from Daiquiri →

Lawton's
Inf Div

creek

cav route

trail

Siboney

hills

Army
HQ

Iron Co. RR

Caribbean   Sea

20

Facing the Elephant

Las Guasimas, Cuba

Friday, 24 June 1898

FOR ALMOST AN HOUR we descended back into that hellish jungle valley. Our pace was much more careful as we constantly looked for enemy ambushes on the ground and up in the trees. Noveno led us around the Mambi traps, several times deciding it was better to leave the goat path and cross some slough or swamp before returning to it.

The incurable naturalist in Roosevelt was fascinated by the flora, though there wasn't much in the way of fauna. He kept an ear out for birdcalls—he is very good at identifying birds by their sounds—and softly told me he hoped to register some rare exotic find in the midst of the war. It would be quite a scientific coup, he said. Tired of his endless enthusiasm, I suggested his pursuit of fame was doomed because any birds that had survived the cannonading had gotten the hell out of here. I further suggested that made them much smarter than us.

In fact, the only ornithological sounds to be heard now were the fake trills of enemy soldiers signaling each other, probably about our progress. Theodore wasn't fooled in the least, promptly judging these to be "mere *Iberian* imposters" and whispering that their efforts were "truly abysmal parodies of the well-documented West Indian Goatsucker, otherwise known as the Greater Antillean, or Cuban,

Nightjar, whose actual scientific name is *Antrostomus cubanensis*. Of course, Peter, that particular bird is a form of nighthawk, and doesn't actually suck on goats, as everyone knows."

I was damn near suffocating from the heat and felt like choking him into silence. "Of course, Theodore. And I'd so been looking forward to seeing a goatsucker."

My sarcasm was lost on Roosevelt, who, momentarily happy in his ornithological diversion, answered, "Oh, quite right, old man. You know, being at war is no excuse for ignoring these unique opportunities for academic progress. Now, where the devil *is* the enemy?"

In a startling coincidence, a new blast of furious shooting erupted to the east, where the white 1st and Negro 10th Regular Cavalry Regiments were fighting their way up the main road. Several far more accurate rounds arrived from enemy sharpshooters closer to us, once again making everyone duck.

Occasionally one of these snipers was successful and a trooper stopped to stare in disbelief at a spreading bloodstain on his uniform. Many were junior officers. Almost all the wounded were left alone where they fell on the path with the empty-sounding promise that someone would come for them afterward. Tellingly, I never heard any of them complain.

Eventually, after sweating gallons, fruitlessly swatting at the bugs that crawled on our bodies *everywhere*, and drinking most of our canteen water—an understandable but serious mistake—we neared the main road. Several times we spotted figures moving in the shadowy distance but were unsure if they were Spanish enemies or Cuban allies, since both wore similar straw hats. Erring on the side of caution, we did not shoot them.

I noticed Theodore was readily asking the men around him for their suggestions, then intently listening to them. He quietly conveyed to me his greatest frustration, which was not being able to *identify* the enemy's location and therefore directly engage him. Nothing was as simple as he had envisaged back at Tampa.

I found his dilemma paradoxical, for guerilla warfare in a tropical forest is a thinking man's game of deception, maneuver, and attrition, as the Mambi tarantula wasp trap demonstrated. Roosevelt, one of the most brilliant men I've ever known, instantly hated this type of combat. He seethed against our situation, uncharacteristically uttering coarse oaths after seeing his men drop from sharpshooters. When a Mauser bullet bored through the tree he was leaning against, inches from his face, he let loose a string of epithets equal to Rork's best. I wasn't even aware Theodore *knew* those words.

In an ironic twist of fate, the first to spot the enemy was not Noveno or one of Roosevelt's western hunters but a famous New York City war correspondent who had tagged along with us in the hope of seeing some action. Richard Harding Davis was an impossibly handsome, composed, and urbane gentleman of the world. Somehow he managed to maintain his savoir faire even in the midst of all the lead flying about him.

Our column had stopped for a brief rest. Reposing comfortably on a fallen log, complete with a notebook on his knee, Davis indicated someone across an open area of scrub bushes. As if watching a competitor in a yachting regatta, he casually mentioned, "Why, there they are, Colonel Roosevelt. Look over there, near that large tree, which I believe is a mahogany. I can clearly see Spanish army hats with red cockade emblems on them moving about in the bushes. The Cubans don't wear those emblems, so I presume there must be Spanish soldiers beneath them. Regulars, I'd wager."

A grimy sergeant crouching nearby wasn't as blasé. "Well, I'll be damned if he ain't right, Colonel. Them's the sonsabitches, sure enough. Now we can start killin' 'em back!"

For the first time that morning, I saw the legendary Roosevelt grin, a welcome sight. He thrust a fist toward the enemy, announcing, "Well now, my lads, it seems opportunity is knocking. Let us use it to show those Spanish scalawags just what an *American* fighting man can do with a rifle!"

And his lads did just that. A couple of the regiment's best shots, Rocky Mountain men, were brought up to our position. After calmly adjusting their rifle sights and measuring their breathing, they let fly with instant results. The hats disappeared. More targets were spotted high up in the foliage. A minute later, two bodies fell out of trees, accompanied by their weapons. The jungle resounded to the cheers of the troopers.

My companions approved, each in his own way. Rork nodded sagely and pronounced his professional judgment: "Damned good shots. This ain't their first time."

Major Fortuna's analysis was, "Difficult trajectory, range, and timing. Excellent results."

Noveno barely moved his head in the affirmative and smiled.

It wasn't over. More hats came into view farther east and were instantly tracked by two dozen rifles. The troopers tensed and leaned into their weapons, but someone quickly called out that these hats were tan felt, not straw. That meant they were American soldiers, regulars of the 1st Cavalry, along with a few black troopers of the 10th who had wandered too far to the west, or left, in their advance northward toward the enemy defense lines. With more jauntiness to our steps we moved toward those felt hats.

Five minutes later we accomplished the goal of our assignment. Our right flank was joined—the army term is "married"—with the left flank of the regular regiments in the rest of the brigade. Following a quick reunion of the brigade's troopers, complete with humorous insults about which side of the brigade was most successful and why, the entire line moved northward, away from the path and into the thick tangle, toward the foe.

It was slow going; damned near impossible to make any headway. Roosevelt quickly decided after a few moments of that exercise in frustration to move toward the enemy via a new direction. Keeping a small detachment closely connected with the other regiments, he went back halfway along the path to a thinned-out place and led his men off the path in an angled course to the northwest, pocket compass in one hand and revolver in the other.

The plan was to obliquely merge with Wood's main body of the regiment, which, judging by their gunfire, was getting closer to the Spanish defenses. This new slog proved more grueling than the previous one but had less distance to go, with the welcome incentive of reuniting with Wood's main body on higher ground with less foliage. Anywhere other than that jungle valley was fine by me. Once reconstituted, the regiment would then go about its primary business of dislodging the enemy from the western side of the Spanish defense line at Las Guasimas, which had heretofore remained largely untouched. Once that was done, the road to Santiago would be open.

Emerging from the claustrophobic forest into the scrubland, we found the hillside trail and the main body of the 1st Volunteer Cavalry Regiment. The enemy's earthworks were only a hundred yards away to the north and higher up on the side of the hill. They were less seen than heard and felt as a deluge of bullets assailed us from that direction.

We also came upon the body of Sergeant Fish beside the trail. Theodore was visibly affected by the sight of his dead friend. Then, conscious of those around him, he adjusted his spectacles, set his jaw, and ordered, "Forward, men. This is just the start. Our time for revenge will come soon."

Moments later we came upon the body of Allyn Capron, his handsome face contorted in death. None of us lingered as Chaplain Brown ran forward and knelt to say a prayer over him, for a hail of gunfire swept over us from the enemy line. We bent down into a lower crouch, dashing forward and to the left, off the trail. The enemy gunfire diminished, and we regained the trail, trotting forward, passing many troopers crouching in the bushes.

Out in front of the column we found Wood. He was coolness personified, telling his cursing soldiers, "Don't swear, men—shoot!" and carefully instructing them, "Sight your target's head or chest, then fire. Do *not* waste rounds."

It was an admirable performance of leadership. It was obvious to me that Wood, who'd been awarded the Medal of Honor for his heroism in an Indian battle years earlier, knew what he was doing. His confidence was visibly inspiring his men, who calmed themselves and followed his orders.

A few moments later, over on the even higher ground to the left, Major Brodie, third in command of the regiment, took a bullet in his wrist, an excruciating wound. We had wandered over there with Wood, who was checking that side's progress. Even Rork winced when he saw the major's wound. Though Brodie insisted on remaining on the front line, Colonel Wood saw the major's intense agony and knew he couldn't last long in command of the regiment's left wing.

Roosevelt was ordered to take over the left squadron of troops and move them along the ridge to higher ground on the Spanish west flank. I told my entourage we were staying with him. The country was more open, akin to what Americans were used to seeing, but that made it far more dangerous, too, because there was less concealment.

From this point onward we were in a full-blown battle, and the ensuing chaos clouds my memory. When facing mortal combat, you quickly descend into a myopia in which you take in only what is happening in the thirty feet immediately around you. A few paces ahead of me, scarcely within my periphery, Roosevelt was leading almost half the regiment, fully four hundred men, toward the Spanish positions.

I could tell he knew this was his moment. Caught up in the intensity, my friend drew his fancy store-bought saber. Waving it over his head, he exhorted his troopers to keep moving forward through the scrub toward the enemy. Opposing us were several hundred Spanish infantrymen, veterans of years in Cuba, securely ensconced within rifle pits, stone walls, and trenches spread across higher ground on our front. They had the perfect defensive position, the very one Colonel Clavel had warned me against assaulting.

This is insane, I told myself as I moved forward with everyone else. I knew it was stupid, for I'd endured similar scenarios fighting Confederates in Florida, Chileans in Peru, and French artillery in Vietnam. But nevertheless I ran toward the killing zone. Why my reason deserted me and I joined the insanity I cannot explain. Nonetheless, there I was, running with Rork and Law beside me to the right and our two Cuban partners on my left. All around us, the western cowboys and eastern athletes followed a crazy, bespectacled romantic into his first battle.

Men went down in ones and twos from a relentless fusillade of Mauser rounds. Incredibly, the attack never slowed. We were hungry and thirsty, our clothing was sopping wet from sweat and abject fear, our skin was ripped open by thorns, but everyone kept their eyes forward, spurred on by a ridiculously high but calm Yankee voice cultivated at Harvard that allowed no other option than getting done what we'd come there to do.

The relentless Spanish gunfire—*how do they have all that ammunition?*—was nothing compared to our lunatic quest of reaching those trenches and ending this misery. I looked over and saw Rork grinning—his jaded soul had been infected too. Youthful Lieutenant Law and middle-aged Major Fortuna both had eyes ablaze with the primordial instinct that had taken over our minds and bodies. Even Noveno fixed his gaze on the Spanish trenches, his machete ready for its grisly work.

We heard cheering to our right—Wood's men on the trail—and Roosevelt responded with his own cheer, waving again his parade-ground saber. He pointed it at a red-tile-roofed farmhouse that had come into view 150 yards to the northwest, the only structure I'd seen since leaving Siboney. With a visible target in sight, the regiment poured rounds into it as we ran. Rork and I blasted buckshot out of our shotguns as the troopers fired their Krags. Law shot his Lee Navy rifle, and Fortuna paused every so often to very deliberately fire his captured Spanish Mauser.

Another storm of 7-millimeter Mauser rounds came at us from an unseen trench line in the grass to the right. We were enfiladed, three more troopers going down. Another half-dozen slumped or clutched their limbs. Someone yelled that Leonard Wood was dead; someone else said the right side was withdrawing. Both were ignored. The men continued rushing, stumbling, trudging forward up that slope.

Then I realized we'd outflanked the Spanish positions. A trench lay empty to our right. I saw several of the light blue uniforms of the enemy moving away to the left, toward Santiago. More followed. The Spanish were retreating from their trenches in small groups as others laid down a field of fire.

I didn't understand it. *Why are the Spanish leaving? They still have other trenches. We don't even have the full regiment on the scene yet. Is it a trick to draw us into an ambush?* Just as Theodore and I reached the bullet-pocked farmhouse the answers to my questions became clear.

Suddenly, inexplicably, everything changed. Our troopers no longer dropped from bullets or heat exhaustion. The continual zinging of the Mausers just stopped. The only enemy soldiers in sight were running down the road. The trenches were unoccupied. So was the farmhouse. Even the thudding of artillery over on the far right had ended. Everything was abruptly silent, as if an electric switch had been turned off.

Colonel Clavel had been right. The whole thing had only been a Spanish rearguard action exacting a heavy toll of American blood, ammunition, and endurance. Now it was over.

My watch showed 9:38 a.m. We'd been in battle for an hour and a half since the artillery rounds began at 8. The farmhouse fight had only taken a few minutes but felt like hours. And now in the aftermath came the assessment, always the same no matter the country's banner.

Officers arrived to report unit positions and casualties to Roosevelt. Sergeants checked on their men's ammunition, food, and water. The troopers, exhausted but still wary of a counterattack, rested on bended knee. Skirmishers were posted out front, on the flanks, and to the rear. Contiguous defense lines were established. Colonel Wood—still alive after all—came up. He congratulated Roosevelt, received his report, then went off to make his own regimental report to the brigade commander.

I dispatched Fortuna and Noveno to report the situation to Colonel Clavel, who, from what I could tell, was only half a mile away on the American far right flank. I sent Rork and Law to find food and water for us. I was left standing next to Theodore. My right knee was wobbly, an old wound revisiting me from the strain and stress. I noticed Theodore's saber hand trembling slightly.

"It seems we've run them off, Peter," he said vaguely, looking over at the trench, now filling with his own men.

It was time for the truth. "No, we didn't, Theodore. They withdrew their forces in good order, which was their plan from the start. This was only a rearguard action to slow us down and kill as many as they could, which they did. We were damn lucky we didn't lose more."

He turned his gaze away from a pile of spent Mauser shells on the trench's parapet, focusing on me with a brooding look. His voice was hoarse and distant. "Yes, I think you may be right. In any event, I finally faced the elephant, Peter, and didn't flinch. I was desperately fearful I would flinch in front of my men."

Images of my first battle, so long ago, came to mind. A skirmish, really, on the misnamed Peace River of Florida back in 1863. My decisions led to sailors dying—my sailors. I nearly died. My hand touched the scar on my right temple. Another quarter of an inch more . . .

It was also a time for empathy. I'd once been where he was now. "No, Theodore, you didn't flinch, not one bit. You led your men under enemy fire and accomplished the mission. And now that you know what it's like to be shot at, you don't have to worry about that flinching stuff anymore, so forget about it."

"Thank you. I am very glad to have it behind me," he reflected.

"Good. But get ready, because today was just a little practice session compared to what's ahead. I've seen those defenses around Santiago. It'll be a long, bloody fight to take them. You'll need to be resolute in preparing your men, smart about planning your part in the assault, and then absolutely ruthless in executing it."

Theodore's voice regained its determination. "Yes, I know."

As I surveyed the carnage around us, there was no doubt in my mind that he did know. Theodore Roosevelt was a naturally quick study. I knew he had better be.

Mistakes in war are measured in the blood of those who trust you.

21

The Butcher's Bill

Near Sevilla, Cuba
Friday Night, 24 June 1898

THERE WAS NO CLOSE pursuit of the retreating Spanish force, a tactic that has been the standard procedure of armies for centuries in order to prevent a concerted counterattack. But by the time the dismounted American cavalry brigade took possession of the Spanish positions at Las Guasimas it possessed neither the manpower nor the energy to pursue the enemy.

So the Spanish left the area unmolested and headed west toward their main lines at Santiago. The 1st Volunteer Cavalry Regiment moved in skirmish formation along the road for less than a mile beyond Las Guasimas, then stopped. We camped that afternoon in a field near the tiny settlement of Sevilla.

Shelter halves offered us some protection against the penetrating afternoon sun and the evening rains. What little dry firewood could be found was gathered for the cook fires started after the rain ended. Roosevelt's troopers paused in their chores to watch the black troopers of the 9th Cavalry, veterans of twenty years of Indian fighting, as they tramped through our area to man the front line. When greeted amiably by the 1st Volunteer Cavalry, the inscrutable Buffalo Soldiers replied with dour nods and grunts—for them, this was just another march in yet another miserable place, in some other war.

In the shadowy dusk of the late afternoon, General Adna Chaffee and a regiment of his regular infantry brigade also came up the road, having hastened all the way from their landing site on the beach at Siboney. As the infantrymen marched through, they were greeted with a few good-natured taunts from some of the volunteers about being late to the war. None of them laughed or retorted with insults, and the heckling stopped.

As the sky turned from peach to magenta a few minutes after sundown, a begrimed and clearly fatigued Theodore Roosevelt drifted over to where Rork and I were cooking dinner over a tiny clump of dry kindling. I'd never seen Theodore this drained of verve. The man was almost asleep on his feet. I invited him to sit down and share our meal, and he gratefully accepted.

Having eaten already, and being a bit uncomfortable around higher-ranking officers, Lieutenant Law excused himself and went off into the gathering darkness to seek his own peers, the junior Army officers. Rork had no such qualms and gestured for Roosevelt to sit on Law's blanket.

Our dinner was not the official rations. That cursed potted meat in tin cans had a rancid smell that would gag a dog. The issued rations hadn't been replenished after we'd run out that morning anyway, for no supplies had made it up to us. Nobody missed them. Instead, dinner was the spoils of war—black beans found in bags on a dead mule beside the abandoned farmhouse, complete with a pot in which to cook them. This discovery was courtesy of Rork, who possesses a petty officer's ingrained talent for scavenging ammunition, food, rum, and other essential items—though not necessarily in that order.

The pot of beans was duly boiled, with the welcome addition of some pepper and the regimental cook's gift to Rork of a tiny morsel of fatback to add to the taste. This entrée was accompanied by cups of strong Cuban coffee spiked with aguardiente and stirred with a stick of sugarcane. Earlier, Rork suggested to me—with a straight face, no less—that the liquor might prove a useful sedative, allowable since our adopted unit was relieved of frontline guard duty and thus of extreme vigilance. I concurred, also promoting its antiseptic qualities. This conversation took place before Theodore joined us. Neither of us told him what was in his coffee.

Theodore lowered himself to the ground and dug into the plate of beans Rork handed him. Never one to care for hard spirits, he nonetheless drained the cup. Incredibly, he showed no reaction. Rork and I exchanged mystified glances.

Looking at the old boatswain, Roosevelt matter-of-factly intoned, "Yes, Rork, I know what you put in the coffee. Your sly look warned me to expect something beforehand, and I smelled it before I even had a sip."

"Ooh, well, hope you didn't mind, sir," replied Rork with actual sincerity. He nodded toward me. "We just needed a wee nip for strength. Never know when it'll be the last."

"Ah, that which hath made them drunk, hath made me bold!" quoted Roosevelt with gusto, before wearily adding, "But tonight it just makes me tired. Been a long day, comrades. Just got back from the surgeon."

Using sailors' traditional dark term for the casualty list, Rork quietly asked, "An' how bad's the butcher's bill, sir?"

Theodore stared at the flames. "Eight of our fine men were killed, including dear Hamilton Fish and Allyn Capron. Thirty-four in the regiment are reported wounded. I'm told another half dozen are wounded in some minor fashion but have chosen to stay in the ranks. Total American losses in all three regiments of the brigade were sixteen killed and fifty-two wounded. We volunteers took a fearful share of that."

It *was* a frightful toll for such a small engagement. And it portended worse for the future, when our troops would face a large-scale battle. Rork frowned, then asked the expected next question. "An' what o' the enemy's losses?"

"Well, Bucky O'Neill and I walked about and counted eleven Spanish dead on the field. I've no accurate idea how many were wounded."

"What about the Cuban army regiment out on the end of the right flank under Colonel Clavel? Have you heard anything?" I asked. "You may remember we were over there with them before your regiment arrived. I sent Major Fortuna and Noveno with a message to them."

"I heard they provided scouts to our regiments along the road but did no real fighting in large formation. You know, Peter, I am beginning to have doubts as to the Cubans' abilities in a stand-up fight against the Spanish."

I didn't argue the obvious—that Clavel's original plan would have been far more successful and without the heavy losses the Americans had suffered. It wasn't the time or place.

"Our dead are buried," Roosevelt murmured. "Chaplain Brown is doing a service at sunrise. Good man, Brown. Even the troopers respect him, a rarity among cowboys."

Theodore paused, poking a glowing ember with a dry papaya leaf. The leaf flared into flame as he continued in a respectful tone. "I must say we are also quite fortunate to have Doctor Church as our regimental surgeon. He and his assistants performed tirelessly today. They're still at it. His little field hospital is filled with our brave wounded."

He glanced up at me, the mist in his eyes reflecting the firelight. "Have you heard what my wounded men did while I was visiting them at the hospital?"

I gestured that I hadn't. Taking off his spectacles to wipe them, he said, "They sang 'My Country 'Tis of Thee.' And the ones who could, stood up at attention. Not a single man among them—not a *single* one of them, Peter—was complaining, though their plight is dreadful due to the Army's appalling incompetence on all matters of supply, even desperately needed medicines. What splendid soldiers these brave American men are. How honored I am to serve with them."

There was a contemplative silence until Rork offered, "Aye, sir, an' the lads're lucky as hell in havin' you an' Colonel Wood for their regimental officers. You take care o' your men, an' they see that. They trust you."

"Thank you, Rork. Yes, I believe they do trust Colonel Wood and me—a blood bond that will last forever. *We few, we happy few, we band of brothers*, so said the Bard of England three hundred years ago."

Trying to change the maudlin atmosphere, I interjected, "So Theodore, you just came back from brigade headquarters—what're the new orders for your regiment?"

Given the losses of the day and Shafter's desire not to move his force forward until all was ready, either along the coast or up this road, I guessed there would be several days of recuperation ahead while the support functions prepared. Rork and I, old men that we were, could certainly use the rest.

Theodore had been quiet for a time after my question, evidently reflecting philosophically on the day's events. Now the old resolute Roosevelt returned. His jaw tightened, his fists clenched, and behind the spectacles those piercing eyes narrowed in barely contained anger. A stranger might think he was about to attack someone. "We are to sit and we wait until reinforcements arrive and the divisions are built up in this area," he growled. "Then, when all is finally judged ready, the corps will advance up this road to the city. I find such inertia frustrating. We should be pressing the enemy now!"

His reply was final confirmation that Shafter had changed his plan of attack. The assault on Las Guasimas was no longer a feint or probe on the right flank—it was now the axis of the general advance. The Army would fight inland, without naval gunfire support.

I didn't share Roosevelt's zeal. "Just be thankful for the opportunity to let your men rest, Theodore. They need time to recuperate from their first action. There'll be plenty of opportunity for more shooting and dying."

He didn't answer, just wagged his head and dug back into his beans. Roosevelt and his exhausted men got their chance to recuperate that evening, but such luxury was short-lived for Rork and me. Two hours after my conversation with Theodore, Shafter sent orders for me and my assistants to return to Siboney immediately. There, we were to rejoin General García, who was arriving on the transports from Asarradero with four thousand men. The Cubans would then become the extended right flank of Shafter's grand campaign across the hill country toward Santiago.

My stomach and bowels, already weakened by dysentery, rebelled as we began the walk. I had to stop and deal with it, restarting our band's journey twenty minutes later. A mile down the road it started to rain. I had to stop in the bushes again. This time so did Rork.

When we resumed the march, Rork said to no one in particular, "I hate this place."

I silently agreed.

22

The Road to Santiago

Oriente Province, Cuba

Late June 1898

THE AMERICANS' DIFFICULTIES continued to increase in the days after the battle at Las Guasimas. Major General Wheeler was laid low by illness and replaced as the cavalry division's commander by General Sumner of the 2nd Brigade. Sumner was a respected regular with a calm demeanor. Many officers saw the replacement as an improvement. Colonel Wood took over as brigade commander, also viewed as a good thing. Thus, command of the 1st Volunteer Cavalry Regiment devolved entirely upon Theodore Roosevelt.

My friend was ready. He'd used his two months as Wood's number two learning how to command hundreds of men. The fight at Las Guasimas had given him invaluable tactical experience. The men had always respected his brains; now they respected his bravery. I had no doubt the regiment was in capable hands with Roosevelt in charge.

However, I did have misgivings about one salient issue. After only a week in Cuba, the dismounted cavalrymen's physical condition was deteriorating rapidly. It wasn't only them. The entire Army corps was in similar shape.

This drastic downturn was due to the climate and, most egregiously, the Army's supply problems. Ammunition, water, and thousands more infantry had arrived—and were still arriving—at the front line; the essentials to keep them healthy had not. Tents, dry-bulk foods, equipment, heavy artillery, and medicines were somewhere within the mound of cargo boxes, barrels, and bales piling ever higher back on Siboney's beach. Some of the supplies were still moldering in the ships' beastly hot cargo holds offshore.

The road transport situation from Siboney to the front was ridiculous. Shafter's revised plan ignored the coastal rail and road route of advance and instead relied on the inland route, in complete defiance of the weather, logic, and my recommendation. Now, the only supply line to the front was a narrow, rutted road that the daily rains and thousands of boots had turned into a muddy morass. Two days after the Americans began using it the road became impassable. In addition, mules and vehicles to carry supplies from the coast were unobtainable locally in the war-ravaged area, and few had been landed from the ships.

And for the wounded and sick? Amazingly, only five ambulances had been allocated for the entire army. Only four of those were ashore. No one knew the location of the fifth. The regiments were running out of medicines, for most of the regimental medicine cabinets were still on board ships. There weren't enough doctors to handle the patients, and there were pitifully few medical orderlies and only a handful of Red Cross nurses.

Once back at Siboney, I rejoined General García. He greeted me heartily and insisted that I accompany him during the march forward to the front line, which was delayed by supply issues. When García's Cuban forces finally plodded up the road from Siboney through Sevilla to Los Mangos, they turned right and headed for their position on the right flank. As we passed the 1st Volunteer Cavalry's bivouac, I received permission from García for a brief reunion with Theodore.

Unlike most of his troopers, who by then had shed their absurd woolen uniform coats, heavy packs, and blankets, Roosevelt maintained his professional military appearance as best he could. He was determined to serve as an example of self-discipline to others, as had his mentor Leonard Wood. The men tolerated this eccentricity, for they genuinely admired his fortitude.

After more than a week in the jungle, however, Theodore's uniform was far from immaculate. Mud, sweat, and the dark brown stains of others' blood splotched the sleeves. That dangling saber, elegant but worthless, had been discarded. He still wore the military tunic, a ridiculous vanity, but the choker collar was unbuttoned. He looked thinner and more haggard, and I worried about whether he had dysentery yet. Rork and I certainly did.

In my conversation with Roosevelt that evening I noticed that the famous voice was quieter, slower. The usual impatient staccato insistence had faded. He displayed a more paternal understanding for disappointing answers. The ready smile and laugh weren't so ready anymore, either. His well-known humor sometimes sounded forced.

That transformation is normal for a new commander after his first battle—I would wonder about any man who didn't show it. But with Theodore, I felt something more was amiss. I soon heard the explanation.

He was angry. Not at the enemy but at his own superiors. He wasn't alone. The entire V Corps was angry. They'd waited in bivouac on the roadside for six days. During that time the nightmare I had long cautioned about finally arrived—the rain and fever season. The climate had taken over the war zone. I knew it would exact a far greater toll on the Americans than the Spanish would.

Without tents the men had no protection from the sun or the daily deluge. By early afternoon every day, the densely humid air reached a vitality-sucking 100 degrees, a fact confirmed to me by a journalist from Maine who had a pocket thermometer. Even the strongest men fell unconscious to the ground from sunstroke.

Every day in the late afternoon a gushing downpour arrived, turning the camp into a soupy mess. After hours of rainfall, the land steamed until midnight, the air so hot and thick you felt as if you were asphyxiating.

Between dawn and midnight, physical exertion had to be done in small increments. Men panted for breath as they cursed Cuba, the generals, and the politicians who had sent them here. Day after day they sat in the mire, slapping mosquitos, trying to keep their weapons and ammunition clean, and waiting for battle orders.

Food, weaponry, ammunition, supplies, uniforms, medicines, firewood, maps and reports, personal belongings—*everything*—was damaged or destroyed by Cuba's rain, heat, mud, insects, and humidity. Roosevelt continually reminded all to keep the regimental area and themselves orderly and sanitary, another lesson of Wood's indomitable leadership. But the climate always won.

The inevitable medical consequences began to spread. Dysentery or malaria or sunstroke had already rendered a tenth of the men unfit for service. The percentage was growing every day.

I left Theodore's camp that evening worried by everything I'd seen. At the time of the Las Guasimas fight, 4,000 Americans were ashore. Six days later, 15,000 U.S. soldiers were sitting in the mud along the road to Santiago, along with more than 4,000 of García's Cuban soldiers. All of them were dependent for supplies on that one damned road out of Siboney. The coastal rail line and vehicle road sat unused. I thought it madness.

Time had run out for Shafter. He faced a terrible dilemma, caught between the growing debilitation of his force and the time needed for his army's supplies and artillery to be brought forward so he could attack. The general had to decide between waiting for supplies before attacking Santiago or attacking the formidable defenses while he still had some effective soldiers. He made his decision on the twenty-ninth of June.

Later that evening, my little team and I were with García's forces in the woods southeast of El Caney, a Spanish hilltop fortification on the northeastern side of Santiago. We stopped for the night on the far right of the campaign front. My assistants were off on a reconnaissance, so I dined with García's staff. After a dinner of mango and plantain, I was about to leave the Cuban officers to their conversation and find a place to lie down for the night when I received a surprise.

General García arrived in camp and called me over. He addressed me in rather good English. "Belated happy birthday, Peter. I understand you turned fifty-nine years of age on this last Sunday, the twenty-sixth. Oh, do not look so surprised, *mi amigo*. Yes, I speak a bit of English, but I choose not to use it except for special occasions. As for knowing of your birthday, the Mambi army may not look as grand as the Spanish, but our intelligence is much better. I bring you sincere felicitations from your Masonic friends in Cuba and elsewhere. They think highly of you."

"Thank you, sir. I am honored to be considered their friend."

"And they yours as well, Peter. Regrettably, we were not able to celebrate the occasion on the proper day in grand style. Perhaps next year, when Cuba is free and at peace. But I do have some Matusalem to share with you as a present. Yes, I even know your preference for that rum! So, would you grant me the distinction of your company as I inspect the night guard of my regiments?"

His servant arrived with two glasses of rum, and García and I walked slowly, he puffing away on a cigar, and each of us enjoying our drink. As we looked over at El Caney a mile away in the darkness, the Cuban commander expressed his concern to me—politely worded, naturally—about the inertia of Shafter's army.

"My conference with General Shafter this morning was most pleasant. We will execute our orders to protect his army's northern flank with élan during the coming attack. But I have a worry ..."

"What is that, sir?"

"General Shafter has waited too long, Peter," he said, the concern on his face visible in the light of a nearby campfire. "The Spanish have been allowed to get into their trenches and fortifications. It will take heavy artillery and cost many men to dislodge them, and yet the siege cannons are not ashore. In addition, thousands of Spanish reinforcements are en route from Manzanillo, and I hear that the fevers are beginning to cripple General Shafter's army." García woefully shook his head. "The hard lesson of 1741 still applies."

I knew that lesson well and had already shared it with General Shafter, who'd made no comment afterward. British major general Thomas Wentworth had invaded Cuba at Guantánamo Bay in the summer of 1741, and his army had made the fifty-mile march toward Santiago through the same jungle where the Americans currently waited. Wentworth brought four thousand men ashore, but by the time he was halfway to Santiago he had lost more than half of them to disease. He never attacked the city. Instead he was forced to withdraw the survivors from Cuba and suffer the humiliation of defeat. It was an accurate and demoralizing analogy to what I was seeing unfold around me.

I could only say, "General Shafter knows about Wentworth's fiasco, sir. He knows he has run out of time and must capture Santiago immediately. Everything hinges on this battle."

General García didn't seem encouraged and changed the subject. For the rest of our walk we spoke only of our children and wives, ignoring the impending clash of 40,000 men. We parted with an *embrazo*, the Cuban embrace between men, and sincere wishes for good luck in the impending fight. I did not see Calixto García again before the battle.

At dawn the next morning, 30 June, García sent orders, via Fortuna, for me to go to Shafter's headquarters, which was now ashore near Sevilla, to procure medical supplies and ammunition for the Cuban forces. Fortuna explained I would be far more successful in dealing with the overwhelmed American staff officers than the Cuban officers had been. As the campaign went on, they had been met with growing resentment by the supply officers, especially if there was a dark hue to their skin. I was told General García considered this assignment a priority. So off I went with my band of followers, back over the same route we'd already endured several times in both directions, to connive or coerce more supplies for the Cuban troops on the front line.

It turned out to be a fateful assignment.

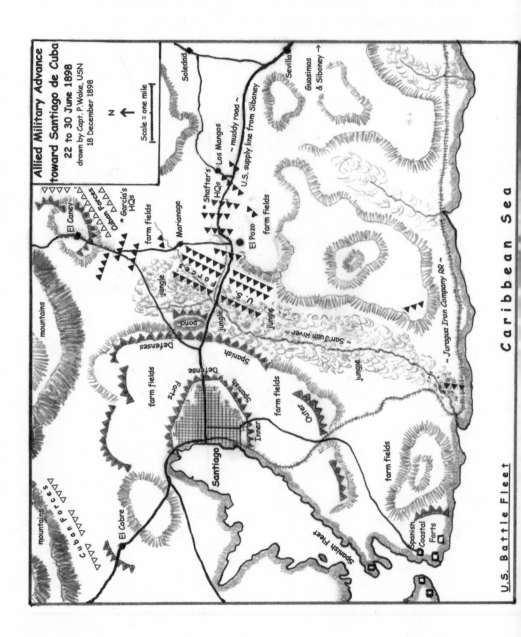

Allied Military Advance toward Santiago de Cuba
22 to 30 June 1898
drawn by Capt. P. Wake, USN
18 December 1898

N

Scale = one mile

Soledad

Los Mangos

~ muddy road ~

~ U.S. supply line from Siboney

Sevilla

Guasimas & Siboney →

El Caney

Cuban Forces

* Garcia's HQs

* Shafter's HQs

farm fields

Marianage

El Pozo

farm fields

mountains

jungle

U.S. Forces

pond

jungle

jungle

jungle

~ San Juan River ~

jungle

~ Juragua Iron Company RR ~

Spanish Defenses

Defenses

Spanish Defense

Spanish Forts

farm fields

farm fields

Santiago

Inner

Outer

mountains

Cuban Forces

El Cobre

farm fields

Spanish Fleet

farm fields

Spanish Coastal Forts

Caribbean Sea

U.S. Battle Fleet

23

A Lovely View of Santiago

El Pozo Hill, Cuba
Friday Morning, 1 July 1898

ON OUR RETURN TO García's command post the next morning, my men and I were stopped at El Pozo Hill, the forward extent of the American advance. With incredibly bad luck, we had managed to arrive at the very place from which the main attack on Santiago was being launched—right then. The road was crammed with troops lined up in column, all anxiously facing west. The road and side paths leading off it were full of Americans. All were waiting for the people in front of them to move. Officers conferred, sergeants growled, and privates quietly grumbled.

My companions discussed how to extricate ourselves from this mass of soldiers and make our way north to García. Fortuna suggested avoiding the roads and going cross-country behind the lines. Law suggested we find a senior officer and get a written pass. Rork thought we should pull our weapons and barge through. I was leaning toward Rork's idea. Noveno just stood there and watched us with an expression of bemused resignation.

As sunrise lightened the sky behind us and I contemplated what to do, Theodore Roosevelt emerged from a cluster of cavalry officers and strode over to us. "The Navy's here! Are you coming with us on the attack?"

I explained that was the furthest thing from my intention. I was trying to get back to the right flank and the Cuban troops facing El Caney Hill.

"Well, it is patently obvious you can't get back to General García's command post now, Peter," said Theodore Roosevelt, flashing his famous grin. His contemplative mood of last night had been replaced by sheer energy this morning.

"Doesn't matter, Theodore. I need to return to the Cubans because—"

But I never got the chance to explain, for the old Theodore was back, and his raring-to-go confidence was on full display. "Impossible! Things are in *motion!* The roads are filled with soldiers heading for Santiago—that's the crucial fight, and it's where you should be."

He waved away my impending comment. "Besides, Lawton and García have already started their attack over there on the right flank. Once they capture El Caney they'll reinforce us at Santiago. I really think it best you come along with us. Once we cross the river in front of yonder heights, you can head off to the right and find García's command as they come over to join us. It'll be a shorter route, anyway."

My fatigue may have contributed to my acquiescence. Our transit from Shafter's headquarters back to García's had taken much longer than I'd anticipated. I'd had to persist in my arguments late into the night with various staff officers, finally reaching the colonel in charge of the depot. He explained there was nothing more allocated for the Cubans, and no transport to get it to them if there had been. I came away empty-handed and in a foul mood. I was also operating without so much as an hour's rest.

Under these circumstances Theodore's suggestion seemed to make sense. The best way to get back to García was to move forward with Roosevelt's regiment, which was heading obliquely in that direction. Once we were across the river, I should meet up with García in a few more hours. For a fleeting, magnificent moment, I imagined the Cuban general and me entering Santiago together in victory.

"All right, Theodore. We'll do just that."

"Good! I feel much better having veterans like you and Rork with us." He spun around, waving a hand toward the east. "I say, this is a glorious morning, isn't it? What a vista!"

He was right. Viewed from our perch on El Pozo Hill, the dawn certainly was glorious. Above the milling mass of men waiting to kill the enemy, the powder blue sky was incongruously peaceful. Fluffy white clouds tinged with rose and lemon serenely floated ashore from the Caribbean several miles to the south. The sea was just visible from the top of the hill—an endless cerulean horizon. Periodically I saw the men look to it for reassurance, for it was our escape route from Cuba if things went badly. But escape was all it could provide, for we were too damned far inland for our warships to provide gunfire support for the attack.

Behind me, the sun peeked over the massive shoulder of Gran Piedra Mountain. Its rays reached out through the mountain mists to the west, illuminating the silver spires and gilded dome of the cathedral in the center of Santiago de Cuba, the original capital of Cuba and the ancient symbol of Spain's empire in the New World. The wind shifted a bit to the west-southwest, bringing the familiar scent of a real breakfast from the Spanish cooking fires. I was instantly hungry.

The growing sunlight brought to mind José Martí's comment to me at dinner one night back in early 1895. The conversation had been about the coming uprising and full-scale war to liberate Cuba from Spain. We had been discussing fate and what we would like ours to be.

"I am a good man, Peter," Martí had said. "And as a good man, I must and will die *facing* the sun."

It was the statement of a man facing combat for the first time, for he was about to embark for the Caribbean and eventually land in Cuba. He died in battle at Dos Rios, about thirty-five miles from where I now stood, only a month after he joined the war. I knew if he'd been standing there with me overlooking Santiago that morning he would've waxed poetic about the beauty of the scene. I missed my Cuban friend. He had the artist's gift for vivid description by way of evocative metaphor. *If only he had lived, things would be different. He had power and influence. The Americans would have listened to him instead of disregarding the Cubans' advice.*

My reverie was interrupted when Rork, standing between Roosevelt and me, grew philosophical in his own way. He motioned to the nervous officers from the cavalry brigade staff who had gathered closer to us. Then he pointed to the city.

"Aye, now just lookee there," he said, forgetting that all of them outranked him. "Best fancy it while ye can boyos, for our next view o' those distant hills'll be pretty damned miserable once this donnybrook starts an' them Spaniardos start slingin' Mauser an' Krupp lead our way. Then we'll see who's what among us."

The Army officers pursed their lips at his impertinence without deigning to look at him. Then, executing a perfect half-right, they marched off in unison to look important somewhere else. Rork, having turned his gaze to the distant sea, didn't even notice their departure.

Theodore swiveled his head around and slapped Rork on the shoulder. "Spot on, my dear man. I thought those useless hangers-on would never leave!"

Rork suddenly realized his breach of military etiquette and glanced at me with embarrassment. "Sorry, sir. Wished no disrespect, me bein' only enlisted an' all. Was just thinkin' aloud."

"Actually, I thought it on target and rather profound," I replied. "And all said without a drop of rum to facilitate your tongue. I am correct in believing that, am I not?"

"Nay, nary a drop, an' right about now I could use one. As for me philosophizin', well, you know 'tis only the Gaelic versifier in me burstin' forth." He gave a flamboyant shrug that would have made a Frenchman jealous. "Aye, sir, 'tis an Irishman's great blessin' an' also his curse, to have such a thing wellin' inside him."

"Yes, well, back to the war, Rork." I pointed to a far hill. "Can that artillery hit us here?"

"Ooh, nay. We're out o' those fellows' range by five hundred yards." He added with raised finger, "O' course, once we commence crossin' that valley an' get closer to those bastards, they'll open up on us with grapeshot like a hurricane in hell. Aye, an' then we'll be as uncomfortable as a Friday night tart in Sunday church."

Roosevelt declared, "That is uncomfortable indeed, Rork. Look there, Peter, I do believe the Spanish will have the perfect flanking enfilade on us. We will have to move fast getting to that far hill."

"We won't be able to move fast, though," I muttered as I looked at the mass confusion around us. "This whole attack is moving far too slowly already. The sun is up. We should have been attacking their lines by now."

To Rork I confided, "I've got a bad feeling on this one."

Rork put his false left hand on my shoulder, its metallic weight reinforcing his solemn expression. "Aye, it'll be dicey, for certain, sir. But we've heard the banshees callin' out our names before—an' they were always wrong. So just ignore the bloody devils when they whisper in your ear this morn. They'll not have us today."

Banshees. I chuckled at the wonder of his imagination. "You're entirely right, Rork. I shall ignore all Irish banshee whispers and concentrate on those damned whispering Mausers instead."

I turned my attention to the enemy spread before us across the length of San Juan Heights. Wispy dark green coconut palms and light green farm fields formed a bucolic milieu for the long columns of Spanish soldiers marching out of the city in uniforms of light blue pin-striped rayadillo cotton heading for their defensive positions. The red-and-yellow regimental flags, flashing steel bayonets, gray blockhouses, and long trenches of terracotta earth created a colorful montage of the enemy menace.

Closer still, a mere mile from us, ominous brown rows of rusty barbed wire snaked across the front of a smaller hill, atop which sat an old farm building. The hill and the building were clearly fortified, manned, and ready for us. The Spaniards' obvious intention was to slow our forward progress enough to enable the Krupp cannon and Maxim machine guns on the heights behind them to kill us before we got close enough to fire our own weapons. It was a sobering sight.

And yet, the whole scene was somehow tempting. The 380-year-old medieval city, romantically shining in the morning light, was right there for the taking. Once inside, we would have shelter, food, comforts, and rest. All we had to do was get past the Spaniards' systematic array of mechanically efficient death.

Standing beside me, Roosevelt took it all in through his Zeiss binoculars. Inserting them carefully back in their case, he threw the Spanish one more defiant look. Then he mounted his horse, Little Texas, and trotted over to his regiment, part of the long column of troops that stretched back more than a mile to the east.

The soldiers at the front of the column began heading forward, down the hill. Then the regiment before Roosevelt's started moving. Calling over his shoulder, he declared to us, "Follow me, gentlemen. It is time to advance to the enemy."

We trailed him on foot. Fortuna crossed himself. From our conversations, I knew he'd followed self-confident officers against Spanish fortifications before, usually with disastrous results. So had old Noveno, who padded over to walk behind his superior, his watery eyes accepting this latest ordeal to be suffered in a long life of them. Our Marine, Lieutenant Law, simply stared at the impressive sight of the enemy host spread out before us as he marched along.

Rork sputtered a profanity under his breath, then said aloud, I think mainly for Law's benefit, "Aye, the hell with it. Let's get the grisly deed done an' go home, me lads. One way or t'other, today's the day for God to make his choices among us. An' the Devil'll take the leftovers."

As if on cue, three American field artillery pieces near us on the hill blasted a salvo, hurling the initial shots of the battle. A thick bank of acrid gun smoke swept over us, burning our eyes. We strained to see the target area, the solitary mound with the fortified house between the two watercourses that trisected the battlefield. Plumes of red earth and black smoke erupted where the triangle of rounds impacted. But there was no spectacular secondary explosion of Spanish munitions, just dirt.

The enemy's battery on the far hill, the one I had asked about earlier, fired back, showing little flicks of light seconds before we heard the echoing boom. There was no smoke from the Spanish guns. The Spaniards' ammunition was more modern than ours. The rounds fell short of us by a quarter mile, just as Rork predicted.

All eyes turned appreciatively to the boatswain, who commented, "Hell's bells, me hearties, the silly sods just wasted three rounds. Guess they're not so smart after all!"

It was pure morale-building bravado, of course, and damned if it didn't work, for everyone around us laughed. The tension was broken. Joining in with Roosevelt's regiment, we became part of the long procession of Americans slowly moving west down into the valley. As we descended, the joking faded. Everyone's mind was on those guns. We were in range now.

The military term is succinct and brutal. We were entering "the killing ground."

24

The Killing Ground

San Juan River, Cuba
Friday, 1 July 1898

THE ATTACK PLAN HAD sounded feasible enough when I'd heard it at Shafter's headquarters the day before—if you ignored the supply, artillery, terrain, signals, and movement factors. As he briefed the generals, I could see Shafter was doing his best to show confidence in his decision. This performance was in spite of his illness, which was now greatly aggravated and apparent to all.

The strategy was deceptively simple. It would begin with an easy victory on the far right at El Caney Hill to capture the Spanish fort there and secure the right flank. Then there would be a combined rush to penetrate the main enemy defenses at San Juan Heights, which stretched for miles across our front. The center and right of the enemy line would disintegrate into a rout, enabling the Americans to enter the city. At that point the Spanish fleet, trapped in the bay, would surrender. The war in eastern Cuba would be over.

I remembered all that as we trudged down into the valley from El Pozo Hill. The sound of fighting three miles to our right at El Caney rolled over the hills as a continual roar of popping rifle fire punctuated by thuds from field artillery. It had been going on for hours, and now the din intensified into a constant thunder as more artillery opened up. Like an onrushing storm, the sound grew stronger and stronger as both sides introduced more batteries.

Fully six thousand men of Lawton's infantry division, supported by three thousand of García's Cuban soldiers, were attacking the six hundred Spanish infantry defending El Caney. At the prebattle meeting of generals, Lawton had estimated it would take only two hours to capture the hilltop and consolidate the victory, eliminating the threat to the allied right flank. Once that was accomplished, Lawton would lead his American-Cuban force four miles to the southwest to join the right side of the main U.S. assault on the enemy lines dug into San Juan Heights. The entire strategy depended on Lawton's forces joining ours in midmorning, building an unstoppable phalanx that would roll up the Spanish defenses in front of the city.

But Lawton's prediction was dead wrong. He accurately estimated the Spanish numbers at El Caney but grossly underestimated their courage and skill. Outnumbered more than eleven to one, their situation seemed impossible, but they were under the command of General Vara del Rey, a true warrior of the old school. We could hear them fighting like tigers, successfully delaying the American advance on the right side. Lawton's men bogged down on the slopes of El Caney and never made it for the midmorning fight at San Juan Heights.

This meant the right flank of the attack on San Juan Heights would fall to the dismounted cavalry division alone. But before we could even get into position to assault the heights we had to capture that small hill right in front—the one covered with trenches and barbed wire and topped by the fortified building.

The farm fields became scrub woods as we went downhill. In the valley's broad bottom the terrain became dense jungle. Somewhere ahead were two streams that flowed from right to left in front of the hill. The lesser one, the Aguadores River, was our first obstacle. The San Juan River, the second stream, was larger. They merged just to the left, or southeast, of the small hill where the Spanish awaited us. Buried in the thick trees, we couldn't see any of that. All we could see was the terrain directly around us.

I knew the muddy road led to crude bridges, ruined by gunfire, across both rivers. They would be bottlenecks for the advance—death traps certainly already registered in advance by the Spanish artillery. I asked Roosevelt if he knew about any fordable areas away from those bridges. He didn't but said he had scouts out looking.

In the entire cavalry division, only a few of the senior officers had gotten their horses ashore. General Sumner, who took command of the division when Wheeler fell ill, rode by us with a couple of his aides. His grim visage softened a bit when he saw Roosevelt, to whom he tossed a jaunty wave as he forced his way through the men on foot to the front of the column, presumably to gain control of the forward progress, which was almost completely halted by confusion.

Ahead of us on the road were the regiments of the 1st Brigade. We in the 2nd Brigade were to support the 1st in the great assault. There were soldiers from infantry regiments on a trail to the left who ended up mixed in with us also, separated from their comrades and plodding forward through the mud like the rest of us.

Even the newest volunteer could see that our army's line of approach was less than militarily sound. The sole road—jungle canopied, shadowy, airless, and mired in several feet of muck from the previous night's rain—was packed with soldiers. Many were already on the verge of heat exhaustion, and it was only midmorning. Regiments comingled, degrading their officers' ability for tactical command and maneuver. The column moved in fits and starts—forward for a few minutes, then at a standstill, then forward again. This went on for quite a while. Comments from the ranks turned from nervous humor to angry derision. Sergeants yelled at them to shut up. Officers exchanged worried glances.

As if the situation wasn't bad enough, a giant Signal Corps observation balloon floated up in the air just behind us. They'd been fiddling with it on the top of El Pozo Hill all morning and finally had it aloft. I'd thought it would stay back at the hill, but instead it bobbed along behind us like an eager puppy, serving as an excellent confirmation to the enemy gunners of our exact location on the tree-shaded road.

Rork shook his head in disgust but said nothing. He didn't have to. We both knew this was exactly how *not* to conduct the line of approach to a frontal assault. The Spanish weren't fools. Our column presented an irresistible target, and I felt like an old, fat pig being led to the slaughter as I waited for the barrage.

The first casualties came a moment later, when we were still almost a mile away from the nearest enemy trench. Men suddenly began dropping—dead or mortally wounded—but not from the artillery fire. Sharpshooters camouflaged in the trees and using smokeless ammunition took them down one by one. The only clue to their existence was the zing of a Mauser bullet and the red spot on a soldier's shirt or forehead as he went down.

Officers initially had urged their men forward with gallant phrases, but it didn't take long for those to lose their effect. Soon, only desperate epithets kept everyone moving. Fatalistically, the soldiers continued toward the Spanish defenders entrenched somewhere to the west, helping each other through the deepening mud. Here and there another man fell, a victim of bullet or heat, to be dragged off to somewhat higher ground off to the side of the road and left there for the medical attendants who were supposed to come later.

Everything about the situation affronted my senses, and I grew angrier by the second. The green tangle of bushes, vines, and trees reduced visibility to a claustrophobic twenty feet. The racket of clanking canteens and rifles and cursing formed the background for the relentless whine of rifle fire and concussion of distant cannons. The stench of rotting vegetation, death, mud, manure, and filthy men filled the air. The entire place stifled rational thought, taking men to the edge of panic even before they could see the enemy.

When the head of the column got close to the Aguadores, the order was passed back to hold in position on the road so that Kent's infantry division, which had advanced along a small path roughly parallel on our left, could form for the attack. Our troopers crowded up to the front of the column, staying to the right side of the road where there was a gap in the trees. We peered to the north. Lawton's infantry regiments, supposedly coming from El Caney on our right, were nowhere in sight. They were still enmeshed with the Spanish on that distant hill.

On our left, Kent's brigades managed to get most of their regiments into an assault line and began running across the shallow river. As we waited for the word to charge, increasingly worrisome rumors circulated along the road: Lawton was defeated to our right and retreating, the Spanish were pursuing him and outflanking us, Shafter was perilously ill and dying in his tent, Wheeler had come from his own deathbed to take command of the assault, the assault had been rescinded, the Spanish were attacking our rear, the Cubans had all run off.

Meanwhile, the Signal Corps balloon was still bouncing along above us. Some senior idiot up in the balloon observing the overall attack excitedly yelled down to us in a stentorian voice that the enemy was now firing at us. As if we didn't already know that. The officer's announcement elicited a raucous round of comments about his eyesight, brains, and military skills.

With perfect irony, this was when the Spanish artillery found us. It wasn't hard for them—they just aimed for the ground under the big, fat balloon. Rork identified the artillery as the 6.3-inch Ordóñez guns on San Juan Heights. Airbursts of shrapnel scythed down around us, sending up clouds of leaves and causing a chorus of maledictions from those lacerated. Within minutes, more men lay wounded or dead on the roadside. The Spanish gunners managed to hit the balloon as well, and we took some satisfaction in watching the damned thing descend out of sight.

We hunkered down and waited. The barrage lasted for almost another hour, during which Roosevelt was like an enraged lion trapped in a cage, barely able to conceal his supreme disgust. My companions and I got off the road and hid from the cannon bursts under a cluster of sabal palms. We watched Theodore as he sent runner after runner to his superiors with requests for orders to move, to attack, to do anything but sit there and die.

Finally, in the late morning, a messenger arrived with orders to move forward to the river. But that was no remedy, for our ordeal got worse. The closer we got, the more accurate was the enemy fire. We were now in rifle range of the small fortified hill out in front of San Juan Heights. Men dropped all around us, some screaming, some cursing.

Roosevelt's orderly, a nice college boy from Massachusetts who enjoyed discussing philosophy, collapsed, mortally ill from fever and heatstroke. His replacement was ordered to run yet another communication to headquarters requesting permission to get completely off the road and advance to the river through the woods to the right. When the trooper stood to salute Roosevelt and acknowledge the order, he fell dead of a round through the throat. When Capt. Bucky O'Neill, Theodore's favorite subordinate commander and a legend among the volunteers, went down with a bullet through his face, we just kept moving slowly forward.

The road at last emerged from the confining jungle into semithick scrub woods and fields. Ahead we could finally see the Aguadores River. We were several hundred yards upstream from where the infantry division was trying to cross under murderous Spanish fire. Suddenly, the command was shouted for us to advance to the riverbank in skirmish order at the double-quick. A shallow area had been found where we could cross the river.

The 10th Cavalry, a Negro regiment, crowded up right behind us. Some got among us. They were grim faced and quiet, their eyes constantly surveying the terrain. Ahead were the 3rd and 1st Cavalry Regiments, already spreading out and moving quickly across the open ground. I could hear Colonel Wood up there calmly calling out commands for his brigade to begin fording the river.

We heard Wood order everyone to assault the hill beyond the river, even though the regiments were still intermingled. We started forward. Our regiment's column stopped suddenly when we ran into the back of the 9th Cavalry. It was apparently the regiment's reserve company, for the rest were attacking. Their captain said his company had orders to hold his position on the road, and he would not violate them.

But they were blocking our progress. Roosevelt argued with the officer for twenty seconds, then simply ignored him and barged his men forward through the 9th, many of whom joined with us. Once past that obstacle, we followed a side trail through the scrub to the right. No one was ahead of us anymore.

Finally in ground open enough for maneuver, Theodore didn't hesitate. He immediately ordered his men to spread out in line abreast and attack. Atop Little Texas he charged toward the river, with my entourage running right behind him. As Roosevelt splashed into the water, the entire regiment, having spread out in attack formation, quickly waded into the shallow and narrow Aguadores. Little jets of water fountained up around us, rifle rounds from the hill directly in front of us.

In the middle of the river we came across one of those memorably absurd sights you sometimes see in a battle. An officer named Pershing from the 10th Cavalry, whom I'd met in Tampa, stood in chest-deep water directing soldiers where to go on the far side, encouraging them on with extremely impious comments as bullets plopped close about him. I found out later it was he who had scouted out the ford and led the brigade across. Seeing my uniform, he bellowed to his black troopers, "Look! The Navy's here, boys, so we know it can't be *that* bad!"

Once on the far bank, our regiment reformed and ran through a marshy field to a barbed-wire fence. As we ripped down the posts and strands of wire, a blast of grapeshot from the fortified house on the top of the hill tore through us. Two men to my immediate left went down. Next to me, Noveno twisted and fell in a crumpled heap. Once down, he never made a sound or movement.

Fortuna checked him, then looked up at me, mouthing the word "*muerto.*" I could see that Noveno's head was gashed open. There was no time to do anything more. Around us, troopers were pushing to get through the gap in the fence. We got up and ran with them, heading toward another line of barbed wire, this one more elaborate. A trooper arrived with wire cutters and began opening a gap, for the posts there were too stout and deeply set to knock down. Twenty feet of wire was cut and trampled down, then more gaps were cut open. The American cavalrymen rushed through. By now the Spanish rifle and artillery fire was a constant noise, just a part of the background. I couldn't hear orders or the screams of the wounded, only the pounding of my own heart. Men were falling everywhere. There was no cover anymore, no place to stop or hide. We could only run forward, and we did. A hundred yards later we came upon the San Juan River.

It was a bit deeper and wider than the Aguadores but still fordable. I was amazed to see Roosevelt still on his horse. He was leading his men into the coffee-colored water, seemingly oblivious to the danger, cursing fluently as I'd never heard him curse before.

After crossing the chest-deep San Juan, we ran into more tangled lines of barbed wire in tall grass at the base of that first fortified hill. More damnable wire! Everyone fell to the ground, trying to get low in the tall grass; some simply collapsed, overwhelmed by the heat and exertion. I cursed Shafter bitterly. Lieutenant Law stared at me, and I stopped.

Battle furor swirled around us. I could barely make out calls for wire cutters and medical orderlies. Finally, after what seemed an hour but was probably a couple of minutes, two troopers with cutters crawled forward and opened several holes in the wire fence. No one leaped up to run through them, though. The Mauser fire was too hot. Lying in a clump of tall weeds, I strained to find Roosevelt. Was he dead? *How will I tell Edith?*

Right then I caught sight of Theodore, and a wave of relief went through me. He'd dismounted and left his horse untethered. Little Texas, skin frothed with sweat and head hanging low, was as exhausted as the rest of us. Ignoring the human chaos, the horse trotted off to gobble up a clump of dark green grass back by the river.

Roosevelt dashed behind me over to the far right side of the regiment, issuing orders we couldn't hear. The word passed back along the line to get ready to charge up the hill. Around me, men who a moment earlier looked like they couldn't go another yard took a deep breath, adjusted their ammunition pouches and bayonets, then crouched at the port arms position, ready to dash forward.

I heard a cheer from the right and saw our men moving up the hill. Roosevelt had remounted and was riding behind the line toward us on the left side, cheering on the troops as he went. They cheered back. Rejuvenated by his brief respite, Little Texas danced about as he gathered himself for the charge.

As he passed me, Theodore yelled, "No more waiting, Peter. We go *now!*"

A volunteer lieutenant nearby howled an Indian war cry. Our part of the line echoed him, rose, and charged up the incline. Several troopers of the 9th Regulars rushed forward next to us, their dark faces scrunched in concentration. On the ridge above us I saw Spanish soldiers pop up from trenches and fire down at us. We had targets at last! In our mile-and-a-half advance so far, we'd taken too many casualties without being able to see the enemy, much less fire effectively at them.

That was about to change.

25

Kettle Hill

Kettle Hill, Cuba
Friday, 1 July 1898

BLACK, WHITE, REGULARS, volunteers, cowboys, Mexicans, Ivy Leaguers, and Indians—the cavalry troopers took matters into their own hands. Within seconds of each other, different groups began running up the slope. The long period of frustration had ended. The entire brigade was going up the hill.

Roosevelt was out in front of us all, galloping up the hill at full speed and croaking out unintelligible commands. Right behind him on foot was his third replacement orderly since sunrise lugging a rifle, pack, and extra ammunition as he ran after the colonel.

Theodore jerked back on the reins when he arrived at another wire fence line halfway up. Two men of the 9th ran up and tried to tear it down to allow the others to get through. On the hill above, an entire squad of Spanish soldiers was blazing away at these easy targets as they struggled with the wire and posts.

Theodore jumped off Little Texas and yelled furiously at the Spanish. The horse had a wild look in his eyes, much as his master did. Once set free, the horse ran down the hill for fifty feet and then stood watching the bedlam. Roosevelt never looked back for him.

Squeezing through the gap in the wire, he yelled, "Follow me, men!" and headed for the Spanish shooters in the trenches near the building at the top. He and his orderly advanced at a fast walk, Theodore methodically spinning toward new targets, firing at them as if bird hunting. Two Spaniards dropped from the orderly's rifle. Theodore's pistol doubled over another. Half a dozen more Spaniards leaped out of their rifle pits and ran to the other side of the hill to escape.

Five more troopers joined Roosevelt beyond the wire, then dozens more. Within minutes an incessant hail of rifle fire was raging *up* the hill, accompanied by a cacophony of various war whoops and epithets from the different American cultures they represented. By this point, the unit cohesion temporarily regained after crossing the river was gone.

At the top, men from five different regiments merged into a chaotic mob. Filled with pent-up bloodlust after enduring the enemy's continuous shooting all day, they gunned down the retreating Spaniards. Officers shouted orders and sergeants cursed to regain control over their men, but it was a free-for-all against the Spanish remaining at the top of the hill, a primitive melee where few prisoners were taken.

My own gallant charge up the hill slackened from a lung-pounding trot to a weary walk. Halfway up, I suddenly wanted to know what time it was and pulled out my watch—one o'clock. That was a mistake. I hadn't had any water since sunrise and was now desperately thirsty. I dared not drink from my canteen that early in the day, however, for I was certain there'd be no replenishment. So with an increasingly parched mouth, I trudged my way through the gap in the upper row of barbed wire and headed for the building on the ridge. Behind me marched my men, and I saw that even young Edwin Law was weary. That made me feel slightly better.

The sound of Mausers had diminished by the time we reached the steep upper slope below the fortified farm building, but both Rork and I were ready for anything as we neared the enemy positions—pistols jammed in our waistbands, ammunition bandoliers crammed full, and shotguns held at the ready. To our surprise, by the time we got to the top there was no one left to shoot. The Spanish were gone. Roosevelt and the cavalrymen had taken the hill.

General Sumner and some of his staff soon arrived on horseback. Looking worried, he kept glancing to the north toward El Caney as he conferred privately with Roosevelt. After a few minutes the general rode off to find his other regiment and brigade commanders, who were scattered across the battlefield to the left.

From the summit I could see the entire panorama of the main defenses to the west on San Juan Heights. The light blue uniforms of the Spanish soldiers dotted the intervening shallow valley between our hill and their main lines along the plateau. I noted they were withdrawing in good order by unit and forming up over there. The battle for our hill had merely been a preliminary delaying affair for them.

Gathering my little crew behind me, I headed for the shade of the building, which turned out to be a sugar mill. I found Theodore leaning against an enormous iron kettle next to the structure, examining a map while straightening his glasses on the bridge of his nose. He wasn't winded at all, greeting us with hearty handshakes and his toothy grin.

"We did it, Peter. Did you see them? My boys damn well did it!"

My congratulatory reply was interrupted by a Spanish artillery shell bursting overhead; the concussion stunned us. Shrapnel thudded into the wooden walls of the building and ricocheted off the kettle, nicking Fortuna's shoulder. Everyone instinctively dove behind the six-foot-high kettle, Rork and me being the last to get under its lee.

I examined Fortuna's shoulder. It would need stitching to close the wound, after the hot metal had been dug out. I told Rork to take the major back to an aid station, but the Cuban refused. I made it an order.

"Captain Wake, I promise to get aid after the battle, but the hot shrapnel cauterized the wound and the bleeding has stopped. And right now, our seriously wounded men need the attention of the doctors far more than I do."

Rork nodded sympathetically to Fortuna, then gave me a look that said to let it go. I did.

More shells burst above us, and sustained rifle volley fire started zinging at us. The rifle fire came from the trenches at the closest point of San Juan Heights a quarter mile to the west. The artillery was from farther away.

"'Tis that same bloody Ordóñez 6.3-inch battery," Rork observed, pointing at it. "A wicked weapon, that. See it? Just a wee bit to the right of that blockhouse way over there an' a bit behind it. Full marks to the bastards for some bloody fine shootin'—that last one damn near did me in. Can ye believe this? Hells'a poppin', an' it's well past time for *our* big guns to have a go at those Spaniardo buggers."

Another Spanish artillery round burst nearby. Lieutenant Law was about to say something when Rork continued his commentary. What had begun with a professional assessment quickly reached high sarcasm born of anger. When Rork gets this way, you can't shut him up, even in the middle of a battle, so I let him rant.

"Ooh, but then again we can't kill 'em back, now can we, lads? An' why is that, you ask? Why, because the ignorant fools in charge'uv Uncle Sam's friggin' army in this blighted hellhole didn't bother to bring the heavy guns ashore! All we've got're light fieldpieces. An' that stupid decision was made *after* they decided to run this giant misbegotten disaster too far inland for decent naval gunfire to help. Those grandee Spaniardo buggers must be laughin' their bloody bollocks off over there. What a royal friggin' cock-up this turned out to be. An' lookee there, we've not even reached the main enemy lines yet."

Roosevelt stared at Rork apprehensively, never having seen him in such an insubordinate rage. Others around us were noticing his rant too. I would have to do something.

"A bit testy today, are we, Chief Rork?" I quietly asked.

"Aye, sir," Rork shot back. "An' with bloody good reason."

"Could be worse, though," I calmly countered. "At least we've got this kettle to hide behind. Better than lying out there in the grass."

"Aye, that's true, sir." He blew out a deep breath in disgust. For a moment he said nothing more. Then a small smile showed on his sunburned face. "Well, I suppose this kettle *is* a bit like havin' our very own ironclad, isn't it?"

"Any port in a storm, Rork," I said, ducking a new volley of rifle fire. One round clanged off the kettle's rim.

Rork sniffed the air, and I saw a glint in his eye. I knew that look. Normally it warned me he was up to something—probably something against regulations and propriety. At this point I welcomed the change of subject.

He smiled. "Ah, but there's a happy side to this here port, sir. Smells like rum to me, an' it's drivin' me mad as a hatter. Me throat's dry as bone dust right now an' could surely use a nip o' nectar. Good for courage, don't ya know. Suppose any's around?"

I chanced a quick peek over into the kettle. "It's only the molasses you smell, Rork. Not rum. They took it with them when they fled."

That ended Rork's happy mood. "Bloody hell an' back—what're the odds? Here we are at a rum mill in Cuba, 'uv all places, an' nary even half a gill o' decent liquor to be had. Damned unfair! How's a sailor to fight properly? What happened to the spoils o' war?"

I said, "I fully agree, Rork. A tot would go down well right now. We're too old for this charging up hills business without a reward at the top."

Another round burst in the air behind us to the east. A piece of hot metal zinged around the rim of the kettle, missing Lieutenant Law's head by inches. He let loose an uncharacteristic string of oaths, which made Rork laugh. "Aye, an' so sayeth the U.S. Marines! By God, now those bastards across the way'll be scared!"

Law reddened, and Rork quickly added, "Lieutenant, you've been saved by a rum kettle; a fine story for your grandkids someday. Come to think on it, that's a right appropriate name for this nasty piece o' real estate—so Kettle Hill it'll be."

While this repartee was going on, Theodore was looking over the kettle's rim at the enemy through his fancy binoculars. After a long perusal he muttered to himself, "Ah, ha . . . I see . . ." Then decisively, "Well, it's got to be done."

I didn't like the sound of that. Fearing he was formulating further heroics, I peered around the kettle's underside, which I judged to be far safer than looking over the top. What I saw through the haze of caustic gun smoke covering our hill was less than reassuring.

Over to our left, General Kent's infantry was halfway up the middle section of San Juan Heights. Thousands of dark blue dots in ragged lines and clusters were ascending the grassy hillsides. Regimental flags waved frantically as their bearers ran up the slope, showing the rate of advance. Banks of gun smoke from light fieldpieces hung over the battlefield from the American lines near the river.

Along the top of the heights were four long lines of light blue dots protected by trenches, several fortified houses, a couple of artillery batteries, and a large blockhouse. The American general assault was being carried out only by the left and center portions of our army, however. The right side of the attack—our side—had been slowed by the still ferocious Spanish defense of El Caney two miles to our right and of the outer hill we currently occupied.

From this vantage point I could see that the fighting at El Caney was still intense. Help from that direction wasn't coming anytime soon. Though I was duty bound to report to General García, right then it seemed better to stay and take my chances with Roosevelt for a while longer. As dangerous as Kettle Hill was, it was better than crossing several miles of enemy-held territory while searching for my Cuban superior, with only three men and without the provisions he had sent me to get, in the midst of trigger-happy soldiers of three armies.

Returning my focus to the main attack, I couldn't see how the infantry on the left and center could overwhelm the heights without an attack against the Spanish from our side of the line. But how could we take the hills on our front without Lawton's thousands of infantry? Our men were worn out. All over our hilltop, troopers

were sprawled on the ground calling for water or Dr. Church's medical attendants. Every minute, the volleys of Spanish rifle fire from
San Juan Heights were wounding more.

It must have easily been 100 degrees by then. The layer of air
just above the ground was shimmering from the heat. I doubted the
men were capable of traversing another quarter mile under intense
rifle and artillery fire, much less climbing an even more heavily
defended hill and dislodging the enemy from their trenches at
bayonet point.

I also had no doubt that Roosevelt was going to order his men do
just that, with him leading the way. He gripped my arm and made
it official. "It appears our brethren over yonder on the left are in
serious need of our assistance, Peter, and we need to provide it post
haste. Don't you agree?"

I damn well didn't *want* to agree, but I had to admit he was right.
Kent's soldiers needed help, and they needed it fast. Our pressuring
this side of the Spanish line would keep the enemy from concen-
trating against Kent on that side. This was it: the decisive moment of
the battle, probably of the entire campaign, which was on the verge
of failure. We had to try.

"Yeah, I agree, Theodore," I said flatly.

Pointing out an area on the far right where there weren't as many
enemy soldiers, Major Fortuna suggested, "Perhaps a flanking move
in that direction would draw enough Spanish off General Kent for
him to gain the heights, Colonel. Upon reaching the top, we could
also sweep the Spanish lines from the side—an enfilade."

Roosevelt curtly shook his head. "No, that would be an advance
of almost a mile, and in this heat it's too much, Major. My men can't
make it that far. As I see it, we'll have to take the shortest distance and
time, and strike the enemy immediately. We'll head for that marshy
pond in this slight valley between us and the enemy, go around the
right side of it, and then run like the dickens at them on that hill."

He swiveled around to face me. I nodded. "You're right, Theodore.
But we'll have to go fast, before Kent's division loses momentum."

He pounded the kettle. "Then so we shall. I'll lead my men right at them!"

Decision made, Roosevelt sent runners out to his subordinate commanders with the new orders, then quick-marched toward our rather meager defense line on the west side of the hill, where men were dodging the constant enemy fire. Oblivious to the bullets zinging all around him, he waved his hat high, shouting something I couldn't make out but doubtless was splendidly glorious. Seconds later, his face tightly drawn in resolve, he went right through our line and strode down the hillside toward yet another line of that damned barbed wire.

He was already far in front of our troops by the time I had gotten my things ready to follow him. Taking a deep breath, I whispered a quick prayer for help and headed for Theodore. I heard my tired men fall in behind me.

I soon regretted my decision.

26

Parker's Guns

San Juan Heights, Cuba
Friday, 1 July 1898

ROOSEVELT'S INTENDED BEAU geste didn't unfold quite as he'd thought it would. With impeccably bad luck, he bounded over the solitary line of barbed wire on the side of our hill facing the enemy just as the Spanish unleashed a new hail of lead toward our lines.

As if miffed by the Spaniards' insolent intrusion into his scene of glory, Theodore stopped, brandished his pistol at them, and cast them a contemptuous look. Then, using his best oratorical voice, which I could scarcely hear above the again-constant thunderous roar of enemy firing, he waved his hat toward his beloved troopers back on the hilltop and shouted, *"Follow me, men!"*

That said, he spun around, returned his attention to the enemy, and headed down the grassy slope toward the pond in the valley. Most of the troopers, busy ducking the Spanish bullets and artillery or tending to their wounds and water, never noticed his grand effort or heard his command.

The enemy did notice, however, and immediately sent a volley to his location, all of which miraculously missed my rash young friend. It was a magnificent performance, this charge of Theodore

Roosevelt toward San Juan Heights, worthy of a Pierre Loti novel. But alas, there was a problem.

Only five of Theodore's men followed—and two of them were quickly gunned down.

Theodore was a hundred yards down the gentle slope when he turned around, suddenly realizing the situation. This was just as my men and I had reached the defense line and were about to step out onto that perilous hillside.

Theodore gestured for the three survivors near him to lie down in the tall grass and stay put. Two of them crumpled before they could do that, shot. The third dove for the grass. Seeing that, I stopped my men and we all dropped to the grass. In seconds Roosevelt was stomping back up the hill toward his regiment, swearing like a boatswain and glaring evilly at the line of troopers. When he vaulted the fence again, his regiment got hit with a full load of scathing Rooseveltian invective, the likes of which impressed even Rork. The troopers were reduced to shocked apologies for not hearing his command to charge.

Recognizing they really *hadn't* heard him, Roosevelt's epithets stopped in mid-word. He laughed out loud and told them, arms outstretched, "Well then, boys, let us do it *now!*"

While all this was going on, the Spanish were not idle. The air was filled with their lead, which cut down bushes and men alike. I still don't know how Roosevelt, who never tried to evade the fire, emerged unscathed.

But he did. As he stood there fearlessly in the bright sunlight, his short and almost plaintive speech worked. This time around, Theodore's entire regiment, augmented by the others on the hill, followed him. Five hundred men headed down that slope toward the enemy-held ridge of hills on the other side of the little valley. More joined in from all along the line, until the entire brigade of two thousand soldiers was moving west.

My men and I ended up in the middle of the horde, carried along by its movement. As we got to the valley floor and neared the marshy pond, Rork proclaimed, "Yea, though us poor bastards're walkin' through the valley of death, we shall fear nary a one o' those damned Spaniardo bullets, cause those dumb buggers are the worst shots me eyes've ever seen!"

Hoots and cheers rose from the men around him, many adding their own vulgar descriptions of the enemy. This derisive élan served to speed up the pace, which I found difficult to maintain. Rork seemed to get his second wind, though, and was jauntily bouncing along on my left, hurling Irish invective at the Spaniards in the heights above us.

The valley was stifling, like a humid oven. The stagnant air and the heat were quickly depleting what little was left of my stamina. There were no trees to offer shade from the sun and concealment from the enemy. The range was much closer now for the Spanish, making it easier for them. More men began dropping, in spite of Rork's joke.

We had to get across and out of the killing ground. As we rounded the northern side of the pond—fetid swamp would be a better description—I pointed to a small, rocky ledge set into the bottom of the hill and told my men, "See that little defilade at the bottom of the hill?" It wasn't much, but if we could reach it we could find some shelter from the enemy's fire and maybe a bit of shade.

"Aye, sir. Gettin' a bit . . . dicey . . . 'round here," quipped Rork, suddenly sounding short of breath. The jaunty expression was gone from his face. His pace was slowing.

We were more than halfway there. Fortuna, who was right behind me, popped off a rifle shot at the enemy and afterward made a nonchalant comment to Law that I made out amidst the din. "A rare mistake on the part of the Spanish. They didn't put their trenches on the military crest; they put them on the top. It provides us that slight defilade ahead and a good silhouette shot at their heads in the trenches."

Law didn't reply, for another storm of Mauser fire swept across the field. The Spanish were firing by volley, a disciplined method to conserve their ammunition. Two volunteer troopers went down on my left, falling into the swampy water. I felt a sting on my right forearm. It was nothing, only a graze, but it hurt like the blazes.

The general pace of the advance slowed when the men ahead began ascending the hill. Clouds of American gun smoke hung in the air, choking my dry mouth and reminding me of my thirst. I saw but could not hear officers shouting for their men to stay with their company and regiment. Wounded men were calling for medical help. Someone far behind me shrieked in pain. But it was all muted by the gunfire from the Spanish above us.

I barely heard Rork cursing the Army and Cuba as a black trooper in front of him staggered toward the swamp, blood pouring out of a hole in his jaw. Rork shouted for a medical orderly. None came. I helped Rork drag the man out of the water; then we headed for the rock outcropping.

I searched for Roosevelt, but in all the confusion I'd lost him from view. Was he hit? It didn't matter then. The rock outcropping was only fifty yards away. In a pause between the Spanish volleys, I rasped out to my companions, "Run for it!"

"Friggin' Army . . . sonsabitches . . . have cocked up this . . . whole . . . damn . . . thing," snarled Rork as he adjusted the seabag to his left shoulder, shotgun in his right hand. He tripped over something and stumbled into me. His face was crimson and pouring sweat. I offered to take the seabag, but he brusquely waved me away. "Just lead us out o' this!"

The soldiers nearest us spotted the defilade too. Soon a dozen dark-blue-clad troopers were running over the swampy ground toward it. Younger and faster, they got there first.

I heard the mechanical rattle of sustained gunfire, sounding as if it came from the Spanish side of the valley. It wasn't rifle shots. It was a machine gun, somewhere close by. My gut clenched into a knot. The Spanish army used German-built Maxim machine guns.

But when it fired again, I knew the gun wasn't a Maxim. The sound of a German navy Maxim was imprinted in my brain, for one of them had nailed me at Samoa nine years earlier. This gun was slower, with a lower-pitched, clanking sound. Maybe the Spanish had Colt machine guns, or a Nordenfelt? And where exactly *was* the damn thing? I scanned the ridge but couldn't locate it.

"Spanish machine guns!" someone yelled. Other men repeated the warning. Around me, fear instantly replaced exhaustion on the faces of the American soldiers. We were completely exposed and all thinking the same thing. We were dead.

"It's the Gatlings, men," I heard Theodore shout from far ahead of us. "*Our* Gatlings!" Then I saw him at the foot of the hill, flourishing his crumpled hat above his head. He turned back toward the enemy and charged up the hillside with crazed momentum.

The rattling Gatling shots increased in volume. Several of them were firing now. The top of the hill erupted in a line of spurting sand and dirt. What a fool I was! I should have recognized the sound immediately, for the Navy used Gatlings. But my brain had been muddled by the overall confusion. That realization startled me. I had to get my wits together.

It was good news, though, and I knew who was responsible for it. Lt. "Blackie" Parker, an Army infantry officer I'd met back in Tampa, was in charge of V Corps' four Gatling guns, each one sporting ten barrels that spit out lead at a prodigious rate. At last I spotted them over to the right. Parker had moved three of his guns forward to the very edge of the attacking force and was using them offensively. That violated Army doctrine, but their effectiveness in this situation was beyond debate.

Parker's guns poured a veritable hailstorm of hot American lead at the Spanish trenches along the hill in front of and above us. Thousands of rounds were tearing the earth and rocks apart. It went on and on, a continuous thudding of mechanical destruction spewing into the trenches.

This was the moment the tide turned at Santiago.

The Americans, reinvigorated, ran forward, cheering the Gatlings. Ahead of us, the 9th and 10th Cavalry Regiments were ascending the hill along with some of Kent's infantrymen who had drifted over from their regiments on the left. The front of our regiment was right among them. The 1st Cavalry was climbing up on the right.

Suddenly the Gatlings stopped. In the ensuing silence I realized the incessant thunder of enemy gunfire had faded. I could hear men around me talking. Slowing down to catch my breath, I took stock of the situation. Behind us, a large American flag had been raised over the kettle on the hill we'd just departed. The sun and a slight breath of wind made it shimmer, a stirring sight even to my jaded soul. I felt my spirits rise for the first time since I'd landed in Cuba. Some potshots came our way, but nothing like the hail of lead earlier.

Then I heard a surprised grunt close behind me. Right afterward came a groan and the thud of a body hitting the ground. I spun around to see what had happened. Surrounded by hundreds of men surging forward toward the enemy hill, Law and I stood there, stunned.

Rork and Major Fortuna were facedown on the ground.

27

Heat of Battle

San Juan Heights, Cuba

Friday Afternoon, 1 July 1898

W ROLLED THEM BOTH over. The small hole in the center of Fortuna's forehead precluded any hope of his survival. Just like old Noveno, the major was dead before his body hit the ground.

"Leave him. He's gone," I told Law. "We'll bury him and Noveno later. Help me with Rork. I think he's still alive."

It was hard to tell for sure. At first, Rork looked dead too. We stretched him out carefully. I put my ear to his mouth, listening for breath. Another flurry of Spanish shots rang out. I couldn't hear Rork breathing above that noise, but I could feel his chest move, slowly. His head began to tremble slightly. His face was a frightening sight, corpselike, bloodless. But his forehead wasn't cold; it was very hot. His eyes were rolled back. I felt his pulse; it was racing.

I searched him for bullet holes or shrapnel gashes but found no apparent wound or blood. As I probed his groin, he twitched angrily and cursed me in a mixture of English and Gaelic.

"Where's he shot?" asked Law, kneeling beside me.

"I don't think he is. Maybe heatstroke," I answered. I passed my hand in front of Rork's open eyes, but they weren't focusing on it.

"Sean, can you hear me?" I shouted urgently into his ear, worried about apoplexy of his heart. I could handle violent wounds, but I knew nothing about treating heart failure.

"Peter?" he mumbled pitifully in a soft voice, like a little boy. In the general commotion around us I faintly heard him say, "I can't . . . see you. It's so . . . bright . . . sun's in me eyes."

Law moved to put his shadow over Rork's face. My friend's eyes finally focused on me. He reached out his right hand. "Peter?"

"I'm here, Sean."

"They get me?"

"Can't find a wound. I think the sun got you."

He took in a deep breath. Then his hand gripped mine hard. "The *sun*, you say? I'm laid low by the bloody friggin' sun? Sweet Jaysus, uv' all the friggin' Mick luck."

"We'll take care of you, Sean. Rest easy, my friend."

Rork's hand gripped me even tighter as he suddenly came fully to and realized he was on the ground near a dead trooper. He hadn't seen Fortuna. "Nay, can't be lollygaggin' here in the midst'uv a battle. The men'll think me a bloody idler."

"Be quiet. You're in no shape to do anything but rest. We're going to cool you down in the pond. That'll make you feel better."

I turned to Law. "Help me get his clothes off and carry him into that water."

Rork didn't like my idea. "You're gonna do *what*?"

"Just shut the hell up, Rork, and help us get your uniform off."

"Nay, 'tis unbecomin' an' I'll not be doin' that."

"Rork, help me get your damned trousers off before I get shot!"

Rork grunted something nasty and started unbuttoning his trousers. I heard the Gatlings resume their firing. Soldiers in the valley cheered again.

Lieutenant Law looked at the fetid pond and shook his head doubtfully. "Wouldn't it be better if we took Chief Rork back to the hospital, sir?"

Damn all! First Rork, now the Marine. Why can't anyone follow a simple friggin' order! Holding my temper in check I explained, "It's too far away, Mr. Law. Rork's burning up inside, so we've got to get him cooled off right away. The swamp water's a little cooler than the air temperature. After that, we'll get him into the shade of the ledge. His wet skin in the shade will cool him faster."

Law stopped hesitating. We dragged Rork's trousers down and got his shirt off as he lay there perplexed, his hands shielding his face from the sun. It took several minutes of fumbling effort. Fortunately, the enemy's firing had dwindled considerably by then, for our soldiers were near the top of the hill. One of them was frantically signaling to the Gatling guns with wigwag pennants to cease firing so the Americans could make the final charge.

Even with our men near the top of the heights, a few Spanish shots landed near us as Law and I dragged Rork into the swampy water. His stark white torso and sunburned face and arms made an easy target against the dark green scum floating on the water's surface. Great gobs of green scum clung to us as we lowered Rork into the mess.

"I'll hold his head up, and you push his body under," I told Law. "We'll hold him here for five minutes, then run with him for the shade."

"Whoa, this is colder than it looks!" Rork blurted out when we put his body under the warm water.

We should have kept him there for far longer than five minutes, but we were in the open. The dead around us were a grisly incentive to hurry. The flies that rose from the water were getting in my eyes.

"Your face is bleeding, sir," said Law.

I wiped my free hand across my cheek and looked at the red smear. The wounds I'd gotten in late April at the battle of Isabela had reopened once again, but they were minor compared with Rork's life-threatening condition.

"Not important," I told Law. "Three more minutes in this water, then we run to the shade with him."

Bullets impacting near us meant nothing by then, just another part of the sights and sounds of chaos. I had no idea of time as we stood in the waist-deep water, no thought to check my watch, which fortunately was in my breast pocket. Time disappears in battle. I'd said three minutes, but I wasn't counting. At some point I simply said, "Now!" and we heaved Rork up and headed for the hillside.

Several hundred men must have passed by us in those minutes after Rork and Fortuna fell, but no one helped us. They had their own troubles. We fell repeatedly as we lost our grip on Rork's wet skin. I remember swearing bitterly at Law for dropping Rork's legs.

At last we got him to the shade of the rock. The sun was starting to lower in the western sky, expanding the rock's shadow. Several wounded men were there calling for water.

The shooting from both sides slowed even more. The Gatlings had shifted their fire somewhere else. As the three of us lay there trying to catch our breath, I tried to figure out what to do next about Rork.

Law raced back to the pond and brought back several soaked rags to spread over Rork's face and chest to help cool him down. I didn't ask where he'd found the filthy rags. He dashed out again to bring back Rork's weapon and uniform, and the seabag. By then the wet rags seemed to have done some good, for my friend's face was less flushed. He sat up on an elbow.

"Here's your canteen, Sean. Get some water inside you."

"Aye, sir. That I will, just as soon as me bones're covered up respectably."

"This is one hell'uva time to be shy, Rork."

"Captain, 'tis embarrassin' for a senior petty officer such as meself to be out here with nary a stitch on an' no blood to show for it. Good Lord, sir, people'll think me gone daft, or a lily-livered faker!"

"You *are* daft, you old coot. Just follow orders for once in your life and drink the friggin' water first. Then we'll get you back in uniform!"

He glared at me but followed my orders. I took my own advice and swigged water from my canteen. Taken from the body of a Spanish infantry officer by the Mambis, it was a large canvas bag bigger than the metal canteens the Americans carried. It had been presented to me with great solemnity when I'd first reported to

García's headquarters. I was told the canvas bag made far less noise when moving through the jungle than the American version, something I'd found to be true.

My intention was to imbibe only half the water, but only a quarter of it was left when I forced myself to stop. My hands were shaking, and I wondered how close I had been to sunstroke myself.

Two more cavalry troopers came into the shade and collapsed among the soldiers. One of them was holding his ear, trying to stop the blood pouring over his fingers. A stretcher party arrived with a man, dropped him off, then headed out again. The space under the ledge was getting crowded.

"Go and find out what's going on out there, then report back to me," I said to Law. "I'll start getting Rork's uniform back on him."

Law took off up the hill as I began pulling on Rork's trousers, a difficult task. He is a big man, they were wet, and my efforts put me in some rather uncomfortable poses. The trousers were about to his knees when Rorked winked at me.

"Ooh, methinks you're a bit slow on this. Why, I've known several wee lasses that could do the job in the opposite direction in half the time. Remember that one on the island in Vietnam?"

I did indeed. "Hell, Rork, I thought you were sick and about dead. Damned if you're not just a giant Irish pain in my ass," I retorted, glad his sense of humor had returned. "Now drink more water and help get this stuff on. And don't ever scare me like that again!"

"Aye, sir. Sorry about me fallin' out like that. An' now, we'd best be gettin' back to the business at hand here. Feelin' fit as a fiddle again, I am, so let's get this job done."

He gave me a determined gaze to cover his lie. But I'd already decided Rork's war was over. "No, you're going to the rear, Sean."

At that point the men in the shade of the outcropping were treated to a farcical scene. Summoning some hidden source of strength, Rork got to his knees, growling ferociously, then stood up at full attention. His trousers fell down, and he stood there with them about his ankles and not a stitch on anywhere else.

Bringing his right hand up to salute, he indignantly bellowed out, "Captain Wake, I'll have you know you're speakin' to a United States Navy *chief* petty officer with thirty-seven years in Navy blue, an' there's more fight still left in me than any ten o' those Spaniardo bastards on yonder hill. So let's stop caterwaulin' about how hot the friggin' sun is an' get this job done in proper naval fashion, shall we? An' by the bloody way, I'm still a better shot than you are, an' I always will be, so you'll damn well be needin' the likes o' this ol' salt right alongside you—*sir!*"

Lieutenant Law returned just as the crowd of wounded soldiers howled at Rork's speech. The lieutenant stood there dumbstruck at the sight of Rork, naked as a newborn with green slime dripping from his hair, yelling at me. Apparently he'd never seen an enlisted man yell at an officer.

I gave up my well-intentioned attempt to classify Rork as a casualty. "Oh, hell, you win, you grumpy old bastard. Get back in proper uniform, Chief Rork. You look positively silly standing there buck naked, and in front of the Army, no less."

"Aye, aye, sir!" His attempt to quickly haul his trousers up made him stumble, which got the Army crowd heckling the Navy once again. With stubborn effort, Rork finally pulled up his own trousers, refusing Law's help.

Once he was squared away, Rork sat down beside me and asked, "Where's Major Fortuna?"

"Dead, Sean. Mauser round in the forehead. Same time you dropped."

"Oh, no. Not him too . . ." Rork let out a long sigh that conveyed a lifetime of woe. "Had big hopes for the major's future, I did. An' now Cuba's lost another good man."

"Yes, a damned shame, like so many others." I wearily looked up at the Marine. "Mr. Law, what did you find out?"

"They've taken the hill, sir," he reported. "Our colors are flying at several places along the crest. I also heard that Lawton finally won over there at El Caney and his men are heading here to reinforce us. Not sure, but I think I saw them several miles off in the distance."

San Juan Heights and El Caney are ours? Is the battle over? I allowed myself a moment of mental relaxation. "Well, some good news, finally. We'll go and report in to General García."

Then I stood and looked down at them. "But first, gentlemen, we've got a sad duty to perform . . ."

28

Facing the Sun

San Juan Heights, Cuba
Friday Afternoon, 1 July 1898

ORTUNA'S BODY WAS WHERE we'd left it near the pond, already covered with flies. I went through his pockets to retrieve his personal effects. There wasn't much, just a crude sketch map of the Spanish defenses of Santiago and a small cotton pouch. Inside were a crucifix, a crinkled photograph of a young woman and a baby boy, a toothbrush, and a medal of Saint Michael, the patron of soldiers. Folded with the photograph was a six-month-old letter from his wife. Stained and moldy, it described his son Jorge's first steps, admonished him to watch over old Noveno, and ended with a reminder that their bed waited for him at home. Except for the map, which I kept for myself, I put everything back in the pouch, which went into our seabag.

Then I quietly said a prayer for a distant young widow and her baby.

After that I studied Rork for signs of relapse. Though he was moving slowly—we all were by then—he seemed to have recovered. I found some sticks, a plank, and a potato vine to fashion together a cross. Rork scratched a crude epitaph on the plank with his marlinespike:

MAJOR ALFONSO FORTUNA
Cuban Liberation Army
Born 1865. Died in battle 1 July 1898
A Hero of Free Cuba

Law found a small shovel among the various infantry equipment discarded during the battle and dug the grave, which I had carefully outlined to be perpendicular to the setting sun.

When Law asked me why, I repeated what José Martí had said to me before he went to fight in Cuba. "Fortuna was a good man, too, Lieutenant—one of the best—and like Martí he died facing the sun. So we'll make sure he's buried that way."

As we gently lowered the body into the grave, a wave of sorrow for Cuba's loss swept over me. I'd held my composure until then, but at that moment all the years of misery, all my dead friends, proved too much for me. I couldn't stop it. I stood there weeping.

Thirty feet away, a line of American infantry from the reserve depot back at Siboney trudged by heading for the front lines on San Juan Heights. Many stared at us. They hadn't fought yet, and obviously they hadn't been in Cuba very long. They were still clean, still burdened with all their issued equipment. They didn't have that tired stare out to nowhere.

Ignoring them, the three of us stood in a line facing the grave. I offered a simple eulogy.

"We gather here to bury the mortal remains of a good man, Major Alfonso Fortuna, of the Cuban Liberation Army. A valiant son of Free Cuba, an outstanding soldier, and our trusted friend. It was an honor to serve alongside Alfonso as we faced the foe. We will never forget him.

"Now the ordeal and pain of war have ended for Alfonso. He sits on the right side of Saint Michael, joining his fellow soldiers and his hero, José Martí. Dear Lord, please take good care of his widow and his baby, and please watch over those of us still in this battle. Amen."

Several of the troops passing by made the sign of the cross; others removed their hats. We quietly walked away toward the riverbank by the first hill, the one Rork had named Kettle Hill. After searching for some time we found Noveno's body. It had been dragged under a bush. His simple trousers had no pockets. He carried no possessions. I wondered if he'd ever had any, for I knew nothing about the man's past except that he had some relationship with Major Fortuna's family. I wished I'd asked when I had the chance.

Law and I carried the corpse back to Fortuna's grave. Rork lashed together another cross while Law and I dug the new grave. Noveno was also buried facing the sun, right next to his major, but his epitaph had a far less personal description. I didn't even know his full Christian name. I said the same prayer over the grave.

Then we joined the column of troops heading up the captured hill in the dimming light. I planned to head along the front line and try to find García's headquarters somewhere about a mile or two off to the right. Roosevelt's regiment should be in our path, so I decided to check on him on the way. I hadn't seen him for hours, since his charge up the heights. After witnessing his reckless behavior in battle I prepared myself for the worst.

Once on the crest, I saw a line of American regimental colors floating in the breeze, stretching more than a mile and a half, from one end of San Juan Heights to the other. Out on the right, or northern, end of the battlefield, two columns were marching toward us from the northeast—Lawton's troops and García's troops, the Cubans in the lead.

Directly behind us, a long column of infantry reinforcements was coming across the valley from El Pozo Hill, interspersed with supply and artillery columns. Engineers were working on a crude bridge over the San Juan River. I surmised that by morning, the hard-won American position on the heights would be consolidated, strengthened, and extended. It was a reassuring view in the gathering dusk.

Occasionally a shot came from the west side of the heights, which the Spanish still controlled, but overall there was a quiet weariness in the air. Even the sergeants spoke softly as they got their men situated along the hilltop. The calm was dense, palpable—a mixture of grief and apprehension.

Looking west, I had a much better view of the Spanish lines than I'd had on my reconnaissance several days ago, or from our distant perusal back at El Pozo this morning, or even from Kettle Hill this afternoon. A chill went through me as I realized the true nature of the day's victory.

Our success was neither complete nor even likely permanent. In fact, the American army was in a precarious position, for it had captured only the first line of defenses on the San Juan Heights. Even with the reinforcements coming up to our front line, a determined and overwhelming Spanish assault on a single point would have no difficulty pushing us off the heights.

Three hundred yards to the west I could see another two complete lines of Spanish defenses echeloned on slightly higher elevations. They had even more trenches, blockhouses, and artillery emplacements than the first line we'd worked so hard to overrun.

I sat there stunned. Casualty rates would be disastrously high in a frontal assault. The Spanish were making the yanqui invaders pay dearly for every inch of territory we gained. Red-and-gold banners of Spain undulated defiantly above their positions, glowing in the final copper rays of the sun.

"The generals won't order an assault on that," said Law, more to himself than to us. "They'll bring up the siege guns and settle in to bombard the Spanish, then starve them out. Might take a month, maybe two."

"Afraid there's no time for that, Mr. Law," I replied. "The siege guns aren't even ashore yet, and fever season has set in. We'll lose half our men to disease in the next month if we stay out here in the swamps. Both the Spanish and General Shafter know that."

Rork groaned and sat down on a rock. "Bad way to go, death by crappin' an' pukin' your guts out from a tropic crud. Nary a touch o' glory in that, Mr. Law. Lads, if such a thing happens to yours truly, just bury me achin' ol' bones back at the beach—with me looking out to sea, mind. I don't fancy seein' this damned Cuban hellhole for all eternity."

He rubbed his stomach. "But we ain't dead yet, are we? So a wee bit o' food would be nice right about now, sir. We've had nothing since afore sunrise."

"Yes, I'm starving too. Maybe Theodore or his people will have some food when we find them."

Rork swayed a bit but quickly recovered, looking to see if I had noticed. Then he lightened his tone. "Aye, now there's a grand idea, sir. That lad Roosevelt surely does know how to eat civilized, even in the bloody jungle."

And so we resumed our trek, heading north along the line of trenches, now filled with Americans grimly staring to the west. The sun disappeared, and the humid tropical night settled over the uneasy battlefield. Over the mountains in the distance clouds were forming. But the air above us only had some small clouds racing along on the last of a sea breeze. Stars emerged to carpet the sky.

Anywhere else, this would have been a romantic evening.

29

Perfumed Moonlight

San Juan Heights, Cuba
Friday Evening, 1 July 1898

W HEN WE FOUND HIM, Roosevelt was sitting on a camp stool. He stood and took a close look at my face, squinting through his specs. "Peter, you look terrible. Have your old wounds reopened?"

I'd forgotten about them. "It's nothing. They opened up a bit today," I replied as we sat down on the ground next to a small fire. Nearby was Theodore's tent, already stained and torn.

"Say, where are the Cuban gentlemen who were with you?" he asked.

"Killed in the attack," I explained. "Noveno went down in front of Kettle Hill. Major Fortuna was hit at the pond."

He removed his spectacles. "So very sorry to hear that, Peter. Good men, those two. Noveno was quite a scout. And Major Fortuna was a Harvard man, if I recall correctly. A sad loss for his people. They'll need men like him to run this country someday." He paused before adding, "We all lost a lot of good men today."

There was nothing for me to say. We sat in quiet and somber reflection. It didn't last long, for Roosevelt was as hungry as everyone else on the hill. "Let's eat. You can go find General García later."

I agreed. Rork in particular needed nourishment. But I hadn't seen much around us. Scavenging for food among the relinquished Spanish fortifications had become the main endeavor for everyone on the trench line. Pretty much everything edible or useful had already been taken. I wondered what Roosevelt intended us to eat but was too polite to ask.

Theodore's abode wasn't quite as civilized as Rork predicted, but he did have some decent food. His orderly's search had yielded tinned peaches from Georgia, of all places. He'd found ten cans of them in a Spanish officer's abandoned trunk and presented them to his colonel. Roosevelt gave all but three to stretcher-bearers to take back to the brigade's field hospital.

Dr. Church arrived at our little circle, and Theodore called upon him to examine me. The doctor, who looked about ready to drop from exhaustion himself, briefly looked me over and pronounced, "Nicely scarred, but fit for duty."

I had him look at Rork. Church did a quick once over and said, "Probably heat prostration. Good thing you were cooled down straight away, Rork. That saved your life. You must get rest tonight. Prognosis: *un*scarred, and fit for duty—tomorrow."

That got a chuckle from Theodore. I gave Rork an I-told-you-so expression, which he acknowledged with a smiling nod.

"Oh, I'll be owin' you a decent drink for savin' me life, sir. Never worry, though. Sean Aloysius Rork pays his debts."

Health concerns alleviated, we ate. The five of us sat in a circle, eating the remainder of the peaches along with other spoils of war: three bananas, two mangos, and four slivers of sugarcane stalk. The meal was accompanied by Spanish red wine, also courtesy of the Spanish army, albeit somewhat soured in its flagon. We also had enough Spanish coffee for a cup each. The entire repast did the trick, raising our spirits enormously.

After dinner, Roosevelt took me aside and quietly suggested, "I think it best you and your men retire here for the night, Peter. Get up early and find the Cubans at dawn. Getting shot in the dark by nervous sentries is a bad way to go. García will understand." He nodded toward Rork and said, "And our friend desperately needs the rest."

"Thank you. We will."

After we returned to the fire, Theodore regaled us with a stirring account, complete with darting eyes, stabbing fingers, and flashing teeth, of how the cavalry brigade had stormed up the hill, met up with our infantry on the left, and together had defeated the enemy at the top. The assault's success was all due to Parker's Gatling guns, he declared, adding that he heard they had fired an incredible 18,000 rounds in the first 8 minutes, overwhelming the Spanish soldiers and allowing the American advance to reach the top. Parker's guns had also defeated an attempted Spanish counterattack and now formed the strongest point in the American line. Everyone wanted to be near those Gatlings.

"I've seen the reinforcements coming up to the line, Theodore, but what about supplies? Have we enough to hold out?" I asked.

"We've received some ammunition and water, but no heavy cannon or additional machine guns yet. What I would give for three more Gatling guns! After we captured this trench line, a few of the generals, who shall remain nameless, thought we were too weak here to hold the place. They even thought we should withdraw back to Kettle Hill."

Roosevelt grew agitated at the thought. "Well, you can imagine how *that notion* sat with us. We'd fought our way up here and weren't in any mood to give it back! When General Wheeler returned to the fight from his sickbed and resumed command of the division awhile ago, he ended any such talk of retreat."

"The men need food, though," opined Dr. Church, sipping some coffee. "The bungling fools sent us no food in the supply column. We've only what we can find in the captured Spanish stores."

Roosevelt pounded his fist on his knee. "Quite right, Doctor! The stupidity of the supply situation is astounding. These brave men are famished, but we are reduced to eating the enemy's leftovers!"

He snapped his fingers. "Oh, wait, I almost forgot one other thing they did send us. For some unfathomable reason, an hour ago we got mail for the first time since we landed in Cuba. Can you imagine that? Mail but no food!"

Theodore leaned over toward me. "My darling Edith wrote me all's well at home and to say hello to you. The children are fine. She says everyone back there is working hard to support our success down here by sending what we need."

"Some heavier artillery would be nice," grumbled Rork.

"I heartily agree, Rork. But first we need food for the troops. And not that canned poison they issue, either. Say, let me fetch my orderly and have him see if there's any mail for any of you naval gentlemen."

Surprisingly, there was. The orderly returned with two letters for us that had been put in the cavalry division's mailbag with the thought they might be passed on to the Cuban headquarters. One tattered envelope was for Law, a letter from his parents. I had one from Maria in Tampa, scented with her jasmine perfume. Poor Rork had nothing.

Law made a sympathetic comment, but Rork shrugged it off. "Nay, Mr. Law—no one to pity here. I'm used to no one writin' me. Uncle Sam's blessed Navy's been me home an' me family for a long time."

Law held his letter up near the campfire light, sniffling as he silently read through the pages. Everyone looked away, giving him some privacy. Roosevelt went off to check his lines and guard posts. I walked off with a dim Spanish lantern to read Maria's letter alone.

I found a safe spot in a shell hole behind a rock where I could be alone with her, even if only figuratively. Longing filled me as I traced her beautiful cursive script slowly with my finger, for feminine softness was only a memory now. The mere sight of her lovely writing nearly reduced me to tears.

> 19 June 1898
>
> My dearest Peter,
>
> Here is a quick note to tell you two things. First, I miss you and worry about you terribly. I won't even ask you where you are, knowing you will be where the armies are fighting.

I beg you take care, darling, for you solemnly promised to come home to me. Do you remember that? I simply cannot live without you, so you must live and return to my bosom— or my heart will fail.

Please give Sean Rork an embrace for me. Bring him home, too. I miss his laughter. No one laughs around here anymore unless they are drunk. There are too many fears of the future, too much sorrow for the past, to be lighthearted when sober. I've had no wine, nor rum, since your departure—there seems no point in it without you.

My second bit of news is more momentous. I have had the honor to be asked by Miss Barton herself to accompany Red Cross nurses to Cuba. As you know, Clara is a wonder of energy and skill and decisiveness. She well knows the situation inside Cuba from her time helping the Cuban sick at the Spanish re-concentration camps last year. Even the Spanish governor appreciated her work and begged her to continue. Then the war started, changing everything.

Since starting my work in Tampa, Clara and I have become dear friends. Still, you may wonder why she asked me, one born into the enemy's culture, to go to Cuba with her. Though I am not a trained nurse, she said my organizational skills and fluency in Spanish are greatly needed in Cuba. Her insistence was so intensely sincere that I agreed to the request. I have tremendous respect for this indomitable seventy-seven-year-old lady. How could I say no?

We are due to depart Tampa this very morning on a hospital ship called the *State of Texas*. They are taking us to Oriente Province, where the news correspondents write there will be a battle to capture the city of Santiago de Cuba. The Red Cross officials say we should arrive there in ten days. Once ashore, we are to organize a hospital on the coast to support the military doctors who will set up regimental hospitals closer to the fighting. We have been warned that the Army will resist our efforts, since they believe women cannot endure in such a place. Miss Barton will prove them wrong, as she has at every war where she has provided comfort and treatment for those in need.

I will admit part of my agreement to go to Cuba was motivated by my desperate hope to see you, if only for a brief moment. Please understand, Peter, and do not be angry with me. I need to touch you, darling. To have you hold me, to feel your strength, and to look into your eyes. I have gone too long without the touch of your hand, the sweetness of your kiss. My heart and my very soul feel so empty without you near me. I pray we will see each other and have a moment of privacy.

With all my love, your adoring wife,

Maria

Only three weeks had passed since I'd last held her in Tampa, but it seemed a year. Suddenly, something struck me. Her letter was written on the nineteenth. Ten days from the nineteenth of June meant she'd been ashore in Cuba for several days already, probably near the main Army hospital at Siboney.

My God, that's only fifteen miles away! The realization was like a jolt of electricity. My mind began conjuring ways to get to Siboney.

When I returned to the campfire, Law was still staring at his letter, unaware of those around him. At the edge of the firelight, Rork snored softly. Roosevelt had returned from his inspections and was stretched out on his back contemplating the nearly full moon rising fast over Grand Piedra Mountain to the east. From the west came sporadic gunfire from the Spanish, sounding almost halfhearted after the massive volleys that day.

Along the mountains to the north of us, lightning flashed inside a wall of translucent clouds. A storm had formed and was heading toward us rapidly. I could already smell its moisture in the wind. We would be wet soon. The few men with canvas or blankets began propping them up into lean-to shelters.

"While you were gone, a messenger arrived for you with a verbal message," Roosevelt informed me while still staring upward. "Captain Peter Wake and his staff must report immediately to General Shafter at El Pozo. And it seems you won't be alone. Leonard Wood told me General Shafter has summoned all division commanders to come to a conference tonight on what to do next. García will be there, so you can rejoin him then."

I had no idea why Shafter wanted me. Maybe he was dissatisfied and planned to return me to the naval effort. That possibility made me smile, for it would take me through Siboney. Catching a whiff of her perfumed letter in my pocket, I imagined holding my darling Maria.

"We'd better get under way now, then. Thank you for the hospitality, Theodore."

He jumped to his feet and favored me with the famous grin. The firelight glinting off his spectacles made him look particularly mischievous. "*Mi casa es su casa, amigo.* Sorry you couldn't get some rest, but I'm glad Chief Rork got a little. Say, maybe it's good news for you at Shafter's headquarters and you're going back to sea, where the food is better!"

I sighed at the thought. "Oh . . . a clean bunk and decent food. I can only hope."

I nudged Rork awake. Law shouldered the seabag. Shaking hands, Theodore and I wished each other luck. Then I led my men out of the camp and along the crest toward the hated road to the rear.

By the time we reached the road, thick clouds covered the moon. Moments later a wave of cold rain swept down over us. The Spanish fired several random artillery rounds to harass the American positions behind us, their concussions mixing in with the thunder.

"Hope we can get back to a ship, sir. *Any* bloody ship. That's where the likes'uv us properly belong," declared Rork as he sloshed forward in the dark. "Don't fancy livin' in the mud even a wee bit longer."

"My sentiments exactly, Rork," I replied, then slipped in the mud.

30

A Glorified Lackey

El Pozo Hill, Cuba
Saturday before Dawn, 2 July 1898

AFTER HALF AN HOUR the downpour slowed to a drizzle. The road, which had been merely muddy following the dry day, was now liquefied into an ankle-deep canal of thick soup. Forgetting the decorum expected of my rank, I gave loud and vulgar vent to my opinions each time I fell. Even Edwin Law, to date usually quite disciplined in his words and gestures, gave in to his frustration.

We had ample reason. The road was crowded with men, mules, and wagons, all struggling in the wet darkness to go west toward the front lines. We continued our way east in the pitch-black night. After managing to cross the two rivers, now swollen and raging, we reentered the jungle portion of the road. There, the westbound vehicles weren't able move at all, mired to their hubs or higher. But the men kept wading. The oncoming soldiers filled not only the roadway but every bit of higher ground on either side as well, forcing us to push our way through them instead of detouring around.

At last we ascended El Pozo Hill, the location of Shafter's forward headquarters. It was still drizzling when we finally found a staff tent at 1 a.m.—having taken three hours to make two miles—and reported our arrival to a surprised minor aide on Shafter's staff.

That tired soul looked at us as if we were from another planet. He'd never heard of me and didn't know there was a naval contingent that far inland.

We were politely told to stay there because the general would be arriving soon. We found a large laurel tree that provided some shelter from the rain. Sitting with our backs against the trunk, we waited. The release of the aching tension in our bodies was a bit too relaxing, though, and within minutes each of us was blissfully insensible with sleep.

At 3 a.m. we were awakened by the same lieutenant, who explained the general wasn't, in fact, coming to El Pozo. He was still at his main command post, a house near Los Mangos. I was to report to him there.

This entailed walking another mile east along the road, which at that elevation was at least drier than the portion down in the jungle. At the crossroads known as Los Mangos we headed north on a path for a hundred yards, where we found another group of staff tents near the dilapidated farmhouse where the general had his headquarters.

As another rain shower swept over us, I found a bedraggled officer who led me to the conference in the largest tent set up for the staff officers in the front yard. It was a chaotically urgent scene—the complete opposite of the Tampa Bay Hotel a month earlier.

It seemed not much was going right. The place was jammed with men. A sergeant in the corner of the tent was explaining to a major that the telephone connection to El Pozo was broken, as was the line back to Siboney. A lieutenant announced that the regimental medicine chests had just arrived ashore—a week late—but there was no transport to get them forward. Right after that, another lieutenant piped up with a message from General Kent demanding more food. A leak in the center of the canvas poured water down into an overflowing bucket on the canvas floor.

I spotted Miley, now a captain, shaking his head at it all. At the allied commanders' conference at García's mountaintop camp a week ago he'd been the very epitome of a diligent staff officer in a starched uniform, handling the military minutiae of the campaign for the great man. When I saw him in the midst of the San Juan Heights battle he was far less spit-shined. He was impressive, darting here and there to deliver commands from Shafter to the brigade and division commanders. Now, Miley looked just how I felt. Exhausted, filthy, and frustrated.

With a weary nod and mumble he suggested I see the staff adjutant, a colonel seated ramrod straight behind a table at the far end of the tent. I headed over and stood before the table. The colonel, it was clear to see, was a recent arrival to the campaign in Cuba. From boots to shoulders, his uniform had a parade-ground sheen without a hint of dirt or dampness. There were actual creases in the sleeves and legs. It was a marvel, that uniform. I had the burning temptation to ask him how the hell he managed it. You couldn't walk ten feet outside without splattering your shoes and trousers with mud.

But I didn't ask, for right then he raised his attention from the report he was studying to the naval officer before him. Before I could introduce myself, he announced, in an unambiguously chastising tone, that the general had been expecting for me for *hours*. He added I'd best not keep the general waiting any longer. This greeting was accompanied by a minute inspection of the mud-caked, stubble-chinned naval intruder from head to toe. His wrinkled expression of disdain and prolonged sniff made it manifestly apparent that I didn't pass muster.

Miserably uncomfortable and borderline mutinous at the colonel's rudeness, I declined to render any of the usual courtesies and instead turned and plodded out the tent to the front door of the farmhouse. The guard stood to attention, bringing his rifle to present arms. After returning his salute, I leaned through the doorframe and peered inside.

The main room of the house was plainly furnished. A pair of lanterns sat on a large table with a cloud of swirling bugs around each. Seated in an oversize folding canvas chair at the table, Shafter was reading some paperwork. His uniform coat and hat were flung on a cot in the corner along with several rucksacks and a raincoat. Two steamer trunks were next to the table, one opened to reveal toiletries and large tins of food.

The adjutant colonel marched briskly by me in the doorway, leaving a trail of strong cologne behind him, and entered the house. I looked down and saw mud on his shoes, which brightened my mood. Without so much as a hello, the colonel placed another pile of papers on the corner of the general's table, which was already covered with neatly organized maps and reports.

"That naval officer has *finally* arrived, sir," he stated to the general, who vaguely acknowledged the information without looking up. I walked inside and stood before the table as the colonel threw me a smug look on his way out. The fervent hope flashed through my mind that a Spanish sniper was somewhere close by looking for colonels to shoot.

For a brief moment I regarded the man in charge of the entire American operation ashore. The sight wasn't reassuring, for William Rufus Shafter didn't look well at all. His straw-colored hair was in disarray. Massive sweat stains spread out from his armpits across his shirt. His face was bathed in glistening perspiration, with rivulets streaming down his nose and chin. The small eyes squinted. His breathing was audible and labored. *Does he have the fever now in addition to his previous ailments? Probably*, I decided.

In regulation form, I announced myself. "Captain Peter Wake, U.S. Navy, Fifth Corps liaison to the Cuban Liberation Army, reporting in as ordered, sir."

"Wake, I called for you yesterday evening and expected you to be with General García when he arrived at the commanders' conference several hours ago. Where exactly have you been? He said he hasn't seen you for days."

The general didn't offer me the small camp chair on my side of the table. The omission was intentional, a pointed sign of his displeasure. I didn't care.

"Sir, yesterday morning I was at El Pozo, on my way from this headquarters to General García's staff, when the attack on El Caney began. Since I couldn't catch up with General García's staff where they had been *before* beginning their attack on El Caney, I headed for where they were supposed to end up, over on the right flank of the cavalry division at San Juan Heights. That course put me with Colonel Roosevelt's cavalrymen during the attack at Kettle Hill and San Juan Heights."

His brow furrowed. "Roosevelt, eh? Hmm."

"Yes, sir. As you know, General Lawton's and General García's divisions didn't capture El Caney until the afternoon. They didn't join the main army on San Juan Heights until last evening. I got word then that you wanted me to report to you during the divisional commanders' conference at El Pozo and set out immediately. Upon arrival after a three-hour march, I discovered the conference was over and was told to wait because you would be returning. An hour ago, they told me to see you here, at Los Mangos."

"Confounded miscommunications." The general's face tightened, and he let out a disgusted *harrumph.* "And yes, that El Caney attack took far longer than anyone thought it would."

He exhaled while wearily shaking his head. "The commanders' conference ended hours ago. They're heading back to their divisions now. Wake, I wanted you at that meeting so you would know the overall situation before embarking on your next task."

"My next task, sir? With the Cubans?"

He looked at me nervously. "No, I've reassigned you from García to me. I've got a job for you to do. To do it correctly, you need to understand my plan. We're going to reinforce our existing lines to hold the line we've already got along the heights. Then we're going to extend our lines to completely encircle Santiago. García's Cubans will handle the northern and western sides of the city while we hold down the eastern side. The Cubans are also going to try to stop a column of five thousand Spanish reinforcements coming toward Santiago right now from Manzanillo, though I have doubts they're up to it."

I thought that plan remarkably ignorant. Did Shafter really not have a basic understanding of the terrain and order of battle of both his allies and his enemies?

"General, the Cubans don't have enough men or artillery to stop a 5,000-man enemy force. Especially if they're also trying to hold down a 12- or 15-mile-long section of the perimeter around San-tiago. General García only has about 6,000 men available to him at Santiago. His other regiments are holding down positions—and Spanish units—all over the eastern end of Cuba while our army has at least 17,000 men ashore to hold only 5 miles of the perimeter."

Shafter wasn't impressed. "Yes, well, the Cuban side of the perim-eter is a temporary stopgap measure. As the siege unfolds, we'll get more of our men ashore to expand American control of the perimeter to include the Cubans' current segments. General Miles is arriving soon with another seven thousand men and some heavy siege artillery."

I could not control my anger—or my tongue. "Siege? General, if you convert this offensive campaign into a siege it'll take months to starve the Spanish out of the city. And the rising rate of fever sick-ness will be at 50 percent of this army by the end of the month—at the very latest."

He bridled. "Captain, I *fully realize* the fever factor. Some officers are suggesting the alternative to a siege—another attack on the enemy's defenses."

"No, sir! A frontal assault would be suicidal. Their defenses are too damned strong and layered in depth. We don't have enough men for any more days like today. The casualty rate was nothing compared to what it'll be if we try that again against the main Span-ish defenses on San Juan Heights. *I was there.*"

As my last comment came out, I realized I'd gone too far. Shafter hadn't gotten closer than a mile to the front line. His face went from blotchy to solidly enflamed. I heard someone's boots scuff the planks outside the doorway. The guards and staff were getting an earful.

Pounding the table, Shafter spat out, "Damn you, sir, I am sick of your continued impudence! I don't need some discarded sailor who couldn't get his own ship to tell me how to run my 23,000-man military campaign on land!

"Wake, your only assignment was to be a liaison for us with the Cuban general and his staff, and you haven't even been able to carry out *that* minor responsibility. So get this crystal clear and adjust your insolent attitude right here and now—you have no authority here. You have no advisory capacity in my staff, you are not commanding any of my troops, and you were not asked your opinion of *anything* regarding strategy. Is that completely understood, Captain?"

It was. Regarding my position and authority, General Shafter was absolutely correct. I was nothing but a glorified lackey, and not even a good one. I heard more boots on the planks. I had no doubt the tirade would be spread all over the army by mouth, telephone, and telegraph within the hour—if those devices even worked. I could hear it now. *Ooo-whee, the general really laid into some Navy officer who told him off about the campaign. Damn, I thought Ol' Pecos Bill was gonna shoot the poor bastard.*

I came to attention, feeling humiliated in my unprofessional dishevelment. It had been awhile since I'd been dressed down by a superior officer, but I still knew the automatic response.

"Aye, aye, sir. Understood completely."

He deflated a bit, leaning back in his chair with a loud exhale. After wiping away the sweat covering his face, he lowered his voice. "Very well, then. Let's get back to what I was about to say before you began lecturing me. I need solid information about the enemy's dispositions, and I need it fast. You are going to provide it."

Shafter paused to catch his breath. I remained silent, though I did relax from the position of attention, for I felt absurd being braced up at my age. He leaned forward with a frown, as if what he was about to utter was distasteful to even consider, much less say.

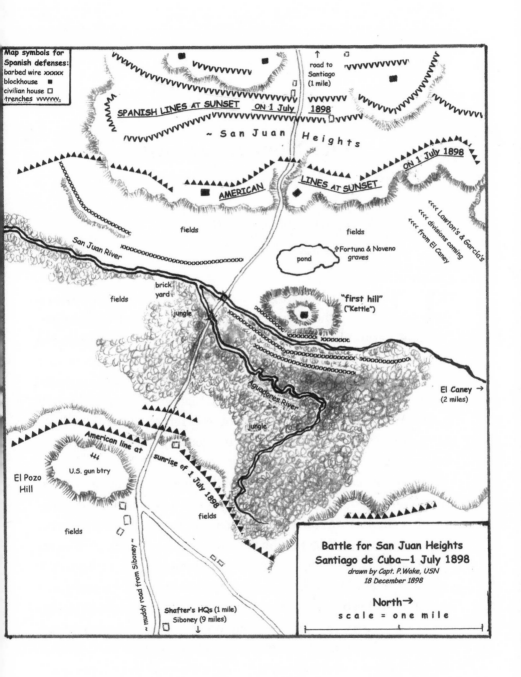

Map symbols for
Spanish defenses:
barbed wire xxxxx
blockhouse ■
civilian house ☐
trenches vvvvvv.

SPANISH LINES AT SUNSET   ON 1 July   1898

road to
Santiago
(1 mile)

~ S a n   J u a n   H e i g h t s

AMERICAN   LINES AT SUNSET

ON 1 July 1898

>>> Lawton's & García's
>>> divisions coming
>>> from El Caney

San Juan River

fields

fields

pond

⚓ Fortuna & Noveno
graves

brick
yard

fields

jungle

"first hill"
("Kettle")

Aguadores River

jungle

El Caney →
(2 miles)

American line at

sunrise of 1 July 1898

U.S. gun btry

El Pozo
Hill

fields

fields

~ muddy road from Siboney ~

Shafter's HQs (1 mile)
Siboney (9 miles)

Battle for San Juan Heights
Santiago de Cuba—1 July 1898
drawn by Capt. P. Wake, USN
18 December 1898

North →
s c a l e = o n e m i l e

31

The Secret Option

V Corps Headquarters, Los Mangos, Cuba
Saturday before Dawn, 2 July 1898

"UNFORTUNATELY, WAKE, you are the only American officer who has seen the entire Spanish defensive line around Santiago. Plus, you know the lingo and how to survive on your own in this dreadful place. So, since you are still under my authority, you are released from your liaison posting with General García's staff. A note regarding that will be sent to him. It is now 3:16. When you leave here you will return to the front line. After sunset tonight you are going to execute a special reconnaissance mission for me, to be completed by midnight."

Shafter turned in his chair and pulled one of the maps from a pile on the bed behind him. He spread it out on the table, flattening it with a thud. It was an 1895 Spanish topographical map, stained and crumpled but showing the terrain, roads, and major fortresses around the city. *Probably captured at San Juan Heights,* I surmised.

The general put a finger on the map at Santiago. "You and your assistants will scout out the area on the southern outskirts of the city. That is, between Santiago Bay on the west, the city's inner defenses to the north, the southern end of our lines to the east, and the coastal forts at Morro in the south. It's an area of four miles east to west, three miles south to north. Specifically, I want to know if there is any weakness we can exploit somewhere between Fort Cañadas on the southeast side of the city and the inland side of the Morro fortifications at the entrance to the bay." The general's finger slid from Santiago to the area south of General Kent's infantry division on the left, or southern, flank of the American line, which had been penciled along San Juan Heights. Someone coughed outside. Shafter glanced at the door and lowered his voice as he continued.

"I am moving some of our reinforcements under General Bates to the far left of General Kent, which will be the new southern flank of V Corps' lines. They'll be opposite Fort Cañadas and in position by late afternoon today. That will give us a continuous line from El Caney to San Juan Heights and most of the way down to the coast."

He looked up at me expectantly, so I nodded my acknowledgment. He continued.

"I repeat that I need to know what you discover by *midnight* tonight. If you find a place weak enough for us to cross, then Bates will attack through that area and assault the coastal forts from behind. That will be at dawn on the morning after I receive your report. The timing of that report is crucial. Understood?"

"Yes, sir."

"His success will secure the entrance to the harbor. The Navy, as you surely know, can't do anything about the Spanish fleet hiding up in the bay until the mines at the harbor's entrance are removed. The mines can't be removed until the forts are destroyed or captured. Our capture of the Morro forts would enable the Navy to remove the mines, enter the bay, destroy the Spanish fleet, and then compel the city to surrender.

"If this possible opportunity can be successfully exploited, we can end this entire campaign without a frontal assault on the city's main defenses and without a protracted siege during the fever season."

He paused and cast me a defiant look, daring me to dispute his brilliant and bold plan. It was all I could do not to laugh. Capturing the coastal forts to enable the Navy to enter the bay was the *original campaign plan*, before Shafter decided on his own to approach Santiago through the inland jungle and hill country, away from the covering fire of our warships at sea.

The forts had to be captured because the minefield at the entrance of the bay was electrically controlled from inside El Morro Fortress. In addition to the mines, the heavy shore batteries from half a dozen forts would wreak havoc on any warship assaying the narrow entrance to the bay. But the coastal forts did have a weakness: their landward sides had no heavy guns.

I hadn't seen any large formations in that area when I'd circumnavigated Santiago a week earlier. The enemy troops I'd seen were concentrated on the northern and eastern perimeters of the city itself. The southern flank was patrolled but empty of significant formations. Once the American invasion had landed, however, the Spanish would certainly have placed troops out in the open countryside between the city's perimeter forts and the coastal forts to prevent an attacking land force from capturing El Morro and its subordinate fortifications from the landward side. I was amazed Shafter hadn't already conducted a reconnaissance.

Shafter added an ominous condition to his orders. "Wake, no one, including the division commanders, knows of my idea on this. Do not tell anyone, not even your own assistants. This secret option must remain secret until I choose to employ it."

"Aye, sir," I parroted, "keep it secret."

"Good. You should start now. The colonel outside will arrange provisions and supplies for you and your men. Remember, it is imperative that I have this information by midnight so I can decide whether to attack. We've strung telephone wire to the front line, so call me immediately upon returning from your mission."

"The line is down, sir. I heard someone on your staff report that minutes ago, on my way in."

His faced tensed again. "It will be fixed. Just get me that information."

"Aye, aye, sir," I said as neutrally as I could. His instruction about secrecy worried me. I'd heard the same sort of thing before in my career. When a superior says *no one else knows what you're doing*, it means he won't be blamed if things go badly. If the mission ends in victory, he grabs the credit and brags about it to the press.

Incredibly, at this point he tried to boost my morale. "Wake, with the Cubans that you have attached to you and your personal knowledge of Cuba and the Spanish defenses, I know you're the best man for this important job. Your mission could mean the difference between ultimate victory or defeat."

That sounded rather lame considering his earlier estimation of me. I kept my sentiments out of my reply. "The Cubans assigned to me are dead, sir. They were killed in the assault today. It'll just be Chief Rork, Lieutenant Law of the Marines, and me."

I expected a reply, but the general was acting as if I'd already left. He was leaning over the map, intently studying the area around El Morro. The colonel came in, wordlessly handed me a signed provisions requisition form, then put another report in front of Shafter.

The general quickly perused it and started a discussion with the colonel about the number and type of available flatbed wagons at Siboney. Obviously, my presence was no longer needed, so without the usual farewell respects to my commander and his adjutant I walked out into the dark.

Neither of them seemed to notice.

32

The Actor

U.S. Army Field Hospital, Siboney, Cuba
Saturday Morning, 2 July 1898

"WELL, IS IT BACK TO the Cubans or back to the Navy?" asked Rork, his voice giving the latter possibility a hopeful lift.

"Neither, Rork. It's back to doing another little job for the U.S. Army. But first, we're going to make a little unauthorized detour."

It was late morning and already hot when we got to the coast. I smelled the sea before I saw it—a fresh, crisp tang of salt air that blew the jungle's miasma of death and decomposition out of my lungs. We crossed the Siboney River on a newly built bridge, courtesy of U.S. Army engineers, and crested a small knoll overlooking Siboney village. The Caribbean Sea was an azure expanse of clean freedom, a stark contrast to the slimy confines of the tropical forest. It was filled with American ships of every type, a sight to gladden the heart of any sailor.

Once down in the village I sent my men on their assignments: Rork to find decent food and drink and Law to find some replacement uniforms. Our clothing had become unrecognizable as American uniforms, a potentially mortal liability should any friendly forces mistake our identity.

The scene at Siboney shocked me. Everything had changed in the eight days since I'd last been there. The sleepy village of a few dozen Cuban peasants was now a city swarming with a thousand American soldiers. Greasy cook tents, bulging supply tents, old staff tents from the Civil War, and soldiers' tiny half tents covered every possible space of high ground from the riverbanks to the hills behind the village.

Amidst the rows of tents were muddy thoroughfares and side streets. Wheel ruts in the main streets had turned into miniature streams, and makeshift walkways of planks or tree limbs meandered about the side streets. I went through the tent town and down to the pier.

Dozens of boats, barges, and lighters competed for docking space on the pier's leeward side, for the surf was up, and landing a heavily laden boat on the beach was impossible. On the narrow pier itself, wagon drivers, stevedores, and supply sergeants argued over the destinations of the cargo, artillery, and livestock being landed. A bespectacled lieutenant was sitting on a bollard swearing aloud to no one in particular.

On the western side of the village the coastal railroad line sat unused. I kept walking. Offshore, troop transports, hospital ships, freighters, and gunboats rolled on the long Caribbean swells waiting for their turn to unload cargo or take on the sick and wounded. I knew their captains were eager for orders to do anything other than sit there wallowing in the shimmering heat.

Siboney was the dreary side of war, that unsung but crucial part that supports the men fighting on the front lines. No medals or fame would be garnered at Siboney, just day after day of hard decisions on impossible dilemmas.

After getting directions from a sergeant, I walked toward the worst of the entire place—the corps' general hospital. Even a thousand feet away I could distinguish the odors of quinine, iodine antiseptic, ether, sewage, and vomit. As I got closer I heard the anguish of those undergoing surgery.

I'd seen it all before. Rork and I had been patients in such places several times. The horror returns when you see it again. At the hospital's front tent, a fresh-faced young medical sergeant with tired eyes stopped berating an orderly to answer my inquiry.

No, he'd never heard of Maria Wake of the Red Cross. But, he hurriedly added, most of the Red Cross nurses were over in the "sickness section" treating soldiers with diseases. He pointed toward a group of tents located farther up the hill, separated from the "wounded section" to prevent the spread of contagion. I headed up the hillside.

Maria was in the third tent I entered. The sign at the entrance labeled it the "Dysentery Ward." A row of cots lined each side, and it was beastly hot inside. Every one of the cots had a soldier in it, and a few more sick men lay on blankets on the ground. Most were naked except for a towel covering their torso. She was at the far end, bent over a soldier curled up on his side on a cot.

I barely recognized her. She was in a white smock with a red cross stitched to the upper left front. A brownish-yellow stain was smeared across her waist. Her silky dark hair, which she usually maintained in an elegant French braid, was a tangled mass pulled up in a bun. In her hands was a white enamel tub, which she began carrying toward the doorway. Her expression was listless, her eyes cast downward as she walked.

"Maria," I said gently to get her attention.

She looked up and stopped five feet from me. Now I could tell what was in the tub, the stench even more awful than the sight. Her hands trembled. I stepped forward and took the tub from her, placing it down on the dirt floor. Then I wiped away the tears that began running down her face. She said not a word as I held her in my arms, the quiet weeping turning to sobs as her last barrier of strength burst. The tent grew quiet, every man watching us.

An older woman's voice came from behind me. "Maria, why don't you and the gentleman take a walk outside for ten minutes before we get these men ready to go out to the hospital ship."

Maria motioned her thanks and led me out by the hand. We followed a path away from the tents and stopped in a clearing above a ravine. Thirty feet below us the narrow Siboney River rushed down from the mountains inland. We sat on a fallen log, and I held her. The sobbing soon ended, but her frailty filled me with worry. I'd never seen her this fragile, even when her son had been killed in Cuba six months earlier. She'd been here only a few days, but was she sick too? I kissed her, caressing her face, willing her to feel better, to smile, to show me any sign she wasn't ill.

"Maria, are you sick too?" I asked. "I didn't get your letter until yesterday and figured you might be working here. I've only got a few minutes, but I had to see you."

She straightened up, took a deep breath, and bestowed her lovely smile on me. "Yes, I am fine, dear. Just a bit overwhelmed. This place is so—and then suddenly seeing you . . ." Her smile crumpled onto a frown. "Oh, Peter, your facial wounds are opened and infected. You look terrible, and filthy, like you have been crawling through mud. I thought you were on a staff with General García. How are your other wounds from before? Show me."

"I'm fine, dear."

"Show me that you are fine. I need to see them, Peter. And while you are doing that, you can tell me how you got here. Were you in the big battle?"

I began unbuttoning my shirt. "I was on García's staff but got separated and couldn't make it back. So during the battle I was with Theodore's regiment. He's fine. Rork is too. He got too much sun and needed to rest, but he's back to his old cantankerous self now."

She minutely studied the scars on my torso, then returned to the open ones on my face.

I tried to mitigate her worry. "Maria, it's just stress from exertion, that's all. They're not badly infected; don't worry."

It didn't work. Maria examined them anyway as I stood there with my ragged shirt and trousers open, hoping her superiors didn't wander along. "Peter, they *are* infected. And these down here on your thigh are too. Here's a new one on your arm."

"That one's just a scratch, dear. I didn't even notice it."

Her brow creased at my dismissive tone. "No, it is *not* just a scratch. It is a *bullet* wound. You need immediate care or the infections will get deadly. First of all, a bath. Then a covering with antiseptic solution will be applied to these wounds. Lastly, bed rest for at least three days."

"Well now, dear . . ."

"Don't you dare tell me you don't have time! This damned war will last at least that long, Peter. You and Sean Rork are far too old for this sort of thing. And where is he right now?"

In spite of her no-nonsense attitude I laughed, imagining Rork's response to her opinion of our age and capabilities. "He's off on a mission to get supplies for us right now, otherwise known as stealing them."

Her mood eased. "Everyone does that here. It is the only way to get anything."

"I can't stay, Maria."

Her anger returned. "Can't or *won't*?" Then she instantly softened. "Oh, I am sorry, Peter. Please stay the night, at least. You're exhausted, and those wounds require attention. I have a cot in a tent with two other nurses who will be working tonight. And there is a real bathtub in the tent next to it. Of course, my cot is narrow, but if we snuggle close . . ." The sentence ended with a pleading look. "Please, I desperately need to have you hold me through the night, Peter."

My heart melted as she held my face in her hands. I came close, very close, to giving in. But visions of the battle went through my mind. I knew I might be able to prevent another frontal assault if I could find a way to take the coastal forts from behind. The lives of thousands depended on it.

"Maria, as much as I want to stay, need to stay, I can't. I have something very important to get done. It'll take a couple of days.

Afterward, I don't know where I'll be—things are very much up in the air right now. I'm here now because I needed to see *you*, to hold you, even if for a moment. I needed to tell you I love you."

I brought her close. We kissed, lost in a long, deep expression of our love. Then she pushed away from me and studied my eyes. "This is not a staff job, is it? You're going back into battle, aren't you?"

We had never lied to each other; there was far too much respect between us. But she knew sometimes I couldn't tell her everything about my work. "No, it's not a battle. But Rork and I, along with a Marine lieutenant named Edwin Law, have a chance to end this entire mess quickly. If I can, I'll return here in a few days. Is that tub big enough for two?"

She didn't laugh at my jest. "No, it's barely big enough for one. I wish you and Rork were out at sea, Peter. You'd be safer there."

"I'd be far more comfortable, that's for sure. Cuba in July—not the most pleasant time of year to be here, is it? Not to mention the war."

Unlike many married couples, Maria and I had always been the closest of confidants. Perhaps it was because we married at a later age and shared similar life experiences. We both felt the freedom to share, without repercussions, our innermost opinions, dreams, and fears. Over the years our conversations on those topics had been cathartic for each and had strengthened our love. She had never been reticent in expressing her thoughts. But now, as we sat there at the edge of the jungle, both of us miserable in our griminess, I knew she was holding something back—something deep, serious, and painful.

"Tell me what you're thinking."

With that, Maria's pent-up emotions came tumbling out.

"Peter, I have learned more about the depths of human nature in the days I have been at this hospital than I ever imagined in my worst nightmares. The sickening sights here have showed me that war is the ultimate expression of madness. I was never naïve before. The death—the brutal murder—of my son showed me the depravity in some men, but I thought that sort of evil was limited to a very few. This place has opened my eyes to the horror and stupidity of the leadership class of every nation."

I was about to agree, but she wasn't done.

"If I ever hear another politician in Washington, including our friend Theodore, glorify war, I will forget ladylike social constraints and slap him right in the face. Peter, you are the kindest and most gentle man I've ever known in my life. I cannot understand how you could have ever devoted your life's work to this—this brutal insanity. Why?"

Her words stunned me. My wife was questioning my life's work, my purpose. Then they angered me. "Maria, the first war I fought was to free black Americans from slavery. Two of my brothers *died* for that cause. I'll make no apologies and feel no remorse for my role in that war.

"After the Civil War I worked for years to get accurate information to the country's executive decision makers so they *wouldn't* make stupid mistakes and go to war in various places around the world."

I held up a hand when she tried to speak. "No, listen to me for a moment. Do not equate me with the glory-mongers in Washington or Madrid. You damn well know I've devoted years of my life to preventing this war. But politicians in charge on *both* sides wanted it, and everyone has known for a long time it was going to happen eventually. Well, it did, and my job is to make sure our country—the side for freedom for Cuba—wins it.

"Right now I have an opportunity to end this damned thing before it drags on and even more men, thousands more, die. And yes, Maria, I wish to hell Rork and I were at sea too, but we're not. For right now we're stuck ashore, smack dab in the middle of this mess."

The absurdity of my wife being ashore in a battle area and me having to leave her made my anger and voice rise even further. "And let me tell you something else, Maria. I am not thrilled that *you* are *here*. I understand you are committed to doing something positive to help our country, but this is *not* what you should be doing or where you should be doing it. I want you out of here on the first ship heading north."

"You suddenly arrive and start ordering me around? I will leave when I decide to leave."

Maria gets defiant when backed into a corner. Unfortunately, my diatribe had done exactly that. Her commitment to help the sick and wounded stemmed from the personal tragedies she'd endured. It was her way to move forward meaningfully in life, to help right some of the terrible wrongs of the world. Her devotion to peace was at the core of her being and a major source of my respect and love for her. And now I'd dismissed that, just as she'd questioned my core beliefs. The war had done this to us, intruding into our bond, something I'd never thought possible.

I took a slow breath and drew her close again, though she resisted at first. Speaking softly into her ear, I tried to soothe the harshness of my words. "Just please be careful here. Remember, on top of everything else, you are Spanish born—and that makes you the enemy in the eyes of some Americans."

She jerked back. "You think I am ignorant of that? Do not lecture me, Peter. I came here to help heal Americans and Cubans and yes, even Spanish soldiers who are prisoners. This is exactly what the Red Cross is doing, in spite of the U.S. Army Medical Corps' outright rejection of our initial efforts. The Army's prejudice didn't last long once the wounded began to arrive by the hundreds, let me tell you. They were glad enough for our help then."

I reached for her hand, determined to end the acrimony. "Please don't confuse me with them, Maria. Don't confuse my worries with a lack of respect for you. I adore you, but I fear for your safety."

"Maria!" the older nurse called out from the tent. "Time to get the patients ready."

The anger in her face eased, and her eyes misted up again. "I know you love me, Peter." She nuzzled close again. "I love you, too. But I have to go now."

She placed my hand against her soft cheek. "I hate these good-byes. I think we should say say *au revoir*, as we did back at Tampa."

The frightful moment was over. We stood, and I wrapped my arms around her tightly. My eyes were misty too. "It'll never be *adieu* for us, Maria. Only *au revoir* until I return for your love."

I had to add a little levity. "And that bath. We haven't had a bath together for a while. Remember the last time?"

With a shy smile, she reminded me, "I do, but this is a very small tub, Peter."

"We'll find a way."

We kissed again, neither of us wanting to part from the embrace. In the end it was Maria who was stronger and walked away first. I watched her head back down the pathway, my heart filled with worry and admiration for her. I sat there for some time thinking about what she'd said about my career choice, my life. And then I left to find my comrades.

They were in the village sitting under a bullet-scarred coconut palm. Their assignments had gone well. Rork had found food, and Law had obtained new uniforms. Rork even gave Law an accolade, proclaiming him a "first-class purloiner, worthy o' the finest swindlers in the fleet."

First, we ate. Since we were in the rear it was real food—roast beef from the Army officers' mess nearby and a flask of whiskey from a medical chest. Then we changed into the new uniforms, putting the coats into the seabag to protect them from the dirty journey back to the front.

Refreshed to the best extent possible under the circumstances, we joined a column heading up the road to Santiago, a regiment of volunteer infantrymen from New York who had just landed. They were quiet, nervously gaping at the alien sights around them as their boots plowed through the mud in the noonday sun. Several stared at the hospital as they passed by. I asked an officer where they were going. He shrugged and said, "The front at Santiago."

From the hilltop I looked back at the hospital, thinking of my wife working with the wretched sick men inside that sweltering tent. A preposterous sight on the beach abruptly drew my eyes, stopping me in my tracks. Rork and Law stopped and studied it too.

Law asked, "What the hell're they doing down there?"

Down on the beach under some coconut palms, with the blue Caribbean as a backdrop, one of Tom Edison's moving picture crews was filming an officer riding a horse. I'd never seen a film being made, though I had heard a rumor the crews would be in Cuba. Dozens of soldiers from the regiments landing at the pier stood watching as well. A small man in civilian attire shouted directions at the cinematic operators and the man on the horse. The officer reenacted the scene several times, each time waving his hat gallantly for the camera while looking sternly at some imaginary enemy in the distance.

"Well, I'll be damned," Rork muttered. "Those buggers're playin' at war for the folks back home while them actually fightin' it 're livin' an' dyin' in trench mud up there at Santiago with nary a decent bite to eat or tent to sleep in. No wonder this army's so bollocks'd up."

The man on the horse was obviously an actor. He was just too crisp and jaunty to be a real soldier. The blatant theatrics, so unrealistic as to be disgusting to us, would be shown to audiences back in the States as a depiction of our noble conflict in Cuba against the evil Spanish. I had no doubt the film would be quite popular—until the hometown newspapers began publishing the casualty and sick lists.

We rejoined the New Yorkers on the road heading back to the real war.

33

Getting the Lay of the Land

Santiago, Cuba
Saturday, 9 p.m., 2 July 1898

THE ONE NIGHT I needed it to rain in Cuba and cloak us in invisibility it didn't. Instead, the sky was clear of clouds, even over the mountains, for the first since I'd landed on the island weeks before.

As we crept through the low hills, a full moon bathed every nook and cranny in silvery light. We wore our uniform coats to show our nationality and profession—a precaution against being shot outright as spies if caught. Though our uniforms were dark, the moonlight lit up our faces as if by stage gaslights.

With me in the lead, then Rork, and Law in the rear, we slowly made our way through the upland scrub west of the San Juan River. By my reckoning we were heading southwest toward El Morro. Our position was about two miles from the river's mouth at the Caribbean and a mile south of where General Bates' infantry division was gathering at the southern, or left, end of the American military lines facing Santiago. We'd left them an hour earlier in the half-light of dusk and followed the riverbank until I decided we should tack to starboard and head toward the Spanish—wherever they were.

A flat, open area came into view ahead, and we made out the Juraguá Iron Company railroad line stretching from the point where it turned inland on the coast toward Santiago to the north-west. Commercial rail traffic had ceased at the beginning of the war, and I was surprised the Spanish hadn't removed the rails to prevent its use by the Americans. The railroad sighting was good news because it provided a geographical validation of my dead-reckoning land navigation.

We'd arrived at a decision point. Should we follow the tracks to the northwest or continue southwest across the countryside toward the coastal forts? Both courses would be valuable in ascertaining whether the enemy had positioned troops in the area to thwart an American advance. By my estimate, about a mile to the northwest the rail line would intersect with the wagon road between Fort Benefico at Santiago and El Morro at the mouth of the bay. Since that road could be crucial in an attack on either El Morro or Santiago, I chose to follow the rail tracks to the road and then turn left to the southwest toward El Morro, reconnoitering for signs of troops, vehicles, and defensive works along the way.

My two companions offered no objections or better suggestions. We stayed slightly off to the right of the track bed, on constant guard for an ambush. For an hour we headed across a rolling countryside of small sugarcane farms and patches of fruit trees. It was slow going but not unduly difficult. We had not seen a single Spaniard, which made me suspicious. Were they well hidden, or were the Spaniards so short of manpower they didn't have the men to occupy the area?

After crossing over to the left, or west, side of the tracks, we followed a shallow ravine that loosely paralleled the railroad to avoid silhouetting ourselves against the horizon. I had just consulted my pocket watch at 9:38 p.m. when our leisurely hike suddenly ended.

Rippling tongues of flame erupted in front of us with a booming roar. The flashes of light blinded me, but I could tell that at least a platoon had fired a volley at us. Volley fire was a characteristic of the Spanish conscript regulars, as opposed to the Cuban pro-Spanish guerillas and the anti-Spanish Cuban rebel *insurrectos*, who preferred individual fire.

We instinctively hit the deck, with Rork immediately scooting off on his knees to the right to see if there was a route to flank the enemy position or escape their fire. Law came up on my left, his rifle pointed to the south, or left, flank, ready in case they approached from that direction.

The next volley was lower and much closer. I heard the rounds zing right above us—Mausers. The Spanish had corrected their elevation. Rork crawled back and reported men moving toward us on the right. That meant our only option was to head along the ravine to the left. I sent Law to scout it out.

A third volley rang out, followed by an officer shouting for us to surrender, calling us "descendants of Spain." They thought we were Cuban rebels. While I tried to figure out how I could take advantage of their misidentification, Law returned and whispered that the ravine was clear for fifty yards. I told him to lead the way.

So far we had not fired a shot, trying to conceal both our exact position and our meager strength. The enemy platoon came at us from the right as we tried to escape to the left. Significantly, their charge was without the usual bugle call. That omission told me we faced less than a company. Probably a sole platoon on patrol and, if we were lucky, led by an inexperienced junior officer. The next volley, fired from the hip as they charged, went right into the location we'd just vacated. I knew we didn't have much time to escape.

When they were still twenty yards away, Rork and I popped up over the edge of the ravine and let loose with our shotguns. Ducking back down, we followed after Law, who had opened fire from farther down, giving the appearance to the enemy commander of a much larger opponent than he'd originally estimated.

The ravine was getting shallower and more serpentine. As it curved around to the west, away from the tracks, I could see a tree line in the distance. We climbed out of the ravine and headed for that, forgoing further gunfire so as to continue confusing the Spanish as to our whereabouts and strength. This tactic seemed to work, for no more volleys were fired at us. I heard the enemy in the ravine behind us discussing who we were and where we were headed. An older voice, perhaps a sergeant, suggested we were probing their defenses to the west. A younger and more uncertain voice averred the patrol had scared off the intruders, who had fled east, toward the protection of the yanqui lines.

After running for another couple of minutes, we stopped and took a breath, listening for the Spanish. The railroad tracks were some thirty or forty yards ahead.

Rork tapped my shoulder and pointed to something on the track. "Do me eyes deceive me, sir, or did the Spaniardos leave their rail handcar transport out in the open? A bit stupid, that."

He was right. Handcars were not just left out in the open in wartime Cuba. This one must belong to the Spanish army patrol we had just encountered. It looked big enough to carry several people—probably the officer in charge, a couple of privates to work the motive levers, and some light supplies.

It was also blessedly perfect for our purposes.

It took but a few seconds to arrive at the contraption and clamber on board. None of us had ever operated a handcar, but how hard could it be? It wasn't as if you had to steer the damned thing.

Law and Rork began to work the seesaw levers. I kept a lookout ahead and astern as we began to roll northwest. Unfortunately, this was an ancient mechanical beast. Clearly, it hadn't had an effective greasing in quite some time. The wheels began to squeak. The faster we went, the louder the squeaking got.

An angry voice shouted in Spanish from the spot from where we'd spied the handcar. They must have followed our footprints then heard the car. Shots, at first ragged, then more regulated, began heading in our direction.

I joined in pumping the lever. The rail track was on a loose bed, and the car swayed like a boat in a beam sea. As we pushed and pulled on the lever, I felt the tracks ascending slightly. Pumping became far more arduous. At last, gasping for breath, we topped a rise and began to coast downward. This allowed us to rest, but I realized I didn't know how to stop or slow our beast. While I was looking for the handbrake, Law spotted a line across the horizon and brought it to our attention.

"I think it's the Morro road," I replied. "The intersection should be just before those hills far on the starboard bow. That puts El Morro only about two and a half miles to our port side."

Somewhat needlessly, Law added, "Except for that patrol, this area looks wide open, sir."

Rork noted, "Aye, that it is, sir. But this thing's squeakin' like a pig in a lion pit, so those buggers back there'll know right where the hell we are. We've got the lay o' the land now, so perhaps we should get off the car here an' go on foot. We can set a southerly course for a mile across this farm country an' then veer to port a bit an' make our way east. We'll reach Bates' division in plenty o' time to report the good news to General Shafter. It's gettin' late, an' remember, he wants it by midnight."

We were rolling faster now, but there was an incline ahead where we could coast to a stop. I was on the verge of agreeing with Rork's idea when a loud thud jolted us. The handcar tilted up and off the rails, careening over onto the track bed to the left and throwing us off into the bushes. For several seconds there was silence, then our muffled cursing as we checked for cuts and breaks. Miraculously, none of us was pinned beneath the handcar.

While Law and Rork searched for our weapons, which had been flung somewhere into the bushes along with the seabag, I looked at the railcar, then the track, to confirm a suspicion. There it was—an iron bar wedged into the track at an angle between two track ties.

The track had been sabotaged. An ambush? At first I thought the Cuban rebels had done it to hinder the Spanish, but that notion was soon dispelled.

"Good evening, gentlemen. I am Comandante Alberto Marino of His Catholic Majesty's Forces in Cuba. Please do not resist me or my soldiers, for it would be a great pity to kill you now that your war is over."

The genteel voice in perfect English came from a nearby stand of palm and papaya trees, accompanied by the sound of at least twenty rifle bolts ramming home in preparation to shoot us. Other forms rose up from the bushes a few yards away—the soldiers were in a classic L-shaped ambush. They kept their distance at five yards, too far away for us to jump them and cause confusion. These were not amateurs. Marino issued orders in Spanish. He spoke rapidly, like a Cuban. From Havana or Matanzas, I guessed.

Not having found our shotguns and rifle yet, we had no choice but to raise our hands in surrender. Rork muttered an indelicate phrase in Gaelic as Law, who seemed to be losing his normal reserve, followed suit in English. The Spanish troops said nothing, their faces grimly watching us. Yanquis were known to be tricky.

Marino stepped toward me, came to attention, and saluted, complete with clicking heels. After I tardily returned the salute, not clicking, he said, "I see by your gold sleeve lace that you are a senior naval officer, sir. Would you be so kind to inform me whom I have the pleasure meeting on this beautiful evening in Oriente?"

Damnation. They had us, pure and simple.

"Captain Peter Wake, United States Navy. This is Lieutenant Edwin Law, United States Marines, and Chief Boatswain's Mate Sean Rork, United States Navy."

"Thank you, sir. It is a great honor to have you all as my prisoners. You will be well taken care of as our professional guests and also kept safe from harm. And now, we shall take you to Colonel Melgar at El Morro. He will also be quite pleased to meet you, I am sure."

I have been a "professional guest" of my opponents several times over the years. One of the most useful strategies in that event is to establish a personal rapport with your wardens. It helps to disarm their wariness.

"Your English is very good, Comandante. Where did you learn it?" I asked.

"I am very proud to say I became conversant with the language of Shakespeare at the Yale School of Fine Arts, class of '93," he said. "In normal life I am a painter. But alas, these are not normal times."

"Did you know a Cuban engineer named Alfonso Fortuna during your time at Harvard? You both graduated the same year."

His face light up in the moonlight. "Why, yes, I did! Alfonso is a fine man. We first met at a sporting event and occasionally met afterward to partake of refreshments in New Haven and Cambridge. I last saw him at Santiago in '95. Regrettably, Alfonso joined the side of the enemies of Spain in this sad war. I, of course, was duty bound to support my sovereign and my country. If you know him, please present my felicitations the next time you see him, though that may be quite a while."

"Sorry to tell you this, but Alfonso was killed in the recent battle at San Juan Heights."

Marino shook his head mournfully. "A tragic, senseless waste."

A sergeant cleared his throat pointedly, bringing the comandante back to the present. The soldiers still had their rifles aimed at our hearts. Marino nodded to the sergeant, who told his men to search us. Their examination of me was cursory, and though they took Law's and Rork's big Navy Colt revolvers, they missed the smaller revolver hidden inside the front of my waistband.

"It is now time for us to go, Captain Wake," Marino said pleasantly. "We have a wagon on the road, so the journey will not be so arduous for you and your companions. I am glad your war is over and you will not face its terror and death anymore."

Rork's eyes met mine. I knew he was thinking the same as me. Marino was a bon vivant, not a warrior, whom societal and familial expectations had thrust into the most uncivilized experience of his life. In peacetime we'd be drinking together, discussing art and history and women. But it wasn't peacetime. Marino was unprepared and sloppy, the enemy's weakest link.

Killing him was going to make me sad, but it was necessary.

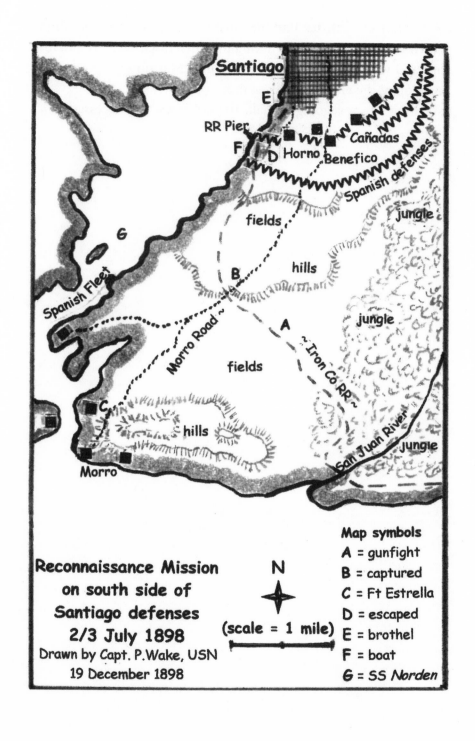

Santiago

E

RR Pier

F
D Horno Benefico Cañadas

Spanish defenses

fields

jungle

G

hills

B

jungle

Spanish Fleet

A ~Iron Co RR~

Morro Road

fields

jungle

C

hills

San Juan River

Jungle

Morro

**Reconnaissance Mission
on south side of
Santiago defenses
2/3 July 1898**
Drawn by Capt. P.Wake, USN
19 December 1898

N

(scale = 1 mile)

Map symbols
A = gunfight
B = captured
C = Ft Estrella
D = escaped
E = brothel
F = boat
G = SS *Norden*

34

An Exquisitely Pleasant Failure

El Morro de Santiago, Santiago Bay, Cuba
Saturday Night, 2 July 1898

ONCE WE REACHED THE seaside ridge along the coast, I noted a fortified battery of four modern field artillery pieces. They appeared to be Model 1895 Krupp 75s, a rapid-fire light fieldpiece with a range of two miles. Their muzzles were pointed inland. Rork and I exchanged worried glances at that development.

I also noticed that sentries along this bumpy road had called ahead, presumably by telephone line, relaying that a high-ranking American prisoner was coming. No one seemed surprised to see us. Many stared with open curiosity. After an hour or so we arrived at the torch-lit entry of El Morro's outer defenses on the inland side.

El Castillo San Pedro de la Rocha, commonly known as El Morro, was an imposing sight with its parapets outlined against the moonlit sea and sky. For more than two hundred years it had kept Santiago safe. For the previous ninety years it had also served as an infamous prison for those considered disloyal to Spain—and now would do so for three foreign prisoners of war.

When the wagon stopped and we disembarked, we were met with solemn pomp and ceremony. A guard of honor was drawn up, and the commander, introduced only as Colonel Melgar, clearly a gentleman of the highest caliber, met us in full dress uniform. He pronounced it an honor to receive such brave warriors of a noble foe. Once this public display was completed, he quietly bid me to enter his private apartments. His invitation included the offer of a cognac, an 1869 Rémy Martin. Taken aback by such hospitality, I found it difficult to remember I was a prisoner of war. I accepted the invitation with sincere gratitude.

Melgar and I strolled sociably through the zigzagged outer walls and over the large drawbridge spanning the twenty-foot-deep and forty-foot-wide dry moat surrounding the main castle. Once through the main gate and inside the massive walls, under the eyes of Spanish soldiers the entire time, we descended some stairs to a small plaza, across which a working party was lugging powder charges to some cannon emplaced on the seaward parapet that were at least a century old.

Melgar saw my reaction and laughed. "For close-in defense. The modern long-range guns are in our accompanying fortifications."

He led the way up another three flights of stairs to his personal quarters. I was drawn immediately to the private patio overlooking the Caribbean. I stood there for a moment, savoring the sight of our inner night patrol of gunboats and light cruisers a mere three miles away, the battleships farther offshore.

"They come in closer at night and return farther out at sunrise," said the colonel, gauging my mind. "But I must tell you they won't be able to come in and rescue you. Our big guns and sea mines worry them."

"Prudent precautions," I replied. "But I must admit, Colonel, that I am of no consequence to the war effort. They have lots of time to wait for your fleet to come out to them. Ships in a harbor are useless in war."

"I agree with your opinion of the American and Spanish fleets but must disagree on your opinion of your worth. Full naval captains do not wander through the night in enemy territory by mistake or for their pleasure. Your excursion was for a profound military purpose."

He chuckled and motioned to a chair, as if we were old friends, a disarming gesture. We relaxed on the butter-soft leather in the warm glow from wall sconces. Paintings by Spanish artists lined the walls, and intricately patterned Moroccan rugs covered the stone floor. The cognac was proffered and accepted, and tasted damn good. A silent orderly served Galician empanadas that proved to be a marvelous pairing with the Rémy. I felt my mood mellowing.

I hasten to add that this unexpected luxury, so vastly different from our recent war experiences, was not limited to me alone. Rork was whisked away to the senior sergeants' quarters for congenial refreshments involving copious amounts of rum. Mr. Law was taken to the junior officers' mess for refreshments that included wine. Admittedly, we had failed in our mission to bring back information to the commanding general by the appointed hour of midnight. But as military failures go, this was turning out to be an exquisitely pleasant one.

A gentleman and epicure of the highest order, Colonel Melgar engaged me for more than an hour in amiable conversation about all manner of things—family, cuisine, travel, spirits—everything except war. Of my family I was circumspect, for reasons the reader well understands. To my immense relief, the colonel didn't seem to have prior knowledge about my marital connection to Spain.

In fact, I can honestly say Colonel Melgar was the most generous prison host I've known during my long career. This is no idle accolade, for I've met an extensive catalogue of prison wardens on six continents.

Of course, all this conviviality was by design. Lubricated by the cognac and the sudden release of anxiety over whether I would be shot as a spy, I relaxed. As the third glass eased the atmosphere, Melgar adroitly turned the conversation to the cultural aspects of the island of Cuba. I could tell he was pleased with his performance and his apparent growing rapport with his prisoner.

Next he segued into empathy for Cuban independence, respect for the goals of the Americans in Cuba, and regret for the carnage both sides were sure to suffer in the event of an assault on Santiago.

To his subtle but insistent queries I pleaded ignorance, maintaining my diminishing masquerade as a mere squadron staff sailor lost ashore who turned in the wrong direction on his way back to the coast and the fleet.

Melgar didn't believe my story in the least, but he never said so, always hoping for a tidbit of information that might prove useful. This gentle inducement and parrying continued for two amiable hours. The level in the bottle had lowered considerably when he mentioned he was now sending my companions and me to the area's commanding officer in Santiago, Major General José Toral. Ignoring the ominous implications of my change in address, I decided to get some intelligence of my own.

Expressing surprise that Toral was now in command, I asked about Lieutenant General Arsenio Linares, the acknowledged supreme commander of eastern Cuba. Without letting on his view of the developments, Melgar explained Linares had been badly wounded in the fighting at Santiago and his survival was in doubt. This was a hitherto unknown piece of information for me and, I surmised, would be for Shafter as well. It cast a different light on the future of the campaign for Santiago. Linares was known as a soldier's soldier, a man who could and would fight. He was highly respected among the senior Americans. Toral was largely an enigma to us. I decided to wax philosophical.

"My dear Colonel Melgar," I said pleasantly, the cognac slurring my words just a bit. "I do hope General Toral understands the futility of further Spanish bloodshed from the American onslaught. I'm certain a respectable armistice could be arranged, one that would satisfy Spanish honor, along with transport for your army back to Spain. In fact, my friend, we could write the document ourselves now, here in his parlor. After all, I see there is still some cognac left. We could have the entire thing done by sunrise and save thousands of lives."

"Surrender?" Melgar's congenial expression instantly hardened into a stone-cold stare, which said it all. I had been an unappreciative and rude guest, divulging no intelligence, drinking his fine cognac, and making a mockery of his interrogation. The faux friendship was over.

The colonel stood and said, "Spaniards do not surrender." And with that he departed.

I was left alone in the room, but not without diversions. Realizing things were most likely about to get far worse, I had another glass of his excellent cognac while analyzing the situation.

We would be transported a fair distance through the night to our new prison inside the city of Santiago. This was an opportunity, for it is far easier to escape from a wagon than from the inside of a cell in the center of a 280-year-old fortress.

When they came for me a few minutes later, the last of Colonel Melgar's Rémy Martin was gone.

35

Memories of Santiago

The Morro–Santiago Road, Santiago, Cuba
Saturday Night after Midnight, 3 July 1898

COMANDANTE MARINO appeared at the doorway with Rork and Law, both of them glassy-eyed with drink. Rork sniffed the air, spotted the decanter of cognac, and edged toward it. When he saw it was empty he sighed his disappointment.

I wasn't worried about my companions divulging secret information. Rork can be falling-down drunk and not let go of his inner faculties, at least where secrets are concerned. Law was young but not naïve, and I'd seen him handle rum well. Besides, neither of them knew the entirety of Shafter's possible secret alteration to the grand campaign plan, for I'd followed orders and kept it to myself. I'd told them that our mission was only a local probe along the river, and that I had to report our findings by midnight. Though he didn't let on, I was sure Rork surmised the real reason for our exploration when we ended up so far beyond the American lines.

Marino was far more subdued now, almost embarrassed, as he silently led us across the drawbridge back to the outer gate, where the same wagon awaited us. No pomp attended our departure, only sullen looks. This time the entourage included an additional cart, in which I saw our seabag with our weapons along with some large boxes and a small barrel. Marino explained the seabag had been found and the contents examined. He added that each item was carefully returned to the bag afterward, including the weapons, for General Toral's personal inspection. There was also a mounted escort of half a dozen cavalrymen, their well-groomed horses glistening in the torchlight.

We departed the magnificent fortress as the night guards were calling out their midnight checks. I began surreptitiously scrutinizing our wagon, the driver, Comandante Marino, the extra cart, and the mounted escort for any opportunities. The escorts were regulars led by a veteran sergeant. They would be difficult to surprise and overwhelm. On the other hand, I had six bullets in my hidden revolver and another six in my pocket.

I decided on a plan to overpower the Spaniards on our wagon as soon as we reached the intersection of the road and the railroad tracks. I would shoot as many of the cavalrymen as I could while Rork and Law leaped on the second wagon to retrieve the seabag and our long guns. We'd then commandeer three horses, shoot the others to preclude pursuit, and ride at full speed to the east along the trail paralleling the tracks to gain the American lines.

If even one of the three of us could make it back, our report would be two or three hours late but still important. Shafter would know the Spanish had left the area vacant of sizable forces but maintained numerous patrols. The attack would shorten the war if there was still time enough to implement his attack plan before the Spanish realized their error and reinforced the area.

My hastily concocted scheme didn't come to fruition, however. As we approached the intersection, Marino and his men got edgy, drawing their weapons and looking keenly about for any ambuscade. After all, it was the area where they'd captured us, and they didn't know if more Americans were lurking. The sergeant watched me in particular, his carbine laid across the saddle, muzzle pointed in my direction.

When we reached the junction with the railroad, instead of continuing straight along the road toward Santiago, as I expected, the driver took a sharp left onto the rough trail alongside the railroad tracks. We were now headed west toward the shoreline of the bay, away from the American lines. Marino offered no explanation for the detour.

I soon realized this deviation had a potential silver lining. We were no longer headed to the city center by the usual direct route, but by a longer one, nearer the bay. Were we to be turned over to Admiral Pascual Cervera, commander of the Spanish fleet in Santiago Bay? Any route close to water was preferable, for water of any kind is a place of relative safety for a sailor. Also, the trail alongside the tracks was much higher and drier than the rutted Morro road, making for far more comfortable riding.

We reached the top of a hill, from which I saw the city to the north and the bay to the west. Visible in the moon-washed darkness was the line of forts and blockhouses arrayed along the edge of the suburbs. Fort Horno was nearest the bay, Fort Benefico farther east. Farther inland to the right was Fort Cañadas. Interspersed between them were smaller blockhouses and trenches.

The trail took a broad right curve to the north, rising in elevation. The bay was only a quarter mile below on our left now. I could see warships at anchor, the famous Spanish fleet. Those ships could devastate the eastern seaboard of the United States within days if they escaped from Santiago. Neither the U.S. Navy nor the U.S. Army had sufficient assets to protect every port from Maine to Texas. I was looking at the primary reason the Americans had even come to Santiago.

A roadblock was ahead, with earthworks and barricades extending to either side. It was one of the few entrances through the city's defense perimeter. There were too many soldiers at the roadblock for us to try anything there. Our opportunity would have to be farther up the track, before we entered the city itself.

I glanced at Rork as we stopped while an officer examined Marino's papers. They exchanged greetings in a friendly manner. The soldiers at the post were chattering as they studied the yanqui prisoners. Rork shrugged slightly and mouthed the words "not here." Law was lying on his side, apparently passed out.

Before waving us through, the roadblock officer offered Marino congratulations on his wedding the next day. My Spanish is less than fluent, but I got the gist. Marino sheepishly thanked him, adding he was the luckiest man in the world.

Rork forced a cough, looking at me with eyebrows raised. Neither of us had wanted to kill Marino before, and now those sentiments were deepened. Law sat up, sensing something was about to happen, and I realized he'd been shamming the drunken demeanor. His eyes darted between Rork and me, signaling he was ready for whatever we came up with.

The column got under way again. The city and its vital defense line were a half mile ahead. A spur line branched off the railroad to the left toward a large pier on the bay, only two hundred yards away. We passed the side path alongside the spur line leading to the pier, ending my hope of being taken out to the Spanish flagship as Admiral Cervera's guest. The main tracks ended a short way beyond, but the road continued toward the city.

We would have to make our move soon. The driver and Marino were up on the box seat forward. The three of us were sitting on the cargo bed behind them Indian fashion. Two horsemen were out ahead, and two were directly behind the wagon, their carbines unholstered and ready for service. Astern of those two fellows was the cart with our seabag, driven by a shriveled man with a sickly wheeze. The other soldiers were riding as a rear guard behind it.

I mentally went over my plan. I would leap upon the driver and Marino, knock them off the wagon, then turn aft to shoot the two soldiers closest to us. I knew—after working with a man for thirty years you are instinctively *certain* what actions he will take in an emergency—Rork would go for the cart and retrieve our long guns, thence to fire at the rear guard. Lieutenant Law was in the stern of the wagon bed, and I trusted him to help Rork when the time came. Though our route of escape to the American lines was cut off, we could get to the bay and escape that way.

If this notion seems impossible to the reader, it sounded equally absurd in my brain. Given the dire situation, though, it was the best I could come up with.

As we got to the midpoint between the outer and inner defense lines, I slowly shifted my position into a kneeling crouch, ready to spring forward. It was now or never. Rork loosened his false left hand, the better to quickly employ the marlinespike concealed therein, and also drew his legs beneath him. I glanced meaningfully at Law and then aft at the cart following us. He followed my eyes and nodded his understanding.

It was time. My hand slowly moved to the sideboard in order to steady my leap upon Marino and the driver.

Suddenly, from a path on the right came the rumbling sound of many hooves. Seconds later, forty horsemen appeared through a fruit grove, loping in a column toward us. The officer at the front hailed Marino with something I couldn't make out as we passed them. The cavalry column wheeled to their right onto the road behind our rear guard, joining the procession toward the city. There were now fifty Spanish soldiers within twenty yards of the wagon.

"Luck o' the ever-bleedin' Irish," growled Rork under his breath.

The city itself and another army checkpoint were directly ahead. Beyond the inner defense works I saw the twin-spired cathedral in the city's center, which I recognized from my last visit inside Santiago de Cuba twelve years earlier. A large building, the city gasworks, was visible closer to us, standing out against the silhouettes of other structures behind it. The sight jogged my memory, sparking an idea.

"Rork," I said barely audibly, so as to not alert our guardians. "Do you remember our time here back in '86?"

"Aye, sir, that I do. Hated every bloody bit'uv it," he huffed back in a whisper. "Except for me little romp at Clara's place, o' course— the one pleasure for me durin' the whole affair. An' then, just when things were goin' grand you came along an' dragged me out o' there. Damned inconsiderate of ye, not to mention bad timin'. Was in me glory, I was, or damned near."

Fortunately, Marino was bantering with the driver about the joys of love, marriage, and having lots of children, and thereby missed his prisoners' discussion. Law, however, was listening intently. For his benefit I briefly recounted that earlier night in Santiago.

"Now, Rork, you seem to have forgotten you were drunk at a whorehouse when you were supposed to be with me, meeting our operative at the Royal Theater. In your absence I had to face some rather irate fellows on my own. But never mind that, it's ancient history and beside the point, which is that the brothel is somewhere near the gasworks, right?"

Instantly catching my intent, Rork cheered up. "Nay, sir, it's in the middle o' town. Why'd ye ask?"

"I'm drawing a blank on the exact location of Clara's place. Can you remember any landmarks?"

"Well, sir, truth be told, that night's a bit'uv a blur. There was considerable drinkin' goin' on." His face furrowed in concentration. "Ah, but I've a foggy recollection o' passin' the cathedral on the way. Aye, an' beyond that, I passed a taverna full o' Spaniardo soldiers. Gunners, if me memory serves, an' drunk as coots, they were. Trod carefully when goin' by that place, let me tell ye."

That rang a bell. I remembered the soldiers' tavern. It was near the artillery barracks, about two blocks east of the cathedral on the main street from the central plaza.

"Yes, and the brothel was in a side alleyway about two streets east of the tavern and four streets south. Then I turned left and the alley was off to the left, halfway down the street. Correct?"

"I think so, but me memory o' that night's mush."

"Understandable, Rork. I was regrettably sober that night. You were regrettably not. The place wasn't much to look at, pretty run down."

"Aye, 'twas a nasty-lookin' place on the outside, but ooh, on the inside it was a veritable palace o' love an' comfort for a lonely soul. Clara her own self met me at the door, an' a true lady she was. From a Spanish colony in North Africa. Melilla, I think. Skin a bit on the dark side. Hell'uva girl, though. I wonder if she's still there . . ."

Up front on the driver's seat, Marino was still in an animated discussion, but the topic had switched to rum. The prisoners' talk among themselves, clearly sprinkled with humor, appeared to generate no worry or interest for our Spanish guardians. After all, we were surrounded and well behind enemy lines. What could we possibly do?

I leaned over and said, "Rork, I really hope you left a good and long-lasting impression on Clara."

He snorted indignantly. "O' course I did, sir! There's nary a cheap bone in me body. Got to maintain me reputation with these lasses, for ye just never know when you'll be needin' their attention next time in port."

Then he caught the hidden meaning of my query. "Oohee, what devilish scheme's brewin' in that head o' yours?"

"I think we'll be needing Clara's attention tonight."

Lieutenant Law smiled.

36

The Wedding Present

Santiago de Cuba, Cuba
Saturday Night after Midnight, 3 July 1898

THE GUARD POST OF THE city's inner defense perimeter on the shoreline road was manned by Cuban militia reservists grudgingly serving their required time in the Spanish army. They were considerably less diligent in their duties than the regulars on the outer defense line. It was late on a Saturday night, and they probably had their minds on more pleasurable endeavors than the subjugation of their rebellious fellow islanders. The dreaded yanquis were still well outside town. Following a perfunctory check of Marino's papers, the lieutenant gave a sloppy salute and waved us forward. The whole thing took a mere thirty seconds.

We rolled on, passing by the gasworks, with its uniquely malevolent smell. Seconds later we went over an equally odorous drainage creek and entered the great city itself. One hundred yards into the city the dirt road became a paved street, the Calle de Cristina. This main waterfront thoroughfare of the city was named for the regent queen mother of the current twelve-year-old king of Spain, Alfonso XIII. Four blocks onward, the cavalry troopers turned to the right up Calle de Santa Lucia toward their barracks on the eastern edge of the city.

At this hour the streets were deserted and dark except for some weak streetlamps. The steady clip-clop of our horses echoed off the centuries-old walls, sounding loud and funereal in the still air. According to the Cuban rebels, many civilian inhabitants had fled Santiago. Those who remained were starving. Few were out in the streets.

I surveyed our remaining escort, now slumped in their saddles. They looked bored. Their carbines were secured in their saddle scabbards. We were in a heavily protected space now, our destination only a quarter mile away. Even Marino had nothing more to say to the driver and had lapsed into a pensive state. I could guess his thoughts. Soon he would be rid of his yanqui charges and could begin his wedding leave.

This moment was our last chance.

The driver's and Marino's silence meant they could hear what was happening directly behind them. Our whispered conversations were at an end. Communication would have to be by gesture and expression, and there wasn't much time.

Catching Rork's eye, I touched my chest and canted my head toward Marino and the driver. Rork's chin bobbed slightly in acknowledgment. I slowly turned my gaze behind us to the cart and the rear guard, then returned it to Rork, giving him a questioning glance. He twisted his false hand for an answer. We both looked at Law, who had been watching our pantomime. I stretched my elbow back at the cart and the rear guard sauntering along behind it. Law took a deep breath and gravely nodded.

It was time. I held up three fingers, then two, then one.

Leaping forward, I used every ounce of my strength to push the driver across the box seat into Marino. Both men sprawled overboard to starboard with arms flailing and landed on the hard road with a thud. Turning aft, I pulled my Merwin-Hulbert revolver, momentarily closing my right eye to preserve night vision but keeping my left open. I fired two shots toward our immediate rear guard of two cavalrymen, the flash and sound shattering the night. The first target, the sergeant, was hit high in the chest and fell backward in the saddle as his horse veered off to the right. The other shot missed, but the soldier was so startled he bungled drawing his own carbine. He fell from my third shot.

I climbed onto the driver's seat and grabbed the reins, whipping them down on the horses' rumps to make them go faster. By this time Rork and Law had jumped off the wagon, bounding two strides before springing up on the flustered old cart driver. Rork managed to grab his arm and fling him off. Law sprang up to the driver's seat and seized control of the confused pony, accelerating the cart up toward the wagon. While all this was happening, Rork jumped up into the bed of the cart and grabbed his shotgun from the bag. Thankfully, it was still loaded. Blasting two shells of double-aught buck astern into the last Spanish mounted troopers who were trying to aim and fire, he knocked down two. The others fired back, then sheered off to starboard, escaping down a side street.

In this sudden pandemonium, the wagon's horses went beyond reason or control, bucking and swerving from one side of the street to the other. It became impossible for me to steer the wagon or return fire astern. The issue was settled when Law brought the cart up alongside to port. Law being clearly more adept at driving, I decided to jump ship to the cart. My leap of faith landed me atop Rork, pushing him backward and damn near overboard. Just then the horsemen reappeared astern, riding full speed for us. Rork threw some cargo boxes at them. One of the Spanish troopers loosed off a round that nearly did me in. The gunfire had the effect of escalating the cart pony's abject fear, and the little devil did his best to flee the scene, outracing the newly vacated wagon.

Off we went, clattering north along Calle de Cristina past a row of dockside warehouses. Behind us, the wagon's terrified horses, now freed from my attempts to drive them, frantically swung to the right to get away from the commotion. The wagon heeled over to port, capsizing an instant later atop a pile of thrashing hooves. The crash blocked the path of the cavalrymen and forced them to a scrambling halt as we raced away.

I heard Marino's angry shout come up the street. "Shoot them! Shoot the damned yanquis!"

In the insanity of the moment I yelled back, "Happy wedding, my friend! Your life is my wedding present to your fiancée!"

There was no answer. A hundred yards ahead we faced another danger. The guards at the Spanish navy's shore headquarters had rushed out into the street to ascertain the nature of the miniature battle they were hearing. In seconds we were among them. Shots were fired by both sides to no obvious effect, but fifty feet dead ahead, an officer had a rifle leveled at me.

Law swerved the cart right onto the most famous street in Santiago, Calle de Catedral. We bounced our way east up the relatively steep incline through the center of the city. Behind us, the cavalrymen had gotten past the wrecked wagon and reached the turn. They fired up the street at us, the shots ricocheting off the walls close around us.

Lamps flared alight in windows. Shouts and police whistles came from every direction. Figures emerged from doorways then ducked back inside. I concentrated on recalling the city's geography, navigating for Law as Rork continued to send blasts of buckshot at our pursuers.

At Calle de San Juan, only a block away from the cathedral overlooking the central Plaza de la Reina, we veered to the right again and raced south for three blocks. This street changes name to Nepomuceno and narrows as you go south. I quickly realized we were heading away from Clara's, or where I thought Clara's was, and back toward the city's inner defense perimeter. That wouldn't do at all, so when we reached Calle de Santa Rita I had Law make an abrupt right turn. Once through the turn, all hands jumped overboard while the cart and pony rumbled down the sloping street toward the bay.

Though bruised and battered from landing on the cobblestones, we had no time to waste. We hobbled toward a narrow alleyway, where we hid behind a stack of empty orange crates. As we regained our breath I took stock of our condition. None of us was hit by the gunfire. We still had the seabag containing our shotguns and ammunition. We were only a few streets from the brothel. Once we got there we could hide until the streets calmed down.

They weren't calm now. A Spanish mounted patrol appeared, cautiously trotting down the street with their carbines at the ready. They came not from our pursuers behind us but from the other direction. Obviously, we'd woken the entire city, and both the army and the constabulary had been mobilized.

A file of infantry approached on a side street. I heard another one call out from a block away. The Spanish were combing the waterfront first, then systematically moving up into the city. I intended to be gone by the time they examined our alleyway. We started moving east through the alleys to the brothel.

It took an hour to get there, one very vigilant step at a time.

37

Madam Clara

La Casa de Placeres Celestiales, Santiago de Cuba
Saturday Night after Midnight, 3 July 1898

A GIRL ATTIRED IN an ill-fitting satin dress and thick face paint answered our furtive knocks. The garish cosmetics couldn't hide her cynical eyes. After coldly calculating our potential for pecuniary gain or physical danger, she flatly asked what we wanted.

In the streets around us, the sounds of soldiers and horses were getting louder. The net was closing in. I nudged Rork to do or say something.

With his kindest voice and most beguiling smile, Rork asked for his old friend Doña Clara, which I thought a rather ostentatious title for the circumstances. His Irish-accented Spanish and ridiculous gallantry worked, however, for without a word in reply the girl opened the door wider. She gestured for us to enter the tiny anteroom, a gloomy space containing four simple chairs along the wall. An even gloomier passageway led off the room. Rork's description wasn't holding up well.

Still studying us closely, she closed the door and slid the bolt home, locking the door against the troubles outside. She obviously connected the commotion with us. Motioning curtly for us to remain in place, the girl disappeared down the hallway.

Misgivings mounting by the second, I held my reloaded revolver under my uniform jacket, ready for use. The three of us stood in the center of the room, back to back in a triangle, with Rork watching the hallway, myself the side door, and Law the front door.

Rork broke the silence. "Maybe this wasn't the best'uv ideas, sir. We're trapped."

My mood was less than charitable. "Brilliant assessment of the obvious, Rork. And this place is hardly the elegant palace you remembered."

"Sorry, sir."

He actually sounded contrite. I tried to sound confident. "All right, men, if things go badly, we'll fight our way to the roof and escape over the tops of the buildings."

"Aye, like Havana in '88," said Rork in a lighter mood. He gave Law a roguish look. "Now *that* was a dicey deal, indeed. Someday over a glass or two I'll tell ye that story, Mr. Law."

The girl returned several minutes later and ushered us down the hallway. We followed her past several closed doors, behind one of which was the room where I'd found Rork years earlier. We headed around a corner toward another substantial door like the one in front, which I surmised was the back door to an alley. This part of the brothel was more genteel, with paintings on the walls and carpet on the floor. We ascended some stairs to the second floor, where we approached yet another thick door, behind which I could hear a woman singing opera rather bizarrely off key.

The girl opened the door and led us into a red velvet boudoir decorated in a plush French style. A bad copy of a Persian carpet covered most of the floor. Wallpaper portraying Parisian scenes graced the walls. On one side, two chaise lounges, a sofa, and three leather wingback chairs were grouped around a coffee table holding a decanter of brandy and four glasses. A large four-poster bed with a red satin coverlet and lace-trimmed muslin draperies took up the other side. Two red-shaded lamps beside the bed provided faint light. On one wall was a large print of a Goya nude. Cloyingly sweet perfume scented the air.

On a table near the bed I saw the source of the strange music. It was a relatively new Berliner gramophone, unevenly playing an Italian opera singer's rendition of the final scene from *Tosca*. Apparently, the summer humidity was affecting the machine's efficiency, and thus the lady's performance. Memories emerged of hearing that same opera performed by my friend Sarah Bernhardt at the Grand Tacon Theater of Havana ten years earlier with the Spanish viceroy at my side.

Taking a moment to sniff the liquor before pouring it, I found it to be a Spanish Jerez of a lesser grade, but serviceable given our straits. I offered Rork a glass, which he gratefully accepted. Law demurred. I poured myself three fingers' worth while surveying the room more closely. It had no other window or door, either obvious or hidden. That was good for privacy—but meant no alternative escape route.

The girl departed, closing the door with a soft thud. Law glanced nervously around the lavish den of iniquity, and I wondered if it was the first he'd ever seen. By his hesitancy to touch anything I decided it was. Having no such qualms and realizing there was nothing more to do, I reclined on the sofa and sipped my brandy, waiting for what might come through the door.

Moments later, the lady herself entered the room just as the recording wound down in a sick wail and stopped. A theatrically ominous entrée if ever there was one. I stood politely and took in her appearance, which was formidable.

Clad in a yellow satin dress that molded her ample form a bit too tightly, Clara looked much older than I remembered her. Her upswept black hair, which appeared to be the result of badly applied bootblack, and the thick layers of powder and rouge on her face could not disguise her age, which I gauged to actually be about forty-five. She might have been treated to the worst life has to offer, but she displayed total self-assurance, her eyes flashing as she studied each of us. I instantly knew Clara would be difficult to coerce or cajole and was capable of any treachery.

I also noted she showed no recognition of Rork, which appeared to deflate my friend a bit. She did, however, recognize American naval rank insignia. Ignoring Rork and Law, who were closer to her, she glided over to where I stood. Holding out her gloved hand to be kissed, she introduced herself to me in rough but serviceable English. "Good evening, Captain. I am Mrs. Clara Aguila. Welcome to La Casa de Placeres Celestiales."

The House of Celestial Pleasures? That's a bit pretentious for this dump, I thought. However, I kept my opinion to myself. My preference is always to start out being nice, so I bowed and took the hand in mine, pecking her wrist.

"It is an honor to meet you, Señora Aguila, and to see your magnificent establishment of love, which is especially needed in this lamentable time of war."

"Yes, war is always to be lamented," she replied graciously. "It interferes with pleasure—and business. To what do I owe the honor of your visit, Captain?"

I poured the lady a hefty slug of her own brandy, presented it to her with a flourish, and extended my arm in Rork's direction. "We arrive here as a result of the recommendation of my esteemed colleague. He still has pleasant memories of visiting your emporium twelve years ago."

Rork stepped forward and reminded her of the circumstances of their last encounter. Clara listened carefully, a slight smile crossing her wrinkled face.

"Ah, yes. I remember now. Your happiness was stopped by this man," she said, giving me a frown before returning her interest to Rork. She reached up and caressed his cheek. "But I remember you still pay me, though, like a gentleman. A very *handsome* gentleman."

Rork threw me an arch glance before returning his attention to Clara.

"Thank you, madam," he said, turning up his charm to its full effect. "Does me a world o' good to know you remember me as fondly as I remember you. 'Twas shapin' up to be a lovely night back then, an' a shame me naval duty interrupted. But better late than never, I say, so I've come back for a visit tonight, an' brought two o' me boyos along too."

She fluttered her eyelashes at Law, leaning forward to better show him her feminine charms, which had seen better days. "And such a nice boy, this one," she said breathlessly. "Very nice boy."

The lieutenant blushed and took a step back, stammering something. Clara went back to caressing Rork and broached the question I knew would be second uppermost in her mind. "I do not see American sailors since last year, before the war. So sad. Why are you boys here now?"

Rork waved away any worries. "Oh, Clara, me dear, it seems we're in a wee spot o' bother with the local lads. Nothin' bad, but we're needin' a place to rest for a bit. Just 'til things pipe down a bit outside, you know."

She continued caressing him. "*No problema, mi amigo. Mi casa es su casa.* Three boys, how many hours? How much rum? How many girls?"

It was already midnight. Behind Clara's back I mouthed "six hours" to Rork.

"Hmm, well let me see," he said. "I think six hours or so, me dear. That would be about 'til sunrise. A wee bit o' rum, you say? What a brilliant idea! A bottle o' Matusalem would do nicely if there's one about. Or whatever you have. And as for the *girls* . . ." Rork swung his attention to me, his right eyebrow raised hopefully.

Some things never changed with him—or with me. A roomful of trollops was the last thing we needed right then. I shook my head no, receiving disdain in return.

He told her, "Ooh, well now, Clara, it seems we won't be needin' any companionship tonight."

"No love tonight?" she cooed. Her left hand went south on him while her right traced his mouth. Rork looked close to capitulation.

"*No*," I announced.

Clara ignored me, but Rork came to his senses and added, "No, dearie, not in the cards—no love for the lonely tonight. We're just needin' a quiet place to rest."

To spare Rork further distress, I gently pulled Clara's hands off him and turned her around to face me. Her expression soured, for Rork was her ally. I was her adversary.

"There's another thing, Señora. I need some good information about neutral ships in the bay. I will pay well for it, of course."

That got her attention.

38

Haggling

La Casa de Placeres Celestiales, Santiago de Cuba, Cuba
Early Sunday Morning, 3 July 1898

I COULD SEE CLARA'S MIND calculating. Though I was an
adversary, I was also plainly in charge of the money, of which
there was evidently more than she had originally estimated. Her
decision took only seconds.

"Yes, I have information on boats. Fishermen and sailors come
here. They tell me much about them."

"Good. Now, as to the ships—"

She wagged a finger at me. "No, you pay me first. This is dangerous business. You are enemy of Spanish, so the price goes up.
Seventy Mexican gold pesos for the room. Good room, my best.
Fifty gold pesos more for the information. Good information, all
true. Everything stay secret, no one know. But you pay first."

Her price was more than the brothel would make in a week off
the Spanish army and navy, but it didn't surprise me. She knew we
were desperate. The demand for Mexican coinage didn't surprise
me either. Gold would be valuable no matter who won the war. I'd
packed some in the seabag for that very reason.

Haggling is an art form in tropical cultures. I kept my expression
deadpan, focusing on those emotionless eyes of hers. "One hundred

twenty pesos is too much. Ninety-five gold Mexican pesos total for room and information. Forty now, fifty-five when we leave," I countered.

"One hundred ten, Captain. Sixty now, fifty later," she snarled.

"One hundred. Forty now and sixty later. Last offer before we walk out, Clara. I'm tired of this. Agreed or not?"

Rork brought his revolver into plain sight and made for the door. Law followed him. I put my brandy down, shook my head in disgust, and turned away from her.

Behind me, I heard, "Agreed, Captain. Where is the money?"

I turned around, saying, "One thing more before I give you the up-front money, Clara. It's important. You will keep our presence here a secret. There will be no other customers inside this place tonight. None. Do not even answer the door. If I see any other man I will kill him. Also, we will use another room, one with a window, and you will stay in that room with us all night."

I quashed the knowing sneer forming on her face with, "No, you will *not* be there to pleasure us. You will be a hostage and the first to die if the Spanish come in here. I will kill you myself. Understand me, Clara?"

She stood there appraising my resolve, then said, "Yes, I understand, Captain."

I handed over four Mexican ten-dollar pieces from my pocket. She slipped them into a hidden skirt pocket, then led us to a back room on the same floor with a window overlooking the alley below. Unlike the previous room, this one was roughly furnished, with only a bed and two chairs. I leaned out the window. Six feet below was the mildewed canvas roof of an old landau parked at the back door. Perfect for our purposes.

There was no horse hitched to it, and I asked Clara where it was kept. She guardedly explained the horse was in the livery barn across the alley, where her driver lived. Then she quickly inserted, "Fifty extra gold pesos to use carriage ten minutes, one-way trip inside the city."

"No. I will pay you forty extra, and only once we get where we are going—if we are still alive. You will be with us in the carriage. Agreed?"

"Agreed," she muttered.

"Good. Now close the place."

She called out for a different girl to come to the room. I caught a whiff of sweet earthiness from the girl that brought to mind the opium addicts I'd seen in Indo-China. Clara told her the place was shut down for the night in the rapid-fire patois of the Oriente countryside. All the brothel's girls were to stay in their rooms until dawn, when they would be paid for their silence. The girl merely nodded her acknowledgment with vacant eyes and padded out of the room. She worried me, for opium addicts live by no loyalty to anything but their dope. She might sneak out of the brothel seeking a reward for information leading to our capture.

With that possibility weighing on my mind, I set up our defenses. Rork was given a chair facing the door, which we left slightly open so he could see and hear any intruder in the hall. He sat down with his shotgun leveled at the doorway and his Navy Colt ready in his belt. Law was positioned at the window where he could survey the alley, his recovered Navy Colt in his right hand. I stretched out on the left side of the bed, my revolver in my right hand and my Spencer shotgun in my left. Both were pointed at Clara, who was on the right side of the bed, sitting upright with her back against the wall, watching her gringo acquaintances' every move. She wasn't fazed in the least by our sudden display of weaponry. I assumed that, like many of her ilk, she probably had a pistol herself concealed somewhere within her dress.

I turned and faced her. It was time to plan the next segment of our escape. "Now, Clara, tell me about any French, British, German, or Dutch ships anchored in the bay."

She seemed happy to tell me how little my money had bought. "Foreign boats all gone for many days. Only one still here. German ship, anchor by Cayo Ratones. Captain in trouble because of cargo."

I knew of only one German cargo ship in Cuba. "What is the ship's name?"

"Her name is *Norden*."

Rork and I knew that ship—and her captain, Bendel. He was the sort who could be persuaded to ignore rules in return for a good fee. Rork perked up at the news. "Interestin' twist, ain't it? That ol' kraut eater could still be o' use."

It was an interesting twist indeed.

How could we get on board, convince Bendel to take us out to the American warships, and steam out of Santiago before daybreak? The Spanish probably wouldn't stop a neutral German ship departing the harbor.

We weren't the only ones thinking along those lines. Clara quietly asked, "You boys leave on German ship?"

"No. That would be impossible," I said with as much fake regret as I could muster. "Bad idea. Better for us to walk back to our lines east of the city at dawn. Much safer. Don't you agree, Clara?"

She thought about that for a while, then said, "Yes, yes, Captain. Much safer walk to yanqui lines. Not far. I take you in carriage halfway there. Only a few pesos more."

In the weak lamplight I saw her thin lips curl into a smile and knew she thought she had me. She would double her money by getting mine first and then selling us to the Spanish for even more.

Which was exactly what I wanted her to think. It's always better if the enemy thinks they are winning. It dulls their awareness of traps.

39

A Dish Best Served Cold

La Casa de Placeres Celestiales, Santiago de Cuba, Cuba
Sunday, 3 a.m., 3 July 1898

T IMING IS EVERYTHING in life and war. I had no intention of waiting six hours to make our move. That was a
simple *ruse de guerre* employed for the confusion of any foe
who might have gained word of our professed intentions. Anything
that disrupts the enemy's timing is to your own advantage.

I'd whispered my plan to Rork and Law earlier so they would be
ready when the moment came to move. During the night I slept
lightly, periodically checking my pocket watch. When it showed
three in the morning I roused my companions. Rork and Law
popped up from their chairs.

Clara wasn't as cooperative. When I touched her shoulder and
said we were leaving, she sat up and in one smooth motion pulled
a derringer from a pocket hidden in the side of her dress. Before I
knew it, the damned thing was in my face.

Her eyes glistened with rage as she hissed, "You try to trick me!"

"No, Clara," I said calmly, diverting her attention by raising my
left hand in submission while surreptitiously easing my right hand
into a ready position by my waist. Rork and Law, pistols in hand,
froze in midstride, watching from across the room as I continued in

my soothing monotone. "I am an officer and a gentleman, Clara," I said. "I make it a point of honor never to lie to a lady. You have my word you will get your money."

She hissed again, a low, animal-like sound, ramming the derringer into the bridge of my nose between my eyes. "No! You try to trick me. I kill you now!"

My unfortunate situation permitted a close-up examination of her weapon. It was a single-shot .41-caliber Remington lady's gun—the favorite of princesses and prostitutes. It had a maximum accurate range of maybe fifteen feet but was quite deadly at this range. I further noted the hammer was cocked back and her trembling finger was tightening on the trigger. She was going to kill me. Whether by intent or accident, the result would be the same. My move would have to be very fast.

It was.

I ducked my head to the right, Clara's left. At the same time, I brought my right hand up and clamped down on the derringer, wedging my index finger into the notch between the hammer and the firing pin just as she pulled the trigger. She tried again, but the hammer wouldn't strike. It couldn't—my finger was blocking it. Our faces were only five inches apart. I saw the rage being replaced by panic as she realized her deadly gambit had failed.

My left hand groped for her other hand before she could pull another weapon on me. I found and crushed the hand in mine. Her terror was real. The type of men with whom she typically consorted wouldn't hesitate to kill her. She tried tears and remorse. "No! Don' shoot me! I am sorry!"

Rork was on her by then, removing the derringer and roughly pushing her back down onto the bed. I twisted her arm behind her back, ordered Law to find something to bind her with, and told Rork to search her carefully for other weapons. Law used a curtain cord to lash her hands behind her back and a towel to gag her. Rork's impolite search yielded two sheathed stilettos, one on each thigh, and a small razor blade within the barrette in her hair.

I leaned close to her ear. "It appears you aren't much of a lady, Clara, so all agreements are off."

Rork's usual relaxed outlook had disappeared. He was in his ruthless combat mode now. Clara was the enemy and quite capable of getting us killed.

"What're your orders, sir?" He said it with the clear insinuation of what *he* thought should be my orders—eliminate Clara as a threat. It would take maybe five seconds, depending on the method. She caught his mood plainly and whimpered through the gag, her eyes pleading against what she knew was coming.

Once again I studied this hideous example of womanhood. She deserved no consideration. No civilized society on earth would welcome her. And yet I hesitated in deciding her fate because that very fact bothered me.

Was I getting old and sentimental? Perhaps. After a lifetime of intimate encounters with death, and my more recent escapes from it, I was tired of the lifestyle. I also knew Clara could be eliminated as a threat without requiring another death by my hand or decision. Per her own orders, the other inmates of her emporium wouldn't try to contact her until dawn, three and a half hours away. In the meantime she could be rendered incommunicado. By the time she was discovered, we would have escaped to sea and she would have a lot to explain to a government interrogator. Those men wouldn't hesitate to torture someone like Clara Aguila.

In the few seconds it took for me to conduct this analysis, her face morphed from terror into miserable resignation. My decision would surprise her, and I knew that soon she would gloat over my weakness. But Clara wasn't thinking far enough ahead to see what was ultimately coming her way.

"Bind her hands, arms, legs, and feet tightly, Rork. Make sure the gag is lashed down tight also. Then leave her alive, under the bed."

While Rork and Law were carrying out my order, I ripped off a patch of peeling wallpaper and wrote a simple note to Clara. It thanked her for helping us escape and promised even more money when she reported the details of the Spanish defenses to me. I put it in my pocket, to be placed later in an appropriate place I already had in mind.

Then I waved good-bye to the trussed form under the bed. Clara's evil eyes glared at me. I thought of the girl she kept zombie-like on opium as her life ebbed away. *What would I do to someone who did that to Useppa?* Clara would find out soon, when she least expected it. As the French say, "Revenge is a dish best served cold."

I led our way out the window, dropping down onto the landau and heading across the alley to find the carriage driver. With any luck at all, by the time the sun came up we'd be having a decent breakfast on board a U.S. warship, my message to General Shafter would have been delivered by messenger, and my Cuban nightmare would be over.

40

Carlito

Santiago de Cuba, Cuba
Sunday, 3 a.m., 3 July 1898

WHEN WE WOKE HIM in his straw bed in the barn, Clara's driver was far more obliging than his mistress. Once I assured him she had fully approved of our enterprise, he was on board with the idea. I neglected to mention the price, and he unwittingly offered us a discount—the ride would be only twenty Mexican gold pesos.

Carlito was a boy of maybe fourteen, with the same worldly eyes as the girl who'd answered the brothel's door but far more vigor. As he got the horse and rig ready, we learned more about him. He'd been working for the brothel for three months, a step up from his previous life as a street urchin, earning the job by stabbing a man he saw hurting one of the girls on the street. He now ran errands for the girls and their clients, tended the brothel's horse and landau, and was the personal servant and self-proclaimed "guardian" of Señora Clara.

He stated the last with a puffed-up chest and lowered voice while fingering the homemade dagger tucked in his rope belt. His work at the brothel had obviously inculcated a strong sense of discretion, for the youngster expressed no surprise at either our nationality or our plan. He wasn't a laggard, either, pocketing the five-peso deposit without a moment's delay. I decided to keep young Carlito in mind for future purposes. One never knows . . .

We got under way at twenty-five minutes past three a.m., with Carlito on the open driver's seat up front and the three of us squeezed inside the small landau. We quickly closed the curtains all around, with one exception. Rork sat right behind Carlito, making sure the kid saw the uncovered spike of Rork's false left hand poking out between the front curtains, just inches from his spine.

The city was quiet as the swaybacked nag lethargically dragged us down the street to the south and the bay. Evidently, the search for us had been called off. We only encountered one group of three constables sauntering along on patrol. They recognized the landau and waved to Carlito. He explained he was taking some drunken officers back to the naval dock.

The policemen laughed, saying the officers would be in big trouble, for the fleet's officers had gotten strict orders to be back on their ships by midnight. That little tidbit caught my ear and started my mind working. *The Spanish fleet hasn't moved in weeks. Are they getting ready to come out and fight the Americans at dawn? What would that do to my plan?*

We rounded the curve of Calle del San Basilio and saw the naval station headquarters building ahead, the same one we'd hurtled past a few hours earlier. It was tranquil now, with only a few sentries, but I saw lights in several windows. Some staff officers were working very late on a Saturday night, which I thought odd. Then I smelled a familiar acrid smoke: funnel gas, a combination of coal smoke and embers. There was a haze of it in the air, coming from the lower bay where the Spanish warships were anchored.

Rork noticed it too. "Spaniardos've fired up the boilers, sir. Just started, by the smell'uv it. Somethin's afoot with their fleet, I'm thinkin.'"

"I'm thinking you're right, Rork. Today might be the day they make their move. We need to get out to sea and warn our ships."

Our conversation was ended when the landau drove up to the naval headquarters' sentry post. Following his orders from me, Carlito casually reported he had three drunken officers from Clara's place in the back, and they needed a boat from the officers' landing to their ship. The boy did it so casually I realized he'd probably said the same thing many times before, a routine occurrence of no importance. The sentry wasn't as casual, though. He nervously asked for the officers' identities so he could report them to his officer of the watch inside the building.

The three of us inside the landau got our weapons ready, but Carlito never missed a beat, spontaneously creating three names for the sentry, adding that the men were heading out to the flagship. It was an inspired addendum, for no one would hinder officers going to the flagship. My respect for the kid went up a notch. Clearly, he would become a famous politician or criminal mastermind someday.

"Get ready to drive out of here fast, Carlito, if they demand to talk with us," I said in muted Spanish through the forward curtain.

The sentry returned moments later and said we could pass onward to the wharf, whence the officers would ride out to the flagship with the captain of the port, who was about to depart in his personal launch. He would meet us at the landing in a few minutes. Then, unknowingly, the sentry dropped a bombshell into my plan when he gave the name of the captain of the port. Boreau.

Rork cursed under his breath. I exhaled slowly, willing myself to remain calm and think logically. Of all the officers in the Spanish navy, the last one I wanted to see was Captain Julio Boreau. As Carlito drove the carriage through the naval depot toward the officers' landing, Law asked Rork why we reacted to the name Boreau.

"'Cause that sonofabitch knows us by sight. An' a truly nasty piece o' work he is. Boreau's father was a lieutenant in the Spanish secret police who tried to kill the good captain an' me a couple o' times over the years. The bastard even came to our home in Florida tryin' to kill our entire family, if you can fathom that."

Law asked, "What happened?"

"Ooh, he got his final comeuppance when Captain Wake gave him the permanent deep six in New York Harbor. That was back in '86, an' ever since then, his son Julio's been after us both. Julio's as bloody crazy as his father, an' damned if the little bugger didn't nearly have us a couple o' times."

"I lost track of him after '95," I added. "He was on a staff assignment at Cádiz, back in Spain. And now he's here in Santiago as captain of the port? This billet's a hell of a demotion for a career navy officer. With his political connections he should have made admiral by now."

Rork huffed, "Nay, even the Spaniardos can spot a bloody lunatic, sir. 'Tis a wonder his own lads haven't shot 'im by now. Bet they want to."

The landau stopped alongside the water's edge. I peeked out the curtain at a steam launch, her little stack puffing away with full pressure as she sat at the landing. The tide was high, and the gunwale was level with the dock, making it easier for us to board in a hurry. The three-man boat crew was standing by. I heard them conversing quietly about the landau's possible passengers.

I whispered up front to Carlito in Spanish, "Do you see a senior naval officer anywhere?"

"No, sir," he whispered back. "It is only us and the sailors by the boat. They are waiting for him but looking at us now. I will tell them there are drunken officers inside the carriage."

My original plan had been to board the launch by pretending we were prisoners under freedom of parole, on our way to breakfast with the Spanish admiral on board his flagship. Once the launch was in the darkness at the middle of the bay, we would commandeer it and go to *Norden*. There, we'd buy off Bendel and steam out of the bay to our fleet offshore.

That was before the unforeseen complications of the Spanish fleet preparing to get under way and Boreau joining us on the launch. As with most of my plans of late, events forced me to cancel this one. We'd have to take action right away at the landing and seize the launch before Boreau appeared.

"The sailors are pointing toward an officer walking this way from the building," murmured Carlito. "I think he is the Captain Boreau the sentry spoke about."

I looked out the side curtain, covertly examining the boat crew. To my mates I said, "We'll have to take the boat now. When I give the word, we rush the crew, knock them out or push them in the water, and get her under way. I'll take the bow man, Rork gets the engine man amidships, and Mr. Law gets the coxswain aft. The coxswain is the only one armed—a holstered pistol in his belt. Remember, no shooting if we can help it. We don't want to alert the sentries and raise the alarm, or we'll never get away from the landing. Quickly and *quietly*, gentlemen."

They both got ready. I placed the wallpaper note about Clara on the floor of the compartment as if it had inadvertently fallen there. Leaning forward through the curtain, I handed Carlito the rest of my remaining Mexican gold ten-peso coins.

In deliberately slow Spanish, I told him, "Your days of working for Clara are over, Carlito. When we jump out, I want you to drive fast out of here. Get away from the naval depot. Leave the landau somewhere on the other side of the city and immediately get far away from it. Try to get out of the city and to the Cuban army. Do you understand?"

"Thank you, sir. Yes, I understand!"

"Good luck, Carlito. Live a good life. I hope we meet again."

Closing the curtain, I noted my pocket watch said 3:35 a.m. I gave the order, "Now!"

The three of us leaped out of the landau. We were on the boat in an instant, knocking the stunned sailors overboard with blows to their heads. Behind us, young Carlito wasn't tardy in seizing his new opportunity. Smacking his horse's rump, he got the old beast into a run toward the entry gate, yelling to the sentries that his horse was out of control—yet another excellent extemporaneous cover story that both allowed him to exit and diverted their attention from what we were doing at the boat.

The sputtering coxswain recovered quickest. Pistol in hand, he reached up for the gunwale to reboard the boat. Rork ended that notion with a roundhouse whack of an oar to the fellow's forehead.

Law cast off aft and took the helm as I cast off forward. Rork engaged the gear, and the launch lurched ahead, gathering speed. Law put the tiller hard over and steered out into the bay. Soon we were moving at five knots.

So far, the commotion of the runaway horse had captured the notice of everyone at the station. Even Captain Boreau—I confirmed it was him when he walked under a streetlamp—headed toward the gate at first. Then the Spanish sailors we left in the water began yelling louder to alert their compatriots.

We were a hundred yards away when the first shot rang out.

41

My New Command

Santiago Bay

Sunday, 4 a.m., 3 July 1898

L UCKILY, THE FIRST Spanish shots were wide. That soon
changed. A discordant series of whistles blared forth. Bellowed commands echoed across the water, and a ragged
volley of rifle shots came down the bay. The riflemen were firing
systematically around the arc of the bay. It was blind firing but
effective. The next volley proved far more accurate, forcing us to
duck below the gunwales. The one after that struck the water to our
left in a near miss.

I had the helm by this point. Law was helping Rork feed coal into
the boiler fire, but the fire was already at its peak. The boat refused to
go faster than about five knots. I did some quick calculations. It was
almost two miles to *Norden*, three and a half miles to the Spanish
fleet anchorage, and eight to the nearest American ship offshore—a
long way to go in a small launch capable of only five knots. With
forts and emplacements on both sides of the bay near the mouth,
the enemy fire would turn into a hailstorm when we reached that
part of the journey. Topping everything else, the eastern sky would
begin to lighten in about an hour and a half—right about the time
we got in front of El Morro. Colonel Melgar would enjoy that.

The timing would be very close. Still, I thought we had a chance at making it most of the way to the fleet offshore, *if* we could remain obscured in the darkness of the bay as we headed south. Fortunately, we were burning coal instead of wood, which would've shown a shower of sparks. Even so, I warned Rork to watch for any telltale embers escaping from our tiny stack and to reduce the boiler fire if he saw them. Other than these efforts there was nothing else to do. We were steaming south as well hidden as we could be.

My hope of concealment ended seconds later.

A white shaft of light beamed out from atop the naval station's headquarters building and slowly swung south along the bay's western shore. We were half a mile away from the dock when it stopped and settled on us. We were lit up as if by the sun. I expected a barrage of artillery fire, but none came.

"No forts on the shoreline this far up the bay," opined Rork. "An' we're out'uv effective range o' their rifles finally. The bastards can see us but not hit us with rifles out here."

Law tapped me on the shoulder and pointed behind us. "Ah, Captain, there's a boat back there close to the naval station, and she's heading this way."

Rork peered back and pounded his right hand down on the thwart. "Oh, hell, Mr. Law's right, sir. An' she's a *Ligera*-class gunboat, like those buggers we fought at Isabela."

Law looked questioningly at Rork, who explained, "Forty-two-millimeter rapid-fire gun on her bow, an' a nasty piece o' work. That was what nailed Captain Wake in the face. They've got a Maxim machine gun on the stern, as well. Her speed'll be maybe nine or ten knots, *if* she's been maintained well, which I'd wager your pay for a month she probably hasn't."

"She'll be on us in ten minutes at the most," I said, glancing aft and then to the shoreline on the port bow. "Look, I think that's the iron company's railroad pier over there. It's just beyond the main defense line outside the city. They'll probably have some small work dinghies. We'll head there, go alongside a dinghy, transfer to it, and set this launch on a course to the west, across the bay. Hopefully, the searchlight and gunboat will follow the launch while we go down the shoreline in the dinghy. Get ready to jump in a dinghy, men."

In the beam of light, Law's face reflected disbelief, but he loyally said, "Aye, aye, sir."

Rork thumped Law on the shoulder, a gross breach of naval discipline. "Aye, nothin' like a wee bit o' piracy to get the ol' blood pumpin'! Right, Mr. Law?"

Law wasn't as enthusiastic. He kept his eye on the gunboat and absentmindedly answered, "Ah, right, Chief. My blood's definitely pumping now."

We headed southeast toward the pier. By the time we reached it, the searchlight's illumination had diminished, for we were now well over a mile from it. The gunboat was only half a mile away, however, and I expected that bow gun to open up on us at any moment. I was sure they could make us out against the shoreline.

As we closed with the pier, Rork suddenly brought out his shotgun, saying he'd seen someone up on the pier. A young voice called out a challenge in Spanish from the deck of the pier.

"Wait!" I urged. "Don't shoot, Rork. He might think we're only Cuban fishermen and let us go by. We'll just have to find a boat somewhere else."

We watched the pier closely, waiting for the flash of gunshots, but none came. I guessed the sentry hadn't gotten the word on our escape and actually *did* think we were fishermen. Then I realized something else. The tide was ebbing fast. I gauged it at over a knot. We'd arrived at the pier much quicker than I'd anticipated, making about six knots over the bottom. The gunboat was approaching fast and would be on us in only a couple of minutes.

It was too late to slow down. We were swept past the dinghies tied up at the end of the pier, which was soon behind us. I surveyed the shore ahead for some small boat pulled up on the rocky shoreline. At last, only fifty yards off our bow, near Cocos Cove, I spied the outline of several fishing smacks clustered around the outer end of a small dock. A couple of them had dinghies. No sentry challenged us, and I saw no fishermen. I steered for the closest dinghy.

Belatedly, I realized my intended target was a sorry excuse for a watercraft, but beggars can't be choosers. In one impressively smooth movement, Rork hopped across into the boat, slashed its painter line with the rigging knife from the seabag, and grabbed our gunwale before we sped past. In another two seconds, Law and our seabag went over into the dinghy. Only I remained on board the steam launch.

The new acquisition dragged alongside the launch's port gun-wale—the side hidden from our pursuers—as I put the helm down hard and veered the little steamer over to starboard. I settled her on a westerly course for the far side of the bay, lashed the tiller in place, and clambered on board the dinghy. Rork shoved us away.

The launch proceeded onward toward the middle of the bay, the opposite direction from our new course. We headed southeast, toward shore.

The Spanish sailors in charge of that menacing beam of light never noticed our switch, keeping it glued to the steam launch. The gunboat followed the light beam, altering course to starboard to cut off the launch somewhere to the west of us.

Pooom . . . pooom . . . pooom . . . pooom—the 42-millimeter bow gun fired its rounds at the launch, which had become merely a gray form since it was beyond the maximum intensity of the searchlight. Though the gunboat was less than three hundred yards from the launch, none of the shots scored a direct hit, although they were close. The Spanish had taken the bait, but once they went on board the launch and realized we were gone, they'd backtrack and search our area.

My new command—all twelve feet of her—was dangerously overloaded, with only a few inches of freeboard showing, and the southerly wind was kicking up a chop against the ebb tide. The worst problem, however, was inside the boat. The bilge was ankle deep in sloshing oily water, threatening our stability. I felt around for something to bail with but found nothing that would hold water. Up in the bow, Law was pulling hard on our only pair of oars, trying to get us going faster. Rork and I paddled with our hands.

I felt water rising around my calves and realized the dinghy was sinking. Obviously there was a leak, and with so much weight in the boat it had gone from a trickle to a torrent. Rork and I began feeling along the inside of the planking, trying to find and plug the leak before it sank us. Our efforts were to no avail. Soon the tiny boat was completely swamped, ready to capsize at any moment. There was only one choice.

I told my crew, "We'll have to go overboard and swim alongside the boat. Even swamped, I think she'll carry the seabag with our stuff on the center thwart."

We removed all extraneous items from the seabag—there weren't many left—then put our shotguns, pistols, and my water-proof-wrapped pocket watch inside. We secured the bag atop the main thwart amidships, the highest and only relatively dry place left in the boat. I led the way into the warm water, and we hung on the gunwale with me aft, Rork on the port side, and Law starboard. With our weight gone, the boat rose in the water a bit. The seabag rode just above the water level.

"Aye, now there's a wee bit o' flotsam we could use quite nicely," said Rork as he pushed off toward a large, leafy mass of tree branches the ebb tide had brought out from some creek ashore. He struggled to bring it back—Rork can't swim well because of his false hand, plus we were all still in our shoes. Law swam over to help. Together they camouflaged the boat into a clump of drifting storm debris.

"Well done," I told them. "Now, let's start kicking. The ebb tide will help us. We've only got a couple of miles 'til we see our ships. Then it's a decent breakfast with Uncle Sam, boys."

To our right I saw two dark forms merge into one. The gunboat had come alongside the launch at the center of the bay. Even above the wind and waves we could hear the excited discussion drift across the water as the Spanish sailors searched the launch. The two forms parted. The smaller one headed north toward the naval station. The larger headed in our direction.

None of us said a word, mesmerized by the growing bow wave of the gunboat.

Suddenly, the warm southwesterly wind off the Caribbean shifted 180 degrees, becoming a strong, cool breeze off the mountains. I smelled moisture in it and almost wept with relief. Seconds later a curtain of dense rain roared across the water, blotting everything from sight. We could hear the gunboat circling nearby, the sound diminishing until the rumble of her engine was gone. The tropical rain shower, the cursed bane of our existence in Cuba, had become our protector. It rained and rained. No one complained.

In the wave action generated by the squall, several braces in the decrepit dinghy's frame worked loose and the little boat began to bend out of shape. It didn't take long for the hull to separate from the thwarts and forepeak. A few minutes later the entire boat fell apart. Law and I perched the seabag precariously within the clump of tree branches, which became our sole source of flotation. Too exhausted to kick and paddle any more after that, the three of us clung to the branches and drifted south down the bay in the deluge.

Our situation was precarious, but I felt we just might make it.

42

Sunrise

Santiago Bay, Cuba
Sunday Morning, 3 July 1898

IT WAS THE STINGING sensation that first woke me. Then Rork completed the job by prodding my shoulder. "Sun's risin' an' the weather's clear, sir. We're doin' fine, exceptin' these damned jellyfish."

"What?" I mumbled. My hands and face hurt, as if burned by a hot iron.

"Drifted into some jellyfish in the night. Sorry to say we all nodded off, sir. An' there's worse news. You won't be fancyin' where we've ended up."

The pain was worse when my face was completely out of the water. Jellyfish, or *aguamala* as the Cubans call them, had stung every inch of my exposed skin, which was now covered with a burning red rash. Rork and Law had it too.

As Rork woke up Law on the other side of the raft of branches, I cautiously and with some difficulty opened my eyes wider. Saltwater, slumber, and swelling from the stings had glued them shut. Once I took my bearings, I realized I was facing east. The sky was light, clear of clouds. But the sun itself was still hidden behind Gran Piedra Mountain far to the east, behind the American lines.

A quarter mile away on the bay's eastern shore lay the Punta Gorda fortress, one of the Spanish forts armed with modern heavy artillery. Rork's prediction of my reaction was accurate—I didn't like sitting in the water right off the fortress. I mentally pictured the chart of the harbor. *We floated for several hours and are only about a mile and a half from where the dinghy fell apart?*

Abruptly, big engines rumbled close behind me—so close I could feel the vibration through the water as well as the air. Startled, I twisted around to see their source.

"Oh, hell."

"Precisely, sir," said Rork. "That's where we are."

We were in the middle of the Spanish fleet.

Law jerked fully awake, quietly letting loose an oath as he registered first the pain and then our location. Rork was a sad sight indeed with his long gray hair, complete with antiquated queue, plastered down around his enflamed face.

"Should'a kept a proper watch as we drifted last night. Damn sorry, sir," he admitted with a weary sigh. "Got weak an' shut me eyes. On top'uv every bloody thing else, we get nailed by friggin' jellyfish. Can ye believe it? It was my watch . . ."

"Nobody's fault, Rork. It was just too much for all of us. Our bodies and brains shut down."

To make the dilemma even more interesting, or perhaps I should say depressing, the tidal current rushing past a nearby channel buoy indicated we were about halfway through a flood tide. That meant we hadn't floated two miles since the dinghy sank; we'd probably floated much farther on the last of the strong ebb. Evidently, fatigue had made us oblivious to what was happening as we floated right through the anchored enemy warships and all the way to the mouth of the bay. In fact, when the ebb tide finally turned and became a flood, we'd probably been only three or four miles from the inshore night positions of the American fleet, but we never knew it.

The flood tide had brought us a couple miles back up into the bay to the Spanish fleet. All six ships were busy weighing anchor, smoke pouring from their funnels and capstans clanking. Men were stowing everything that could be an impediment in battle and bringing up ready ammunition for the secondary and tertiary guns. Officers were shouting commands through speaking trumpets. Boatswains' whistles twittered. Sailors cursed. A bugle blared. Over on the parapets of the fortress I made out a line of uniforms—the army was watching the navy prepare for battle.

The lead ships were already steaming slowly in tight circles near Cayo Smith, the round island just inside the mouth of the bay, their anchors streaming water and mud as they came up to the hawse pipes in the bows. The closest of the Spanish warships was only fifty yards away from us—and was nothing less than a large armored cruiser.

I recognized her at once. *Cristóbal Colón* was a heavily gunned and speedy cruiser built in Italy. In April and May she had been one of Spain's most feared warships along the U.S. East and Gulf Coasts, where they expected to see her any day, destroying shipping, docks, and factories. They had good reason to fear her.

Colón was a state-of-the-art warship, in service for only a year. Everything about her was intimidating. At 8,000 tons she was larger than our exploded battleship *Maine*. *Colón*'s speed was twenty knots, and 5-inch armor plating covered her waterline, deck, and conning tower. Even her main turrets had nearly two inches of armor. And inside those main turrets she had a 10-inch and two 8-inch guns. The secondary battery consisted of no fewer than fourteen 6-inch guns, ten 3-inch guns, and four torpedo tubes. The third set of weapons on board was an array of six 47-millimeter rapid-fire guns and at least two Maxim machine guns.

But then I spotted a glaring—and potentially disastrous—defect in her armament. Her heaviest gun, the 10-inch in the forward turret, which had an effective range of seven miles and enough explosive power to sink any American ship smaller than an armored cruiser, was missing from her foredeck.

I had read intelligence reports stating the Spanish navy had faulted the original Italian-designed mounting and had refused acceptance until it was changed. The reports concluded that the gun and mount would be ready in May 1898. Many American naval officers, myself included, thought the Spanish might have accomplished this installation at a secret rendezvous while *Colón* was en route to Santiago. Since her arrival at Santiago Bay she'd been hiding behind headlands and islands, and our Navy hadn't gotten a good look her.

From my current vantage point, however, there was no doubt she was still missing that gun. In its place was a Quaker gun, as the Americans and British called them—a fake wooden gun barrel that couldn't hurt anyone. The significance of this was enormous: *Colón* could be outranged by smaller American ships if they came at her from ahead.

As I assimilated this information, the sun emerged above the mountaintop, illuminating the bay in shades of aqua and jade. Several sailors on *Colón* paused to look east at the sunrise—and right toward us. I held my breath, wondering how they could miss us. There couldn't be many clumps of tree branches floating in the bay. Fortunately, we were in our blues, and our jungle-stained seabag was various shades of black and brown. Maybe they wouldn't notice us.

"Get as far down into the water as you can," I told the others. "We'll paddle slowly west away from here, toward the opposite shore. This flood current will take us astern of the cruiser and toward the northwest part of the bay. There are some isolated coves over there with far fewer Spanish soldiers, I think. Once we get ashore we'll make our way to General García's forces in the Sierra Maestra west of the city."

Rork spit out some saltwater. "Could fancy a wee squall for some cover right about now. It'll be a long swim past that bloody big cruiser. I'm feelin' like a friggin' strumpet tryin' to sneak past the abbot."

"Hell, Rork," I retorted, trying to improve the mood, "you'd just offer the abbot a tot of whiskey and charm the wrath right out of him."

He laughed. "Well, there *was* that one time . . ."

We began kicking our feet and paddling with our hands. Between the tide and our efforts we got the branches started moving in the right direction. Behind us, the sun rose quickly, turning the water translucent. I guessed the time to be somewhere between 8:30 and 9 a.m.

Colón's anchor was up and almost secured. She altered course to make a wide circle to starboard. We'd been heading away from her, but the new turn would take her back around toward us, right across our escape course.

I recognized the irony of all this. The great battle for which both navies had prepared for years was about to begin. My only son was out there in *Oregon* waiting for these very ships to emerge. Soon he'd be in the thick of it all. But here I was, his father and a senior naval officer, ridiculously clinging to a tree branch as the tide floated me away from the scene of the impending battle.

"Hell'uva way to fight the bloody war, ain't it?" said Rork as he retightened his loosened false hand. "If me mates could only see me now."

Law bobbed his head toward the cruiser. "Ah, Captain, I think those fellows are pointing at us."

43

Men in a Tree

Santiago Bay

Sunday Morning, 3 July 1898

L AW WAS RIGHT. Spanish sailors on the cruiser's foredeck *were* pointing at us. One of them shouted aft to officers on the bridge about men in the floating tree.

"Right enough, Mr. Law," said Rork. "The little buggers're indeed talkin' about us, an' none too kindly, I'm thinkin."

The Spanish didn't waste any time. *Colón*'s steam launch was halfway up on its davits being squared away for battle when it was stopped, quickly raised to the main deck, manned with a crew, and lowered back to the water. There was still steam in the boiler, and they set out immediately for us. I noted the crew wasn't armed with rifles. Maybe there was a chance we could take the boat.

As the boat came up to us I heard the coxswain tell the others in Spanish, "Get those traitorous dogs on board so they can go out and die for their country like everyone else."

Then it dawned on me. Carlito had told the sentries at the naval shore station that we were drunken Spanish officers. The launch crew we'd dumped in the water hadn't heard us speak, and in the dark probably hadn't had enough time to recognize our uniforms as American Navy rather than Spanish. So naturally they concluded that we were Spanish naval officers who had deserted to avoid battle, very much a capital offense. Evidently, the Spanish army hadn't told the Spanish navy of their own embarrassment—our escape from army custody.

The boat arrived at our branches. I was about to explain to Rork and Law my realization of this humorous but potentially fatal twist when a Spanish sailor leaned down and grabbed me by the collar. He yanked me up and over into the launch. It took two of them for Rork, who also got a solid thump on the head with a belaying pin for being perceived as uncooperative. Such a hit would've rendered me unconscious, but Rork has had more than his share of thumps on the head during his thirty-seven years in the Navy. He weathered it without obvious trauma, replying with a stream of invective.

Our Marine tried to swim away to fight another day but was harpooned by a boathook and dragged back. He wasn't impaled—it was a dull-pointed boathook—but he was bruised badly. The lieutenant uttered some very ungentlemanly comments at the Spanish sailor who got him, then got his own thump on the head in return.

The all-important seabag containing our gear was lifted on board far more gently than any of us and put aft. The Spanish coxswain briefly poked through its contents and got quite a surprise. Then he looked at me again, focusing on the four gold stripes on the cuff of my sleeve. I could see his mind working. Clearly, we weren't the deserters he'd assumed we were. He ordered us herded to the forward bilge, where we were held at pistol point by a nervous youth with a trembling gun hand. It was the coxswain's pistol, the only firearm in the boat.

The Spanish sailors were mystified. We weren't deserters. We weren't even their countrymen. We were, in fact, quite the opposite. The bedraggled derelicts they'd fished on board were actually the dreaded yanqui enemy! But how had we gotten there?

The coxswain, recognizing my senior rank, was at a loss for what to say to me. Like most veteran petty officers in such a predicament, he straightened up and saluted me. Not to be outdone by this show of chivalry, I straightened up, returned the salute, and introduced myself in Spanish.

"Captain Peter Wake, United States Navy. Thank you for the ride to the ship, Coxswain. My compliments on your fine steam launch. It is much better than our last one from the port captain's office."

My Spanish is not without considerable defect, but I can be understood. The coxswain seemed to appreciate my attempt at dry wit. It also got his crew chuckling, leading to a general calming of tension and the trembling trigger finger. Rork gauged the moment right and made a self-deprecatory comment in Spanish about our obvious lack of warlike skills.

The Spaniards thought him sincere and assured us our capture was merely bad luck. The sailor who thumped him apologized for roughing him up. The sailor holding the pistol wagged his head in sympathy, allowing the muzzle to drop a bit. The stoker even patted Rork on the shoulder.

I knew Rork's intent was to lull them into complacency as he inched aft toward our bag of weaponry. My impression was cemented when I spotted a malevolent glint in his eye when he glanced at the sailor who'd bashed him. To be sure, a plan for retribution was brewing in that Gaelic brain.

Rork's opportunity for revenge came to naught, though, for the Spanish coxswain was a wily old salt himself and was not deceived one whit by our affable behavior. He watched our every move like a hawk, never allowing us to edge close enough to our seabag or get into a position from which to jump the crew. The crew was admonished to stay alert and act professional. Thus thwarted, our pretended conviviality faded as we went into captivity for the second time in less than twelve hours.

"Ah, friggin' bad Irish luck again," lamented Rork to the sky. "I'm so bloody tired o' this place . . ." He let out a long, sad sigh.

"Steady on, Rork. We're not dead yet," I reminded him gently.

We came alongside the moving cruiser, and as the boat was being hauled up to the main deck the coxswain excitedly shouted up at the junior officer of the watch, "Sir, the men hiding in that tree are yanqui naval officers!"

Before the astonished lieutenant could reply, a deep baritone boomed out from the bridge in Andalusian Spanish. "Bring them to me!"

I knew that voice.

44

A Choice of Deaths

Santiago Bay, Cuba
Sunday Morning, 3 July 1898

I'D FIRST MET Emilio Díaz-Moreu y Quintana at a diplomatic
reception in Cádiz, Spain, back in 1885. I was on a port visit
there with our Mediterranean squadron. He was a lieutenant
commander in the Spanish navy and about to begin a period of
convalescence at Alicante, across the country on the central Mediterranean coast of Spain, for some undisclosed illness. He didn't
look ill to me at the reception. In fact, I was surprised to hear of the
man's intention, for his large physique was imposing, his wit was
acerbic, and his eyes were unnervingly penetrating. I immediately
sized up Díaz-Moreu as a man to watch for in the future and predicted his recuperation would be quick.

I met him again in 1894 at Málaga, on the southern coast of
Spain, at yet another of the innumerable soirées American officers
had to suffer through ashore when serving in Europe. In addition to
his naval status Díaz-Moreu was well known by then as a member
of the Cortes, Spain's parliament. He had recently expressed his candid, and somewhat unpopular, assessment of Spain's navy to Prime
Minister Sagasta's government in Madrid, insisting the navy should
be modernized.

The cocktail conversation at that party had him destined for higher rank and command. I heard from other Spanish naval officers not only that he was a respected captain and staff officer but also that his combat exploits during the recent Rif War in North Africa had garnered him notice in royal circles.

By 1895 I heard a rumor from British acquaintances that Díaz-Moreu would be getting command of one of the much-coveted large cruisers Spain was buying from foreign yards in Europe. It turned out to be correct. The following year he was sent to Genoa, Italy, and given command of *Colón* even as she was being completed at the yard.

Now, four years after Emilio Díaz-Moreu and I shared polite cocktail conversation at a boring social affair filled with international poseurs of every class and type, I was a prisoner on his ship. By then the cruiser had completed her 360-degree turn and was following the other ships out the channel.

Once we were brought to the main deck, a junior officer and guard detail hurried us up several sets of ladders to the portside bridge wing. Inside the wheelhouse, an officer was calling out to the helmsman to straighten the rudder and follow the ship ahead. Status reports, acknowledgments, and observations were being reported in preparation for the battle.

It all stopped cold when they saw me. Someone belatedly announced, "The yanqui officers have arrived."

Officers and petty officers cleared the space around me as if I had a contagious disease, or perhaps because I was dripping seawater. Rork and Law waited at the open hatchway to the outside ladder. Behind them were two armed guards.

Law looked anxious. Rork appeared calm, almost glum, as he stood at parade rest. But he cast a slight sideways look, moving his eyes from me down to the water, and I read his meaning—*Do we jump for it once we're out of the bay?*

My shrug was equally slight. *Maybe. We'll see.*

Attired in his dress uniform, Díaz-Moreu entered the crowded wheelhouse from the starboard wing, and everyone, including me, came to attention. Among the baubles on his chest I saw the Grand Cross of the Naval Order of Maria Cristina, the Grand Cross of Military Merit, and several other prestigious decorations and awards. If he lived through the day ahead, I imagined another medal would join them and his future as a political and naval leader in Spain would be assured.

Díaz-Moreu's strong nose, thick moustache, and imperiously arched eyebrows were the same as I remembered, but his hair was grayer and thinning. He'd also gained a bit of weight, which showed in his jowls and waist. I recalled he once said something about being born in 1846, seven years after me, but standing there on the bridge the man looked older than his early fifties.

Diaz-Moreu was the very beau ideal of his nation's naval manhood, ready and willing to defend the honor of Spain against the upstart gringos. Those dark, evaluating eyes silently studied the soggy wreck of a naval officer, complete with jellyfish-burned face, before him. Would he remember me?

When Díaz-Moreu spoke, it was with the same self-assurance I'd noted years before. Unlike our previous encounters, this time he spoke in very good English. I mentally awarded him a point, for his fluency was such that he must've had it before. Excellent tradecraft for cocktail parties.

"I am Captain Emilio Díaz-Moreu y Quintana, commanding officer of this ship. Allow me to welcome you aboard the armored cruiser *Cristóbal Colón* of His Catholic Majesty's Navy. You are Captain Peter Wake, of the American Navy. We have met twice before in Spain. You were quite highly regarded in naval intelligence work, as I recall."

I bowed slightly. "Yes, sir. We did indeed meet many years ago in your wonderful country. As for my reputation and work, I am but a humble servant of my nation, Captain, as you are of yours. Though I must admit you are far more professionally successful."

He bowed slightly at my compliment. I continued.

"May I introduce my subordinates standing behind me? They are Lieutenant Edwin Law, U.S. Marines, and Chief Boatswain's Mate

Sean Rork, U.S. Navy. We thank you for your remarkable hospitality. As fate has made me a prisoner of war, I am greatly honored to be a prisoner of one of the most highly regarded naval officers in Europe."

"Thank you, Captain Wake. We will endeavor to make you as comfortable as we can, given our current circumstances. And I must congratulate you on gaining access into the interior of Santiago's defenses. It was no small accomplishment."

His next comment was accompanied with a chuckle. "I understand you even captured a brothel."

Oh, so he knows about that, does he? What else does he know? The Spaniard was clearly enjoying the repartee, so I countered in like vein. "It's amazing what you can learn in the enemy's brothels. But I must ask, how did you know I was at Clara's? I don't remember seeing any Spanish naval officers there."

"I should hope not. We have much higher standards! I had breakfast ashore this morning with a friend in the army. He told me the tale of your escape and refuge at Clara's notorious house of ill repute, all of it *en voce sotto*, of course. The army is embarrassed, to say the least. They very much wanted to recapture and execute you as a spy and attempted saboteur."

I smiled. "Actually, we weren't really going to blow up anything. I was just checking on how Spanish morale was doing."

He laughed. "Yes, of course. I hope you found it high. I think the army made up that part to make you sound more formidable and difficult to recapture. But, luckily for you, it was our *navy* who got you. Disguised as a floating tree, no less! Well done, Captain Wake—a glorious way to end your active participation in this war. If I somehow live through the battle today, I shall dine out on this story for a long time."

One can't help but smile under such circumstances, and I did so while replying, "Thank you, sir. I hope the soldiers don't get in trouble because of our escape. One of them was getting married today."

"Oh, I think they are very much in trouble, having vastly outnumbered you. Now, as to the matter at hand for us. In a few minutes we will be confronting your magnificent American fleet, which has us outnumbered and outgunned. There is every chance we will all die within the hour, and this beautiful ship will sink to the bottom of the Caribbean Sea.

"Therefore, I have a decision to make about my newly arrived prisoners. Do I lock you below in our ship's jail, or do I grant you parole under your word of honor not to escape or to hinder the operations of this ship and allow you to stay here to observe the battle? There is not much time for deliberation, Captain Wake. Which do you prefer?"

What he didn't say was that if we were locked below, we'd never get out when the ship sank. If we were standing on the bridge under parole, we stood every chance of dying by the shrapnel or concussion of American high explosives.

It was merely a choice of deaths.

45

Sunday Routines

Santiago Bay, Cuba
Sunday Morning, 3 July 1898

I TOOK THE OBVIOUS OPTION. "Captain Díaz-Moreu, you have our word of honor as naval officers and a naval petty officer. We will abide by the internationally accepted norms of parole and not hinder the ship, harm your men, or attempt to escape."

He shook my hand again, his eyes suddenly somber. "Then it shall be so. You and your companions will stand in the after starboard corner there, where you can watch everything. I truly hope you will survive, Captain Wake, for someday I would enjoy relaxing with you over bottles of decent Cuban rum and Spanish brandy. We can discuss our careers, our women, and our children. I venture to say we would discover some interesting commonalities."

I replied, "I would like that also, sir," but he had already turned and was issuing orders to his executive officer. In an instant the wheelhouse returned to systematic commotion. Last-minute preparations were completed, commands were acknowledged, armored hatches were clanged shut, and viewing ports were lowered with massive thuds. Instantly, all air circulation ended. Two battle lanterns and flat shafts of eerie light from the observation slits provided the only light inside the armored citadel. The scene of tense faces and hushed voices was almost surreal.

Through the viewing slits I could see the Spanish ships in line ahead. The lead position was occupied by the armored cruiser flying Admiral Cervera's flag, *Infanta María Teresa*. She had a main battery of two 11-inch guns forward and another ten 5.5-inch guns around her upper decks. *Teresa* was also rated at twenty knots, but her top speed was closer to sixteen or seventeen, as I knew from an espionage operation I had directed the year before.

Second was her sister ship *Vizcaya*, also slower than advertised. *Colón* was third, the sole cruiser capable of nearly the design speed, followed by another slow sister ship of the flagship, *Almirante Oquendo*. Bringing up the rear of the line were two lightly armed torpedo boat–destroyers, *Furor* and *Pluton*. They were designed for twenty-eight knots but could do twenty-two at most.

We steamed seaward with increasing velocity, passing Cayo Smith to starboard, surging past Fort Estellas on the eastern shore to port. Next, to starboard, were the Socapa batteries. At the narrow mouth of the bay loomed my temporary abode the previous night, El Morro. Ahead of us was the blue Caribbean Sea, its waves glittering in the intense morning sunlight.

It was a vision of endless beauty, except for the menacing black shapes scattered across the horizon. Squinting through the forward viewing slits I tried to make out the number and type of ships in the American fleet. From where I stood I couldn't see any details, much less identify my son's ship, *Oregon*.

The officer of the watch passed along to Díaz-Moreu a signal flag report to the Spanish fleet from the lookouts at El Morro. Three American ships—the battleship *New York*, Admiral Sampson's flagship; the battleship *Massachusetts*; and a small auxiliary vessel, *Suwanee*—had departed the blockade. They were a couple of miles east of the main fleet and steaming toward Siboney. The fortress then reported the remaining U.S. ships on the blockade line. In a monotone the officer listed them in order, from west to east.

The first was the yacht-gunboat *Gloucester*. The next in line were an auxiliary ship, *Resolute*, and two battleships, *Indiana* and *Oregon*. My heart skipped a beat.

The officer went on with his recital. Although the men on the bridge spoke Spanish rapidly, I was able to follow without too much difficulty. In the center of the line, directly opposite the mouth of Santiago Bay, was another battleship, *Iowa*. The eastern side of the American line consisted of the battleship *Texas*, the cruiser *Brooklyn*, the small yacht-gunboat *Vixen*, the torpedo boat *Ericsson*, and the yacht-gunboat *Hist*.

Díaz-Moreu peered through a forward slit during the report, then turned to me. "It certainly appears Admiral Sampson has tried to even the contest. How very generous of him to depart the scene just as we are coming out to do battle. But it is odd, do you not agree?"

"Probably had a luncheon engagement with General Shafter," I quipped, while wondering that very thing myself.

I wasn't worried. In the absence of Admiral Sampson, Commodore Winfield Scott Schley in *Brooklyn* was the senior officer in command of the blockade. Like Sampson, he had a reputation as a fighter. Even without *Massachusetts* and *New York*, Schley had enough firepower and speed to destroy all the Spanish ships.

Colón and the other Spanish ships were charging at full speed past the headlands now, giant gold-and-red battle flags streaming aft from their masts. Only three hundred yards separated each Spanish vessel in the line, an impressive show of seamanship. They presented a brave and thrilling sight—until I thought of the imminent cost of their glorious act. The clock on the bulkhead above me read 9:35 when a speaking tube whistled.

The officer of the watch announced that the masthead lookout reported *Brooklyn* had run up a signal in her halyards. Within seconds the American ships were turning toward the entrance to the bay.

"Ah, I expected that much sooner," said Díaz-Moreu. "They are late in recognizing our sortie from Santiago." He motioned for me to come and stand beside him. When I did so, he beckoned me to view the American fleet close up through the forward slits. Huge plumes of smoke were beginning to roil up from their stacks. The entire fleet had turned toward us.

"Do you know, Captain Wake, why we chose this time and date?" Díaz-Moreu asked while I searched for *Oregon*. There she was, five miles away. The sight of her so far away from the scene of battle was a relief—maybe my son would miss the worst of it.

"Because you know tomorrow is our annual Declaration of Independence celebration and you wanted to participate?" was my sarcastic answer. I was tired of his genteel banter. The man was just too composed for me. He didn't even seem nervous, much less fearful.

He merely laughed at my acerbity. "Oh, no, but what a good idea! No, we chose this moment because in the thirty-three days you Americans have been waiting offshore here we have studied your naval routines, which are followed to the minute. So we know your crews are preparing for Sunday church service at this very time. Almost all the men on your ships are mustered aft on the main deck in their best white uniforms, ready in their minds for peaceful worship, not for war. We thought this would give us an advantage in beginning the chase. We are sure God will understand this transgression of the Sabbath—he is, after all, on our side."

Though he said the last without conviction, and theological appropriateness aside, I had to admit Admiral Cervera had brilliant timing. The surprise would gain the Spanish only a few minutes at most, but when dealing with complicated machines of war at sea, sometimes that's enough.

My reply, which was intended to be a compliment on the Spanish navy's tactical surprise, was interrupted by a column of water erupting dead ahead of us, followed by a distant boom. It was a ranging shot, soon followed by another.

Rork and I both looked at the clock. It had taken the U.S. Navy eight and a half minutes from warning signal to main batteries firing—a very respectable period of time to man battle stations for men beginning church service. The Spanish element of surprise was over.

The long-awaited sea battle for Cuba was about to begin.

46

A Storm of Steel and Lead

Off the Santiago Coast, Cuba
Sunday Morning, 3 July 1898

FOURTEEN MINUTES LATER, the Spanish ships had executed a perfect right turn and were still in column-ahead
formation, now settling on a westward course along the cliff-
lined coast. More impressive, they did it while under heavy gunfire.

Within thirty seconds of the first two American rounds, a profu-
sion of airbursts, near misses, and direct hits exploded among the
Spanish cruisers. The sea around them erupted in geysers of water,
and shrapnel clanged against their armor. The leading ship, Admiral Cervera's *Infanta María Teresa*, was soon alight and smoking
heavily along her weather decks. The initial range between the fleets
was short—three or four miles at most—and closed rapidly as the
American warships turned west in pursuit.

The Spanish shore batteries, including Melgar's ancient cannons
at El Morro, did their best to help their naval brothers, but they
didn't seem to be scoring many hits on the American ships. From
my previous intelligence work on Spanish military capabilities, I
knew Spain's modern ammunition was bad and the ancient stuff
was a joke. We had discovered numerous official complaints from
Spanish commanders that powder charges had been shorted, and

even that sawdust had been found inside the shells delivered to Cuba. Unscrupulous contractors were not only an American curse.

Freed from the confines of the channel, *Colón* and her sisters steamed even faster as they raced along the coast. The close formation loosened as some ships made better speed than others. From now on it would be every ship for herself. Dense black smoke poured from every funnel. Gray smoke belched from every gun that bore on the Americans. Our ship—yes, I strangely thought of her as such—was speedier than those ahead and began drawing up to them. The last two Spanish vessels in line, the diminutive torpedo boat–destroyers, veered off to the west upon emerging from the bay, then began a circle. I thought it a tactical mistake that would end badly, but I kept silent.

"We have high-quality Cardiff anthracite coal for our fuel," explained Díaz-Moreu to me. "I think today we shall show what this fine ship can do."

"You seem to have thought of everything, Captain," I commented. "Proper planning is crucial."

"Thank you, but I cannot accept your kind accolade, Captain. Fortune alone favored us in our acquisition of such fine fuel, not any decision on my part. And under the present perilous conditions in which we find ourselves," he added, "as a brother naval captain of previous acquaintance, I insist you call me Emilio. After all, we are in the same boat, as they say."

I held out my hand. "Very well, Emilio. I am honored. Please call me Peter."

He gripped it strongly. "May we both survive to someday enjoy rum and brandy, Peter."

As if to mock our mutual amity, at that point *Colón* became a main target of the Americans. A storm of flying steel and lead pounded against our armored citadel. Everyone inside the armored wheelhouse instinctively ducked away from the slits—except Díaz-Moreu.

"Bring the course left ten degrees!" he ordered firmly with his face pressed to a slit. "We will go past the admiral and *Vizcaya* on their port sides."

I peered out the slit closest to me. Up ahead on the starboard bow, the Spanish flagship was completely engulfed in fire and was altering course to starboard, toward shore. Beside us, *Vizcaya* also had explosions rippling along her decks from the American gunfire. A detonation somewhere aft suddenly rocked *Colón*.

"Damage report?" demanded Emilio. "And pass the word to the engineers to disregard normal pressure limits and make all speed possible."

It appeared the Spanish ships had concentrated their initial fire on Schley's *Brooklyn*. I could see she was hit, with flames and smoke billowing from among her secondary guns. But she had not stopped or even slowed, and kept on coming at us. Other American ships were now behind or beside us, shifting their fire from *María Teresa* and *Vizcaya* to *Colón*.

As we passed the two lead Spanish ships, someone shouted, "We can outsteam the yanquis! We are gaining distance from them."

A cheer erupted in the confined space. Díaz-Moreu smiled. "Of course we can, men. It is a chase now, and our engineers will be the heroes."

Incredibly, it seemed true. *Brooklyn* had veered away from a near collision course with *María Teresa* and was completing a 270-degree turn. The unexpected maneuver forced *Texas* to slow down to avoid Schley's ship. Meanwhile, *Iowa* was steaming parallel to the Spanish ships on their port quarter, firing at us. Farther astern I could see *Oregon*, her bow wave white against the blue-green sea, heading right for us.

Emilio ordered the entire portside secondary battery to fire into *Iowa*. Several rounds hit her on the main deck and the waterline. *Iowa* slowed, and *Colón* forged ahead, now in front of everyone, Spanish and American.

"*Infanta María Teresa* is out of the fight and heading for the beach, sir," reported an officer at 10:20. Only half an hour after the first shots of the battle were fired, Cervera's flagship was a burning hulk.

Emilio seemed almost to ignore the report, instead ordering, "Alter course five degrees to port. Steer for that headland in the distance—Cameroneito. We will pass very close by it."

"Mother of God, no!" someone cried, to an accompanying chorus from the after end of the wheelhouse. We turned around in time to see a large explosion erupting on the ship behind us. She veered quickly toward the rocky shore.

"Poor *Oquendo*," said an officer. "She is gone."

The litany continued. This time it was the Spanish destroyers. "Look, *Furor* is sunk!" "*Pluton* is beaching herself."

Colón was hit twice more, aft and amidships. The gunnery officer reported all secondary 6-inch guns on the port side—the side engaging the Americans—were out of commission, except one. It still exchanged fire with the American ships, but the increase in range diminished the accuracy on both sides. In another few minutes our guns stopped firing. The Americans stopped wasting ammunition too.

By 11 a.m. *Colón* had been racing at full speed for more than an hour. The engineering reports every fifteen minutes were full of warnings about extreme boiler pressures, overheating bearings, and coal consumption. Díaz-Moreu told them to keep on pushing as hard as they could, for they were increasing the distance from the American ships. That observation was no hyperbole for morale, for *Colón* was actually pulling off the impossible. The lone Spanish hare was escaping the entire pack of yanqui hounds.

Schley in *Brooklyn* was six miles astern and dropping farther back. *Oregon*, which had been farther east and therefore had to steam much farther than *Brooklyn*, was proving herself the fastest American ship in the fleet. Racing along on Schley's starboard quarter, she was starting to catch us, slowly but surely. *Brooklyn*'s 8-inch guns couldn't accurately hit us anymore at the current range, but we would soon be well within range of *Oregon*'s forward 13-inch main guns. My heart pounded—that was my son's battery.

And what of the rest of the American fleet? Far behind the two leaders were *Indiana*, *Iowa*, and *Texas*. Next came Sampson's *New York*, rushing west from Siboney past the slower ships. All of them were out of the real race, though. It was now down to *Colón* versus *Oregon* and *Brooklyn*.

"*Vizcaya* just blew up, sir," an officer reported to Díaz-Moreu at five minutes past eleven. "They are beaching the wreck." It grew quiet in the wheelhouse.

The Spanish captain's voice was like iron. "Gentlemen, our comrades are gone. We are the only ones left to uphold the pride of Spain. We have outrun every enemy ship except *Oregon*. Now *Colón* must outrun her. Our freedom lies beyond that headland to the west."

For another hour the three ships plunged westward through the ocean swells.

Although the men around me were the enemy, that appellation didn't come immediately to my mind as I watched them. I found myself wanting these brave men to live through their defeat.

Emilio ordered the armored ports on the unengaged starboard side opened to ventilate the wheelhouse, then invited his American prisoners to take a stroll with him around the upper deck. I was embarrassed by my sloppy appearance, but not so much that I declined an opportunity to escape the citadel's coffin-like interior. I wanted to gain an unobstructed view of the overall situation unfolding along the coast and see how *Colón*'s crew was coping with battle conditions.

We descended the starboard ladder to the boat deck and walked aft, trailed by my subordinates and two Spanish sailors as guards. We were interrupted by a messenger from the bridge who handed his captain a note. Emilio read it, then turned aft to study *Oregon* for a moment with those hooded eyes. He dismissed the messenger with no reply.

He looked me and dispassionately stated, "We have run out of our Cardiff anthracite coal, Peter. So we must use Cuban bituminous from here onward. Not as efficient, as you know, but one must make do with what one has at hand."

I glanced aloft. *Colón's* exhaust smoke was no longer dark gray from the cleaner-burning anthracite. It was now black. It could only be a matter of time before *Colón* began to slow.

Seizing the moment, I tried to convince him to yield to reason. "Emilio, you and your men have done all, and even more, than could ever be expected of you. The honor and bravery of the Spanish navy has been unquestionably proven today. There is no shame in ending this now, my friend, without further loss of life."

"No, not yet, Peter. We are not beaten yet. In fact, we are still winning the race."

And with that said, Emilio changed into a sociable mood. As if to displace the ugly reality around us with professional camaraderie, he showed me various appliances and equipment on deck, introduced me to his officers, and discussed the diverse duties involved in captaining a warship. Walking behind us, Law and Rork stayed dutifully silent, their faces showing no emotion as Emilio and I carried on about the common burdens of naval command. It was a surreal experience for me, all this unanticipated friendliness in the midst of a life-and-death struggle.

From therein came a peculiar conversation, the likes of which few warriors have experienced.

47

The Ultimate Irony

Off the Santiago Coast, Cuba
Sunday Morning, 3 July 1898

THE GENERAL MELEE BEHIND us now, a curious normalcy descended upon the ship. While the occasional ranging shot was still fired unsuccessfully at them, *Colón's* crewmen partook of their usual noonday meal and rum ration as we walked aft among them.

Since the ship was at battle stations and the galley fires were out, the only food was stale bread and congealed rice and beans. Their real sustenance was the pure rum in their cups, a serious temptation for Rork. I had to glower severely to prevent him from trying to make off with some of the stuff. We needed our wits about us, for the worst was surely still to come.

Even though they'd already had a double tot that morning, I saw no drunkenness or false bravado among the Spanish enlisted men as they took their rum—the day had progressed far beyond such empty rhetoric and gesture. I also noted no despair. The sailors were as personally composed, and as professionally determined, as their officers. I heard one of them tell another the situation wasn't hopeless yet, suggesting what a fine tale they would have when they escaped and made it home. I noted he said "when," not "if."

As we went around, Emilio inspected the battle damage, spoke encouragingly with his men, and inquired of his officers about their guns' readiness and their men's well-being. At each interview he introduced me as their "honored prisoner" and allowed me to hear their reports. I was profoundly touched by the gesture but couldn't help wondering why. *Would I do this? No.*

I grew more and more impressed with Díaz-Moreu. He was a rare example of a true natural leader, one who instinctively understands and can motivate his men. He knew how to focus their attention and efforts with positive comments that applied specifically to them. Several times he urged the sailors not to look aft at the fleet chasing them but to keep looking forward to the west, toward the empty horizon and freedom. They seemed to be heartened by his words. Even the grizzled old petty officers, who knew the odds better than anyone, visibly appreciated his efforts.

Heading aft past the second funnel, which had smoke escaping from shrapnel holes all over it, we reached the mangled after end of the boat deck. Below us was the main deck where the secondary 6-inch guns were emplaced along both sides of the hull. Several on the port side were wrecks, their barrels askew.

On the boat deck, where the smaller-caliber guns were located, I saw three or four guns damaged beyond repair, with pools of blood where their gun crews had once stood. A bloodied sailor, his arm in shreds, was brought past us on a stretcher. He had been trapped in the wreckage and just then freed. Emilio called him by name and touched his good shoulder, thanking him for helping to keep the enemy at bay long enough for *Colón* to escape.

Near the mainmast boat booms amidships, Emilio once again checked *Oregon*'s position. I could tell he was estimating the rate of closure between the ships by the relative bearings.

"Peter, would you happen to know the captain of *Oregon*?" he suddenly asked me. "I believe his name is Clark, is it not?"

"Yes, I know him. Charles Clark is a decent man, an excellent seaman, and a veteran warrior. Fought at Mobile, back in '64. Like you, he's respected by his officers and men."

"Ah, yes, with the respect of his men, a captain and his ship can achieve wonders. I have noted *Oregon*'s gunners must be well trained, for they have been quite successful in their work this morning."

Emilio surveyed the shoreline then pointed at a beach. "Ah, we are already passing Asarradero. I think we have made very good speed for a ship with a foul bottom, encrusted boiler tubes, over-worked bearings, and funnel damage; sixteen or seventeen knots, maybe a little bit more. But, oh, you should have seen her when she was new—four knots faster." His face brightened at the memory, then fell. "But times changed. We could not maintain her, just as we could not maintain Cuba."

He motioned toward another section of the shore. "Look over there. I think the Cubans are cheering, and not for us."

A thousand yards to starboard was the same beach with hot, white sand where Shafter had come ashore to meet García for the first time. It was crowded with Mambi warriors, my allies, watching the sea chase. In the bright sunlight and sea breeze, Cuban flags flapped from bamboo poles in the village behind the beach.

I could see the trail winding up the hill to the plateau above and remembered the poor mule struggling to carry an American general who outweighed him. The tall, green ridges of the Sierra Maestra came right down to the sea on this stretch of the coast, covered everywhere with primordial jungle. It struck me that the terrain must have looked the same to Christopher Columbus, namesake of this ship, four centuries earlier.

Emilio broke into my thoughts.

"Our speed has diminished because of the change in coal. *Oregon* is closing the range. Her big guns will fire at us very soon. From what I have already seen of her gunners, they will eventually hit us."

He said it without rancor or fear. It was a professional observation, a fact. They would open fire with individual ranging shots within minutes. Those would be followed by volleys.

I imagined my son at his battle position that very moment—receiving reports from his gun captains, chief loaders, and the chief petty officer of the forward magazine. Sean would be busy double-checking the range to *Colón* through his new Fiske optical sight, calmly gauging the pitch and roll of the ship for the optimal firing moment. Then he would call into his communication tube to the ship's gunnery officer, who would pass along to the executive officer on the bridge the report that *Oregon's* forward main guns were loaded, locked, laid on target, and ready to fire. Captain Clark would then give the order.

Since it was a moot point anyway, I decided to enlighten Emilio about the ultimate irony of the day. "I suppose you might as well know about a rare paradox today, Emilio. My son is *Oregon's* assistant gunnery officer. He commands her forward main battery."

His eyes opened wide in shock. "Peter, I am stunned. This is terrible. You must not be subjected to gunfire from your own son! I cannot permit it. I am sending you forward to the armored bridge, where there is more protection from *Oregon's* shells. I must return to my position there now anyway. Follow me."

He was already striding forward as I mentioned to Rork behind me, "It really *would* be ironic if my own son ended up—"

Bright white light and a deafening *crack* took the words from my mouth. I was flung backward off my feet, my spine smashing into what felt like an iron cliff. Everything went black as a wall of water inundated me.

48

Two Degrees

I CAME TO A MOMENT later crumpled sideways around a
main ventilator cowl. Rork and Law were sprawled on the
deck by the mainmast. I saw them moving hesitantly, then
getting up. Díaz-Moreu wasn't in sight. Nor were our sailor
guards. The buzzing in my ears was so loud that the voices of the
Spanish crewmen yelling nearby sounded faint. Rork, Law, and I
cautiously stood.

I looked around for major structural damage, expecting to find
part of the ship gone from the blast. But *Colón* was still steaming
forward on a level keel. There was damage, however. A gale of shrapnel had punctured hundreds of holes everywhere along the deck.
A six-inch-long jagged gash was ripped into the ventilator about a
foot above where I had collided with it.

Two sailors lay on the deck, doubled over and cursing in pain. I
went over and knelt to help them. Blood poured from their wounds,
and I started binding a handkerchief around one man's shredded
hand. Rork said something I couldn't hear, then touched my face. I
felt liquid coursing down my cheeks. *Damn it, not again!* The splinter
wounds were pouring blood.

Spanish sailors arrived and took over attending to their shipmates, ignoring the Americans. With difficulty, I stood up and surveyed the scene, realizing what had happened. A pair of 1,100-pound shells from *Oregon*'s forward 13-inch gun turret had impacted the water on either side of *Colón*'s stern, detonating when they hit the surface of the sea and sending steel shards in all directions. If they had struck the ship squarely, I would be dead and the ship sunk.

Rork shouted in my ear. "Near miss!"

His false hand had a chunk out of it, and there was a stain on his right calf. He didn't care, he was gleefully shouting into my ear. "Oohee, sir! But didn't me darlin' *Oregon* bracket us just as she should! Damned fine example o' shootin' by our dear Sean. Aye, an' the next pair o' rounds'll be right on target."

"Where's the captain?" I asked, ignoring the obvious implications of Rork's comment.

Law pointed toward the bridge. "Captain Díaz-Moreu is in the wheelhouse, sir. He was just about there when we were hit. Shrapnel must've barely missed him."

My hearing was coming back. I belatedly noticed the lieutenant had dark stains on his arm and chest.

"Are you two hit bad?" I asked them.

They both shook their heads. Law said, "Only nicks on me, sir. Your face looks worse than my wounds."

I looked questioningly at Rork. "And you?"

"Fit as a fiddle, sir," he roared. "These're just wee scratches on me hide. An' now that me own lads on *Oregon*'re takin' care o' business in proper naval fashion, things are finally lookin' up. Took 'em bloody long enough to get in range!"

A petty officer ran by, cursing at his men aft of us but disregarding us completely. So did the stretcher party who took the wounded men away. We were on our own.

I tried to remember the rate of fire for a 13-inch gun. Two and a half minutes, I seemed to recall, for a well-trained gun crew. We had maybe sixty seconds before Sean's next rounds arrived.

I started heading forward. "Come with me!"

Colón heeled over to port as she veered sharply to starboard. I knew Díaz-Moreu was trying to throw *Oregon*'s aim off, or rather, *my son's* aim. *Colón* had very little sea room to maneuver in, though, for the rocky coast was close aboard to starboard. We couldn't head farther out offshore or we'd lose even more ground to *Oregon*. It was the classic quandary of the pursued. Every twist or turn on our part allowed the pursuers to close the distance on us.

Two more rounds rumbled through the sky toward us and exploded in our wake. They lifted the stern, but we were just far enough forward that the shards didn't get us. This was my first time on the receiving end of 13-inch guns, and even the concussions were mind stopping. They sounded like a train approaching, not at all like the high-pitched scream of smaller calibers.

"Fifty feet short. Next one'll do it once an' for all," exclaimed Rork.

I could imagine the entire American fleet, thousands of sailors, watching *Oregon*'s forward turret to see if the guns could do what had to be done. Sean's next step would be simple. Elevate his guns' trajectory another two degrees to the maximum of fifteen degrees elevation and send a plunging trajectory right down into *Colón*'s stacks.

Our ship would disappear in a flash of light and a volcano of debris. The wreckage would continue moving forward for a moment, rapidly settling down into the water before sinking completely. The suction of the sinking hull would take the few initial survivors down with her.

A change of two degrees, and the battle would be won.

49

Let Us Do This with Dignity

Off the Santiago Coast, Cuba
Sunday, 3 July 1898

WHEN WE REACHED the armored citadel on the bridge, all the ports had been shut again. After the glaring sun outside, it was dark as a cave in there and I stumbled into an officer. He swore savagely at me. A stern voice in the gloom admonished the officer to stay calm.

Amidst the constant drone of battle reports and acknowledgments I heard Emilio's voice rise above the others. "Peter, I thought you were killed! Stay safe in that corner."

Rork, Law, and I wedged ourselves together against the bulkhead as our eyes began to adjust to the dim light of the battle lanterns. The air was thick with smoky haze and human desperation. From what little I could make of the reports coming in from around the ship, the scenario was bleak. *Colón* was taking on water from opened seams, electrical and firefighting water lines were severed, hydraulics for the guns' training mechanisms were failing, fires had started in the after storage rooms, the engine shafts were beginning to warp from overheated bearings, and more than two dozen wounded were crammed into the surgeon's room.

I looked at the clock, which showed 1:12 p.m. We'd been running for our lives for three and a half hours. The race was ending. I braced for the inevitable.

It was a single shot. The sea just ahead of the bow erupted in a gigantic burst of blinding light, black smoke, white water, and white-hot steel. The hail of steel fragments swept across our foredeck, ricocheting off the armor plating like some berserk percussionist was banging away on it. Spray sluiced through the slits, soaking the officers peering out.

The shell's flight must have barely missed the corner of the citadel in which we hid. If it had struck the structure full on, no amount of plating would have saved us. No one commented on the obvious fact that the citadel was the intended target.

The Spanish officers followed Emilio's guidance: unemotional adherence to procedure. They passed along concise damage, engineering, and gun mount reports, each of which their captain acknowledged in his slow, deep voice. They were determined to play out this performance to the bitter end, for the curtain had not yet dropped. It was unlike anything I'd ever experienced. Dreamlike, almost absurd.

Rork counted down the next two minutes. Five seconds after he predicted it the next round arrived. This one exploded right under the stern, two hundred feet aft of where we stood, with a massively thunderous sound. It was far more damaging than the last shot. The blast lifted the entire hull, twisting and shaking it. I felt the vibration of the interior bulkheads buckling. Cabling and pipes fell from the overhead. Battle lanterns shattered. The chart table collapsed. Charts, pencils, navigation instruments, coffee cups, reports—anything that wasn't secured—were thrown into the air. Those inside the small space were thrown against one another, some ending up down on the deck. Spontaneous curses and cries for God filled the darkness until their captain imperturbably reminded them to give their reports.

There were none. All communications from other parts of the ship were gone. Messengers were sent to get reports. Emilio opened the hatch and went out onto the starboard bridge wing. Looking out through the door, I could see the shoreline. I gauged our speed at eight to ten knots and dropping. The stern seemed to be squatting.

Emilio reentered the wheelhouse and quietly ordered a course change, which was echoed by the officer of the watch and the helmsman. "Full right rudder, steady on course 350 degrees. Steer for the mouth of that river you see below the peak of the tallest mountain."

Everyone knew what that meant. He was running his beloved *Cristóbal Colón*—the ship he'd commanded since she was born in the builder's yard—ashore. It was her final act. The destination was the riverfront beach below Mount Turquino, at more than six thousand feet in elevation the highest peak in all of Cuba, and a landmark of great symbolic value to the islanders.

After the order was acknowledged, no one said a word. The ship sluggishly turned north. She was slowing rapidly. I debated internally what to say, but there was little time. Another shell would come in seconds.

At last, I spoke up. "Captain Díaz-Moreu, is it time, sir?"

"Not yet, Peter. But very soon."

He passed the word for all hands to hold on tightly and stand by for grounding. Then he told his officers they could get their personal belongings from their cabins if they wished. None of them left the bridge.

A breathless messenger from the engine room arrived. He reported flooding and that the engineers said they could no longer ensure engine control. The signalman reported the gaff flying the national battle flag as having collapsed, but added that another ensign was set on the mainmast. Another messenger reported the surgeon was moving the wounded topside.

The mountain loomed over us as we closed in on the beach.

Captain Emilio Díaz-Moreu, who had served his country for forty years since he joined the navy at the age of twelve, stood tall in the open doorway. He took a breath and turned to his executive officer, calmly uttering the words no naval officer wants to even think about saying.

"Strike the national colors and deliver them to me. Send officers to all guns and compartments to pass the word that we have surrendered. Upon grounding, they will abandon the ship and make their way to the beach."

He waited while the officers showed their understanding, then continued. "Engineers will open all sea cocks and flood the ship when she grounds. Put Jacob's ladders over the starboard bow and assemble some rafts. Officers will muster their divisions on the foredeck and depart the ship by division, with the medical division and wounded men first, followed by the engineers, the deck division, the gunnery division, then the rest. The wounded will float ashore on the rafts. The senior staff officers will remain aboard to make sure all our men are off, then they will depart. The executive officer will go ashore first and set up a camp for the wounded."

The executive officer hesitated.

Emilio put a hand on the man's shoulder. "I know it is difficult, my friend. But you need to get to work now. I am depending on you."

The executive officer saluted and stepped away to send officers off on their missions. None said a word as they departed. Most of the watch personnel emptied the wheelhouse, leaving only the senior officers and a few petty officers remaining.

My men and I stood there quietly watching our approach to the shoreline. Legally, I suppose we were the victors at that point. As senior American officer present, I could have started issuing orders. I didn't feel like a victor, though, and just stood there, mute.

I felt a gentle rasping as the bow slid across the sandy bottom in twenty feet of water, then a thud as it hit a coral reef. The ship stopped. The bow was aground, but the stern was still afloat, settling down as the flooding increased with the opened seacocks.

"The Americans have stopping firing, sir," a petty officer reported. "They are still approaching at full speed."

Emilio nodded thoughtfully. "Very well, gentlemen. We have surrendered and are now under the protection of the Americans. But remember we are still the officers and sailors of Spain. Let us do this with dignity. Keep order and discipline. I will be in my cabin for a moment and will see you ashore once I know everyone else is off the ship. Captain Wake, would you care to join me briefly in my cabin? I had your belongings placed there for safekeeping when you came aboard."

"Aye, aye, sir," I said with instinctive respect.

I heard grown men weeping as they exited the wheelhouse to fulfill their final duties to their captain, their ship, and their men. It was an unforgettable scene. I'd never been on board a ship when she surrendered, but now I understood that each man there felt the abject humiliation to his very marrow.

I should have been jubilant, but I wasn't. There were tears in my eyes too.

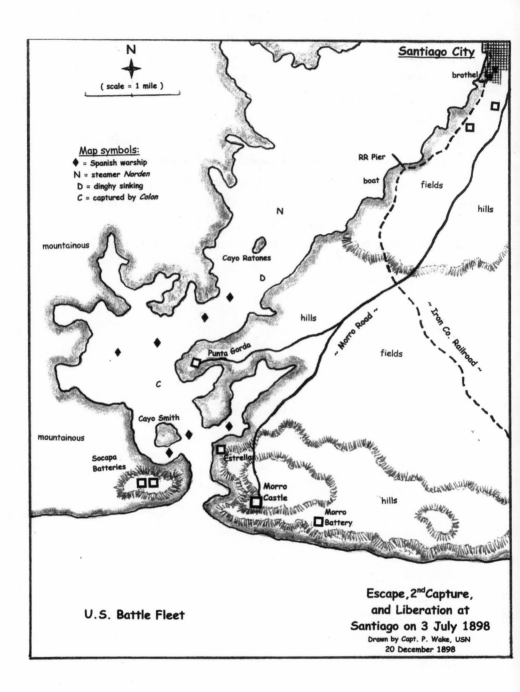

N
(scale = 1 mile)

Santiago City

brothel

Map symbols:
◆ = Spanish warship
N = steamer *Norden*
D = dinghy sinking
C = captured by *Colon*

RR Pier

boat

fields

hills

mountainous

Cayo Ratones

N

D

hills

~ Morro Road ~

~ Iron Co. Railroad ~

fields

◆

◆

◆

Punta Garda

◆

C

mountainous

Cayo Smith

◆

◆

Socapa
Batteries

Estrella

Morro
Castle

Morro
Battery

hills

U.S. Battle Fleet

Escape, 2nd Capture,
and Liberation at
Santiago on 3 July 1898
Drawn by Capt. P. Wake, USN
20 December 1898

50

Honoring the Enemy

The Mouth of the Turquino River, Santiago de Cuba, Cuba
Sunday Afternoon, 3 July 1898

THE CAPTAIN WAS ALONE in his cabin, said his orderly, who stood faithfully in the passageway outside. Leaving Law and Rork with the orderly, I knocked on the door and stepped inside.

Emilio stood there, sword and scabbard in hand. "I believe this is the part where you take my sword, Peter."

"No, Emilio. I did not defeat you, Captain Clark did. I was your prisoner after you defeated me, remember? It's an archaic practice anyway. Nobody uses swords anymore, so why even give them away after a battle?"

"Because it is romantic, Peter, and naval officers are a romantic breed. We cling to our archaic practices as few others do. But I can see your point about the expectations of others. I will present it to Captain Clark when I meet him."

I wasn't sure what to say, wanting to offer something positive. "I would imagine they will be here soon. Your people will be treated with respect, and your wounded will be attended to immediately."

"Yes, of all that I am sure. Peter, I am glad I met you again, and that you survived this ordeal. Please congratulate your son for me.

And do not forget our future evening of sea stories. I look forward to it and to introducing you to my dear Martina."

"I also look forward to our future reunion, Emilio. And it will be my pleasure to buy the first two bottles."

"Ha, as you should!" It was a sad laugh.

He gestured toward the seabag on his bunk. "This is yours. I took the liberty of looking through it and am a bit jealous of your collection of weaponry. The coxswain of my steam launch should be thankful you chose not to employ them on him."

"No, I could see it was time for me to surrender, Emilio. Old sailors know when it is time."

I called Rork in to get the seabag. He returned to the passageway, leaving us alone again.

"It is time for me to go, Emilio. Thank you for your kindness and hospitality. I am privileged to be your friend, and Spain should be honored to have you as a son."

After we shook hands, I stood at attention and saluted my Spanish adversary. He returned the salute. When I left the cabin, he was staring at the sword and scabbard in his hands.

51

_____

Triumphant Glory

Turquino Beach, Santiago de Cuba, Cuba

Sunday, 3 July 1898

DOWN ON THE MAIN deck ten minutes later, Rork pointed over my shoulder. "Aye, sir, an' here come our lads." *Oregon* and *Brooklyn* had stopped a quarter mile away and were already sending armed boat crews to take possession of the ship and custody of the prisoners.

"The wounded are ashore by now, so let's go."

I wanted to get off that ship and go home to my Navy. I led the way to a Jacob's ladder, passing through clusters of still stunned Spanish sailors on the deck. None showed us anger, but their officers, especially the junior ones, gave us cold looks. We shouldered our way past them and descended the ladder to a raft loaded with the last of the wounded. Once ashore, we stood at the water's edge and waited for the American boats, ignoring the stares of the Spaniards around us. Another ten minutes and it was over. The U.S. Navy in all its triumphant glory arrived and took control. A half dozen launches and cutters landed a hundred men in blue on the beach, with more coming.

Within seconds the beach was a chaotic scene. American officers took over the prisoners, now guarded by armed yanqui sailors uneasy in their new role. The Spanish sailors had been mustered by division and remained there dolefully on the sand, waiting for orders from someone. Several other launches clustered alongside *Colón*. I saw a tall Spanish officer on her main deck speaking with the American officers clustered around him. It was Emilio Díaz-Moreu. He followed them down a ladder to a boat.

Looking farther east, I saw *New York* a few miles away, charging in our direction. Sampson was coming. I wondered what he was thinking at the sight of the entire Spanish fleet destroyed.

Nearby, an American lieutenant commander explained through pantomime to several senior officers from *Colón* that they would be taken to the admiral's flagship when she arrived. They finally nodded their understanding and calmly awaited their fate as the American went to another group.

American petty officers began organizing boatloads of enlisted prisoners to be ferried out to *Brooklyn* and *Oregon*, eventually to be transferred to one of the transports. Farther up the beach at the makeshift Spanish aid station, U.S. Navy surgeons and their assistants helped their Spanish counterparts ready the wounded for the long trip to the hospital ship at Siboney.

In all this bustle no one particularly noticed the three of us. I realized they didn't recognize us as Americans, which was understandable. Unshaven and disheveled, we looked like ragged Cubans dressed in cast-off uniforms.

Needing to report in to Admiral Sampson right away, I began looking for a way to get out to *New York* when she arrived. I was about to intrude upon the lieutenant commander when Rork banged my shoulder and gestured toward a group of men down the beach.

"Well lookee there, sir. Is that not a sight to make two tired old men glad?" He gazed up toward the heavens, his right hand outstretched. "Thank you, Jaysus!"

52

Reunion and Defiance

Turquino Beach, Santiago de Cuba, Cuba

Sunday, 3 July 1898

COLÓN'S JUNIOR OFFICERS were being assembled by an American lieutenant who spoke Spanish passably. His back was to me, but I had no difficulty recognizing his voice. I walked over to him.

"Sean . . ." Overcome with emotion, I could say nothing more.

He turned around, his face draining of color. "*Dad?*"

My heart swelled with pride as I hugged him. It was all I could do not to blubber like a fool. He was taller and stronger than me now. He held me by the shoulders and looked me over. I felt old and frail. "Dad, your face is hurt. You look terrible. And how did you ever get *here*?"

Rork walked up and embraced him as well. "Oh, laddie, you're one hell'uva welcome sight for me sorry ol' eyes! Been a wee bit dicey lately for your dad an' me."

My son looked questioningly at me. "I thought you were a staff officer with General García someplace near Siboney."

Rork laughed. "Well, now, Captain Wake, why don't you go right ahead an' tell the lad what his ol' man's been up to—an' dragged my sorry ol' arse into as well!"

All that was too much to explain right then, so I simply said, "Uncle Sean and I got captured by the Spanish at Santiago, son."

"You were captured by the Spanish navy?" As he realized what had happened, his expression changed from surprise to horror. "Good Lord, you were prisoners on *Colón!*"

"Yes, we were. It's a long story, which I'll tell you later when we have more time. By the way, you did fine today, son."

It was my son's turn to be overcome. He couldn't take his eyes off the wreckage that was *Colón*. Dwelling on what might have happened wouldn't do any good, so I changed the subject to more pressing matters.

"Sean, I see *New York* is arriving now. I need to report to Admiral Sampson and get an important message back to General Shafter. Can you get me out to the admiral?"

He snapped back around to me. "What? Oh, sorry, Dad, I was just thinking about what could've . . ."

"All's well that ends well, son. Don't get into the *what-ifs*. They're a waste of time. Now, how about that ride out to *New York*?"

"Right. Of course, Dad." Then, with a shy, apologetic grimace, he converted from my son back into a naval officer. "Ah, I mean *aye, aye*, sir."

Edwin Law, Sean, and I sat in the stern as *Oregon's* steam launch chugged out to the flagship. Once I was sure my reconnaissance report was headed for Shafter, I would somehow get to Maria. I desperately needed to be alone with her, to hold her and have her hold me.

"Any word from Maria?" I asked my son.

"Oh, hell! Sorry, Dad. I should've told you right away, but seeing you *here* shocked me out of my wits. Yes, I got a short note from Maria yesterday. She's been ordered to *Seneca*, a converted Ward Line passenger ship taking our wounded back home. She wasn't sure when they were getting under way or for which port."

Seneca? The one they were loading with wounded when I left Maria? That ship and her master, Captain Decker, were familiar to me. She'd run the Havana route for many years before the war. Maria and I'd even sailed on her from Key West to New York. Three months earlier, when I was commanding the Special Service Squadron on its ill-fated mission, the Navy had obtained *Seneca* and turned her into a troopship. I'd last seen the vessel in June. With the rest of the transport fleet, she was lying off Siboney waiting to disembark her seasick soldiers and pack animals.

This, at long last, was good news about Maria. She was leaving Cuba. My spirits lifted. As soon as I reported to the admiral, I'd find my wife before she departed for the United States.

Up in the bow, Rork sat on the forward thwart. His queue had come loose, and his long gray hair was tangled and flying about in the wind. Beside him was his false hand and its prosthetic base. Swaying easily with the motion of the boat, he was slowly massaging the stump of his left arm. Periodically, especially in the humid tropics, he rubbed talcum powder on the stump to prevent rashes, but he'd run out in Cuba.

The saltwater and jellyfish stings made it worse. His arm was red and swollen. I knew he was in pain. I'd also noticed him limping on the trail. That old right foot injury was acting up, too. He stopped his massaging and dipped his arm into the bow wave. Then he brought it up and vacantly stared aft at Cuba. The eyes had no twinkle; the mouth no ready smile. His frame was slumped. The brave façade was gone.

My oldest and dearest friend looked worse than exhausted. We were all exhausted. But for the first time since we'd met thirty-five years earlier, Sean Rork looked physically and mentally *weak*. He'd never recovered from his heatstroke in the battle two days earlier, and now I saw the stark reality of his health. Rork was an old man. He would never recover from all the wounds and ailments he had accumulated during his long, hard life.

Back at San Juan Heights, I'd thought it was time for him to go on leave and rest. I acquiesced when he put up a vigorous argument. But now I knew it was time for him to retire. I considered ordering him to go home on Maria's hospital ship. It would anger and embarrass him, but I was ready to endure his resentment to save my friend's life.

Seeing me studying him, the old goat quickly went back into his usual persona. He sat up straighter on the thwart and strapped on his marlinespike appliance. The rubber hand was still on the thwart. The marlinespike, that stealthy weapon he'd carried for fifteen years, gleamed in the sun as he inspected it.

The old devilish smile returned as he glanced at me. "Well, sir, seems we cheated death one more bloody time."

The launch's crew, who had been watching Rork adjust his wicked-looking strap and spike, broke into grins at his performance. I'll admit it worked on me, too. *Maybe I misjudged his condition and he really is just a bit tired.* That's what I desperately wanted to think.

"Down but never out!" Rork growled to the waves as he squinted into the sunlit horizon. It was the old Rork. Law looked over at me and grinned.

In that instant I made the decision—knowing it would haunt me for the rest of my life. "Aye, Bosun, and damned lucky at that, I say!" I shouted back over the roaring boiler and clanking piston as we charged along.

He retorted as I knew he would. "Lucky hell, sir! We're the most cold-hearted sea-goin' bastards who ever trod a deck! Enemies tremble at our name!"

By this time everyone was laughing, and I yelled out my part in the running joke we'd had for more than thirty years. "That they do, Rork! But we can't quit now, can we? There's more enemies to be vanquished, ladies to be loved, and wrongs to be righted!"

Rork stood up in the bow, swaying with the swells, and raised his unsheathed marlinespike toward the flagship. "Aye, sir! An' all done in proper naval fashion!"

Everyone in the launch, officers and men, cheered a lusty, "Aye!" in answer. Rork showed the merest flicker of self-satisfaction as he sat down. He sat there, nonchalantly watching the closing gap to the giant warship as if nothing had just transpired. He knew he didn't have to say anything more.

Chief Boatswain's Mate Sean Rork, U.S. Navy, had once again made his point, loud and clear.

53

Living in the Mud No More

Flagship New York
Sunday, 3 July 1898

THE FLAG LIEUTENANT announced my arrival to Admiral Sampson. I stepped past the Marine sentry in the passageway and into the admiral's opulent day cabin. Now that the ship was no longer cleared for action, the space looked more like a society parlor than a commander's spartan quarters. The ports were open, but in the midday of a Cuban summer the cabin still was oppressively hot, no matter how luxurious the fixtures.

Sampson was in shirtsleeves. He looked up from his desk, a genuinely happy grin on his usually taciturn face. "Dear Lord, is that really you, Peter? I heard the news but couldn't believe it! You look awful. We'll get the doctor in here to look at those wounds on your face. And that rash!"

The admiral threw a questioning glance at the lieutenant, who quickly disappeared to find the staff surgeon.

"It is indeed me, sir," I said. "Sorry about my appearance. I haven't had a chance to find new uniforms for myself or my men, or to bathe. My wounds are negligible—just old ones that have reopened. And the rash is from last night when we got stung by jellyfish, of all things, while floating in Santiago Bay."

311

"Well, first and foremost, you need some medical attention."

"Please don't worry about me. I fully understand you're over-whelmed with responsibilities right now, so I won't intrude for long. Just needed to report to you and make sure that my reconnaissance report gets to General Shafter as soon as possible. It's important, and he's been expecting it since midnight last night."

Sampson motioned to the chair by his desk. "Reconnaissance? Peter, please sit down. Twice in the last week I've heard the wildest gossip about you being killed on some sort of skullduggery ashore. Now I'm hearing you were a prisoner on *Colón* during the battle."

It hasn't taken long for that *to get around. Probably from Rork visiting his cronies up in the CPO mess.*

"Well, yes, we did have some trouble ashore, sir, but we got through it. And yes, we were captured while we were trying to swim past *Colón* to the American fleet and ended up on board her during the battle. A very long story."

He shook his head in wonder. "I imagine it *is* a long story. Obviously, we need to get you back in Uncle Sam's Navy before you get yourself killed for real!"

"No arguments from me on that, Admiral. About the report for General Shafter, sir. He's been waiting for it since last night, but I was prevented from getting it to the American lines. Once I got on board *New York* I took the liberty of asking your flag lieutenant to have it typed up. It's right here, sir. And this is your copy." I handed both to him. "He didn't want an extra copy made, but I think you should see it since you need to know the situation ashore too."

"Thank you. I'm heading for a meeting with Shafter later, but we'll get his copy of your report to him straightaway. And we'll keep my copy confidential. Now, I want to hear what's going on ashore—after our doctor looks you over. And we're getting new uniforms for you and your men. Can't have you looking like vagabonds on the flagship, can we?"

Sampson called for the lieutenant, gave him the original of the report to have taken ashore, and told him that he didn't wish to be disturbed for an hour. Then he leaned back and said, "Peter, I haven't seen you since the meeting with García. I want to hear everything."

Strengthened by Navy coffee and leftovers from the admiral's pantry, I began with my liaison with the Cuban and American armies. At Sampson's insistence I included my impressions of the personalities and geography of the fighting ashore.

The doctor, a disagreeable sort with tiny eyes set far back in his head, arrived as I was relating the battle at Kettle and San Juan Heights to Sampson. The physician poked about my body as I continued, interrupting with harrumphs about the jellyfish stings, my facial and torso wounds' appearance, lack of hygiene, bad breath, and the ragged appearance of several very old scars. When Sampson asked about my overall condition, the doctor admitted that I was in no grave danger of death—somewhat disappointedly, I thought. Before departing, he prescribed a bath for the hygiene, a cream solution for the rash and wounds, and bed rest.

Funny how I keep hearing that. At some point, maybe I can do all those things.

Once Sampson and I were alone again, I conveyed the details of my reconnaissance mission at Santiago and subsequent captures by the Spanish army and navy. I also explained the reason for my urgency in getting the report to Shafter: the intelligence I gained could shorten the land campaign.

After I concluded my recitation, Sampson, who had been a rapt audience the entire time, gave me his view of the American strategic situation. "Your assessment of the enemy's position seems spot on, Peter, but the strategic significance of Santiago has been superseded by today's events. Now that the enemy fleet is destroyed, the Army's campaign has been rendered moot."

"Yes, sir, I suppose it is," I said, thinking bitterly about the men I'd seen die ashore and afloat, on both sides. Still, as callous as Sampson's statement was, I saw his point. The Spanish fleet was always the nemesis at Santiago, for it alone could attack the United States. The U.S. Army and Navy were now freed for action elsewhere.

Sampson continued, "General Shafter's plan will probably change from an attack to a siege of the city. And not a long one. Troops en route for him will no doubt be sent to other campaigns. Washington wants Puerto Rico as the next target."

It was the first I'd heard of it. "To capture San Juan?"

"Yes, in an overland flank attack from Fajardo. But Puerto Rico isn't the only possible target. The capture of Havana, maybe even a naval raid on the coast of Spain itself, are also being discussed in Washington. All these potential fights require me to be ready for any eventuality." He looked down at his desk for a moment before continuing.

"Therefore, I need more ship captains to command the dozens of ships being procured for the Navy. I need experienced men I can trust to make spontaneous and correct decisions—like you. Peter, you're going back to sea in command of a ship."

The admiral paused, his attention narrowing on me again. "That's why your days of living in the mud are over, Peter. As I have complete command over all naval personnel in this theater of the war, your orders as liaison to the Army are hereby rescinded. A message to that effect will be sent to General Shafter and to General García."

It was great news. But there were other factors. *That won't bother Shafter, but I'm not exactly loved in Washington. Some folks up there won't like my getting a ship.*

Sampson must have seen a wary look on my face, for he said, "I don't care what enemies you have in Washington. I need an experienced ship commander, and you're getting command of the cruiser *Dixon*. Her captain is slated for a flag posting back in the States."

It was hard to keep the astonishment out of my voice. "*Dixon*, sir? The old Morgan liner the Navy bought in April?"

"Yes, the very same," he said with a grin. "She's large and relatively fast. The Navy has fitted her out as a large auxiliary cruiser with two 6-inchers, ten 3-inch gun mounts, plus several smaller rapid-fire guns. She's screening the transports at Siboney now, which is what you'll do for the invasion at Puerto Rico. I think you may have a fight there with Spanish torpedo boats, but *Dixon* should be able to deal with that menace."

"Thank you, sir. When?"

"Tomorrow morning, after you get some rest. And yes, you can take that old reprobate Rork with you. How is he?"

"As incorrigible as always, sir, but damned handy to have around when things get rough. He's enjoying the hospitality of your chief petty officers' quarters right now. What about the Marine assigned to me, Lieutenant Edwin Law? Good man. I'd like to take him with me to *Dixon*."

"Sorry, but with so many Marines busy ashore at Guantánamo we're short of them out here in the fleet. He'll be going to one of the battleships."

I was about to ask for more details on *Dixon* when the flag lieutenant returned to the cabin and handed the admiral a message from the bridge. Sampson's face darkened as he read it.

"Peter, I'll have to get this idiocy sorted out, and then I'll be right back."

As the admiral stood to go, he explained briefly, "It appears an Austrian cruiser, *Kaiserin Maria Teresa*, entered our area of operations. That was no error, I'd wager. But one of our ships mistook her for a Spanish battleship headed in to sink our Army transports at Siboney. They're just about to engage her. I don't have time for an accidental war with Austria on top of everything else!"

I waited an hour. The admiral never did return from his efforts to prevent another war. Since I heard no gunfire or alarm, I presumed he was successful. And probably sidetracked by some other problem. Finally, I headed off for my assigned cabin, which had been vacated by some unfortunate commander.

The admiral's steward showed up, saying Sampson was still up on the bridge and had ordered him to prepare me a bath in the admiral's private tub. I didn't hesitate one second. In a flash, I returned to the wonderfully luxurious world of an admiral to let my aching body soak away the pains and tension of Cuba. Unfortunately, unlike the bath at Olga's home, there was no rum on the side table. After my soaking I donned my newly arrived uniform and enjoyed a sumptuous late lunch in the empty wardroom.

As *New York* steamed east toward Santiago, I succumbed to the soft berth waiting in my cabin. The effect was instantaneous and total.

For the next ten blissful hours I dreamed of being home with Maria.

54

A Pretty Morning

Off Siboney, Cuba
Monday, 4 July 1898

A FTER SPENDING THE NIGHT with the battle fleet off Santiago, *New York* arrived at the transport fleet's crowded anchorage off Siboney just after dawn. She slowly threaded her way among the tugs, water hoys, barges, freighters, transports, tenders, and gunboats sitting off the Army's tent city ashore.

There wasn't a cloud in the sky, and the slanting rays of the rising sun brought out the water's palette of jade and aqua, blue and purple. A gentle sea breeze from the southeast kept the stench of the Army's latrines and hospital away from us. No sounds of battle were in the air anymore. It could've been a peacetime fleet visit if you didn't look at the military mess ashore.

Standing on *New York*'s boat deck, I spotted *Dixon* in the distance. She was by herself, well offshore to the south. At over 6,000 tons she was larger than most of the ships, and the newly installed gun mounts were clearly visible along her main deck. Smoke drifted from her after funnel as she slowly steamed back and forth guarding the transports from a surprise Spanish attack. The Austrian warship was nowhere to be seen, having been warned off the previous evening. I wondered if the Austrians knew how close they'd come to dying from American guns.

I went up to the bridge. Borrowing a set of binoculars, I searched for Maria's ship. I found *State of Texas*, the Red Cross' chartered hospital ship, her hull painted with large red crosses, anchored close in to the beach. But there was no sign of *Seneca*.

My worry mounted. Had Maria heard the same rumors Sampson mentioned about my death ashore at Santiago? Was she already grieving? After the loss of her son in the war and the horrors of the field hospital, I feared it might be too much for her heart.

As we passed each ship, the officers on their bridges saluted the flagship, calling out effusive congratulations on the great victory. Deck crews added gutteral praise to their usual insults to their counterparts on *New York*. Commodore Schley's *Brooklyn* steamed in after us, also receiving cheers.

New York stopped a mile off the beach, thunderously letting go her anchor and chain in a cloud of rust. Simultaneously, the admiral's gig, a nicely trimmed-out little steam launch, was swayed out from the starboard side. When she reached the water, her tiny stack was already puffing, ready to convey Admiral Sampson ashore for his meeting with General Shafter. The ship's accommodation ladder was lowered down to the gig. No swaying Jacob's ladder for the admiral.

The officer of the deck approached me with a puzzled look. "Sir, I have a letter for you. It's not from home; it just arrived in the Army mailbag from Siboney for the admiral. It's addressed to you, marked general delivery to the fleet."

I tore open the envelope and read the note inside.

> 7 a.m., 4 July 1898
> Darling Peter,
> I am leaving this morning on the hospital ship *Seneca* to help care for the sick and wounded who are being taken home. They say we're heading to a special quarantine camp at Long Island, which may be near Theodore's home.
> You were right. This hospital and the war have been too much for me. I have done my duty in Tampa and here, but I am going home now. You and I will be grandparents soon,

and I want to help bring that wonderful new life into the world and nurture it. I am so tired of insanity and misery and death.

You may hear that I am ill. Please don't worry. It is only the dysentery everyone here has, and with rest and the proper diet I will be fine. The best medicine I could hope for would be seeing you come through the front door of our home. I pray for it each day. I live for it.

Come home as soon as you can, darling.

Your loving wife, Maria

My mind raced with the salient question of whether Maria's ship had already departed. I hadn't seen *Seneca*, but the anchorage was so crowded I might have missed her.

"Ah, excuse me, sir?" the officer of the deck repeated himself.

I looked up from the note. "Yes?"

"The launch to your ship is standing by alongside the quarter-deck, sir. Your gear and Chief Rork are already in it."

"Be right there," I replied and headed down to the main deck.

It took more than half an hour to chug out to my new command. The ship was stationary, rolling back and forth on the swells. As we approached, Rork stood by the coxswain and held up four fingers, signifying to *Dixon*'s boatswain of the watch that an officer of the rank of captain was about to come on board. Then he let them know I was an unattached captain, as yet, by shouting, "Captain Wake."

I could hear the boatswain of the watch growl at somebody, "Ah, hell, he's early. Quick, tell the lieutenant the new captain's here! And for God's sake, make sure word gets topside to the Old Man."

I knew there would be consternation on *Dixon*, from the deck watch up to the captain, at what some would consider my rude-ness. I wasn't expected to arrive and begin the process for taking command for another hour. The timing didn't matter to me. I was beyond caring what they thought. I just needed to get away from Cuba, away from the staff politics of the flagship, and back into the well-ordered and logical life of a navy warship captain.

55

The Woman in White

Cruiser Dixon, *off Siboney, Cuba*
Monday, 4 July 1898

I'D BEEN ON BOARD ONLY two hours. During that time the captain and I had agreed to delete some parts of the traditional change-of-command procedures and accelerate the legally required ones. Fortunately, the captain being relieved understood my insistence and acquiesced with my unusual request. It helped that he was an old ONI friend. He was also anxious to get away from Cuba's heat, up to Washington for his promotion, and out to his new command on the Pacific Coast.

However, I could see the alterations were confusing some of the officers and senior petty officers. The Navy is bound by tradition, and deviation from it invites concern. There was no luncheon with my predecessor, no preceremony inspection tour of the ship, no hours-long study of readiness reports and personnel evaluations. I had no doubt the mess decks, gunroom, and wardroom were abuzz with discussion about this strange new commanding officer with the scarred and swollen red face.

At 11:20 a.m., more than two and a half hours earlier than planned, hundreds of officers and crew mustered by divisions in their best dress whites on the foredeck. By naval regulation, they had to witness the legal transfer of command. The outgoing captain dutifully read aloud his orders of detachment from *Dixon* from Rear Admiral Sampson. I then read aloud my orders from Sampson to take command of *Dixon*.

My predecessor saluted me and announced, "I am ready to be relieved, sir."

I returned the salute and stated, "You are relieved, sir."

At that instant I became captain of *Dixon* and assumed total responsibility for everything about her and the men on board. The national ensign was broken out from the masthead, ending the ceremony. I dismissed the crew. Ten minutes later, after we shook hands on the quarterdeck, *Dixon's* previous captain departed to begin his new chapter in life.

During this entire time, *Dixon* had been loitering offshore. I passed the word to prepare the ship for getting under way. There wasn't much time for what I had in mind.

I didn't yet know the name of any officer or man in *Dixon's* crew, other than the second in command, Cdr. John Belfort. We'd not met before my arrival, but I noted with appreciation that he did not appear ruffled by my unorthodox first couple of hours.

"Steam is up, the watch is standing by, and the ship is ready for sea in all respects, sir," Belfort reported as we stood on the starboard bridge wing under the hot Caribbean sun in our dress whites. "Standing by for orders, sir."

Just as I was about to provide orders to get under way, the foremast lookout called down from above. "Lookout to bridge! Hospital ship *Seneca* in sight two points off the port bow—a mile off. She's outward bound to the southeast, sir."

I let out a long breath. We were in time. Prior to the change-of-command ceremony, while still a guest officer on board, I'd made a request to the captain for the lookouts to notify me if they spotted *Seneca*. By now, everyone in *Dixon* knew the new captain's wife was a nurse on the hospital ship. I guessed this was courtesy of Rork, who let it slip in a conversation with me that the boat coxswain overheard on our way out to the ship. Such is the way of a small community of men at sea. There are damn few secrets.

I brought the long telescope to my eye. The ship was *Seneca*, all right. She was slowly steaming out from behind several other ships on the far side of the anchorage. A large white flag with a red cross flew from her main gaff.

"Kindly get *Dixon* under way, if you please," I told Commander Belfort. "Steady on course zero-five-zero. Make revolutions for ten knots. We will intercept *Seneca* as she emerges from the anchorage and turns eastward."

As convention and efficiency required, my subordinates on the bridge echoed my orders exactly. *Dixon*'s bow turned to the northeast and steadied on a point a mile offshore of Punta Berracos. *Seneca* turned, steering for the same area. I did some quick calculations. We'd intercept her in thirteen minutes.

When we'd reached half a mile distance from her I said to Belfort, "Please signal to *Seneca* this message: *Godspeed on voyage home with wounded. Captain Peter Wake.*"

Seconds later the signalmen hoisted the code flags up into the rigging above us. I could hear them snapping in the breeze, and soon colorful flags appeared on *Seneca*'s halyards. Some were the usual number and letter code, but there were several others, evidently spelling out words not in the standard naval code. I watched as *Dixon*'s senior signalman wrote down the flags in his notebook, then stopped and peered at *Seneca* again. He called for the naval signal book, skipping rapidly through the pages. Softly whistling in amazement, he slid down the ladder and approached me on the bridge wing.

Standing at attention, the first-class signalman cleared his throat and drily announced the other ship's message. "Sir, *Seneca* signals to Captain Wake: *Thank you.*" Then he nervously cleared his throat and added in a lower tone. "Ah, sir, the message then says, *Maria sends her love.*"

I couldn't help grinning at his embarrassment. I knew "Maria" and "love" were the words he'd had to double-check and spell out.

"Thank you. Send this reply to *Seneca*: *Please advise Maria: both Seans and I are fine.*"

The signalman raced up the ladder to send the message. Moments later *Seneca* acknowledged.

"*Seneca* is slowing, sir," said Belfort. "Looks like they want us to come alongside."

I was suddenly aware that the main deck below us was filled with off-watch men. They were studying *Seneca*, occasionally looking up at me. When we were only a hundred yards from *Seneca*'s starboard side, I reduced *Dixon*'s speed to match the other ship's, altering course to steam parallel eastbound. Belfort and I went out on the bridge wing.

Hundreds of soldiers lined the rails of the hospital ship, some in bandages, but I saw no woman. Then a slender form in a white smock came out on *Seneca*'s promenade deck. She gripped the railing, her eyes scanning *Dixon*. Beside her, an officer pointed to our bridge.

Dixon's crew buzzed with excitement at the sight of the lady in white, their heads swiveling between her and their new captain. The men on the bridge grew quiet. Belfort backed away to give me some privacy.

My heart was thrilled at seeing her, at letting her know I was alive and well. Energy raced through me. Then I saw that Maria's smock was discolored across the front. Bloodstains. Her beautiful long hair was done up severely in a tight bun. She looked thin, almost frail. Tears formed in my eyes. I tried, but I couldn't hold them back. I waved to her.

She touched her heart and waved back. The sailors on *Dixon*'s deck erupted in cheers. The soldiers on *Seneca* echoed them.

Rork suddenly materialized beside me with a speaking trumpet. As he put it in my hands, he quietly said, "Thought you might want this, sir."

Without another word, he went down the ladder, back to his watch station on the foredeck. Ignoring the men around me, and those over on *Seneca*, I lifted the trumpet.

"*I ... love ... you, ... Maria!*"

She shouted something I couldn't hear and waved madly. From *Seneca*'s bridge came the disembodied voice of Captain Baker through his trumpet.

"Must go now, Peter. No more time to yarn. Good luck."

With a belch of smoke, *Seneca* picked up speed. Maria turned away and went back inside the ship. For several minutes I stood there watching the hospital ship steam away.

Then I returned to the scene around me. The show was over. Belfort reappeared at my side. *Dixon*'s men began to disperse. Naval routine returned. The oncoming bridge watch took charge of the ship in the time-honored ceremony. It all had a reassuring predictability.

I was back at sea, where I belonged.

Acknowledgments

I've wanted to tell this story for many years. It took a lot of research, which led me to Washington, Tampa, Havana, and eastern Cuba. After five years of research and writing, and a lot of help along the way, it is finally finished, and I want to say thank-you to some wonderful people, without whom it wouldn't have happened.

First and foremost, I thank my brilliant wife, Nancy Ann Glickman. In addition to being my morale and welfare officer when the bureaucratic and logistical odds get overwhelming, she is also my business manager, publicist, lecture/book tour facilitator, and critical reader. Her invaluable influence is evident throughout this book.

I am so blessed to have my worldwide team of volunteer researchers (the legendary Subject Matter Advance Research Team, or "SMART Wakians"). In America, Randy Briggs and Rich Rolfe helped me find and understand academic research on Germany's role in Cuba in 1898. I am also indebted to Mario Cano and Chaz Mena of Miami for historical insights and academic research information from both the Spanish and the Cuban sides of this story.

The staffs and websites at the U.S. Naval Institute, Michigan State University Library, Theodore Roosevelt Association, U.S. Naval History and Heritage Command, Library of Congress, Port Tampa Library, University of Nebraska, and Dr. Antonio Rafael de la Cova's Latin American Studies Project at Indiana University are invaluable resources for historical facts about the Spanish-American War. They have my congratulations and appreciation.

In Havana, *un mil gracias* to Roberto Giraudy (Ministerio de Cultura), Ela López Ugarte (Centro de Estudios Martíanos), Dr. Justin White (professor of Spanish linguistics in Florida and coordinator of my readers' tours in Cuba), Victor Avila (director of the

Museum of the Grand Masonic Lodge of Cuba), and George Fernandez (historical guide in Havana). They have become far more than professional colleagues who have helped my understanding of Cuban history. They are dear friends.

Through the kind introduction of my aforementioned friends I was fortunate to meet with some renowned historians at Santiago de Cuba: Dr. Miguel Ronald Moncada (who spent days with me in various offices and also out in the field), Dr. Omar López Rodriguez (Oficina del Conservador de la Ciudad de Santiago), Dr. Olga Portoundo and Juan Manuel Reyes (Oficina del Historiador de la Ciudad de Santiago de Cuba), Juan Antonio Tejera Palzado (president of the Asociación de Cine, Radio y TV), and Dr. Carmen Montalvo Suárez (director of the Centro Estudios Antonio Maceo Grajales). All these talented people helped me understand not only the historical facts of 1898 but also the unique cultural flavor of the area and the people of Oriente.

My driver in Oriente, Antonio "Tony" Tejeiro Montesino, was nothing short of amazing. He somehow got our little expedition up 3,500-foot mountains, down potholed backcountry roads in the jungle, around ubiquitous mule carts and sudden goat herds, and through roadblocks and narrow city streets, all of which was accomplished in a 1952 Chevy sedan! My hosts in Santiago's Reparto Vista Alegre, the Tejera family, welcomed my fellow explorers and me into their home, a wonderful refuge of comfort, tranquility, and magnificent breakfasts.

My gratitude and respect go to the proficient and pleasant team at the Naval Institute Press who got this book launched: Director Rick Russell, Senior Acquisitions Editor Jim Dolbow, Senior Production Editor Emily Bakely, and copy editor Mindy Conner.

I cannot end the acknowledgments without expressing sincere gratitude to my readers around the world, the famous Wakians. There are a lot of frustrations in the book-writing profession, but for the last seventeen years you have inspired me to never give up my quest to illuminate the crucial events that long ago shaped our current world. You are also great fun to be with at our many Reader Rendezvous around the world!

Onward and upward, my friends, toward those distant horizons.

Robert N. Macomber
The Boat House
St. James, Pine Island
Florida

Sources and Notes by Chapter

Chapter 1. The Hotel

The Tampa Bay Hotel building is now the iconic centerpiece of the University of Tampa, with a section of the building beautifully restored to its 1890s opulence. The hotel is described in *The Assassin's Honor* and *An Honorable War*. It is well worth a visit. See www.ut.edu /plantmuseum.

Joseph Herrings wrote a book, *Kuba und der Krieg* (Cuba and the War), in 1899 about his observations during the war. It described the disciplinary problems, lack of preparedness, and general lack of efficient equipment but also commented on the bravery of the American soldiers.

Wake's exploits at the beginning of the Spanish-American War are depicted in *An Honorable War*.

Chapter 2. The Army

William Rufus Shafter (1835–1906) was born in Michigan and was a career Army officer from 1861 to 1901. In 1895 he was retroactively awarded the Medal of Honor for his actions at the Civil War battle at Fair Oaks, Virginia. After the Civil War he served in Indian campaigns, making brigadier general in 1897. At the beginning of the Spanish-American War he was in very bad physical condition, weighing in excess of three hundred pounds and suffering from severe gout and other ailments. He died in California five years after his retirement in 1901 and is buried at San Francisco National Cemetery. Fort Shafter in Hawaii is named for him.

Chapter 3. Breakfast with a Hero

Leonard Wood (1860–1927) was born in New Hampshire, educated in Massachusetts, got his medical degree from Harvard, and became an Army doctor in 1886. Awarded the Medal of Honor for his heroic actions in commanding an infantry unit whose officers had all been lost during an 1886 battle against Apaches, he subsequently decided upon the career of combat soldier. His distinguished career included service as physician to President Grover Cleveland and President William McKinley, regimental and brigade commander in Cuba, combat commander in the Philippine Moro Insurrection, and chief of staff of the Army from 1910 to 1914. He retired in 1921, becoming the governor-general of the Philippines until 1927. He died at Boston in 1927 and is buried at Arlington National Cemetery. Fort Leonard Wood in Missouri is named for him.

Theodore Roosevelt and Peter Wake became friends in 1886 at a political dinner in New York City. Wake was twenty years older and thus became a mentor to Theodore. They remained close friends for the reminder of Wake's life. This friendship is depicted in *The Darkest Shade of Honor, Honor Bound, Honorable Lies, The Assassin's Honor,* and *An Honorable War.*

During the 1890s in Cuba, the pro-Spanish Cuban militias were known as guerillas. The pro–Cuban independence rebels were known as *insurrectos.*

Col. Michael Woodgerd, a former U.S. Army officer-turned-mercenary, and Wake became friends in Italy in 1874. Since then they've encountered each other in various dangerous corners of the world, as depicted in *An Affair of Honor, Honor Bound,* and *An Honorable War.*

Chapter 4. The Spreading of Joy

Lafayette Street in Tampa is now Kennedy Boulevard. The original bridge has been replaced.

Barbancourt is still Haiti's finest rum. I spent a wonderful afternoon at the Barbancourt distillery in the mountains outside Port-au-Prince thirty-five years ago.

Colonel Isidro Marron, head of the Spanish secret police in Cuba, was Peter Wake's mortal enemy since their initial confrontation in 1886. Read *The Darkest Shade of Honor* to see how the hatred between them began. Read *An Honorable War* to see how it ended.

Read *Honor Bound* for Wake's perilous exploits inside Haiti in 1888.

Chapter 5. *Au Revoir,* not *Adieu*

Read *The Assassin's Honor* and *An Honorable War* for more about Wake's remarkable wife Maria and her influence on his life and work.

Maria had two sons. The oldest, Francisco, was a Franciscan priest in Havana murdered by Colonel Marron in February 1898. Juanito was a colonial bureaucrat and reserve army officer captured in battle by Wake, his stepfather. Read *An Honorable War* for details.

Modern naval opinion is that *Maine* was destroyed by an accidental spontaneous explosion of gases inside her coal bunker that ignited the adjacent ammunition magazine.

Chapter 8. The Society of the Night

Loma Quemada means "burned hill." It is 643 feet high.

The Abakuá are still present in Cuba as well as in Cuban exile communities around the world, most notably New York City.

Chapter 9. Africa

Changüí music is still quite popular in Cuba, and many consider it to be the predecessor of salsa. You can see a video on YouTube at: www.youtube.com/watch?v=CvxWYQSHUYg.

Chapter 10. Civilization

Matusalem rum is still around. Since the 1959 revolution in Cuba it has been made in the Dominican Republic. I consider it to be the finest sipping rum in the world.

Chapter 11. Reinforcements

Wake's friend Bowman Hendry McCalla (1844–1910) was one of the most famous U.S. naval officers of the latter nineteenth century. His naval service began at Annapolis in 1861 and included leading men in combat during the Civil War, the 1885 Panama Crisis, the 1898 Spanish-American War, and the 1900 Boxer Rebellion in China. He was promoted to rear admiral in 1903, retired in 1906, died in 1910, and is buried at Arlington National Cemetery. Two U.S. warships have been named after him as well as McCalla Hill at the Guantánamo U.S. Naval Station.

"Goat locker" is an old sailor slang term for the senior petty officers' quarters. It is still used. The colorful term comes from the days of sail, when ships carried goats and other livestock for food, milk, and eggs. They were kept near the petty officers for safety from thieves.

A "gam" is a conversation between sailors, frequently filled with unverifiable sea stories.

Read *The Honored Dead* to learn the details of how Rork lost his hand in Vietnam and subsequently gained his unique "appliance" courtesy of the French navy.

Chapter 12. The Great Man Himself

Calixto García Iñiguez (1839–98) was born in eastern Cuba in August 1839, only two months after Peter Wake was born in Massachusetts. García joined the struggle for Cuban independence in 1868, when the first phase of the war for independence began. The scar on his forehead was from an attempt to commit suicide with his pistol when captured by the Spanish in 1878. The wound gave him severe headaches for the rest of his life. For thirty years he served the cause of Cuba's independence, becoming a senior general, second only to General Máximo Gómez, the commander in chief of all forces in the Cuban Army of Liberation. Like José Martí and so many other Cuban leaders, García was a Freemason.

When General Shafter and the American army entered Santiago de Cuba upon the surrender of the Spanish defenders in late July 1898, General García and his troops were not allowed to participate in the entrance procession or the ceremony. This intentional snub by Shafter caused enormous and lasting ill-will among the Cubans.

García died of influenza on 11 December 1898, only a few months after the war ended, while in Washington, D.C., on a Cuban diplomatic mission. He was temporarily buried at Arlington National Cemetery with full military honors. Afterward, his remains were taken home to Cuba by the gunboat *Nashville* with full naval honors. He is still revered by the Cuban people.

Andrew Rowan (1857–1943) was a career Army officer from West Virginia who entered West Point at the relatively old age of twenty, graduating in 1881. Long interested in Cuba and fluent in Spanish, he wrote a book about the island (*The Island of Cuba; a descriptive and historical account of the "Great Antilla"*) in 1896. At the beginning of the Spanish-American War he was sent on a harrowing courier mission to take a message from President McKinley to General García assuring him of U.S. support. Later in the war, Rowan commanded black American troops in Cuba. He retired from active service in 1909 and died at San Francisco at age eighty-five. A famous essay, "Message to García," was written in 1899 about Rowan's exploits on his courier mission.

Details of Wake's spy mission in Havana are included in *An Honorable War*.

Chapter 13. Decisions of War and Love

Oregon was a 10,000-ton *Indiana*-class battleship commissioned in 1896. This formidable warship mounted twin 13-inch guns, four 8-inch guns, four 6-inch guns, twelve 3-inch guns, twenty 6-pounder guns, six 1-pounder guns, and four torpedo tubes. *Oregon*'s dash around South America to get to Cuba in time to fight became legendary.

William Thomas Sampson (1840–1902) was a naval officer from New York who graduated from the Naval Academy in 1861. After a typical career, he served as president of the board of inquiry into the *Maine* sinking in early 1898. Afterward he was promoted to rear admiral and given command of the North Atlantic Squadron, the main battle force against the Spanish in the Caribbean. In 1901 Congress created the Sampson Medal, to be given to all naval personnel who served in combat actions under Sampson's command in the war. Sampson thus became one of only four members of the U.S. armed forces ever to be authorized to wear a military decoration with his own image on it. Adm. George Dewey, Gen. Pershing, and Rear Adm. Richard Byrd are the others. Sampson retired in 1902 and died a few months later.

Gloucester was originally the yacht *Corsair* owned by financier John Pierpoint Morgan. *Corsair* was launched in 1891. At 240 feet and almost 800 tons, with a speed of 17 knots, she was one of the largest and fastest yachts in America. In April 1898 she was obtained by the U.S. Navy and commissioned *Gloucester*, under the command of Lt. Cdr. Richard Wainwright. *Gloucester* was armed with four 6-pounder guns and served the U.S. Navy in various capacities until 1919.

Richard Wainwright (1849–1926) was a career naval officer, originally from Washington, D.C., and an 1864 graduate of the Naval Academy. In 1896 he was head of ONI. In February 1898 he was executive officer in *Maine* when she exploded. He subsequently commanded *Gloucester*. He retired in 1911 and died fifteen years later at age seventy-seven.

Chapter 14. Find a Bigger Mule

Wake is referring to the Battle of Fredericksburg on 13 December 1862, when the Union army under the command of Maj. Gen. Ambrose Burnside suffered 12,653 casualties during a stupid frontal assault on the fortified Confederate defenses. Burnside's reputation never recovered.

Chapter 16. The Liberators

The Daiquiri cocktail, a mixture of rum, sugar, and lime juice, is named for the village. Jennings Cox, an American mining engineer who worked near Daiquiri, is usually given credit for inventing the drink in the early 1900s. William Chanler, a wealthy American adventurer, businessman, and politician who served with the U.S. Army V Corps in Oriente, Cuba, in 1898, subsequently bought the copper mines near Daiquiri, learned of the drink, and introduced it to the social scene in New York City.

Chapter 17. In the Arena and Daring Great Things

Captain Bucky O'Neill (1860–98) was a gambler, sheriff, friend of Wyatt Earp at Tombstone, Arizona, and politician. He volunteered for Theodore Roosevelt's "Rough Riders" cavalry regiment and was appointed a captain. In 1907 seven thousand people gathered at Prescott, Arizona, to unveil a monument memorializing him and the other Rough Riders. He is buried at Arlington National Cemetery.

Some may fault Roosevelt's memory of the famous proverb of Solomon. The word usually used in Bibles of the period is "stalled," not "fattened." They mean the same.

"Facing the elephant" (or "seeing the elephant") was a nineteenth-century military slang term for experiencing combat. It is generally thought to be from the classic descriptions of infantry facing an assault by war elephants in the ancient world—a terrifying experience.

Chapter 18. The Grand Strategy

Gen. Joseph Wheeler (1836–1906) was an American military officer, politician, and author. After graduating from West Point in 1858 he served in the U.S. Army until 1861, when he resigned and joined the Confederacy. He served with distinction in the Confederate army, during which he was wounded three times and had sixteen horses shot from under him. After the Civil War he represented Alabama in Congress for twenty years. He was also the author of six books on military subjects. His oldest son served in the U.S. Army during the fighting in Cuba, and one of his daughters was a Red Cross nurse there. General Wheeler is one of the few former Confederate officers buried at Arlington.

The 9th and 10th Cavalry Regiments are storied units of the U.S. Army, part of the fabled "Buffalo Soldier" regiments formed after the Civil War to fight Indians. The 9th and 10th were activated in 1866 as segregated black regiments and served continuously until 1944. Gen. Benjamin O. Davis Sr., the first black general in the U.S. Army, served as a young lieutenant in the 9th Cavalry. Both regiments were reactivated in 1958, this time as integrated units, and both still serve today.

While trudging through the Las Guasimas jungle, I encountered the interesting plants and animals described in this chapter, with explanations provided by a dear Cuban friend. The wasps reminded me of the modern exile Cuban slang for Communist Cuban spies in Miami: *avispas* (wasps). The "wasp network" in Miami still exists.

Chapter 20. Facing the Elephant

Richard Harding Davis (1864–1916) was a well-known American journalist, war reporter, world adventurer, and author from New York City. Davis was a close friend of Theodore Roosevelt and promoted the image of Roosevelt's regiment in Cuba. Because of his reports from a U.S. warship early in the war, the Navy banned reporters from its ships for the rest of the war. Davis died of a heart attack at the young age of fifty-one.

Chapter 21. The Butcher's Bill

Roosevelt's quote is from Lady Macbeth in Act 2, scene 2, of Shakespeare's *Macbeth*, written in 1605.

Chapter 23. A Lovely View of Santiago

An "enfilade" is when weapons are fired from a flanking position down the lengthwise axis of an enemy's position or formation, as in a trench.

A banshee is a figure of Gaelic folklore said to be a spirit woman (sometimes ugly, sometimes pretty) who mourns the death of a clan member by wailing loudly. The more banshees heard wailing, the more important the person who died; the louder the wailing, the more tragic and unexpected the death.

Chapter 24. The Killing Ground

Gen. John J. "Black Jack" Pershing (1860–1948) graduated from West Point in 1886. He got the then-derisive nickname "Black Jack" because he served with black regiments in the Indian and Spanish-American wars. In World War I Pershing commanded American Expeditionary Forces in Europe. He retired in 1924 with the rank of General of the Armies of the United States. He died at age eighty-seven.

Chapter 26. Parker's Guns

Pierre Loti was the pen name of Louis Marie-Julien Viaud (1850–1923), a French career naval officer and novelist who became a lifelong friend of Wake after they met at the 1883 Battle of Hué in Vietnam, where Rork lost his hand. Loti wrote forty-two books, many of them set in exotic locales around the world, and became a celebrated literary figure.

The "military crest" of a hill is a line just below the actual geographical crest. Defenses on the actual crest are silhouetted and thus easily seen and engaged. Those on the military crest are less visible.

For Wake's exploits in Samoa, read *Honors Rendered*.

John Henry Parker (1866–1942) was originally from Missouri. An 1892 graduate of West Point, he became an expert in, and proponent of, the offensive use of machine guns. Lieutenant Parker was initially prohibited from landing his unit in Cuba, being ordered to wait his turn because he was only a lieutenant. He appealed to General Shafter, who believed in Parker and his machine-gun tactics and sent a special launch to land the machine guns. Parker had to spend his own money for Cuban mules to get the guns to the front, where they more than proved their worth in saving the day for the Americans. Parker saw combat again in World War I and retired as a brigadier general in 1924.

Chapter 29. Perfumed Moonlight

Clarissa "Clara" Harlowe Barton (25 December 1821–1912) was a teacher, pioneering professional nurse, founder of the American Red Cross, and founder of modern military nursing. In her early adult life she was a teacher. She began nursing soldiers at battlefields during the Civil War, something relegated at the time to male medical orderlies only. After the war she ran the Office of Missing Soldiers, searching for the remains of soldiers buried anonymously or missing in the war. She found and properly buried more than 20,000 soldiers during the next 4 years. Barton was a battlefield nurse in the Franco-Prussian War (1870–71). Ten years later she started the American Red Cross. In the mid-1890s she served as a nurse in the concentration camps where the Spanish government interned Cuban civilians before the United States joined the Cubans' fight against the Spanish in 1898. Her Red Cross work with the U.S. Army in Cuba saved thousands of American, Cuban, and Spanish lives. Due to internal politics within the Red Cross she retired in 1904. In her later years she wrote several books about her life and causes. She died at age ninety at her home in Maryland, which is now open to visitors. See www.nps.gov/clba/index.htm.

Chapter 32. The Actor

Between 1898 and 1901 the Edison Manufacturing Company and the American Mutoscope & Biograph Company made sixty-eight films about the Spanish-American War and the Philippine Insurrection against the U.S. Army. These films were very short, usually about two minutes, and none had sound. Many were reenactments rather than live footage. Visit the Library of Congress' collection at www .loc.gov/collection/spanish-american-war-in-motion-pictures /about-this-collection/ to see these fascinating films.

Chapter 35. Memories of Santiago

Melilla is an ancient (since 1497) Spanish enclave and colony on the Mediterranean coast of Morocco. It is still Spanish territory.

Chapter 37. Madam Clara

Emile Berliner invented the gramophone in 1887 and was the first to use a flat disc (of hard rubber) to reproduce music. This was the forerunner of modern records. By the Spanish-American War ten years later, gramophones had become very popular around the world.

Chapter 40. Carlito

For more about the mortal feud between Wake and the Boreaus, both senior and junior, read *The Darkest Shade of Honor*, *Honorable Lies*, and *The Assassin's Honor*.

Chapter 42. Sunrise

Flood tides bring seawater into harbors, bays, and rivers. Ebb tides take it out. Tidal heights and current speeds are not that great on the Cuban coastline but do affect vessels and swimmers.

Chapter 44. A Choice of Deaths

Emilio Díaz-Moreu y Quintana (1846–1913) was a Spanish career naval officer and politician. He joined the navy in 1858 as a twelve-year-old naval cadet. By the 1890s he had earned an impressive record and was highly respected by his peers. He also was a member of the Spanish parliament (the Cortés) and a proponent for modernizing the navy. After the naval Battle of Santiago he was held as a prisoner of war at the U.S. Naval Academy until August 1898, then repatriated to Spain in early September. At age sixty-seven he died at his home in Alicante. His descendants have continued his tradition of serving Spain in the government. Interestingly, one of his descendants is a well-respected senior U.S. naval officer (and reader of the Honor Series) who just completed a successful tour in command of an American cruiser. Emilio Díaz-Moreu y Quintana would be very proud.

Chapter 45. Sunday Routines

The Spanish lookouts seem to have missed two other ships, *New Orleans* and *Newark*, which had already steamed eastward. *Newark* was Wake's command in 1897. For more on that, read *An Honorable War*.

Rear Admiral Sampson was steaming away from Santiago to attend a meeting with Major General Shafter at Siboney. The Spanish didn't know of this meeting or plan their sortie for it.

Chapter 46. A Storm of Steel and Lead

Anthracite coal is relatively smokeless and burns at a higher temperature, producing more steam and greater power. Bituminous coal is the opposite and far less efficient.

There is only one ship from the Spanish-American War left in the world, *Olympia*, Admiral Dewey's flagship at the Battle of Manila Bay on 1 May 1898. She was retired from service in 1922 and became a museum ship in 1957. She is moored at Philadelphia's Independence Seaport Museum and is well worth a visit. To read more, go to the museum's website at www.phillyseaport.org/.

Chapter 47. The Ultimate Irony

Charles Edgar Clark (1843–1922) was from Vermont and graduated from the Naval Academy in 1863. His career was routine until he took command of *Oregon* in March 1898 and shortly thereafter made his epic voyage. Clark retired as a rear admiral in 1905. He wrote a fascinating autobiography, *My Fifty Years in the Navy*, in 1915 and died seven years later at age seventy-nine.

Chapter 52. Reunion and Defiance

SS *Seneca* was a 2,700-ton steamer built in 1884. She was a passenger ship for the Ward Line from 1894 to 1914, mainly working the Cuban routes. In April 1898 the U.S. government chartered her and transformed her into a troop transport. In June she took troops to Cuba. In July she was hastily turned into a hospital ship and took sick and wounded troops to the United States. The voyage home was harrowing for her passengers, for there were few medical supplies or personnel on board. From 1914 onward *Seneca* was used as a cargo barge. In 1928 she was sunk in a collision with the ironically named SS *Siboney* off Sandy Hook, New Jersey.

Chapter 53. Living in the Mud No More

Kaiserin Maria Teresa was a 5,300-ton cruiser commissioned in 1894, with a dual 9½-inch-gun main battery. *Resolute*, a newly acquired former merchant steamer–turned–auxiliary cruiser, spotted her approaching the transports off Siboney and signaled a nearby battleship, *Indiana*, that a Spanish battleship was about to attack. *Indiana* intercepted the foreign cruiser and was about to open fire when *Indiana*'s captain recognized her at the last minute. At the end of World War I *Kaiserin Maria Teresa* was allocated as a prize of war to the British, who sold her for scrap.

Bibliography of Research Materials

Theodore Roosevelt and His Service in the Spanish-American War

The Arena, volume 95, number 2, Newsletter of the Theodore Roosevelt Association, March/April, 2015.

The Autobiography of Theodore Roosevelt, 1920 edition, Theodore Roosevelt (1913).

The Bully Pulpit: Theodore Roosevelt, William Howard Taft, and the Golden Age of Journalism, Doris Kearns Goodwin (2013).

Colonel Roosevelt, Edmund Morris (2010).

Grover Cleveland: The 24th President, 1893–1897, American Presidents series, Henry F. Graff (2002).

New York Times, 1897 and 1898 newspaper articles (website), http://spiderbites.nytimes.com/free_1897/articles_1897_02_00001.html.

"The Right of the People to Rule," 1912 Roosevelt campaign speech recording (recorded by Thomas Edison), Vincent Voice Library, Michigan State University.

The Rise of Theodore Roosevelt, Edmund Morris (1979).

The Rough Riders, Theodore Roosevelt (1902).

Theodore Rex, Edmund Morris (2001).

Theodore Roosevelt's Naval Diplomacy, Henry J. Hendrix (2009).

William McKinley: The 25th President, 1897–1901, American Presidents series, Kevin Phillip and Arthur M. Schlesinger (2003).

Cuba and Cuban History

Abakuá, (De)Coding of a Symbol, Ramón Andrés Torres Zayas (2015).

Commercial Cuba, William J. Clark (1898).

Cuba in War Time, Richard Harding Davis (1897).

Cuba, or the Pursuit of Freedom, Hugh Thomas (1971).

History of Cuba: The Challenge of the Yoke and the Star, Jose Canton Navarro (2001).

Insurgent Cuba: Race, Nation, and Revolution, 1868–1898, Ada Ferrar (1999).

José Martí, Cuban Patriot, Richard Butler Gray (1962).

José Martí, Selected Writings, edited and translated by Esther Allen (2002).

Martí, Apostle of Freedom, Jorge Mañach (1950).

Santiago de Cuba, Leocésar Miranda Saborit (2015).

Una Derrota Británica en Cuba, Olga Portuondo Zúñiga (2015).

Naval Operations in the Spanish-American War

Admiral Pascual Cervera's Report to the Spanish Ministry of Marine of the Battle of Santiago, in the Spanish newspaper *La Corresponcia* (August 1898), translated and printed by the U.S. Government Printing Office (1899).

The American Steel Navy, Cdr. John D. Alden, USN (Ret.) (1972).

Battles and Capitulation of Santiago de Cuba (War Notes, number I: *Information from Abroad*), Office of Naval Intelligence (1899).

A Century of U.S. Naval Intelligence, Capt. Wyman H. Packard, USN (Ret.) (1996).

Characteristics of Principal Foreign Ships of War: Prepared for the Board on Fortifications, Etc., Office of Naval Intelligence (1885).

Coaling, Docking, and Repair Facilities of the Ports of the World, Office of Naval Intelligence (1909).

Conway's All the World's Fighting Ships, 1860–1905, Robert Gardiner, editorial director (1979).

Dictionary of Admirals of the U.S. Navy, volume 2: *1901–1918*, William B. Cogar (1991).

En Guerra con Estados Unidos: Cuba 1898, Antonio Carrasco Garcia (1998).

The Fate of the Maine, John Edward Weems (1958).

Guerra de Cuba: Atlas Ilustrado, third edition, Juan Excrigas Rodríguez (2012).

McKinley's Bulldog: The Battleship Oregon, Sanford V. Stemlicht (1977).

The Naval Annual of 1891, T. A. Brassey (1891).

The Naval Aristocracy: The Golden Age of Annapolis and the Emergence of Modern American Navalism, Peter Karsten (1972).

"The Naval Base at Key West in 1898," Cdr. Reginald R. Belknap, USN, U.S. Naval Institute *Proceedings* 41/5/159 (September–October 1915).

Navalism and the Emergence of American Sea Power, 1882–1893, Mark Russell Shulman (1995).

The Office of Naval Intelligence: The Birth of America's First Intelligence Agency, 1865–1918, Jeffry M. Dorwart (1979).

Rear-Admiral Schley, Sampson, and Cervera, James Parker (1910).

"Record of the *Oregon*," *New York Times* (29 June 1900).

The Spanish-American War: Blockades and Coast Defense (War Notes, number VI), Office of Naval Intelligence (1899).

U.S. Cruisers, 1883–1904, Lawrence Burr (2008).

USS Olympia: *Herald of Empire*, Benjamin Franklin Cooling (2000).

With Sampson through the War, W. A. M. Goode (1899).

Military Operations Ashore in the Spanish-American War

"The Capture of Santiago," Maj. Gen. William Shafter, USA, *Century* magazine (February 1899), pages 612–30.

"Cuba in the Spanish-Cuban-American War," *Desperta Ferro*, Spanish historical magazine (2017).

The Cuban and Porto Rican Campaigns, Richard Harding Davis (1899).

Cuban Battlefields of the Spanish-Cuban-American War website, University of Nebraska–Lincoln, http://cubanbattlefields.unl.edu/.

"The Fight at Las Quasina," *Tarrytown Argus* (2 July 1898).

"Incidents of the Operations around Santiago," *National Tribune* (30 June 1898).

In Cuba with Shafter, John D. Miley (1899).

In Darkest Cuba: Two Months Service under Gomez along the Trocha from the Caribbean to the Bahama Channel, N. G. Gonzalez (1927).

Kuba und der Krieg—Eine Darstellung de Spanish-Amerikanischen Kreiges Nach Eigener Anschaung des Verfassers (Cuba and the War: The Spanish-American War Based on Personal Observations of the author), Joseph Herrings (1899), translated by Richard Rolfe (2016).

Marching with Gomez, Grover Flint (1898).

A Message to Garcia, Elbert Hubbard (1899).

The Official War Report of Major General Calixto Ramón García Iñiguez, translated by Larry Daley, Spanish-American War Centennial website, www.spanamwar.com/Garcia.htm.

The Spanish-American War, Albert A. Nofi (1997).

Under Three Flags in Cuba, George Clarke Musgrave (1898).

United States Army Logistics, 1775–1992, volume 2, Charles R. Shrader (1997).

War Map and History of Cuba, Ebenezer Hannaford (1898).

"With Lawton at Caney," Frank Norris, *Century* magazine (June 1899), pages 304–9.

Maps, Charts, and Sailing Guides

A Cruising Guide to the Caribbean and the Bahamas, Jerrems C. Hart and William T. Stone (1976).

Cuba, a Cruising Guide, Nigel Calder (1997).

Eastern Coasts of Cuba, British Admiralty chart number 3865 (1939).

Gulf Stream–Caribbean, Gulf of Mexico, Atlantic Ocean, Lt. Matthew Fontaine Maury, USN, U.S. Office of Coast Survey (1852).

Map of American and Spanish Positions as of 3 July 1898, U.S. Army Corps of Engineers (1898).

Map of Cuba and the Provinces, in *Commercial Cuba* (1898).

Map of Havana, in *Commercial Cuba* (1898).

Map of Santiago de Cuba in 1898, McElfresh Map Company (1998).

Map of Santiago de Cuba Province, Oficina Turístico Provincial (2009).

Map of Santiago Province, in *Commercial Cuba* (1898).

Map of Tampa, Sanborn Fire Insurance Map (1899).

Mapa Carreteras de Cuba, Ediciones GEO (2015).

Sketch Map of Regimental Camps in Tampa, Port Tampa Library (1898).

Sketch Map of Tampa Military Encampments, Port Tampa Library (1898).

Southeastern Bahamas and Eastern Cuba, British Admiralty chart number 1266 (1889).

Spanish Map of the Battle of Las Guasimas, within *Cronologia Critical de la Guerra Hispano-Cubanoamericano*, Felipe Martinez Arango (1950).

Straits of Florida and Northern Cuba Coast, U.S. Office of Coast Survey (1895).

Upper Caribbean Sea and Gulf of Mexico, American privately published chart with U.S., British, French, and Spanish survey data (1860).

About the Author

Robert N. Macomber is an award-winning author, internationally acclaimed lecturer, Department of Defense consultant/lecturer, and accomplished seaman. When not trekking the world for research, book signings, or lectures, he lives on an island in southwest Florida, where he enjoys cooking the types of foreign cuisines described in his books and sailing among the islands. Visit his website at: www .RobertMacomber.com.

The Naval Institute Press is the book-publishing arm of the U.S. Naval Institute, a private, nonprofit, membership society for sea service professionals and others who share an interest in naval and maritime affairs. Established in 1873 at the U.S. Naval Academy in Annapolis, Maryland, where its offices remain today, the Naval Institute has members worldwide.

Members of the Naval Institute support the education programs of the society and receive the influential monthly magazine *Proceedings* or the colorful bimonthly magazine *Naval History* and discounts on fine nautical prints and on ship and aircraft photos. They also have access to the transcripts of the Institute's Oral History Program and get discounted admission to any of the Institute-sponsored seminars offered around the country.

The Naval Institute's book-publishing program, begun in 1898 with basic guides to naval practices, has broadened its scope to include books of more general interest. Now the Naval Institute Press publishes about seventy titles each year, ranging from how-to books on boating and navigation to battle histories, biographies, ship and aircraft guides, and novels. Institute members receive significant discounts on the Press' more than eight hundred books in print.

Full-time students are eligible for special half-price membership rates. Life memberships are also available.

For a free catalog describing Naval Institute Press books currently available, and for further information about joining the U.S. Naval Institute, please write to:

Member Services
U.S. Naval Institute
291 Wood Road
Annapolis, MD 21402-5034
Telephone: (800) 233-8764
Fax: (410) 571-1703
Web address: www.usni.org